ULTRALAZER

Horb & Booko 1

Written by
Maxence Henry and Pauline Giraud

Background Art
Yvan Duque

Character Art
Maxence Henry

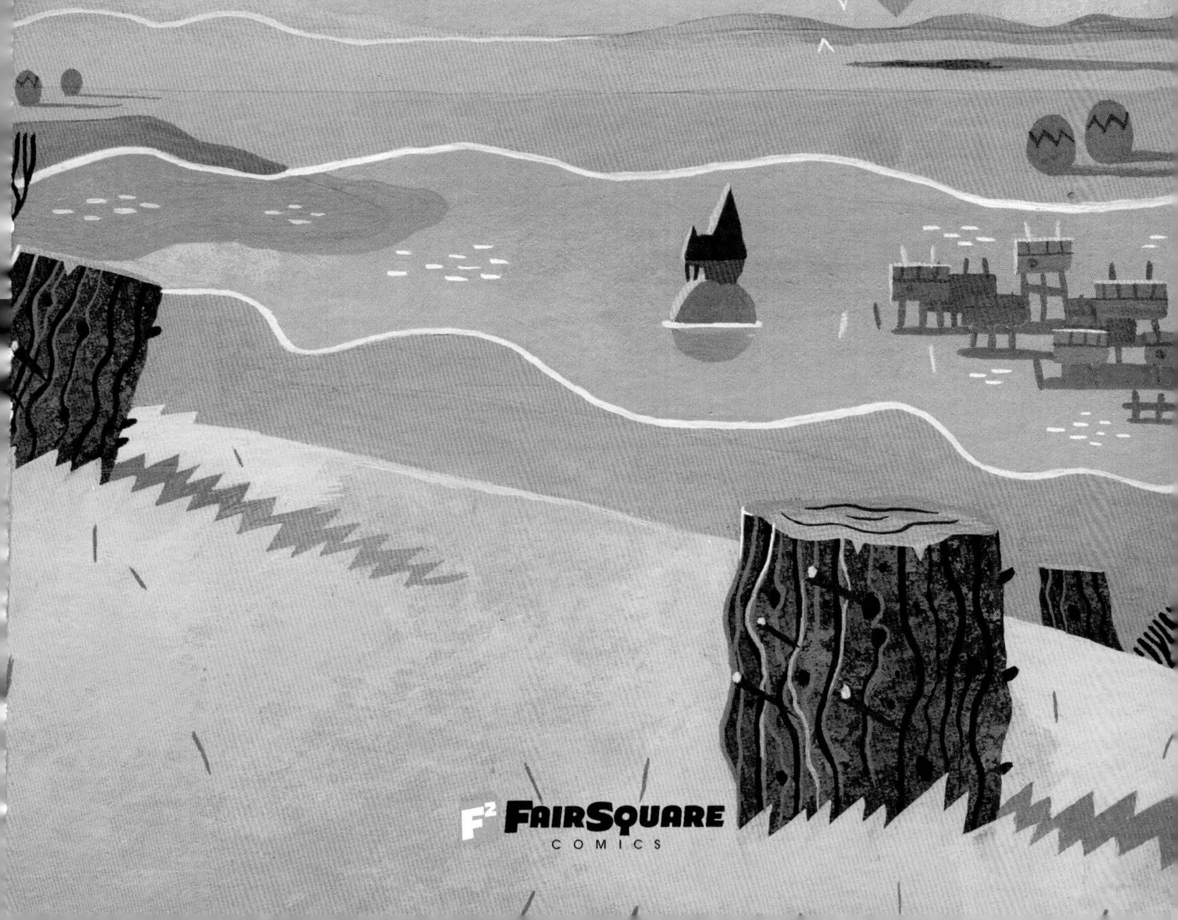

F² FAIRSQUARE COMICS

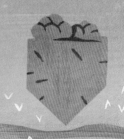

M·P·Y
Thanks to Stéphane Melchior.
Superthanks to Fred for his support and encouragement. To our first young
readers who have helped us improve this graphic novel:
Noé, Mel, Mathias, Titi, Jean-Léon, Hortense, Fanette.

M
To Pauline ♥
To my parents and grandparents,
To my little brother who, all these years, has shared his passions with me.
Thanks to the Maison Fumetti team for welcoming me as a resident artist and to
my friends at the workshop for their good mood and kindness.

P
Thanks to Maxence, mi corazón
Thanks to my family and our friends for supporting us in the making of this
project and big up to Loulou who's still here!

Y
Thanks to Maxence and Pauline for making me a part
of this adventure and thanks to all who are encouraging us.

ULTRALAZER Volume 1. First Printing.

This title is a publication of FairSquare Comics, LLC.
608S Dunsmuir Ave #207, Los Angeles, CA 90036.
Copyright © FairSquare Comics. All Rights Reserved.

Originally published in French under the following title:
Ultralazer, volume 1, by Pauline Giraud, Maxence Henry and Yvan Duque
© Editions Delcourt, 2019. Published under license.

The story and characters presented in this publication are fictional.
No portion of this book can be reproduced by any means without the express consent
of Editions Delcourt or FairSquare Comics, LLC.
Printed in Canada

CEO & PUBLISHER | Fabrice Sapolsky

BRAND AMBASSADORS & CO-OWNERS | Kristal Adams Sapolsky, Ethan Sapolsky

LETTERING & DESIGN | FairSquare Studio

TRANSLATION & PROOFREADING | Nikki San Pedro

PUBLICITY & RETAILER RELATIONS | Sean Wynn, Strange Solutions

CONTACT | fairsquarecomics@gmail.com, +1 (888) 307-0211

COMICS FROM THE REST OF US
WWW.FAIRSQUARECOMICS.COM

This graphic novel has been partially created
at the Manu Manu workshop set up at the
Maison Fumetti (Nantes, France). Original
Editor: Fred Blanchard

1

HORB & BODKO

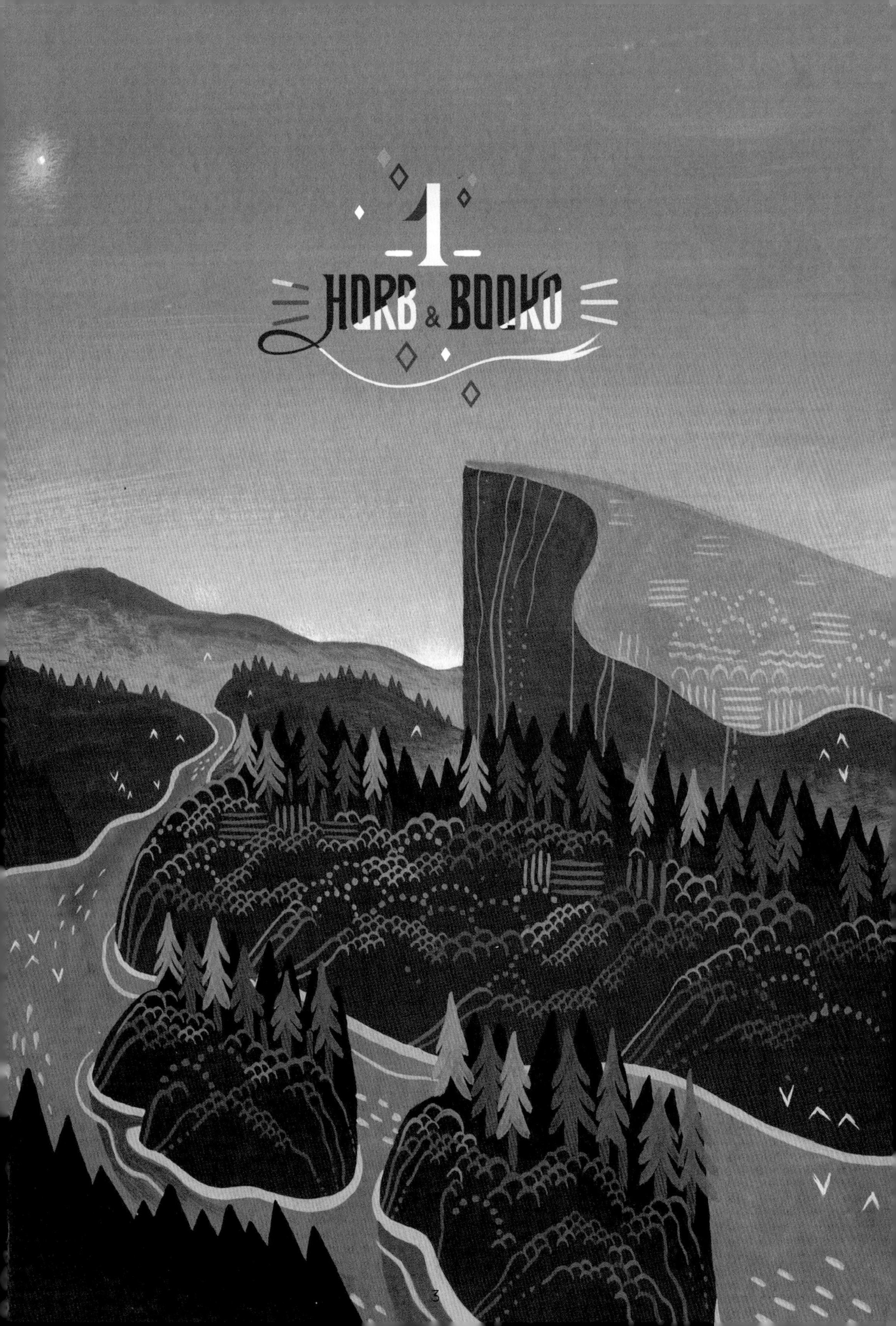

THE LITTLE PLANET OF TOPOY IS A MAGICAL PLACE FULL OF GREEN FORESTS AND PEACEFUL PEOPLE.

BUT NOTHING WOULD BE SO PERFECT WITHOUT THE POWER OF SPECIAL STONES WHOSE SECRETS ARE ONLY KNOWN BY SOME...

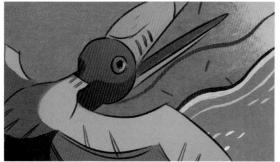

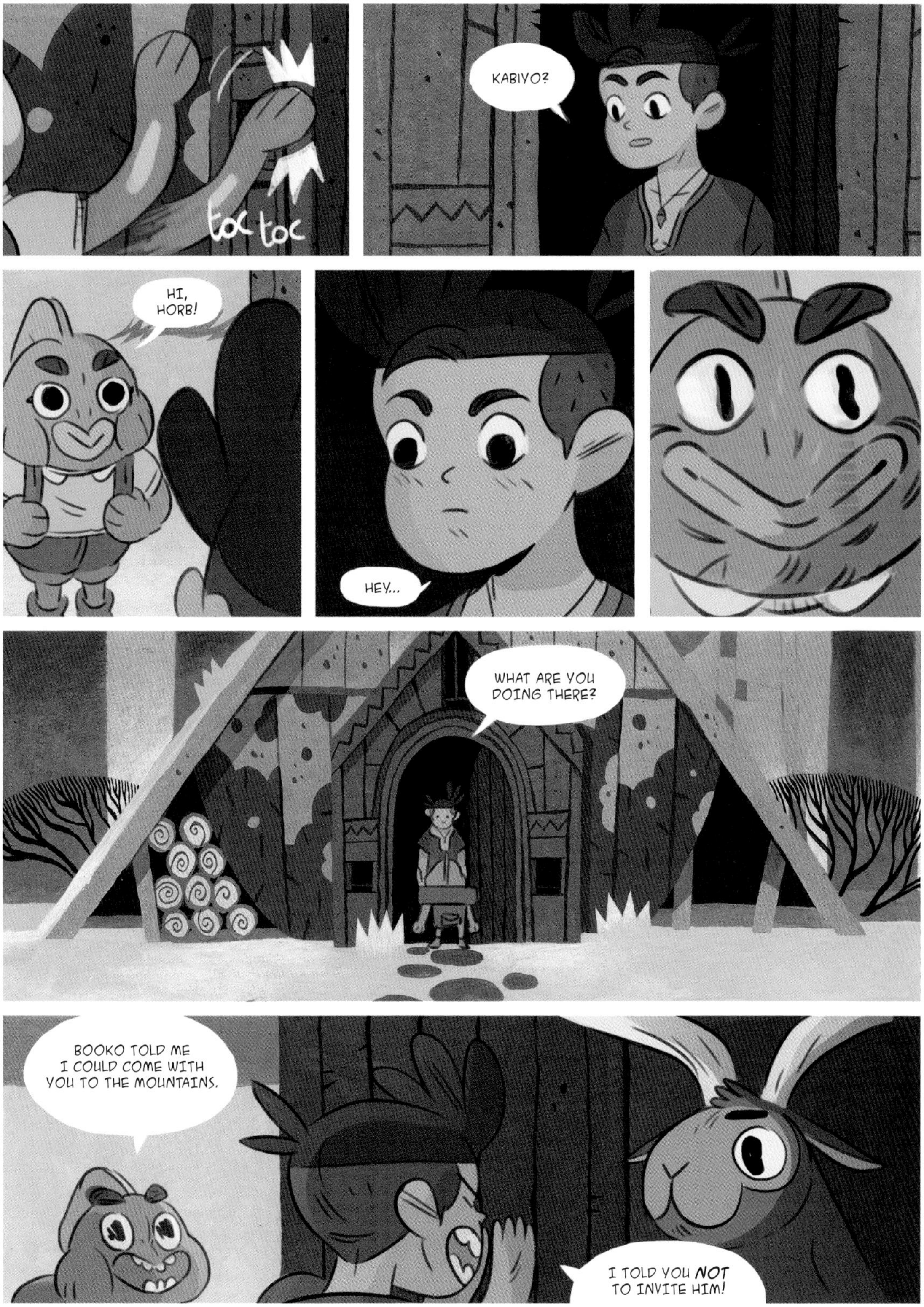
toc toc
KABIYO?
HI, HORB!
HEY...
WHAT ARE YOU DOING THERE?
BOOKO TOLD ME I COULD COME WITH YOU TO THE MOUNTAINS.
I TOLD YOU ***NOT*** TO INVITE HIM!

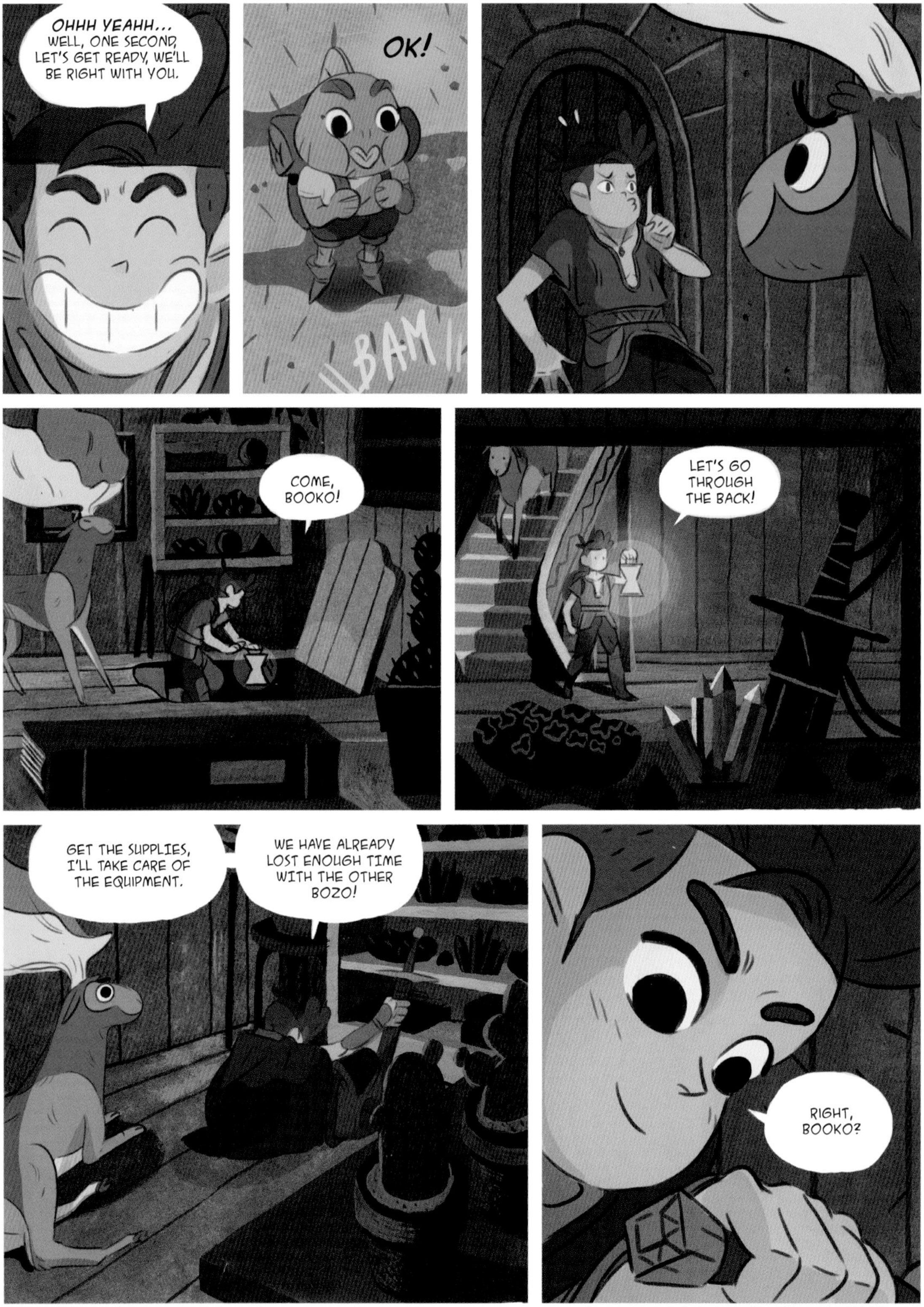
OHHH YEAHH... WELL, ONE SECOND, LET'S GET READY, WE'LL BE RIGHT WITH YOU.
OK!
BAM
COME, BOOKO!
LET'S GO THROUGH THE BACK!
GET THE SUPPLIES, I'LL TAKE CARE OF THE EQUIPMENT.
WE HAVE ALREADY LOST ENOUGH TIME WITH THE OTHER BOZO!
RIGHT, BOOKO?

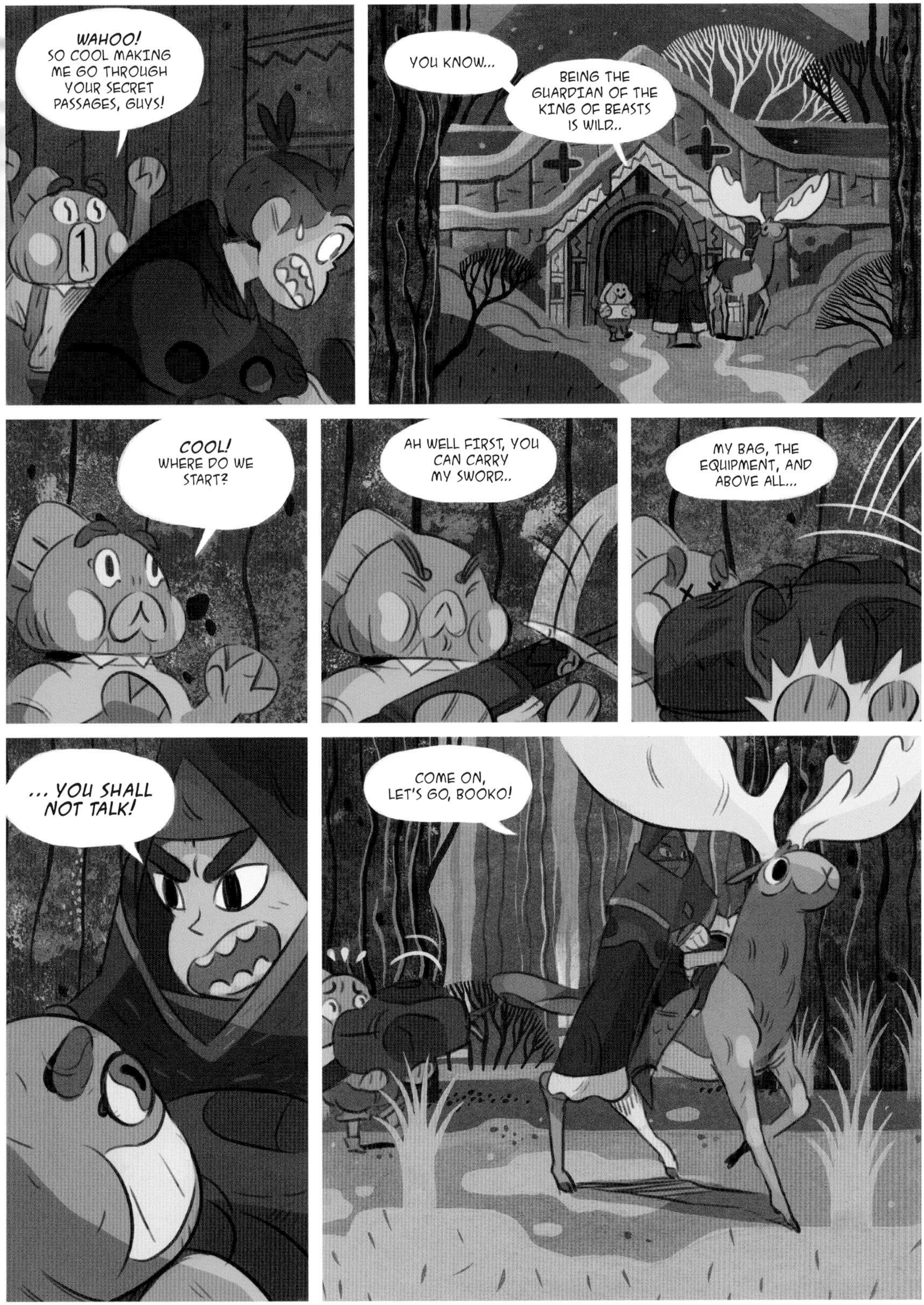
WAHOO! SO COOL MAKING ME GO THROUGH YOUR SECRET PASSAGES, GUYS!
YOU KNOW...
BEING THE GUARDIAN OF THE KING OF BEASTS IS WILD...
COOL! WHERE DO WE START?
AH WELL FIRST, YOU CAN CARRY MY SWORD...
MY BAG, THE EQUIPMENT, AND ABOVE ALL...
... YOU SHALL NOT TALK!
COME ON, LET'S GO, BOOKO!

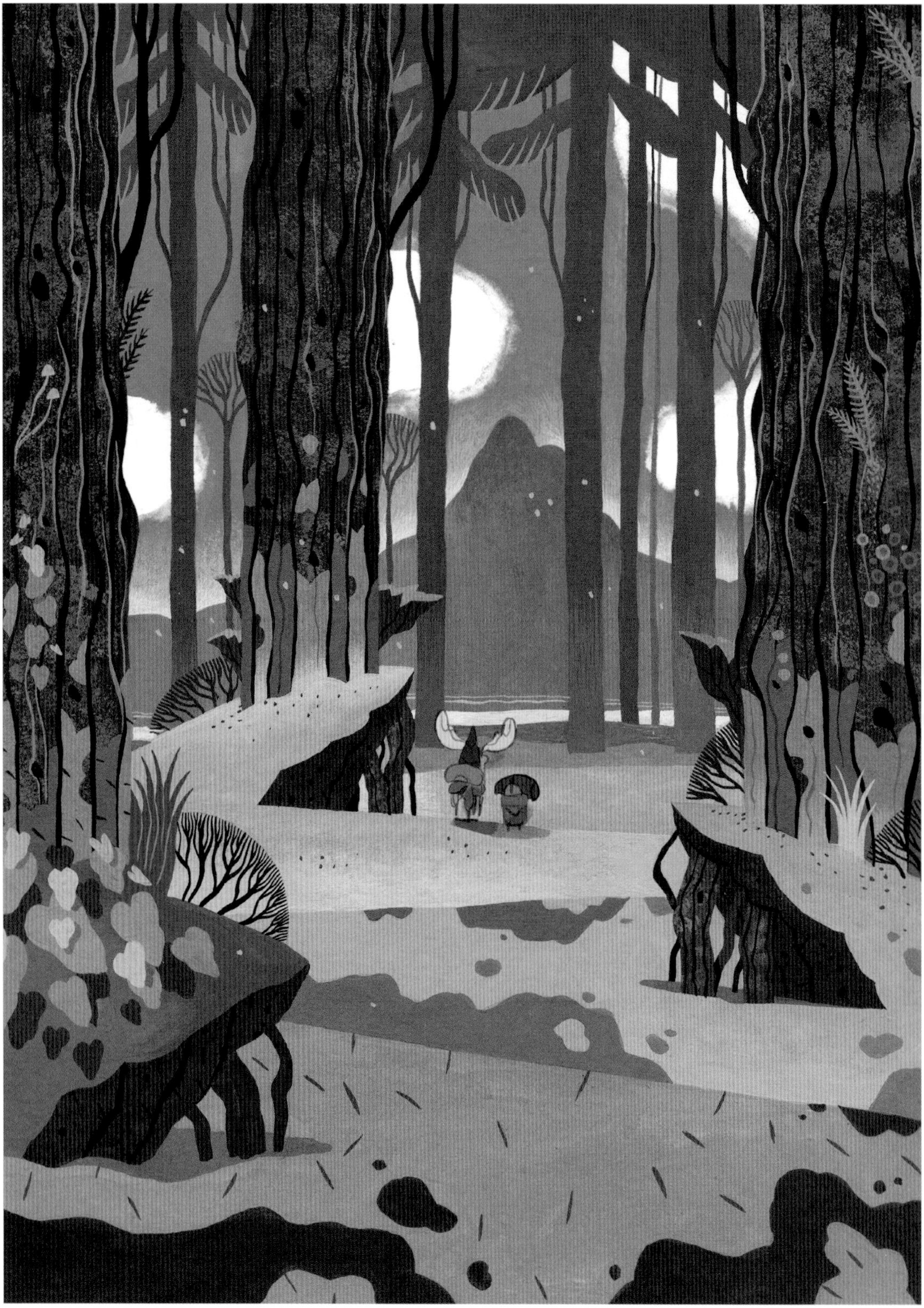

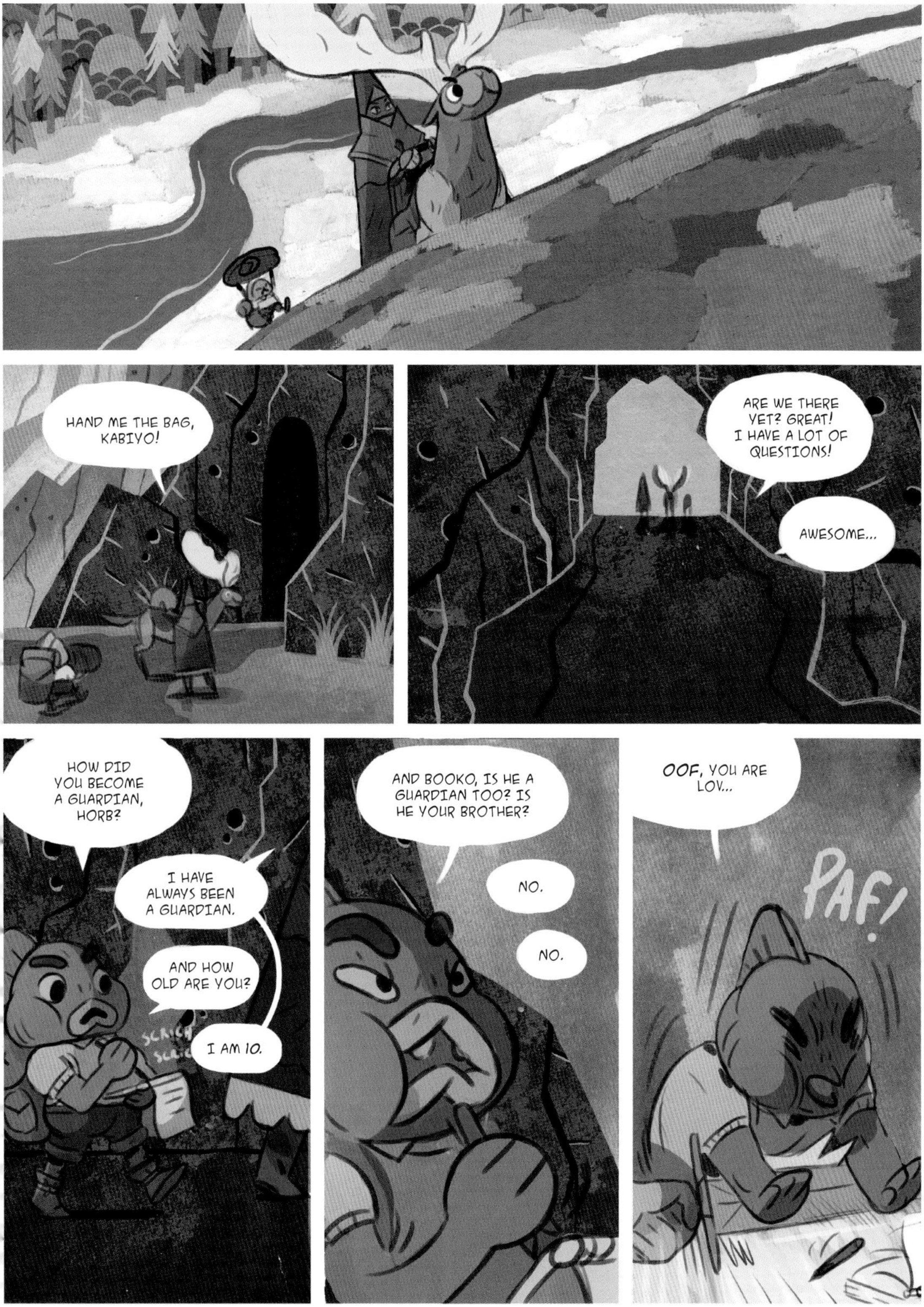

HAND ME THE BAG, KABIYO!
ARE WE THERE YET? GREAT! I HAVE A LOT OF QUESTIONS!
AWESOME...
HOW DID YOU BECOME A GUARDIAN, HORB?
I HAVE ALWAYS BEEN A GUARDIAN.
AND HOW OLD ARE YOU?
I AM 10.
AND BOOKO, IS HE A GUARDIAN TOO? IS HE YOUR BROTHER?
NO.
NO.
OOF, YOU ARE LOV...
PAF!

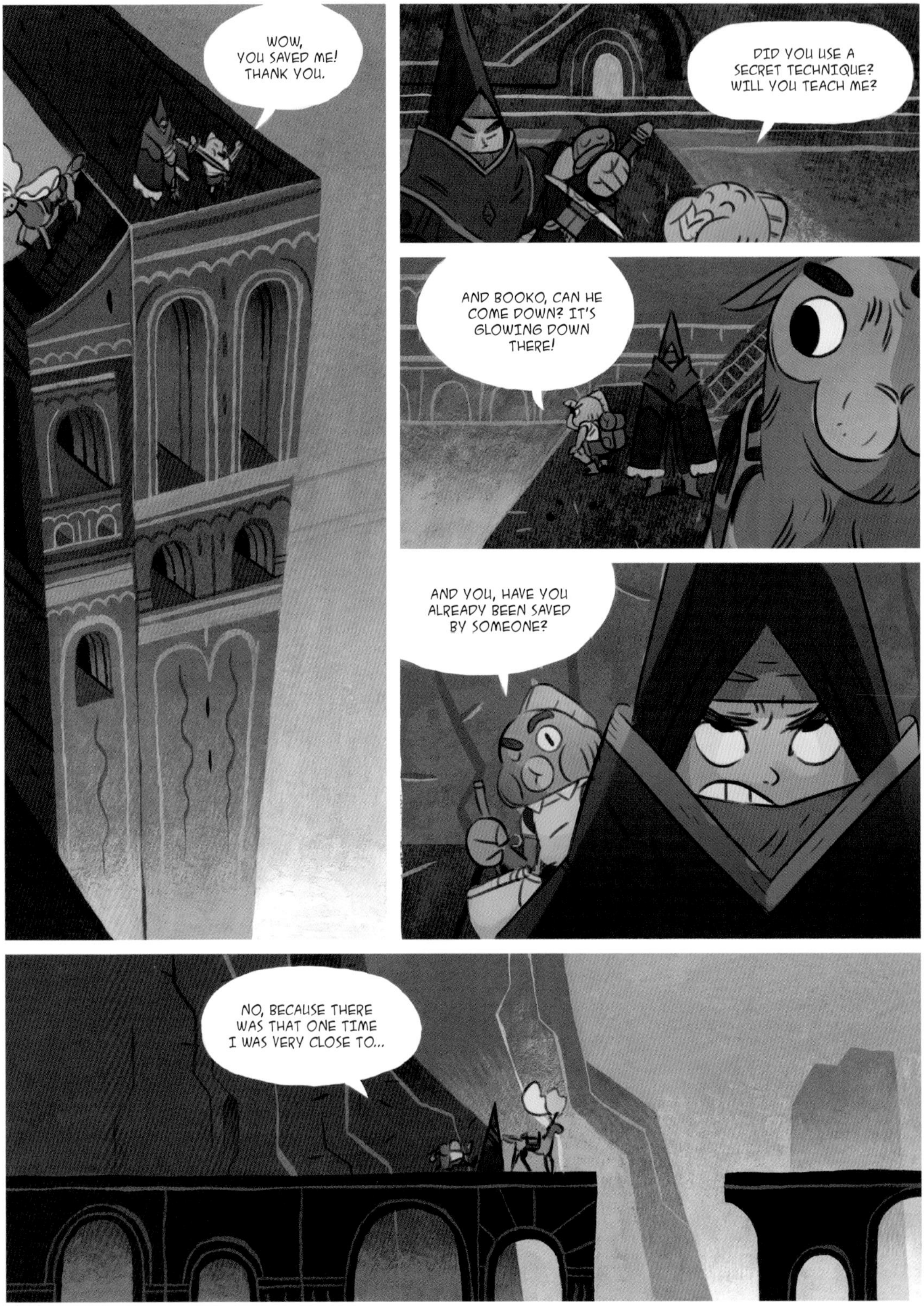
WOW, YOU SAVED ME! THANK YOU.
DID YOU USE A SECRET TECHNIQUE? WILL YOU TEACH ME?
AND BOOKO, CAN HE COME DOWN? IT'S GLOWING DOWN THERE!
AND YOU, HAVE YOU ALREADY BEEN SAVED BY SOMEONE?
NO, BECAUSE THERE WAS THAT ONE TIME I WAS VERY CLOSE TO...

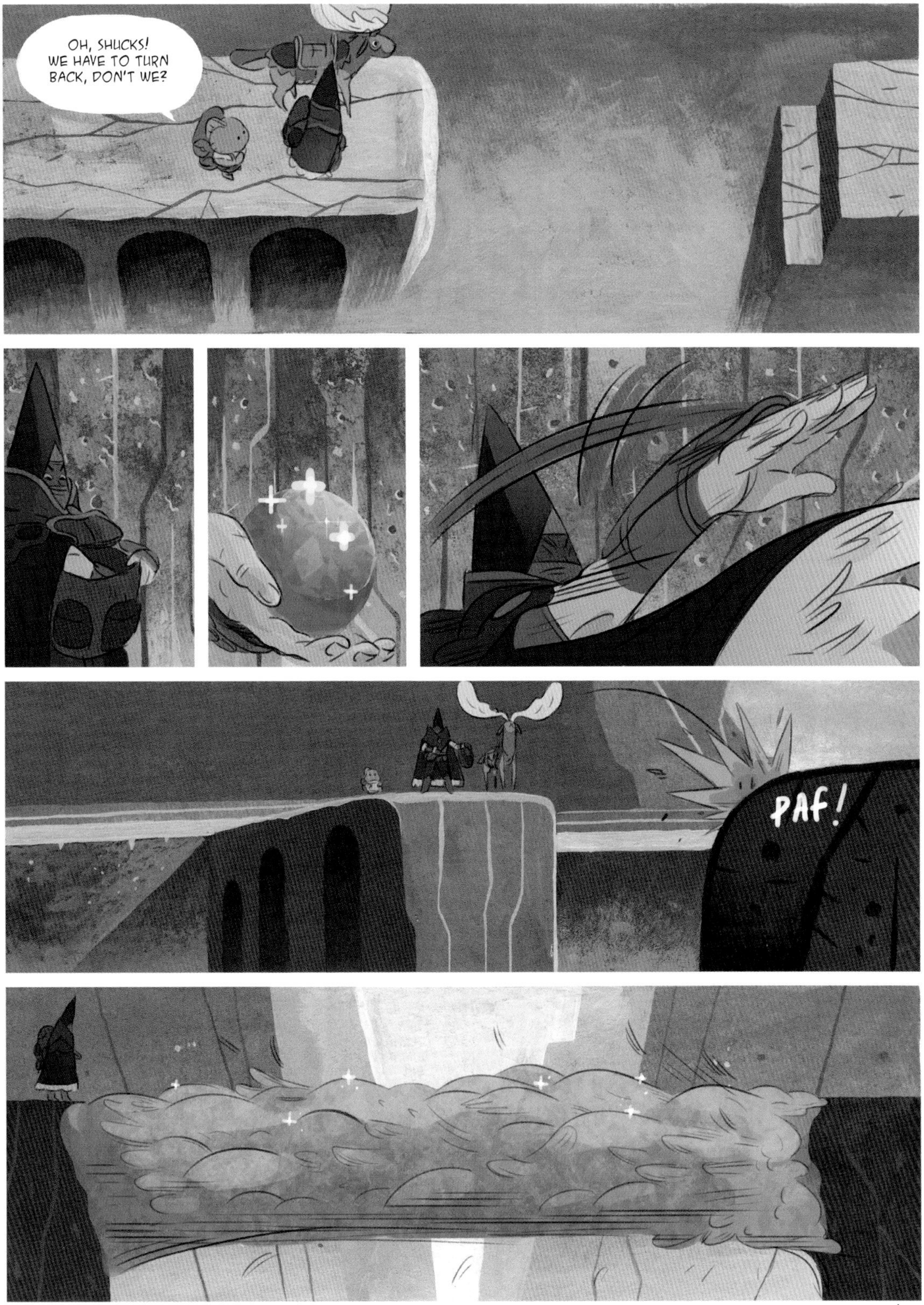
OH, SHUCKS! WE HAVE TO TURN BACK, DON'T WE?
PAF!

SO THIS IS IT... **THE POWER STONES ??!**

WHICH ONE IS THIS? CAN I HAVE A SMALL ONE? PRETTY PLEASE!

IT'S A HEMIMORPHITE, OR MOSS STONE IF YOU PREFER...

TOO LAME A NAME.

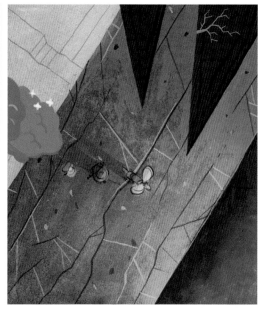

E-M-I...

KRAK

M-O-R-F-L...

HEY!

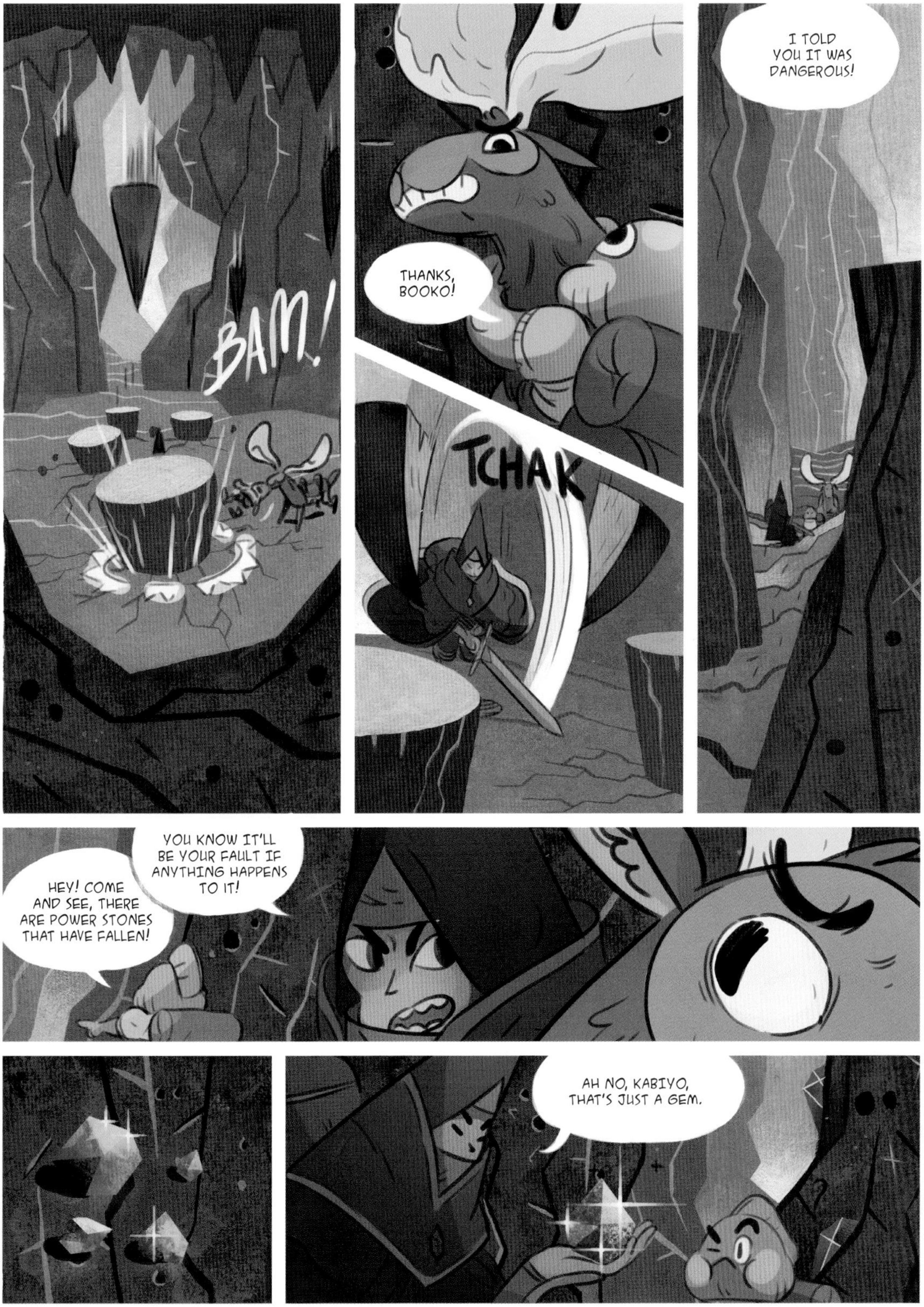
BAM!
THANKS, BOOKO!
TCHAK
I TOLD YOU IT WAS DANGEROUS!
HEY! COME AND SEE, THERE ARE POWER STONES THAT HAVE FALLEN!
YOU KNOW IT'LL BE YOUR FAULT IF ANYTHING HAPPENS TO IT!
AH NO, KABIYO, THAT'S JUST A GEM.

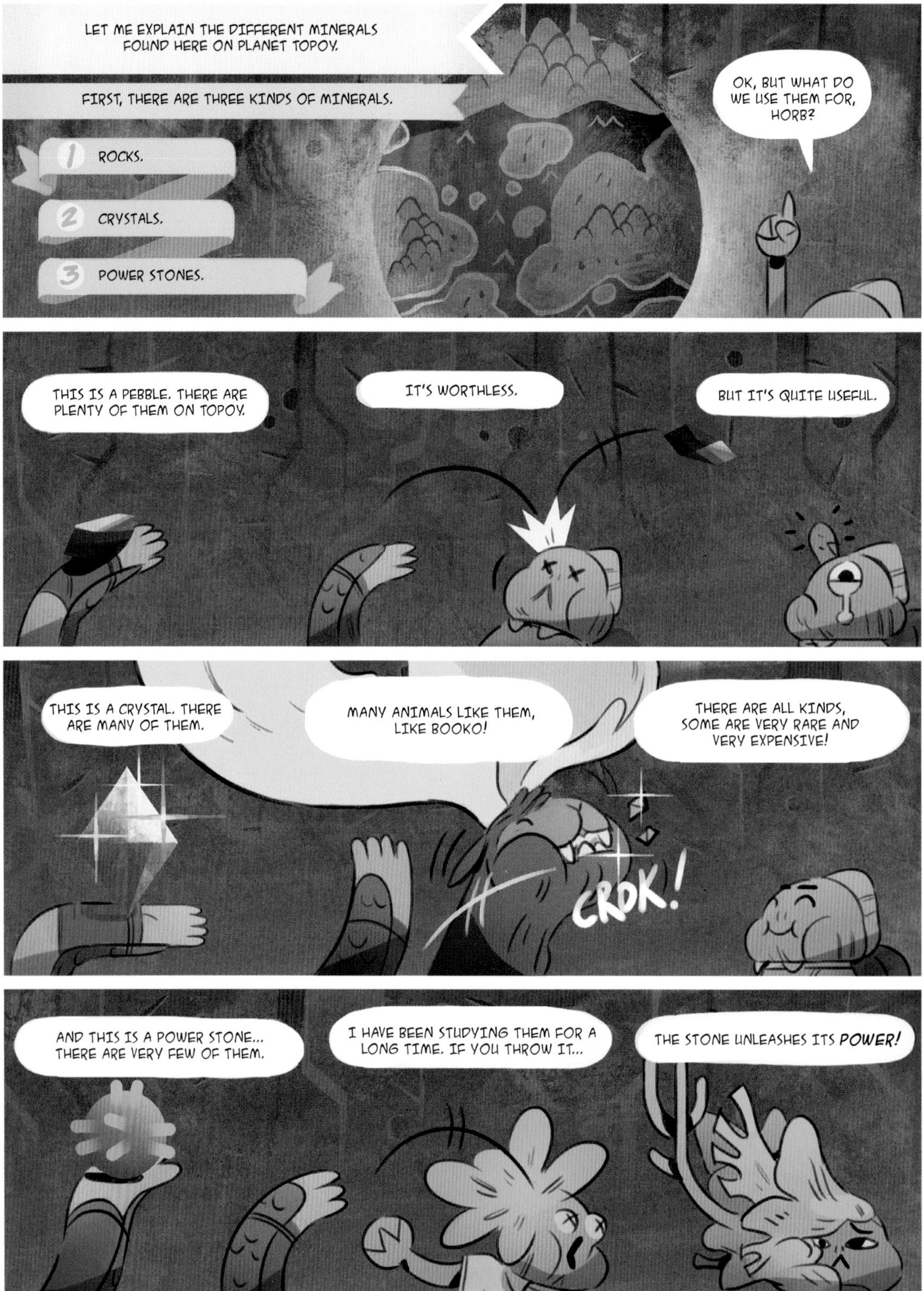
LET ME EXPLAIN THE DIFFERENT MINERALS FOUND HERE ON PLANET TOPOY.
FIRST, THERE ARE THREE KINDS OF MINERALS.
1 ROCKS.
2 CRYSTALS.
3 POWER STONES.
OK, BUT WHAT DO WE USE THEM FOR, HORB?
THIS IS A PEBBLE. THERE ARE PLENTY OF THEM ON TOPOY.
IT'S WORTHLESS.
BUT IT'S QUITE USEFUL.
THIS IS A CRYSTAL. THERE ARE MANY OF THEM.
MANY ANIMALS LIKE THEM, LIKE BOOKO!
THERE ARE ALL KINDS, SOME ARE VERY RARE AND VERY EXPENSIVE!
CROK!
AND THIS IS A POWER STONE... THERE ARE VERY FEW OF THEM.
I HAVE BEEN STUDYING THEM FOR A LONG TIME. IF YOU THROW IT...
THE STONE UNLEASHES ITS POWER!

BUT BEWARE! IMPROPER USE CAN BE FATAL!

THEY CAN CORRUPT YOUR SOUL AND TURN YOU AWAY FROM YOUR PATH.

NEVER SWALLOW A STONE OF POWER!

OK, BUT WHERE DO WE FIND THEM?!

HE DOESN'T LISTEN...

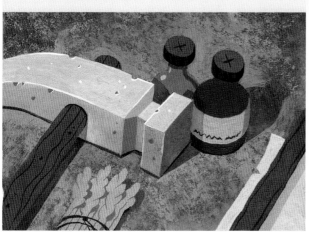

FIRST OF ALL, YOU NEED DIGGING TOOLS, AND ALSO FOOD BECAUSE IT CAN TAKE A LONG TIME.

AND THEN YOU NEED HUGE BICEPS, LIKE ME.

COME ON, BOOKO AND I WILL SHOW YOU A PERFECT PLACE TO DIG!

SAY, BOOKO, DO YOU THINK I'LL BE A GUARDIAN TOO ONE DAY?

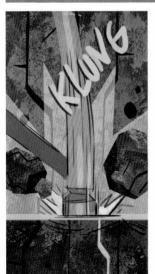

KLONG

Pfiuu...

GNiii...

WELL, HE IS MOTIVATED, THE LITTLE KABIYO!

16

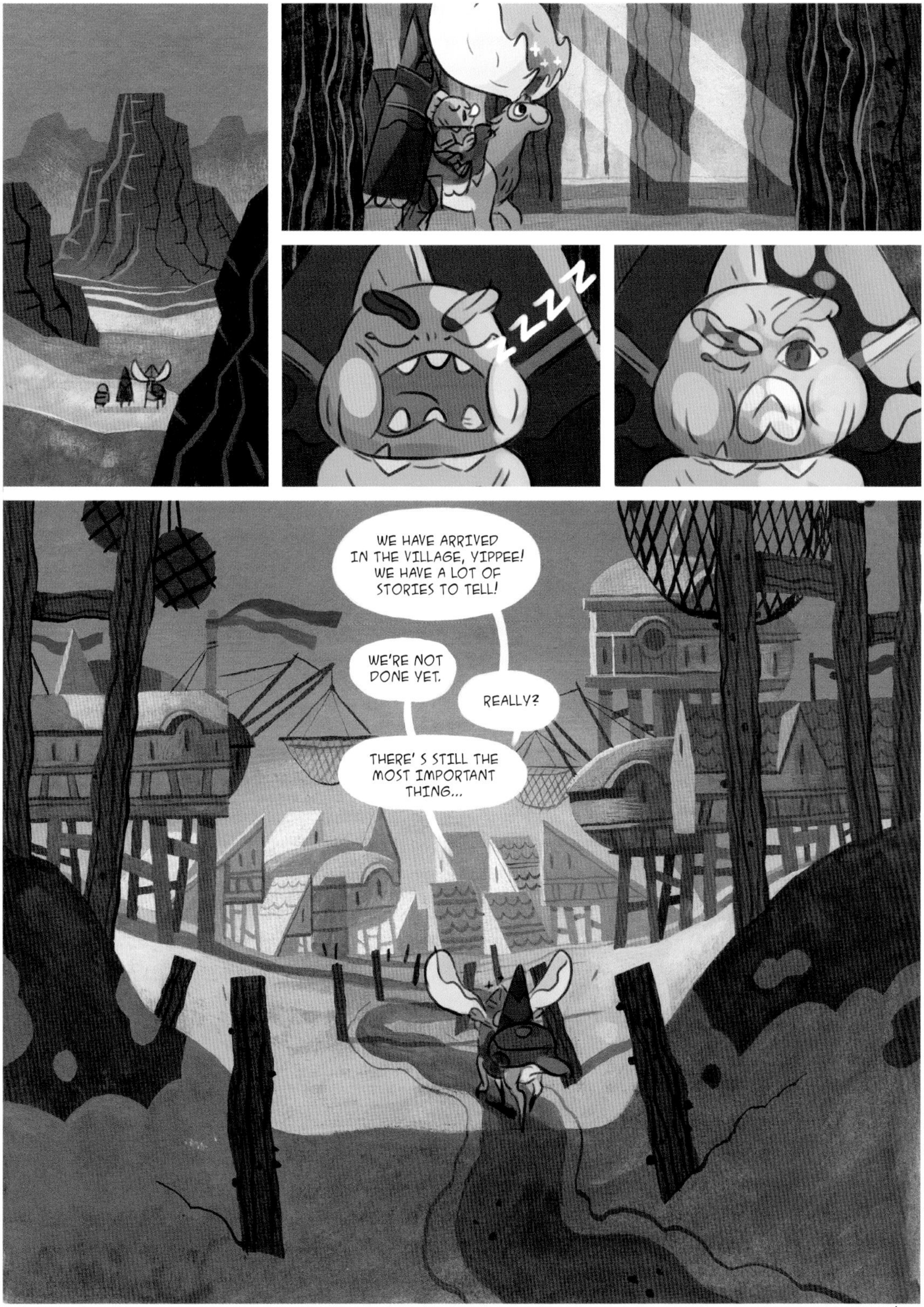
ZZZZ
WE HAVE ARRIVED IN THE VILLAGE, YIPPEE! WE HAVE A LOT OF STORIES TO TELL!
WE'RE NOT DONE YET.
REALLY?
THERE' S STILL THE MOST IMPORTANT THING...

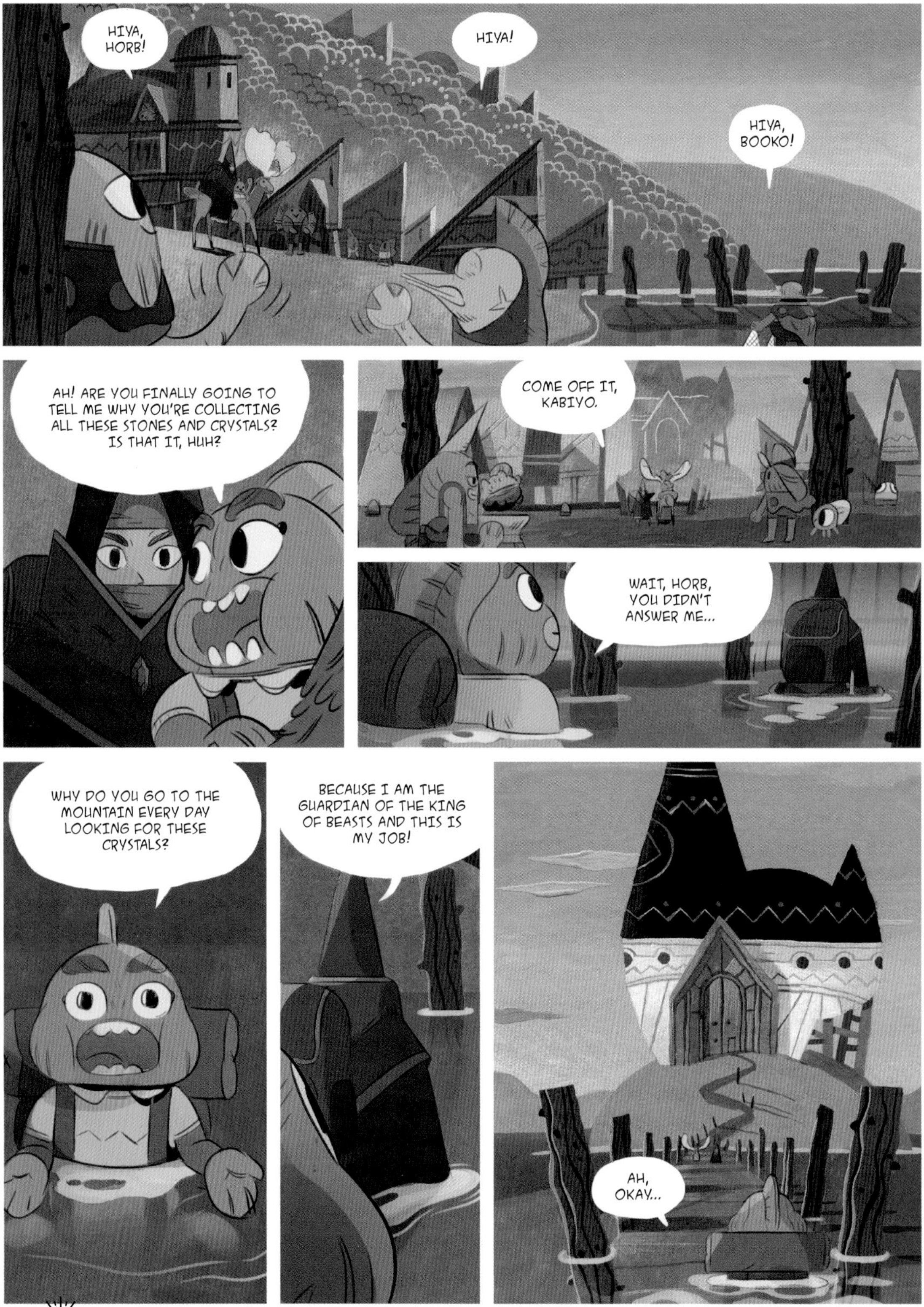
HIYA, HORB!
HIYA!
HIYA, BOOKO!
AH! ARE YOU FINALLY GOING TO TELL ME WHY YOU'RE COLLECTING ALL THESE STONES AND CRYSTALS? IS THAT IT, HUH?
COME OFF IT, KABIYO.
WAIT, HORB, YOU DIDN'T ANSWER ME...
WHY DO YOU GO TO THE MOUNTAIN EVERY DAY LOOKING FOR THESE CRYSTALS?
BECAUSE I AM THE GUARDIAN OF THE KING OF BEASTS AND THIS IS MY JOB!
AH, OKAY...

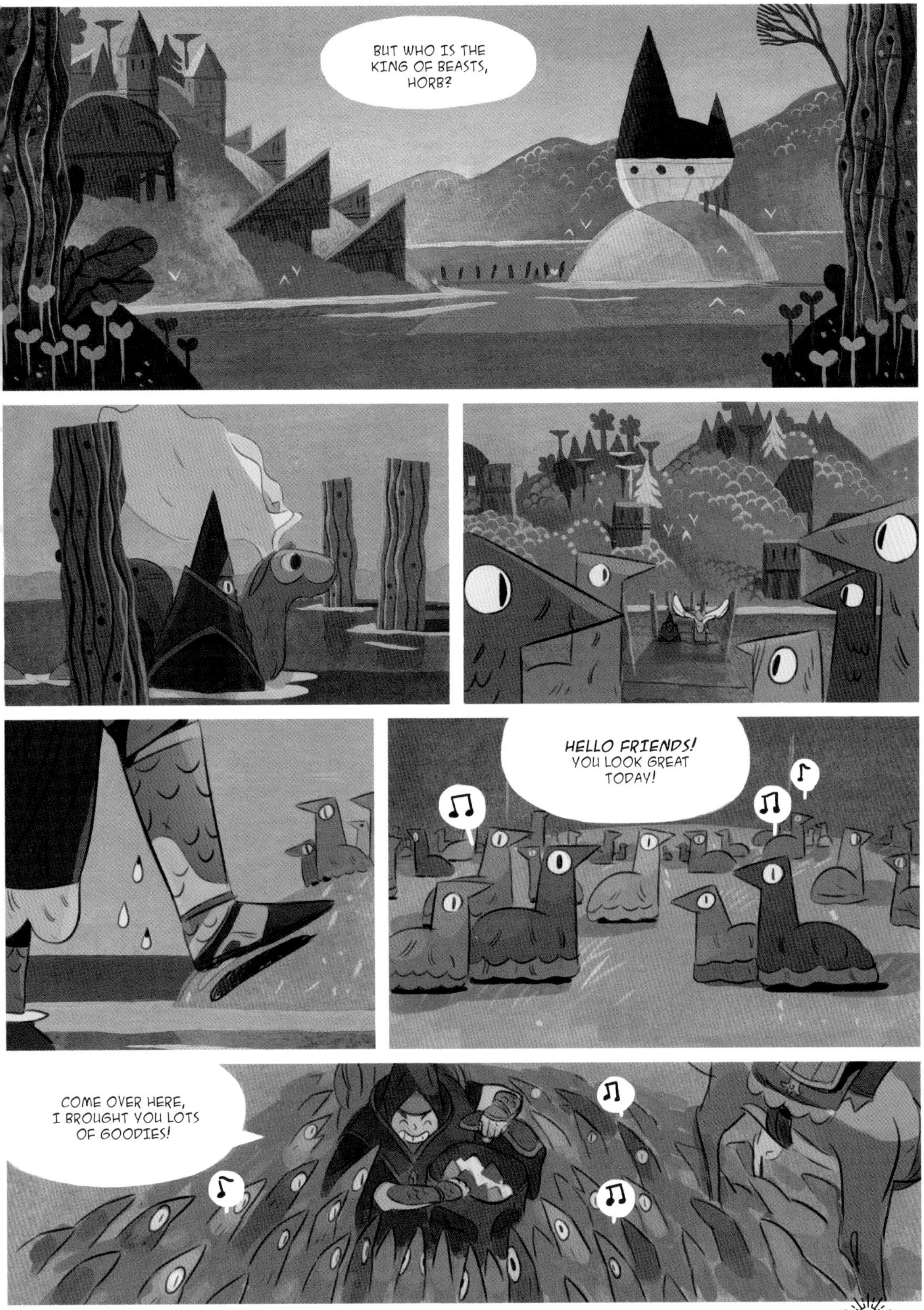
BUT WHO IS THE KING OF BEASTS, HORB?
HELLO FRIENDS! YOU LOOK GREAT TODAY!
COME OVER HERE, I BROUGHT YOU LOTS OF GOODIES!

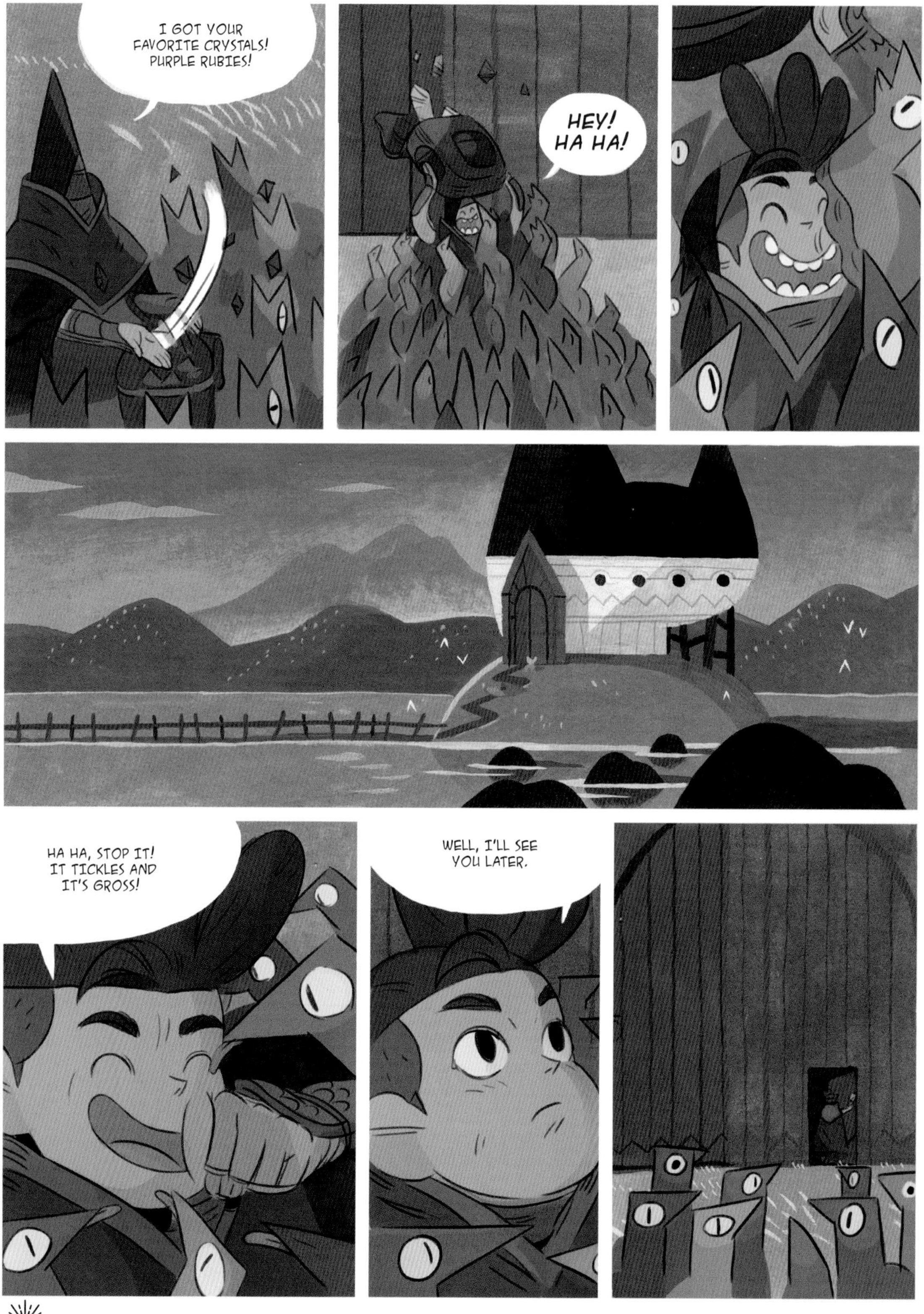
I GOT YOUR FAVORITE CRYSTALS! PURPLE RUBIES!
HEY! HA HA!
HA HA, STOP IT! IT TICKLES AND IT'S GROSS!
WELL, I'LL SEE YOU LATER.

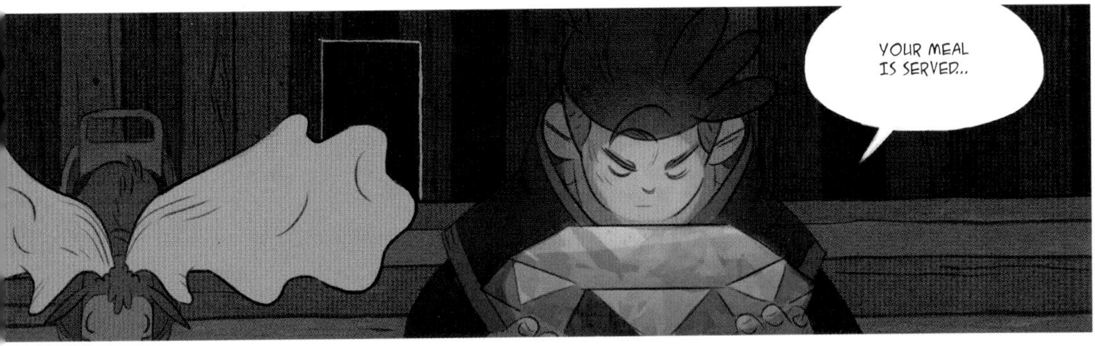
YOUR MEAL
IS SERVED...

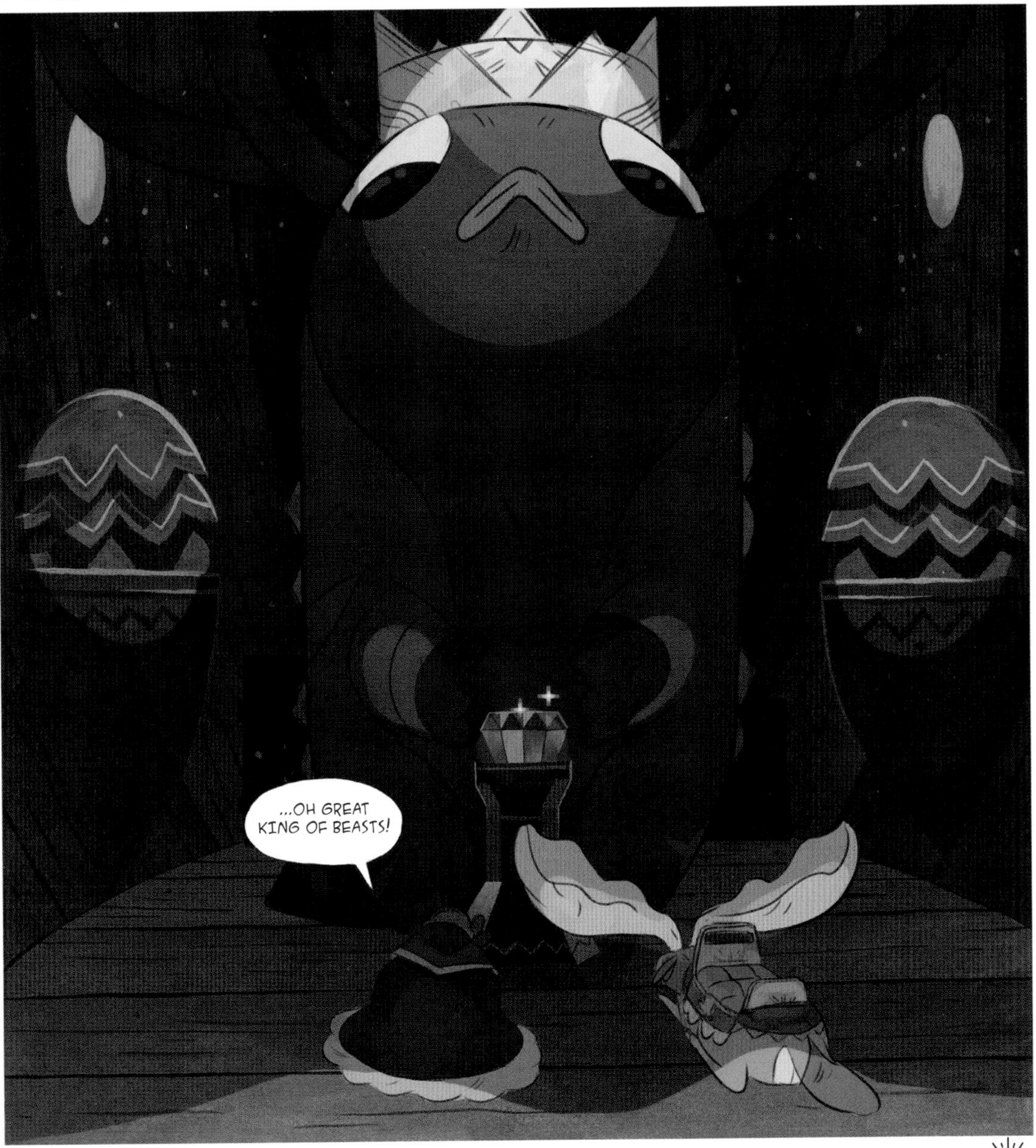
...OH GREAT
KING OF BEASTS!

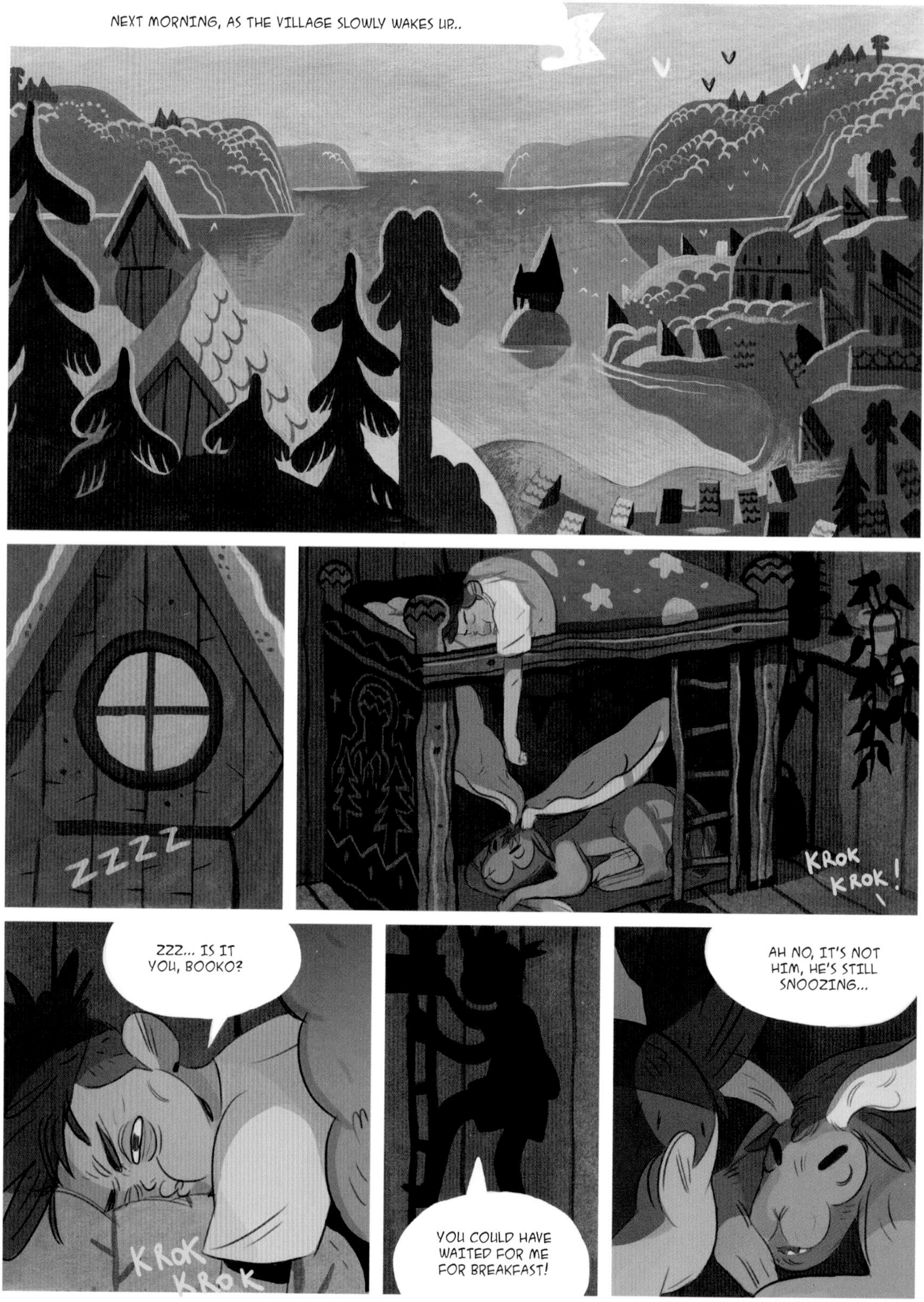
NEXT MORNING, AS THE VILLAGE SLOWLY WAKES UP...
ZZZZ
KROK KROK!
ZZZ... IS IT YOU, BOOKO?
KROK KROK
YOU COULD HAVE WAITED FOR ME FOR BREAKFAST!
AH NO, IT'S NOT HIM, HE'S STILL SNOOZING...

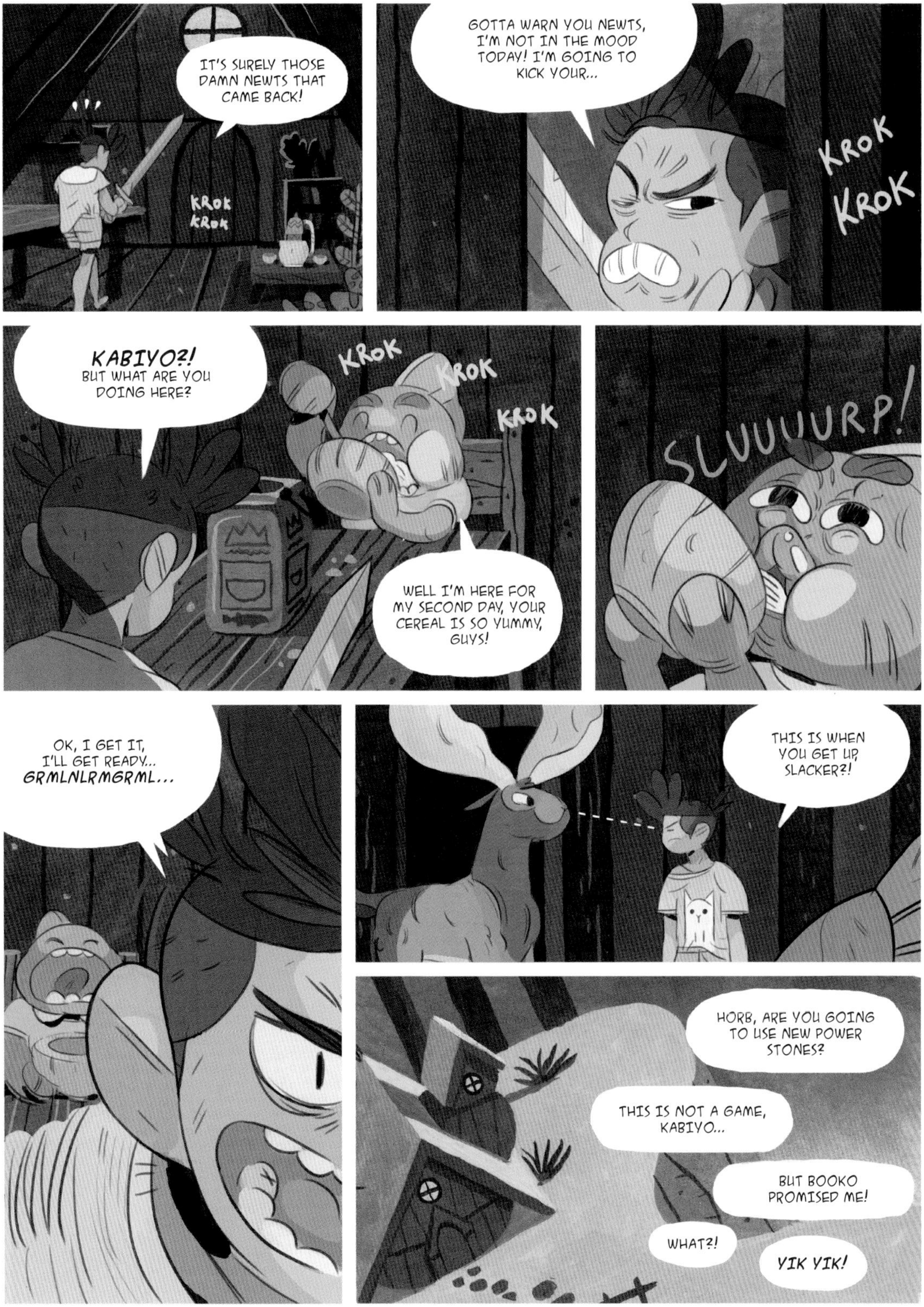
IT'S SURELY THOSE DAMN NEWTS THAT CAME BACK!
KROK KROK
GOTTA WARN YOU NEWTS, I'M NOT IN THE MOOD TODAY! I'M GOING TO KICK YOUR...
KROK KROK
KABIYO?! BUT WHAT ARE YOU DOING HERE?
KROK KROK KROK
WELL I'M HERE FOR MY SECOND DAY, YOUR CEREAL IS SO YUMMY, GUYS!
SLUUUURP!
OK, I GET IT, I'LL GET READY... GRMLNLRMGRML...
THIS IS WHEN YOU GET UP, SLACKER?!
HORB, ARE YOU GOING TO USE NEW POWER STONES?
THIS IS NOT A GAME, KABIYO...
BUT BOOKO PROMISED ME!
WHAT?!
YIK YIK!

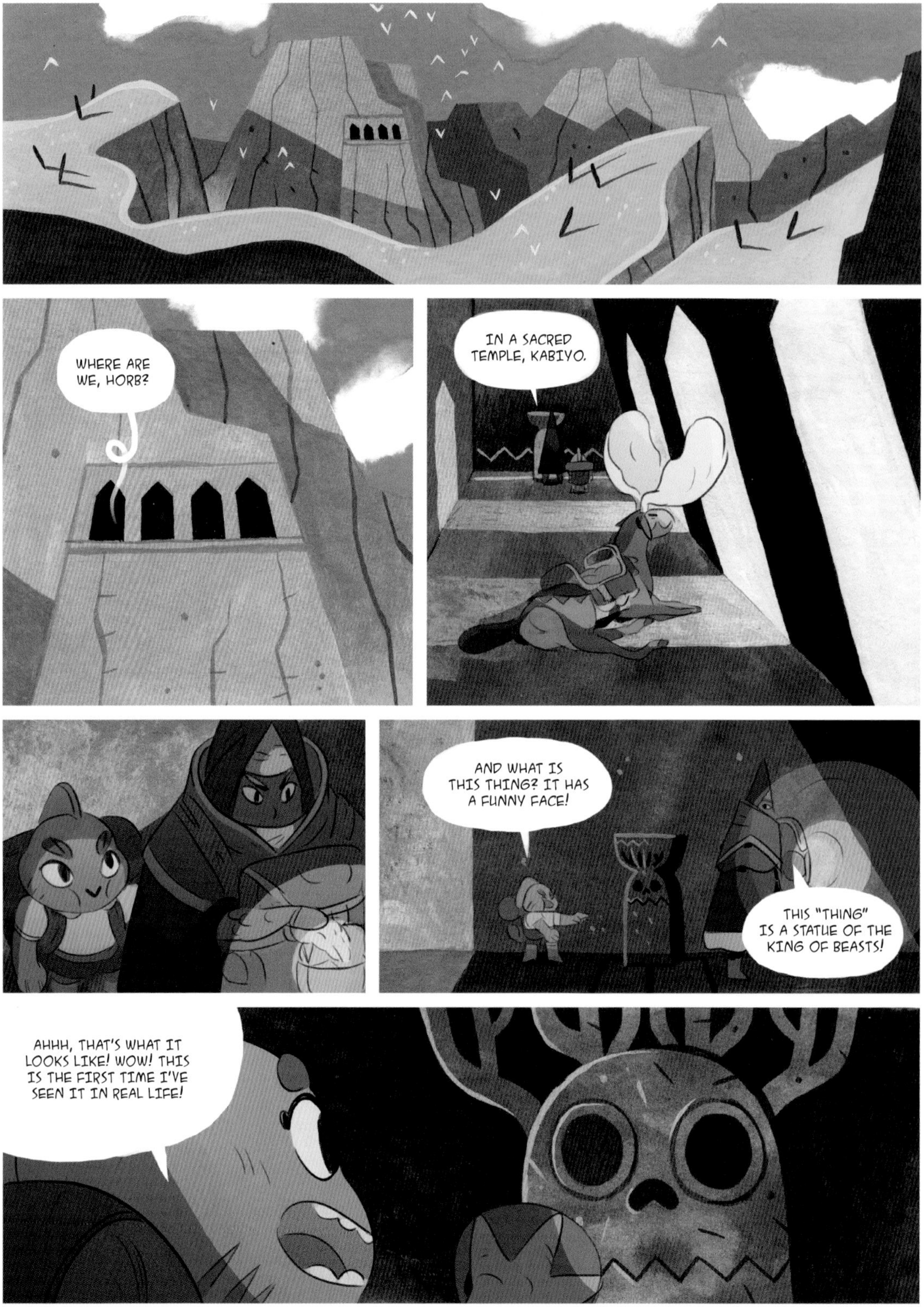
WHERE ARE WE, HORB?
IN A SACRED TEMPLE, KABIYO.
AND WHAT IS THIS THING? IT HAS A FUNNY FACE!
THIS "THING" IS A STATUE OF THE KING OF BEASTS!
AHHH, THAT'S WHAT IT LOOKS LIKE! WOW! THIS IS THE FIRST TIME I'VE SEEN IT IN REAL LIFE!

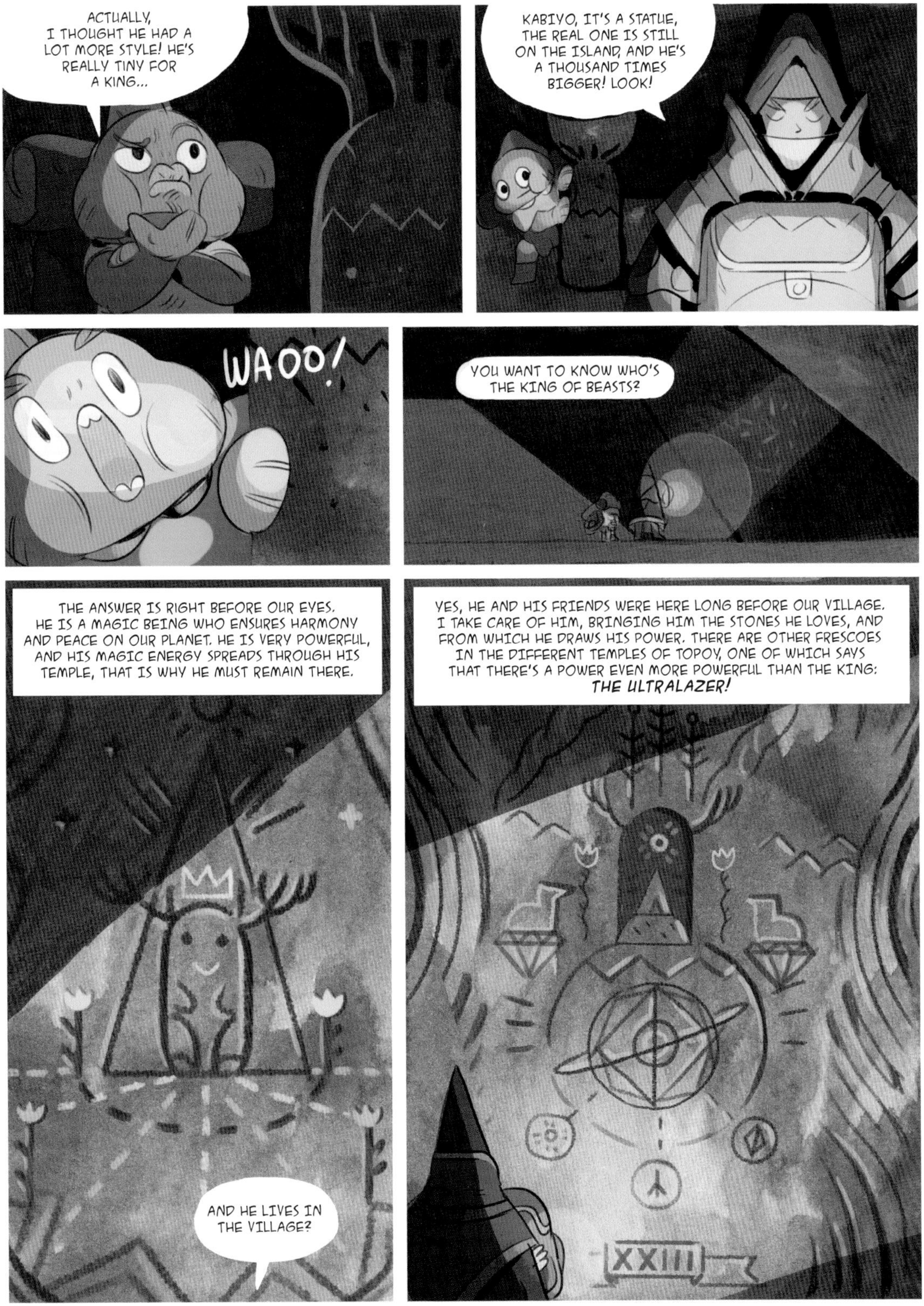
ACTUALLY, I THOUGHT HE HAD A LOT MORE STYLE! HE'S REALLY TINY FOR A KING...
KABIYO, IT'S A STATUE, THE REAL ONE IS STILL ON THE ISLAND, AND HE'S A THOUSAND TIMES BIGGER! LOOK!
WAOO!
YOU WANT TO KNOW WHO'S THE KING OF BEASTS?
THE ANSWER IS RIGHT BEFORE OUR EYES. HE IS A MAGIC BEING WHO ENSURES HARMONY AND PEACE ON OUR PLANET. HE IS VERY POWERFUL, AND HIS MAGIC ENERGY SPREADS THROUGH HIS TEMPLE, THAT IS WHY HE MUST REMAIN THERE.
AND HE LIVES IN THE VILLAGE?
YES, HE AND HIS FRIENDS WERE HERE LONG BEFORE OUR VILLAGE. I TAKE CARE OF HIM, BRINGING HIM THE STONES HE LOVES, AND FROM WHICH HE DRAWS HIS POWER. THERE ARE OTHER FRESCOES IN THE DIFFERENT TEMPLES OF TOPOY, ONE OF WHICH SAYS THAT THERE'S A POWER EVEN MORE POWERFUL THAN THE KING: ***THE ULTRALAZER!***
XXIII

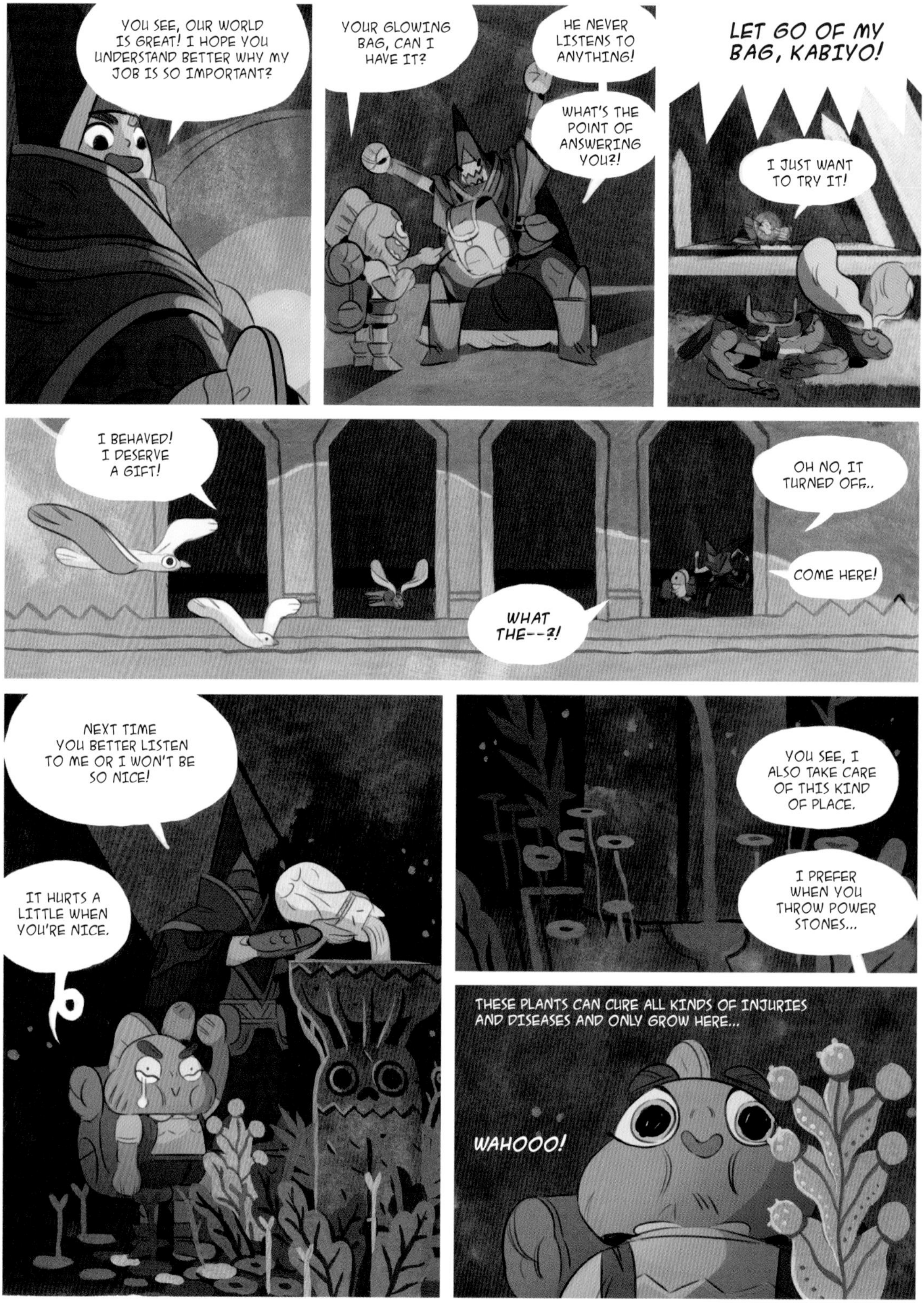
YOU SEE, OUR WORLD IS GREAT! I HOPE YOU UNDERSTAND BETTER WHY MY JOB IS SO IMPORTANT?
YOUR GLOWING BAG, CAN I HAVE IT?
HE NEVER LISTENS TO ANYTHING!
WHAT'S THE POINT OF ANSWERING YOU?!
LET GO OF MY BAG, KABIYO!
I JUST WANT TO TRY IT!
I BEHAVED! I DESERVE A GIFT!
WHAT THE--?!
OH NO, IT TURNED OFF..
COME HERE!
NEXT TIME YOU BETTER LISTEN TO ME OR I WON'T BE SO NICE!
IT HURTS A LITTLE WHEN YOU'RE NICE.
YOU SEE, I ALSO TAKE CARE OF THIS KIND OF PLACE.
I PREFER WHEN YOU THROW POWER STONES...
THESE PLANTS CAN CURE ALL KINDS OF INJURIES AND DISEASES AND ONLY GROW HERE...
WAHOOO!

AND WITHOUT ME TO WATER THEM...

BRRRRRR

AN EARTHQUAKE?

RRRRR RRR

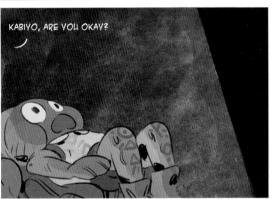

KABIYO, ARE YOU OKAY?

YES, I'M FINE, BUT THERE ARE SOME SHINY THINGS ON THE WALLS!

I HAVE A BAD FEELING ABOUT THIS...

DO YOU SEE ANYTHING, BOOKO?

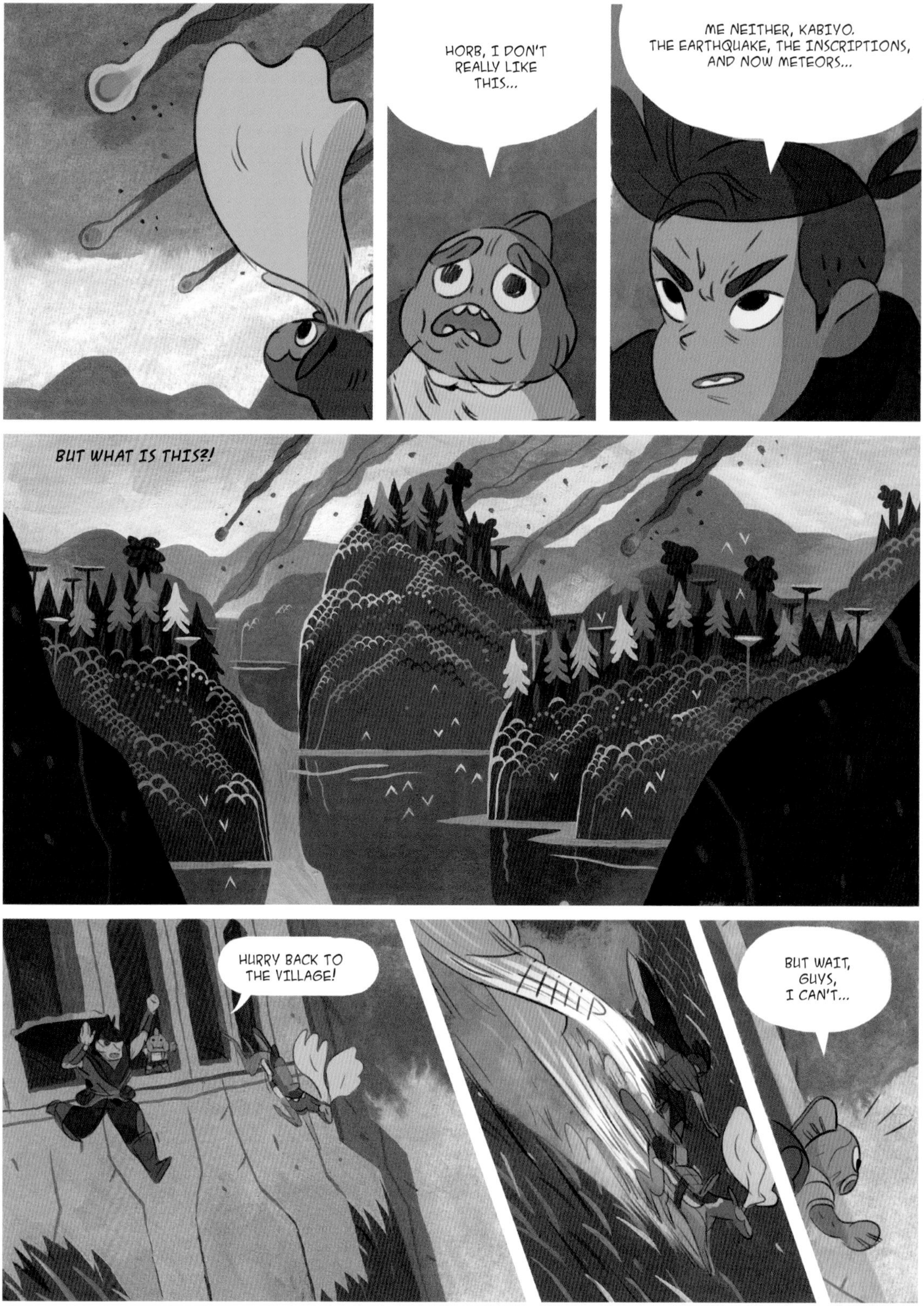
HORB, I DON'T REALLY LIKE THIS...
ME NEITHER, KABIYO. THE EARTHQUAKE, THE INSCRIPTIONS, AND NOW METEORS...
BUT WHAT IS THIS?!
HURRY BACK TO THE VILLAGE!
BUT WAIT, GUYS, I CAN'T...

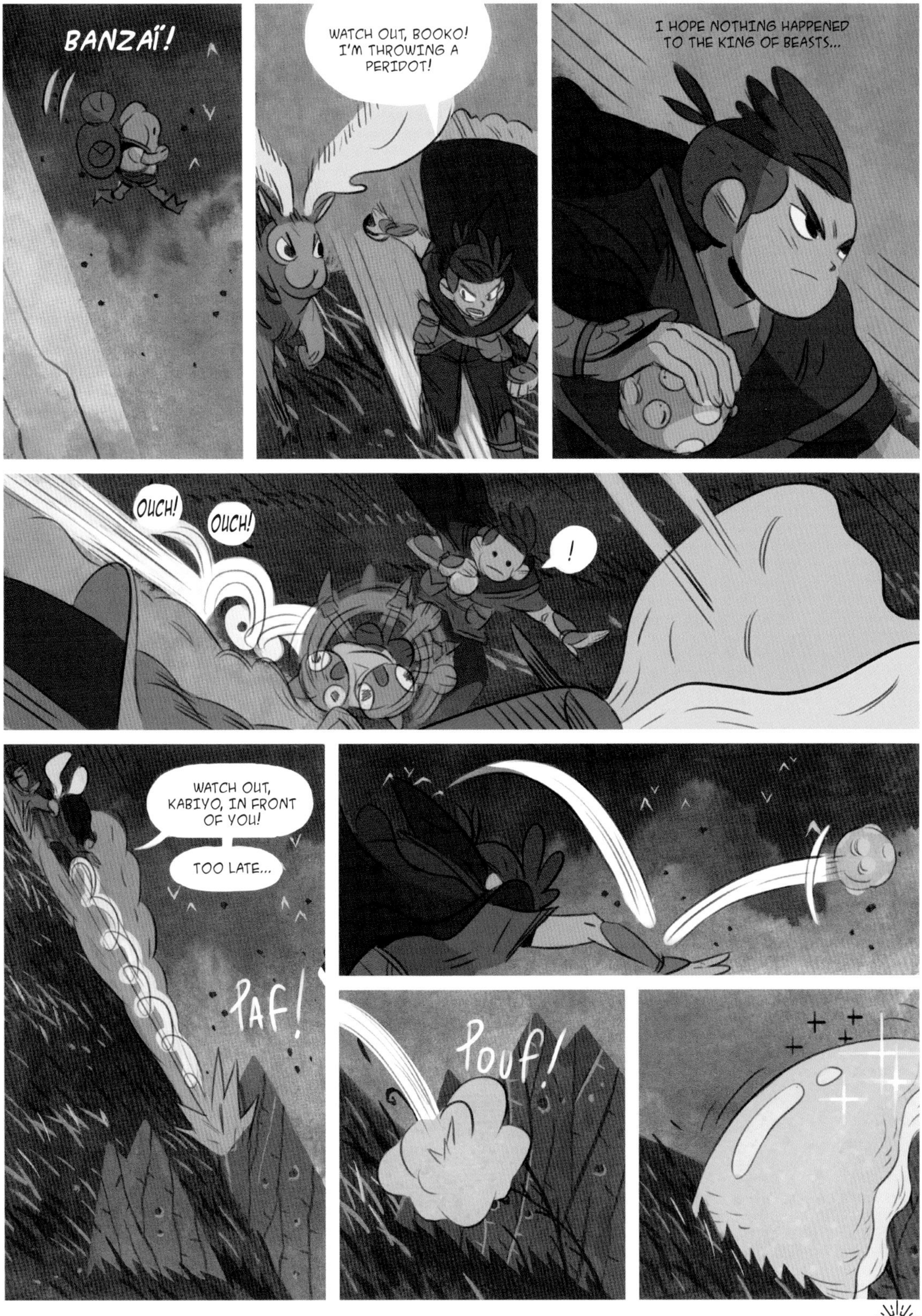
BANZAÏ!
WATCH OUT, BOOKO! I'M THROWING A PERIDOT!
I HOPE NOTHING HAPPENED TO THE KING OF BEASTS...
OUCH!
OUCH!
!
WATCH OUT, KABIYO, IN FRONT OF YOU!
TOO LATE...
PAF!
POUF!

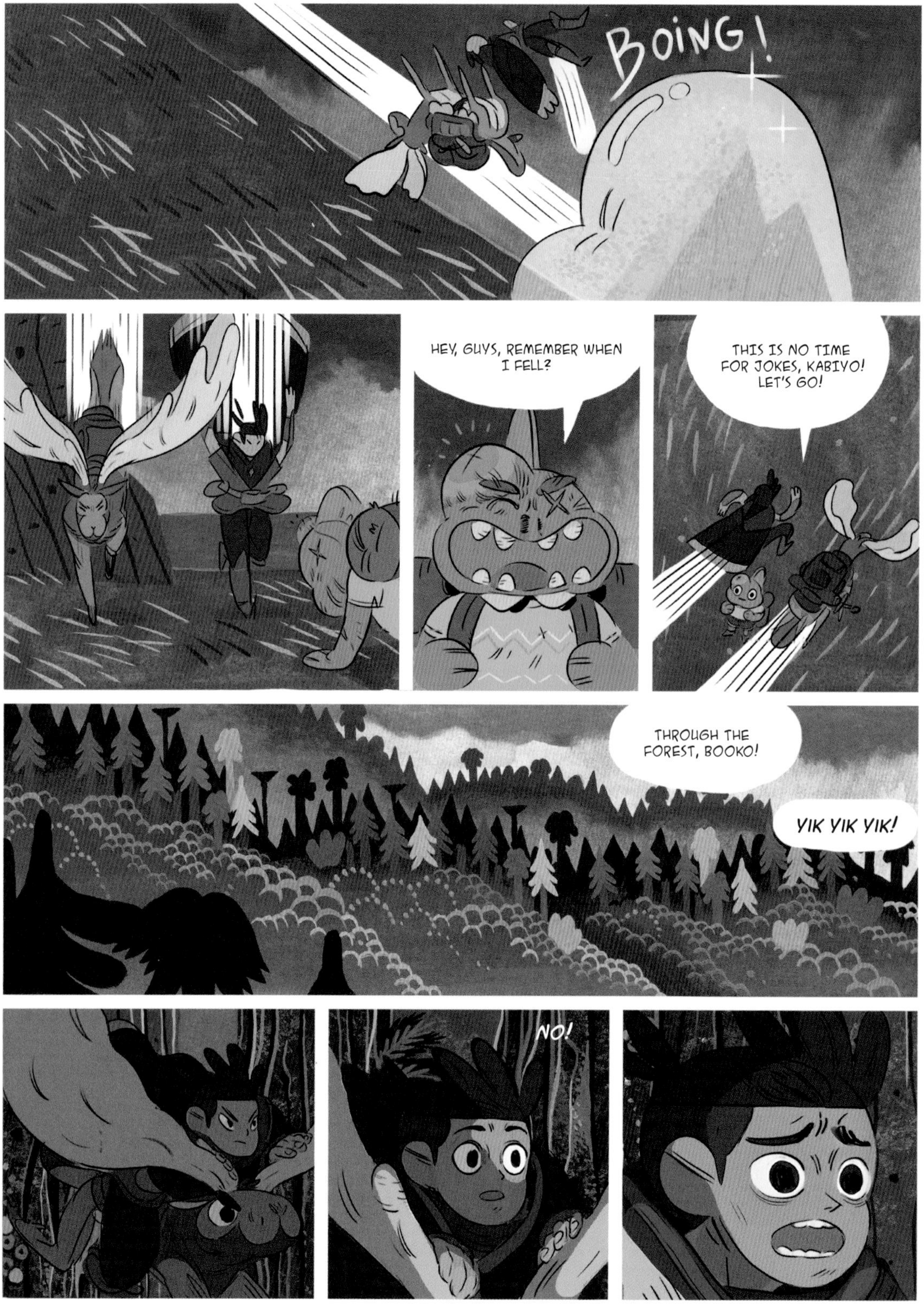
BOING!
HEY, GUYS, REMEMBER WHEN I FELL?
THIS IS NO TIME FOR JOKES, KABIYO! LET'S GO!
THROUGH THE FOREST, BOOKO!
YIK YIK YIK!
NO!

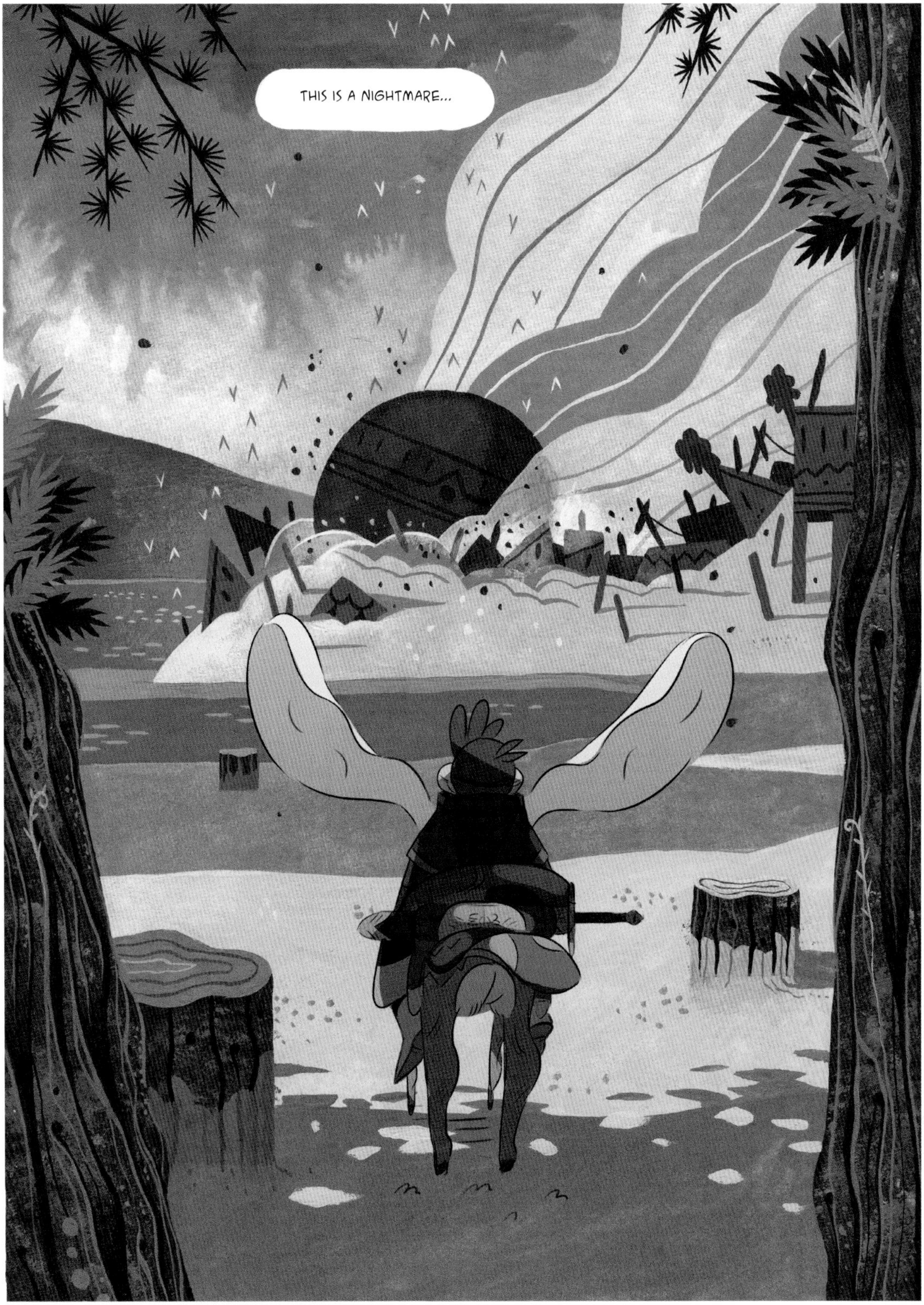
THIS IS A NIGHTMARE...

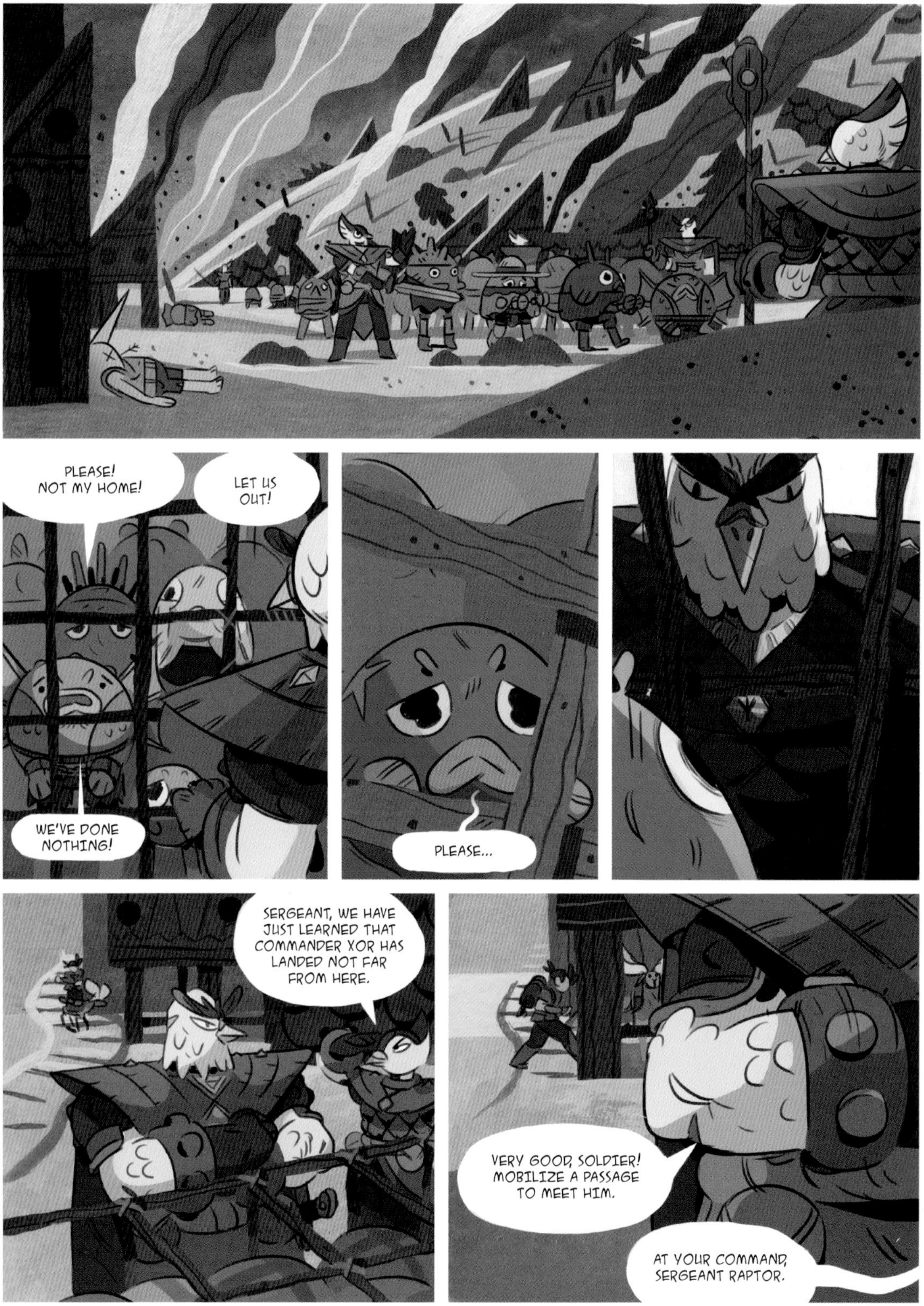
PLEASE! NOT MY HOME!
LET US OUT!
WE'VE DONE NOTHING!
PLEASE...
SERGEANT, WE HAVE JUST LEARNED THAT COMMANDER XOR HAS LANDED NOT FAR FROM HERE.
VERY GOOD, SOLDIER! MOBILIZE A PASSAGE TO MEET HIM.
AT YOUR COMMAND, SERGEANT RAPTOR.

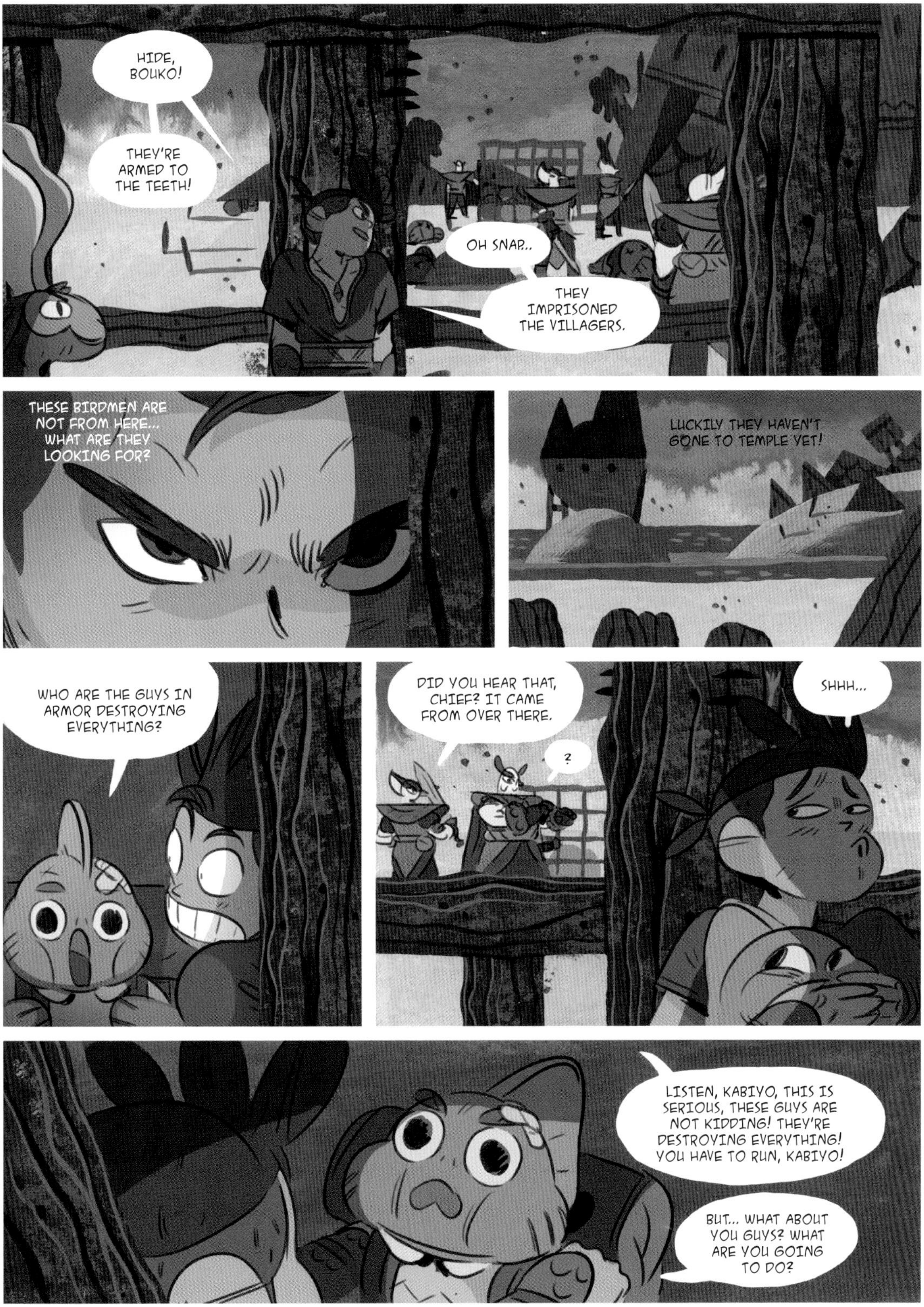
HIDE, BOUKO!
THEY'RE ARMED TO THE TEETH!
OH SNAP...
THEY IMPRISONED THE VILLAGERS.
THESE BIRDMEN ARE NOT FROM HERE... WHAT ARE THEY LOOKING FOR?
LUCKILY THEY HAVEN'T GONE TO TEMPLE YET!
WHO ARE THE GUYS IN ARMOR DESTROYING EVERYTHING?
DID YOU HEAR THAT, CHIEF? IT CAME FROM OVER THERE.
?
SHHH...
LISTEN, KABIYO, THIS IS SERIOUS, THESE GUYS ARE NOT KIDDING! THEY'RE DESTROYING EVERYTHING! YOU HAVE TO RUN, KABIYO!
BUT... WHAT ABOUT YOU GUYS? WHAT ARE YOU GOING TO DO?

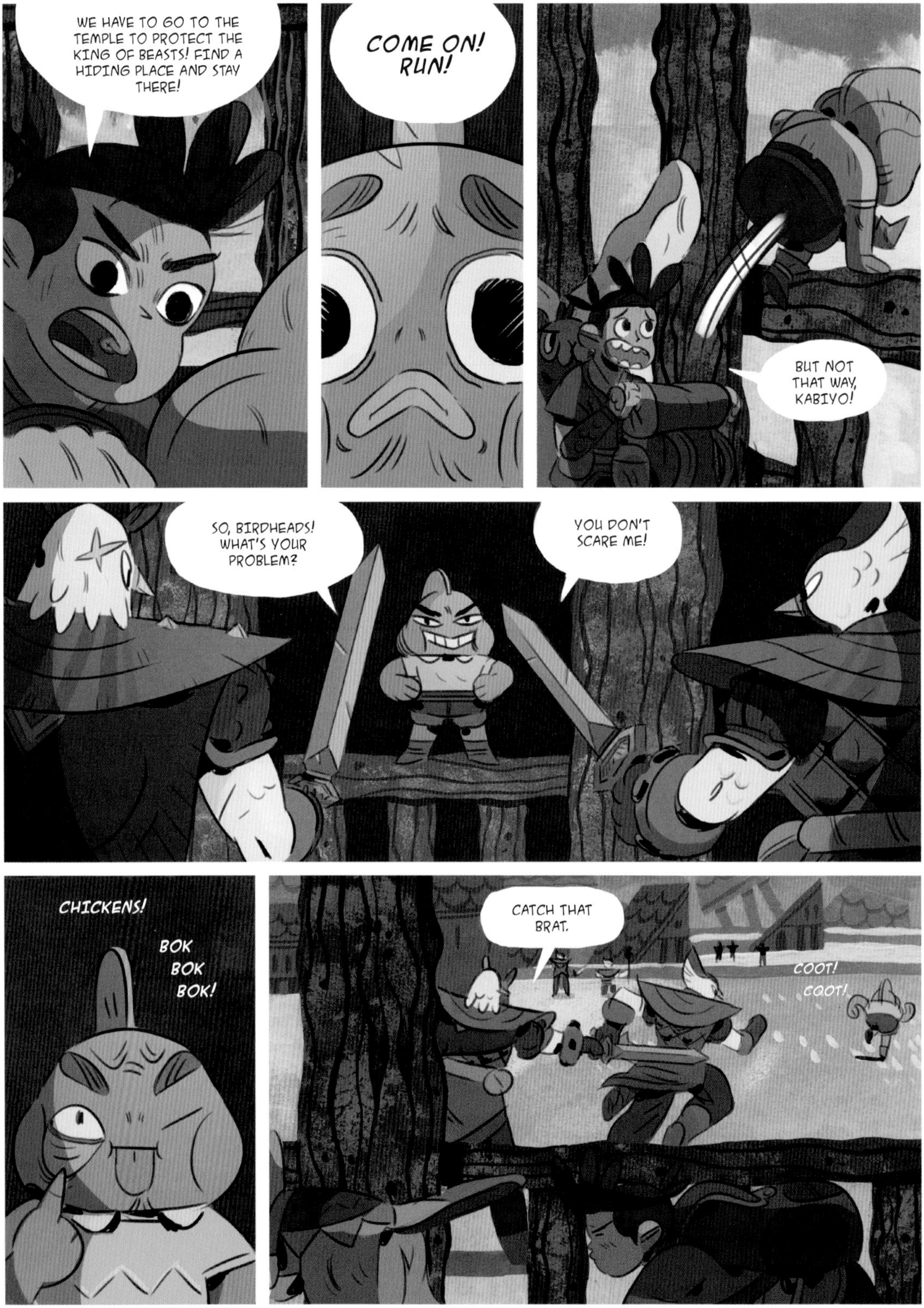
WE HAVE TO GO TO THE TEMPLE TO PROTECT THE KING OF BEASTS! FIND A HIDING PLACE AND STAY THERE!
COME ON! RUN!
BUT NOT THAT WAY, KABIYO!
SO, BIRDHEADS! WHAT'S YOUR PROBLEM?
YOU DON'T SCARE ME!
CHICKENS!
BOK
BOK
BOK!
CATCH THAT BRAT.
COOT!
COOT!

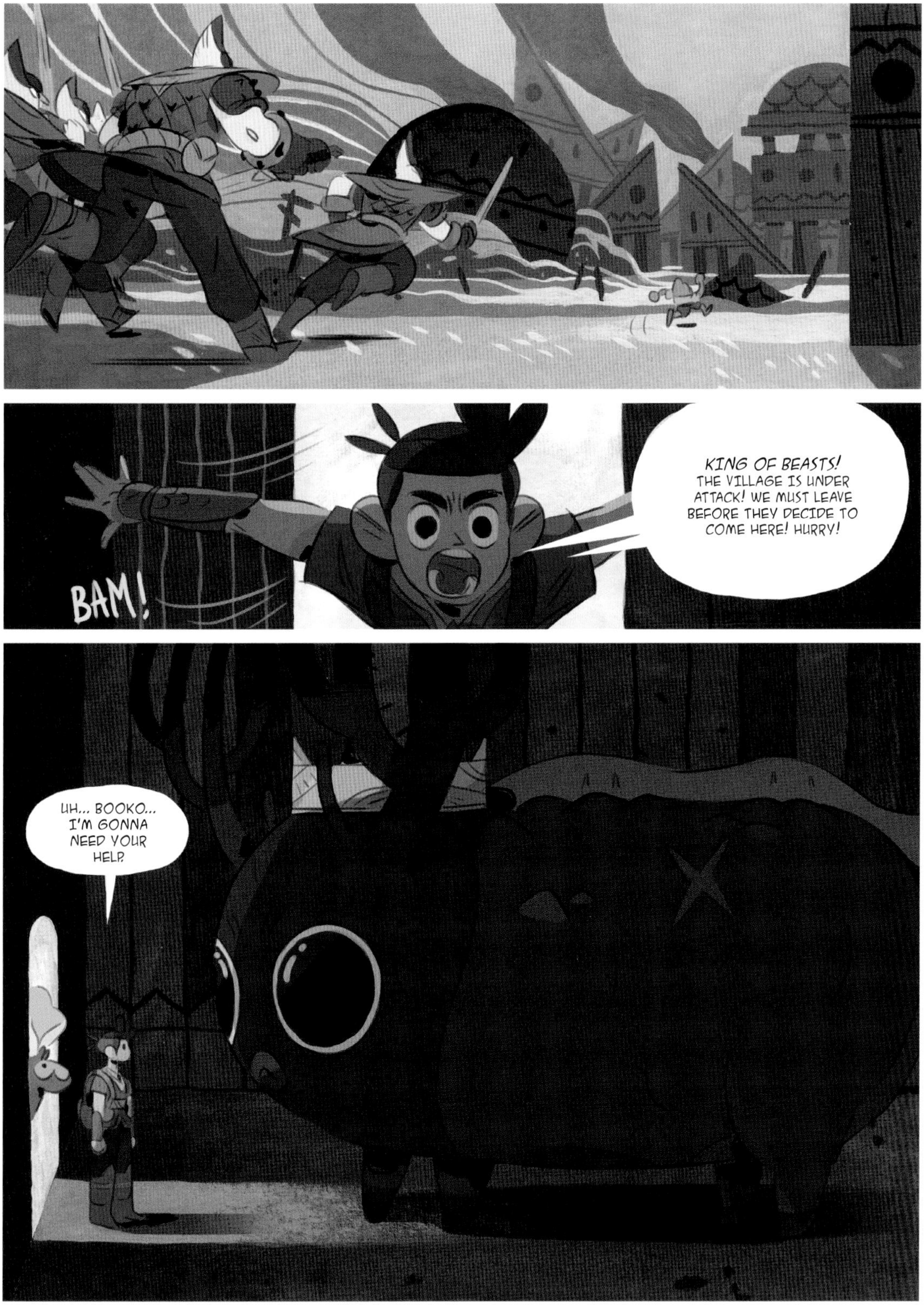

BAM!
KING OF BEASTS! THE VILLAGE IS UNDER ATTACK! WE MUST LEAVE BEFORE THEY DECIDE TO COME HERE! HURRY!
UH... BOOKO... I'M GONNA NEED YOUR HELP.

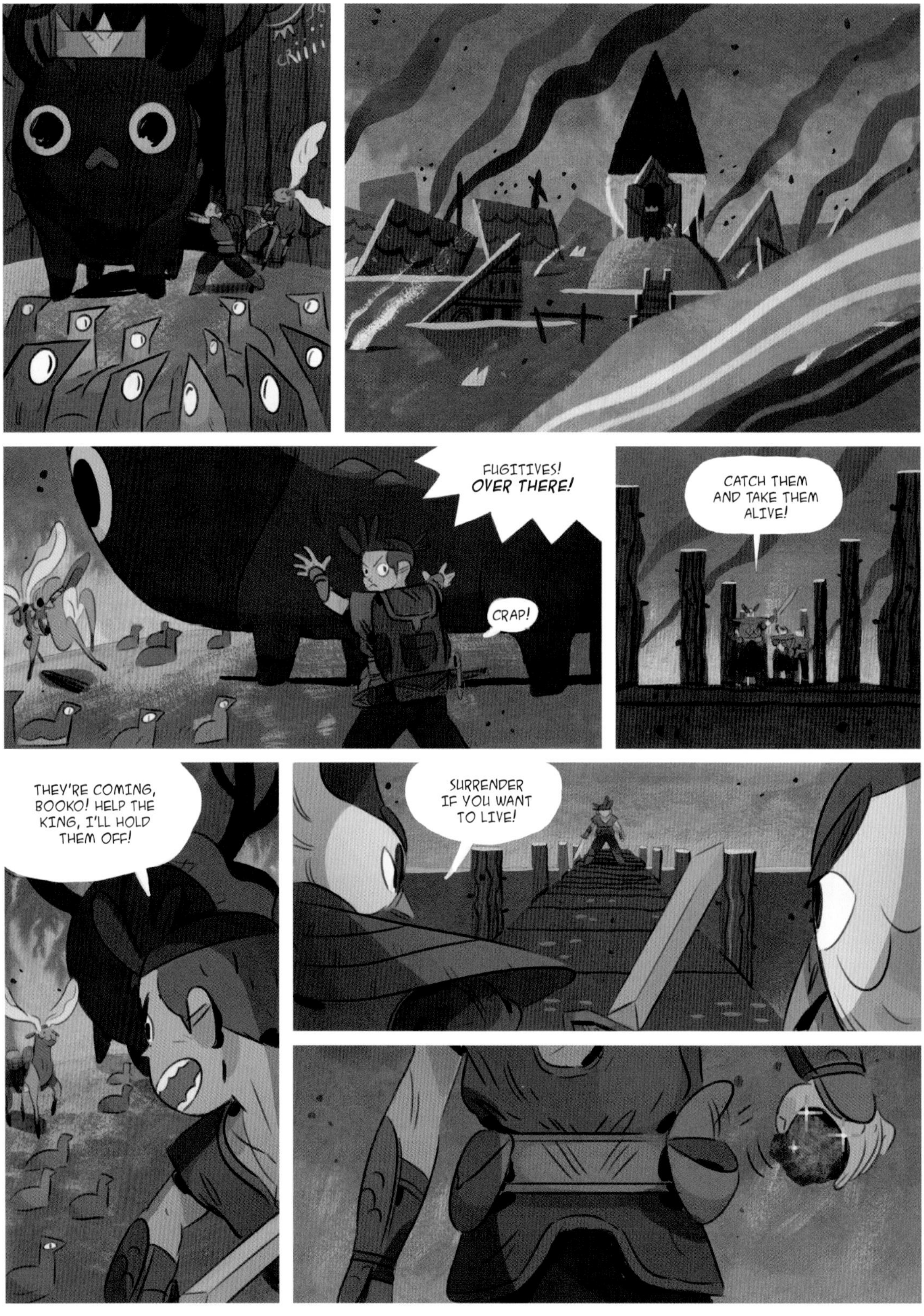
FUGITIVES! **OVER THERE!**
CRAP!
CATCH THEM AND TAKE THEM ALIVE!
THEY'RE COMING, BOOKO! HELP THE KING, I'LL HOLD THEM OFF!
SURRENDER IF YOU WANT TO LIVE!

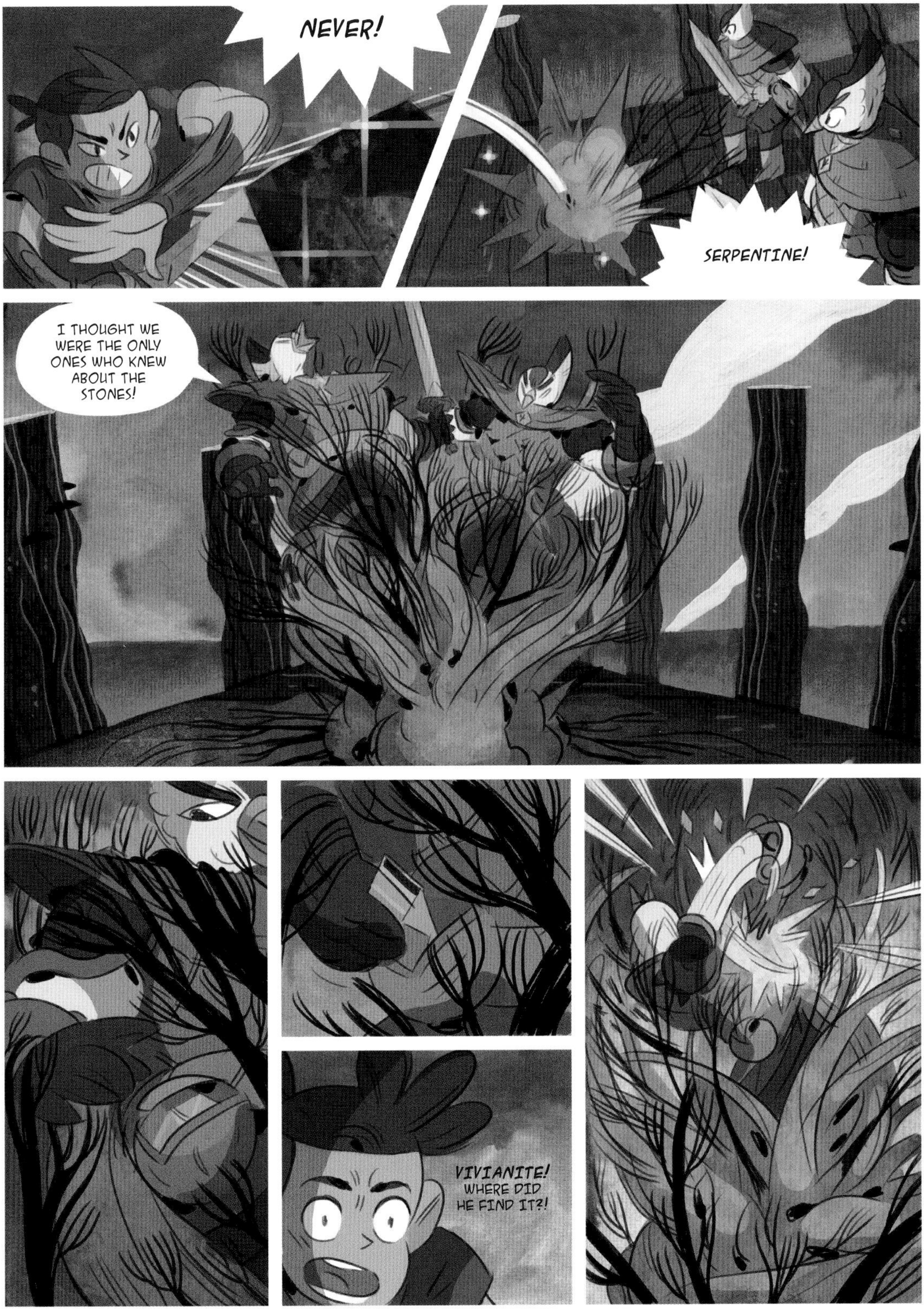
NEVER!
SERPENTINE!
I THOUGHT WE WERE THE ONLY ONES WHO KNEW ABOUT THE STONES!
VIVIANITE! WHERE DID HE FIND IT?!

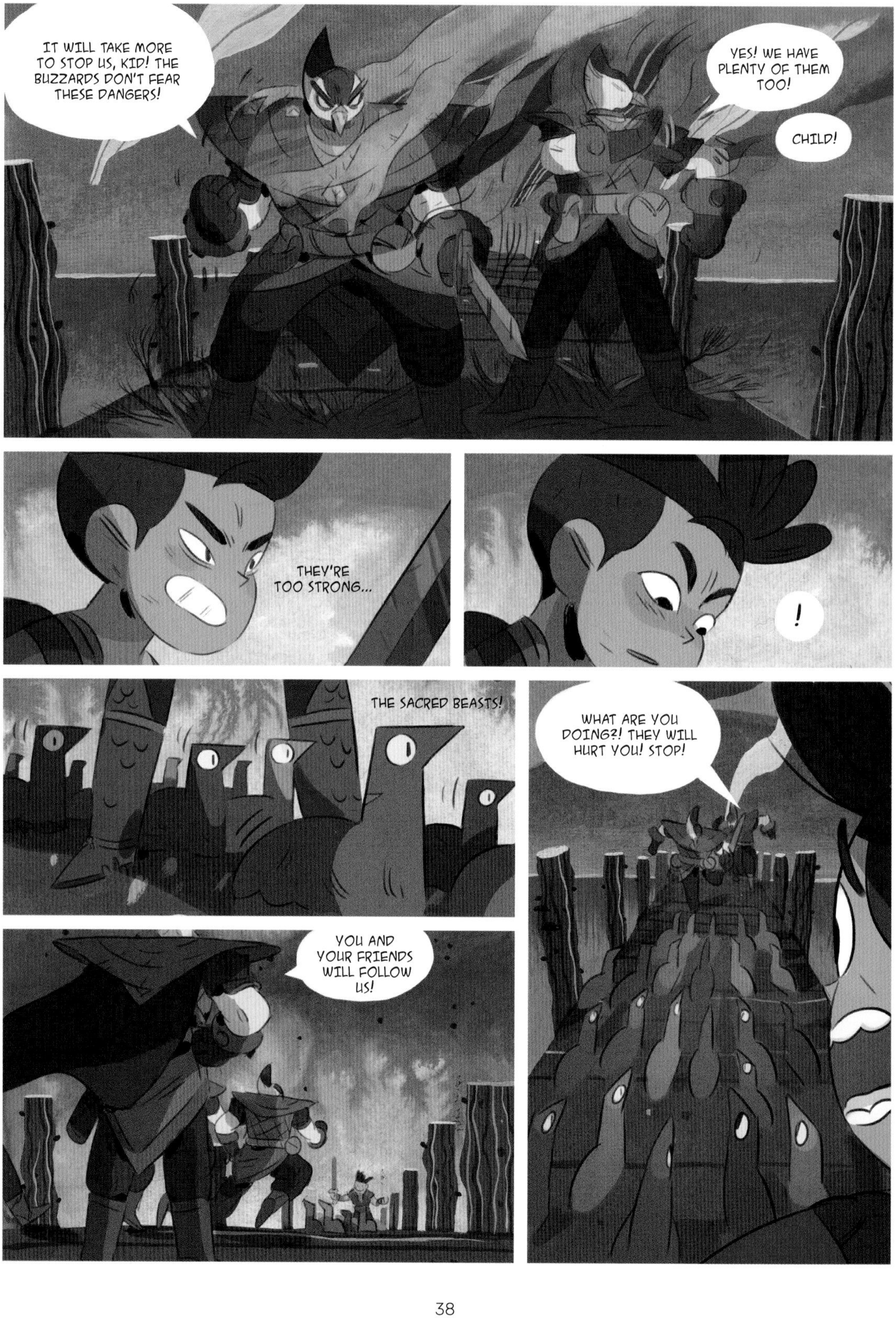
IT WILL TAKE MORE TO STOP US, KID! THE BUZZARDS DON'T FEAR THESE DANGERS!
YES! WE HAVE PLENTY OF THEM TOO!
CHILD!
THEY'RE TOO STRONG...
!
THE SACRED BEASTS!
WHAT ARE YOU DOING?! THEY WILL HURT YOU! STOP!
YOU AND YOUR FRIENDS WILL FOLLOW US!

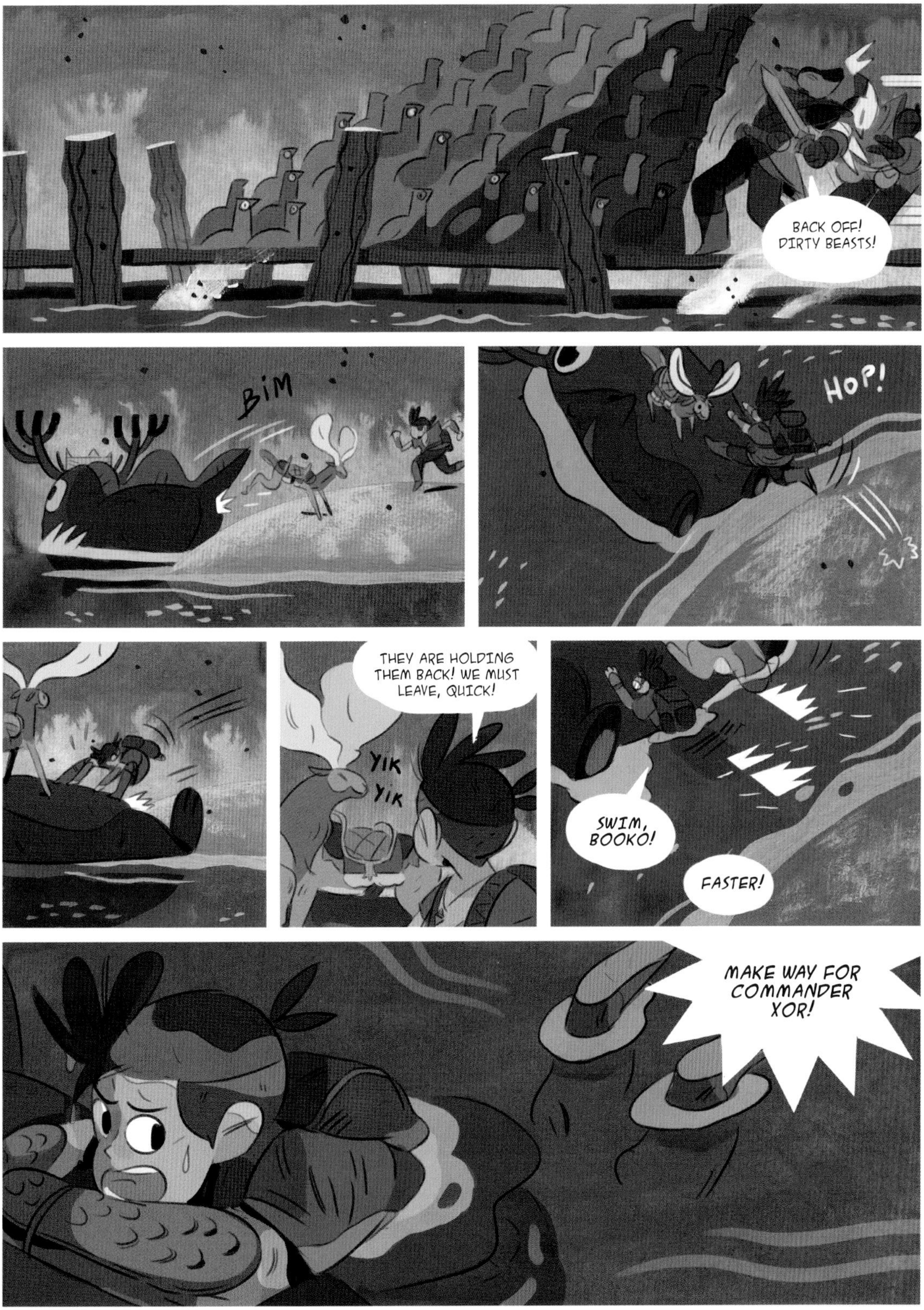
BACK OFF! DIRTY BEASTS!
BIM
HOP!
THEY ARE HOLDING THEM BACK! WE MUST LEAVE, QUICK!
YIK YIK
SWIM, BOOKO!
FASTER!
MAKE WAY FOR COMMANDER XOR!

COMMANDER, THESE CREATURES ARE BLOCKING OUR WAY!

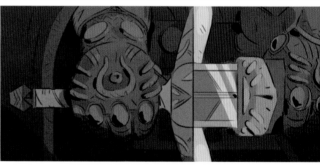

NO!

THEY HAVEN'T DONE ANYTHING TO YOU! DON'T HURT THEM!

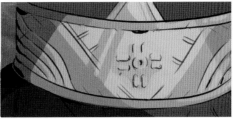

THE SYMBOL!

IT'S THE BIG BEAST WE'VE COME FOR, YOU MORONS!

NO! WAIT!

PLEASE! THEY'RE HARMLESS!

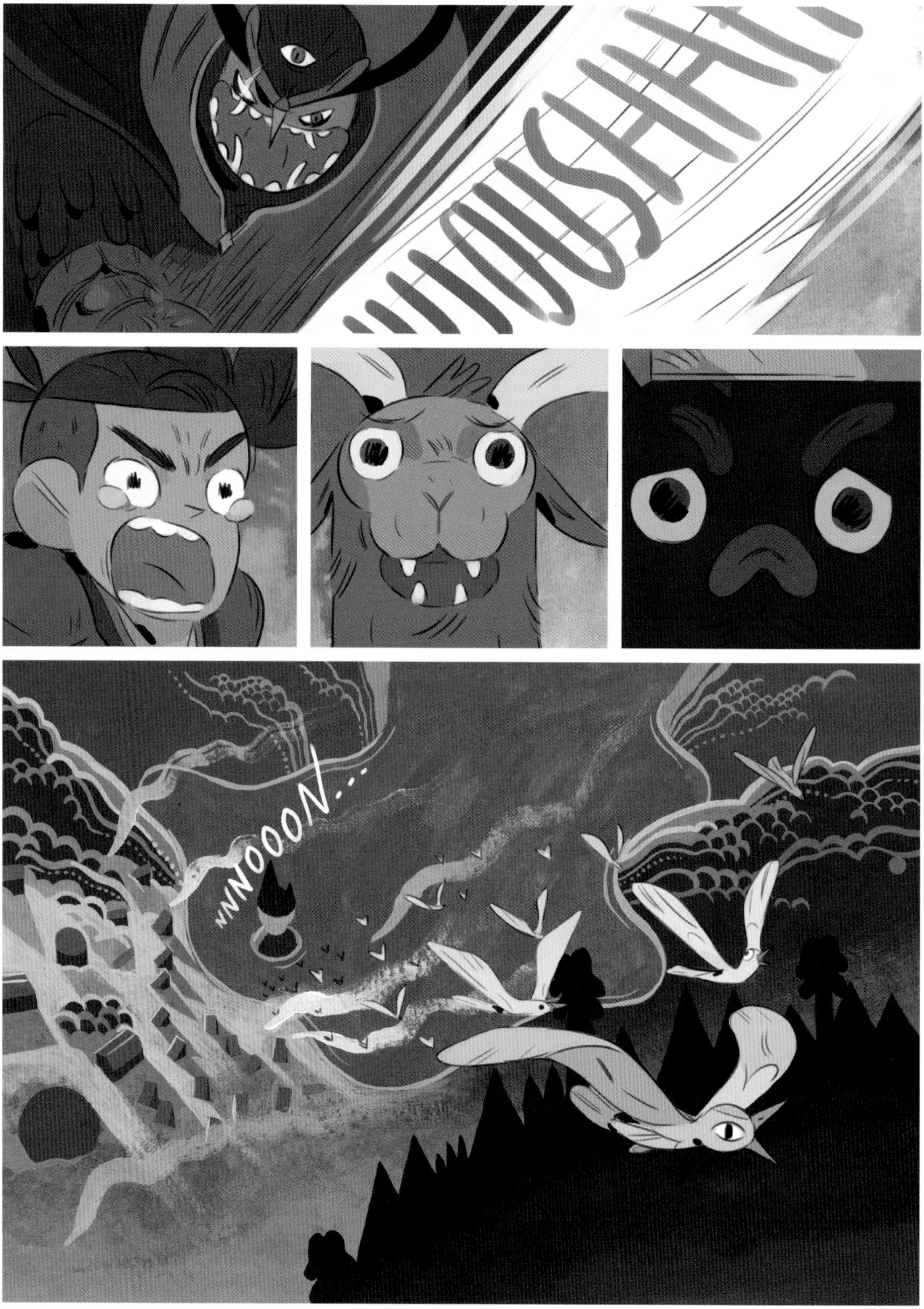
NNNNOOON...

SET FIRE TO THE TEMPLE AND TAKE CARE OF THE BEAST!

YES, SIR!

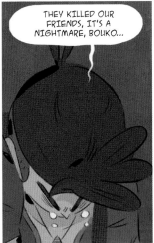

THEY KILLED OUR FRIENDS, IT'S A NIGHTMARE, BOUKO...

frot frot

SNIFF.. WE HAVE TO TAKE THE KING AS FAR AS POSSIBLE FROM THESE MONSTERS.

I GOTTA HAVE AN OPAL LEFT!

HAAA

VLAA

WOOSHHH!

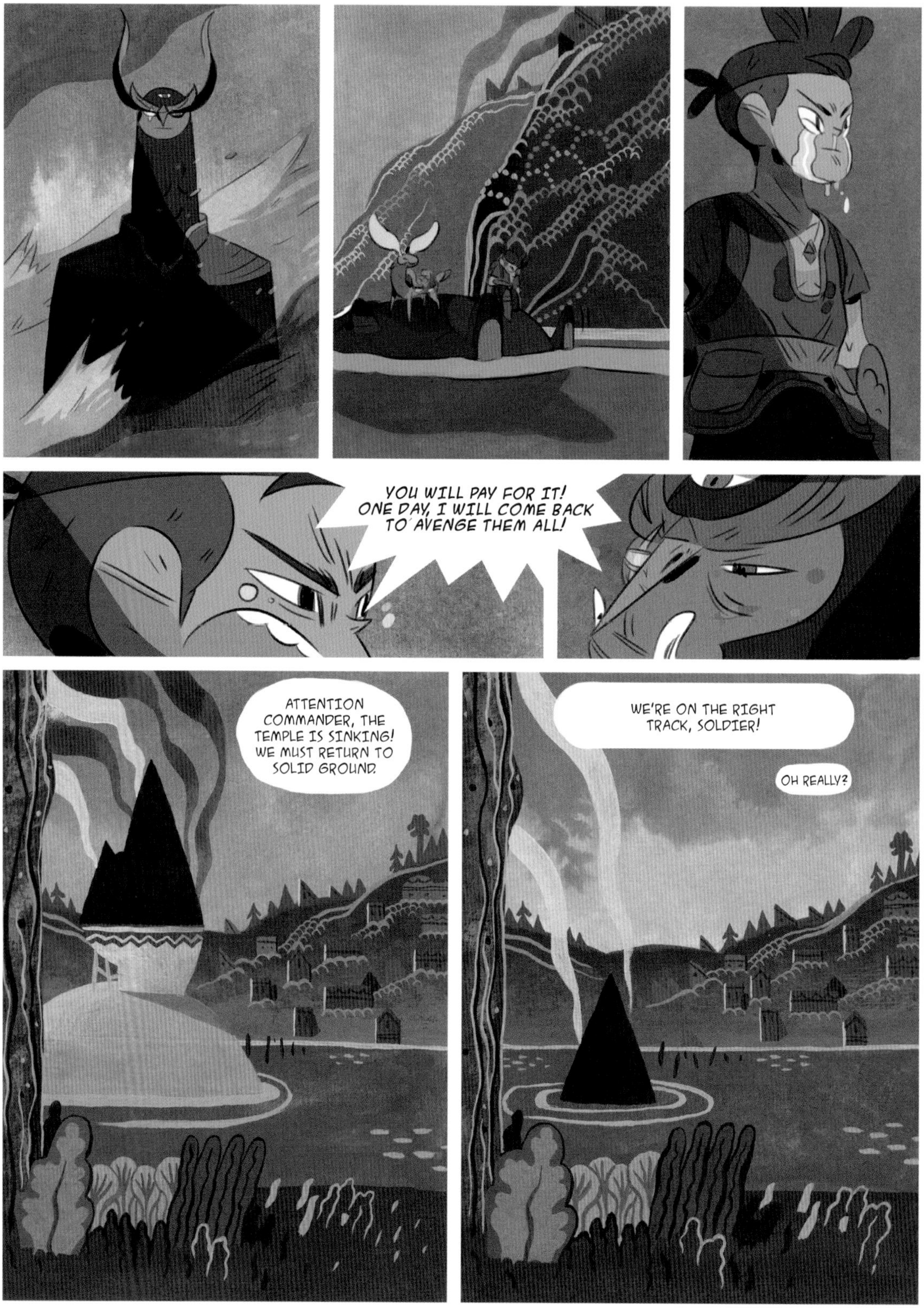
YOU WILL PAY FOR IT! ONE DAY, I WILL COME BACK TO AVENGE THEM ALL!
ATTENTION COMMANDER, THE TEMPLE IS SINKING! WE MUST RETURN TO SOLID GROUND.
WE'RE ON THE RIGHT TRACK, SOLDIER!
OH REALLY?

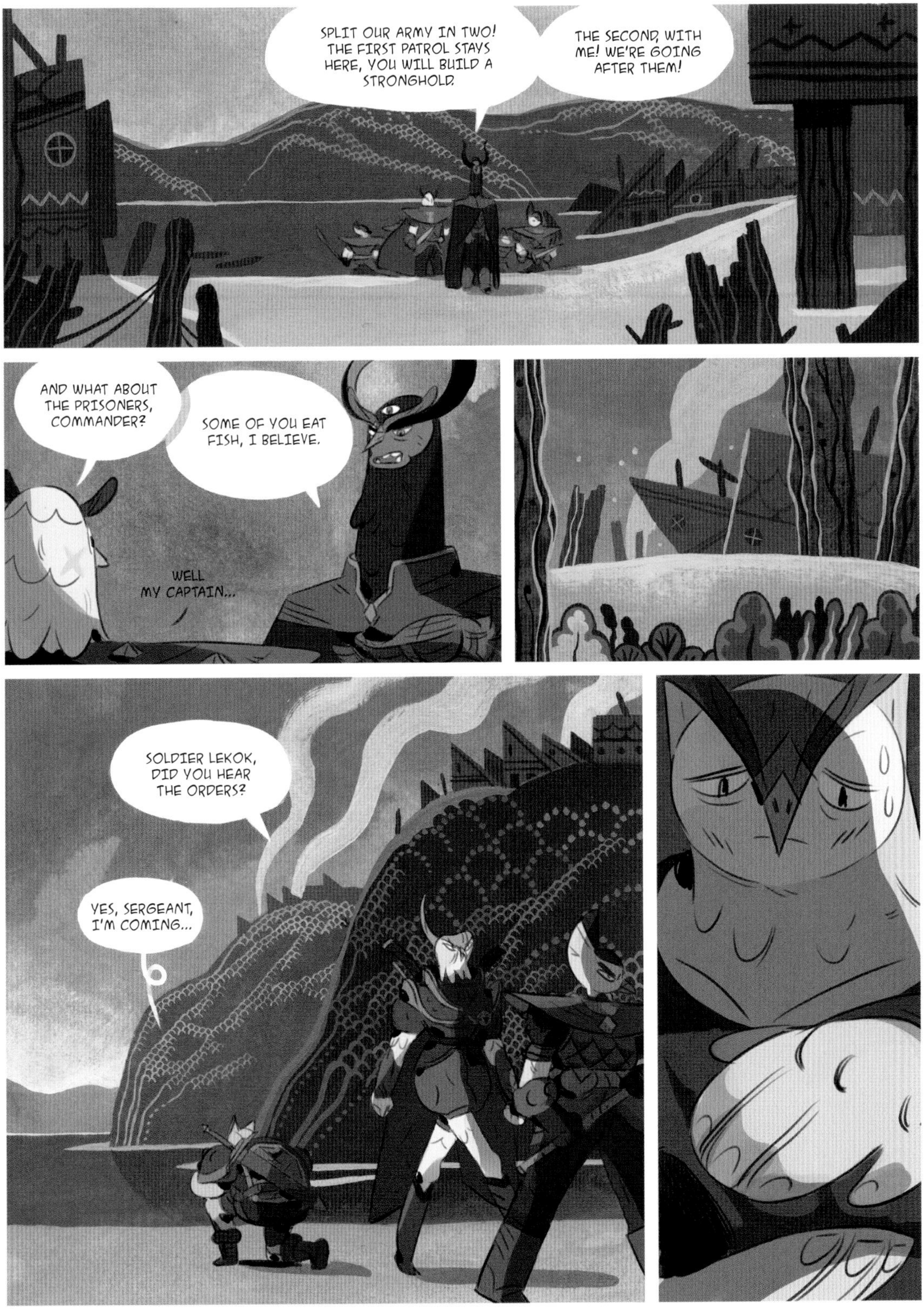
SPLIT OUR ARMY IN TWO! THE FIRST PATROL STAYS HERE, YOU WILL BUILD A STRONGHOLD.
THE SECOND, WITH ME! WE'RE GOING AFTER THEM!
AND WHAT ABOUT THE PRISONERS, COMMANDER?
SOME OF YOU EAT FISH, I BELIEVE.
WELL MY CAPTAIN...
SOLDIER LEKOK, DID YOU HEAR THE ORDERS?
YES, SERGEANT, I'M COMING...

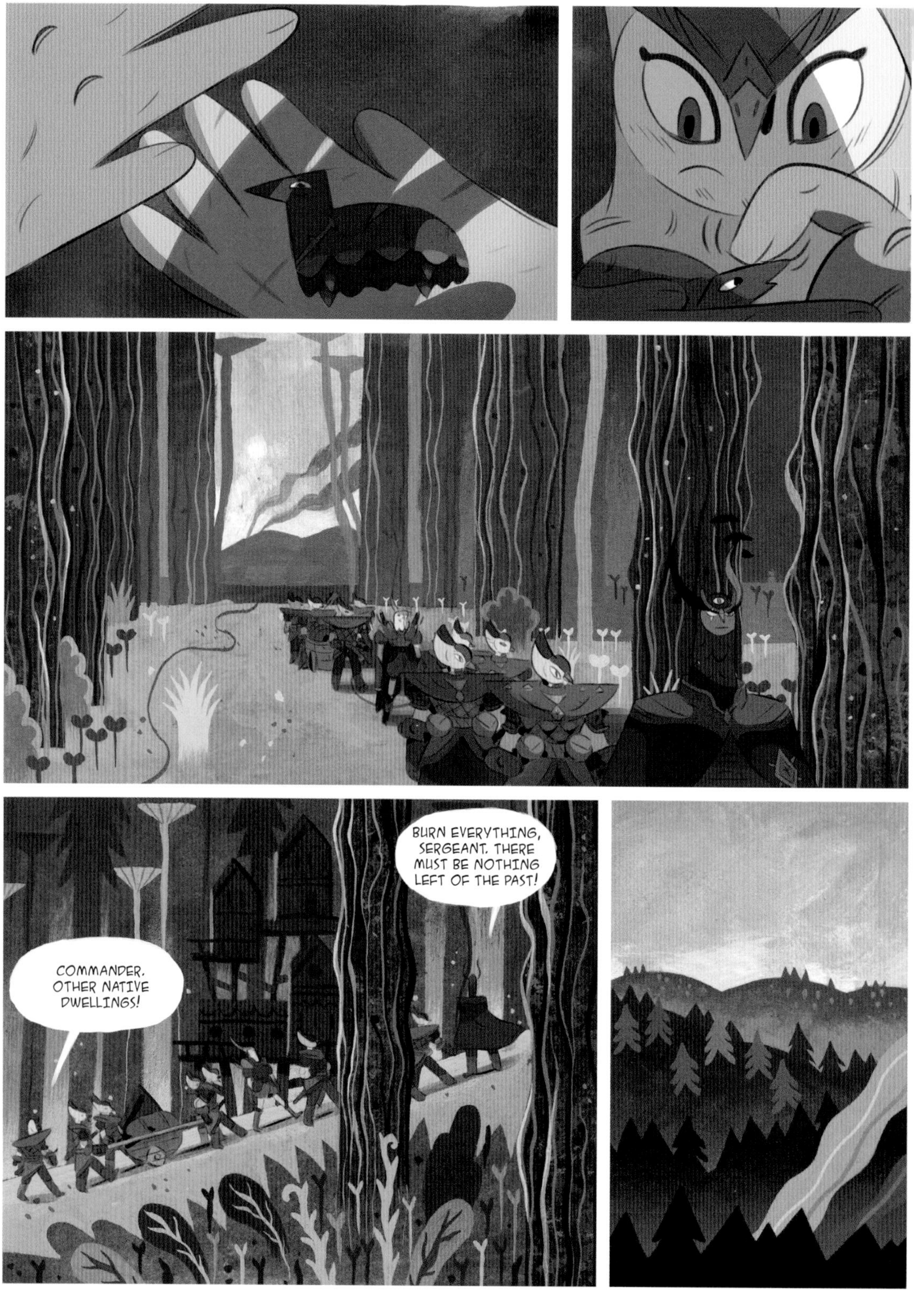
BURN EVERYTHING, SERGEANT. THERE MUST BE NOTHING LEFT OF THE PAST!
COMMANDER. OTHER NATIVE DWELLINGS!

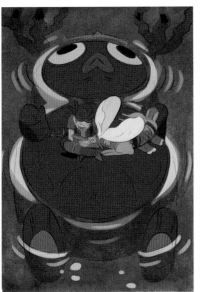

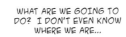

WHAT ARE WE GOING TO DO? I DON'T EVEN KNOW WHERE WE ARE...

WE LOST EVERYTHING, BOOKO...

OUR FRIENDS SLAUGHTERED... AND IF SOMETHING HAPPENS TO THE KING?

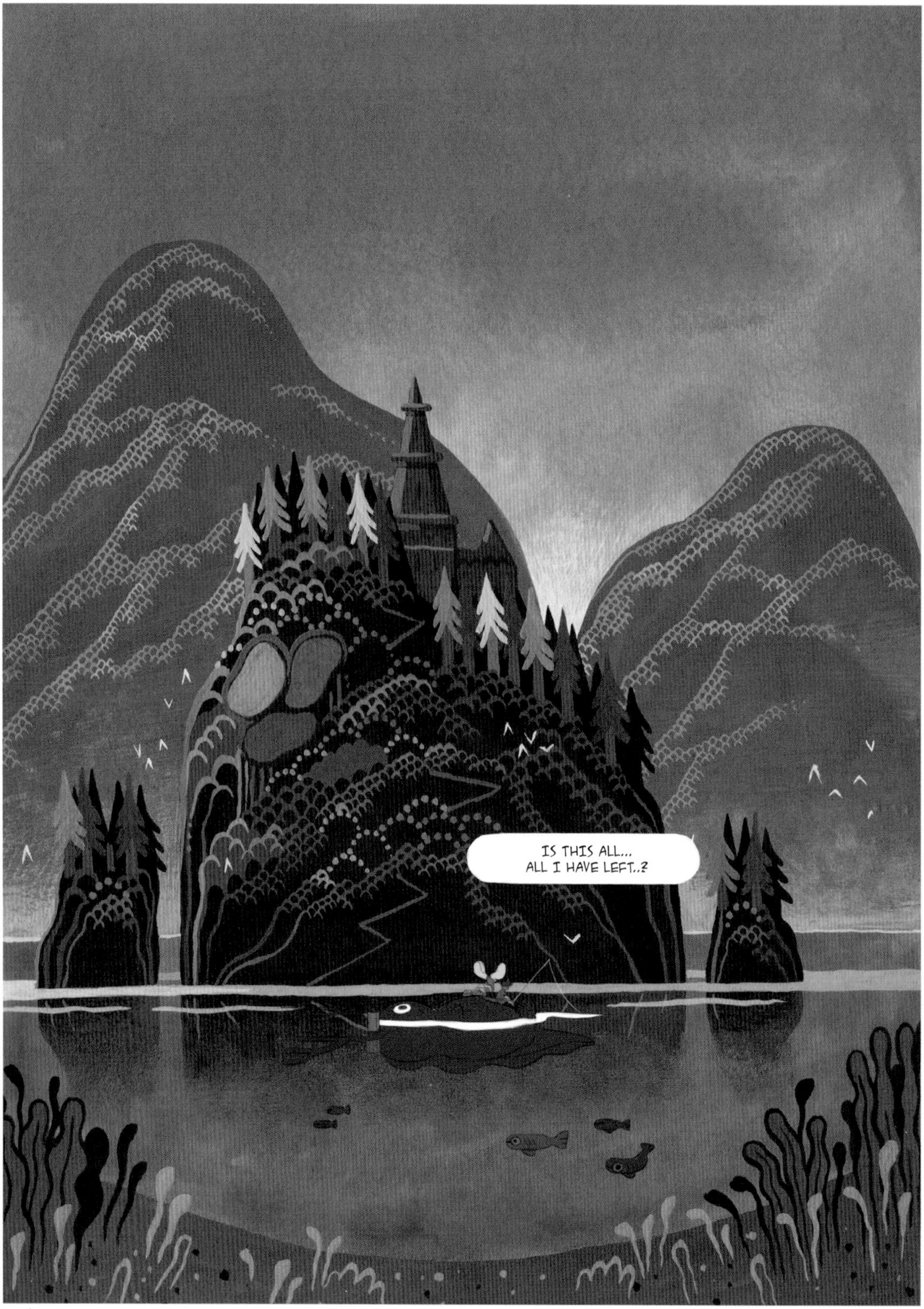
IS THIS ALL...
ALL I HAVE LEFT..?

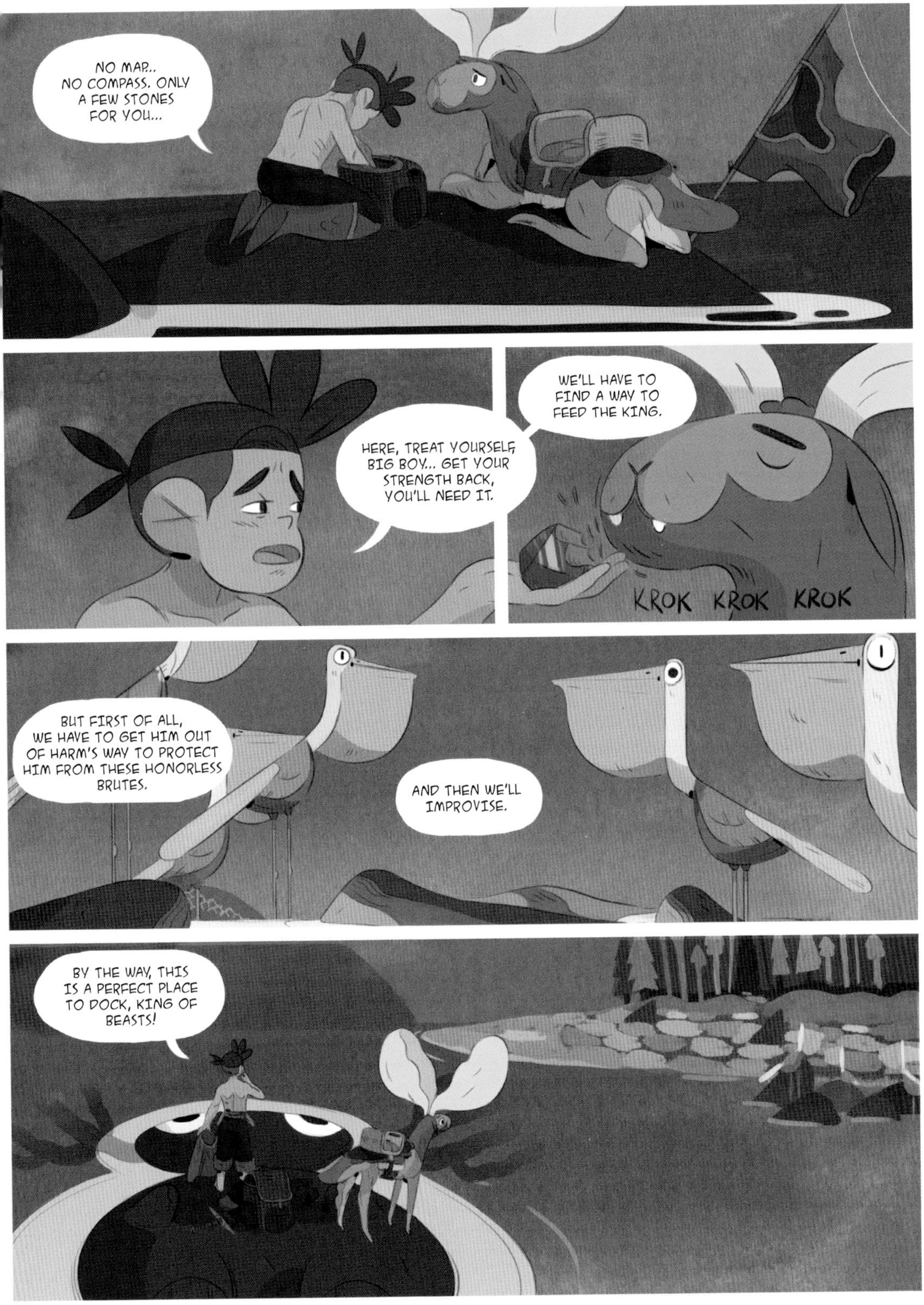
NO MAP..
NO COMPASS. ONLY
A FEW STONES
FOR YOU...
HERE, TREAT YOURSELF,
BIG BOY... GET YOUR
STRENGTH BACK,
YOU'LL NEED IT.
WE'LL HAVE TO
FIND A WAY TO
FEED THE KING.
KROK KROK KROK
BUT FIRST OF ALL,
WE HAVE TO GET HIM OUT
OF HARM'S WAY TO PROTECT
HIM FROM THESE HONORLESS
BRUTES.
AND THEN WE'LL
IMPROVISE.
BY THE WAY, THIS
IS A PERFECT PLACE
TO DOCK, KING OF
BEASTS!

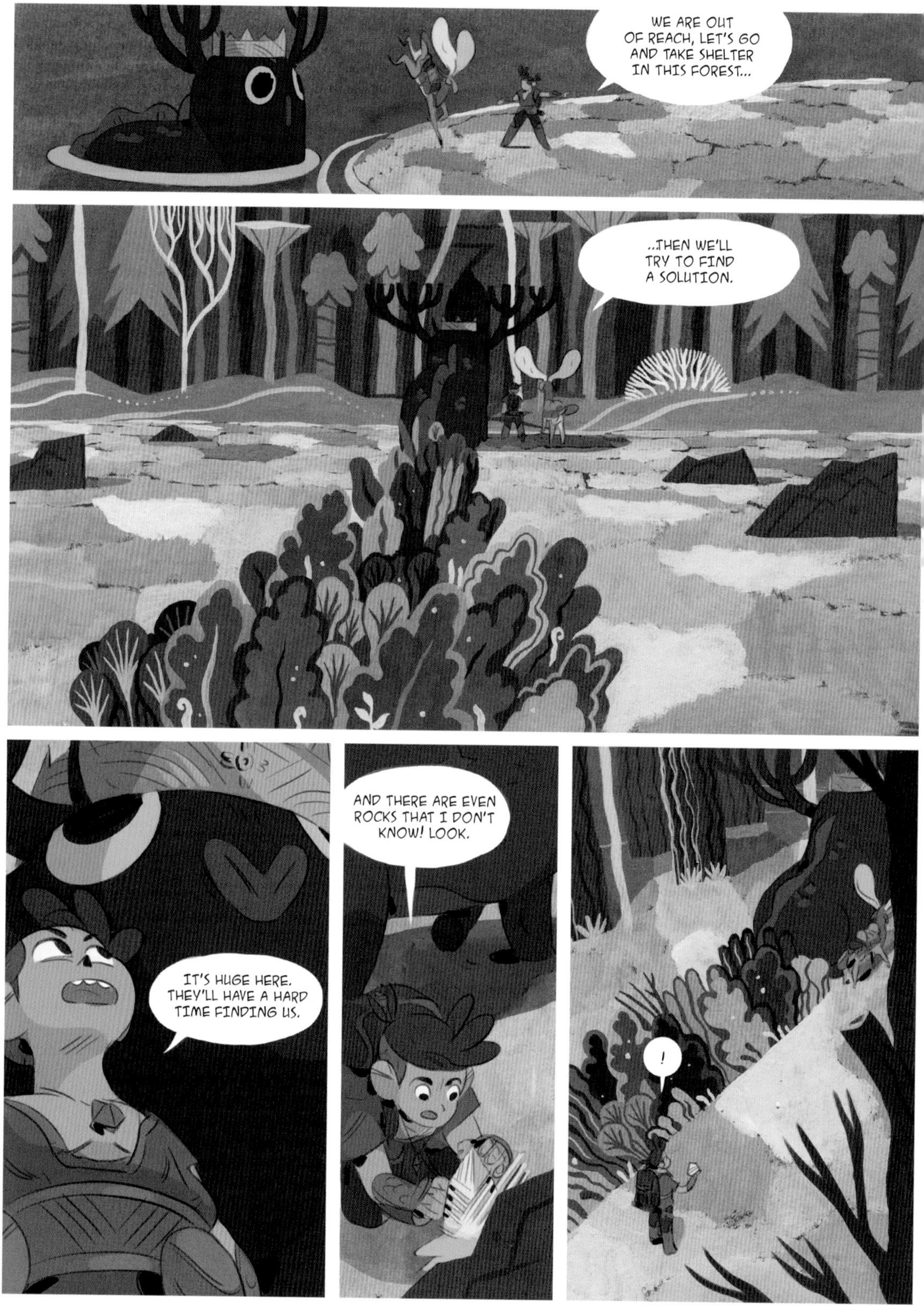
WE ARE OUT OF REACH, LET'S GO AND TAKE SHELTER IN THIS FOREST...
..THEN WE'LL TRY TO FIND A SOLUTION.
IT'S HUGE HERE. THEY'LL HAVE A HARD TIME FINDING US.
AND THERE ARE EVEN ROCKS THAT I DON'T KNOW! LOOK.
!

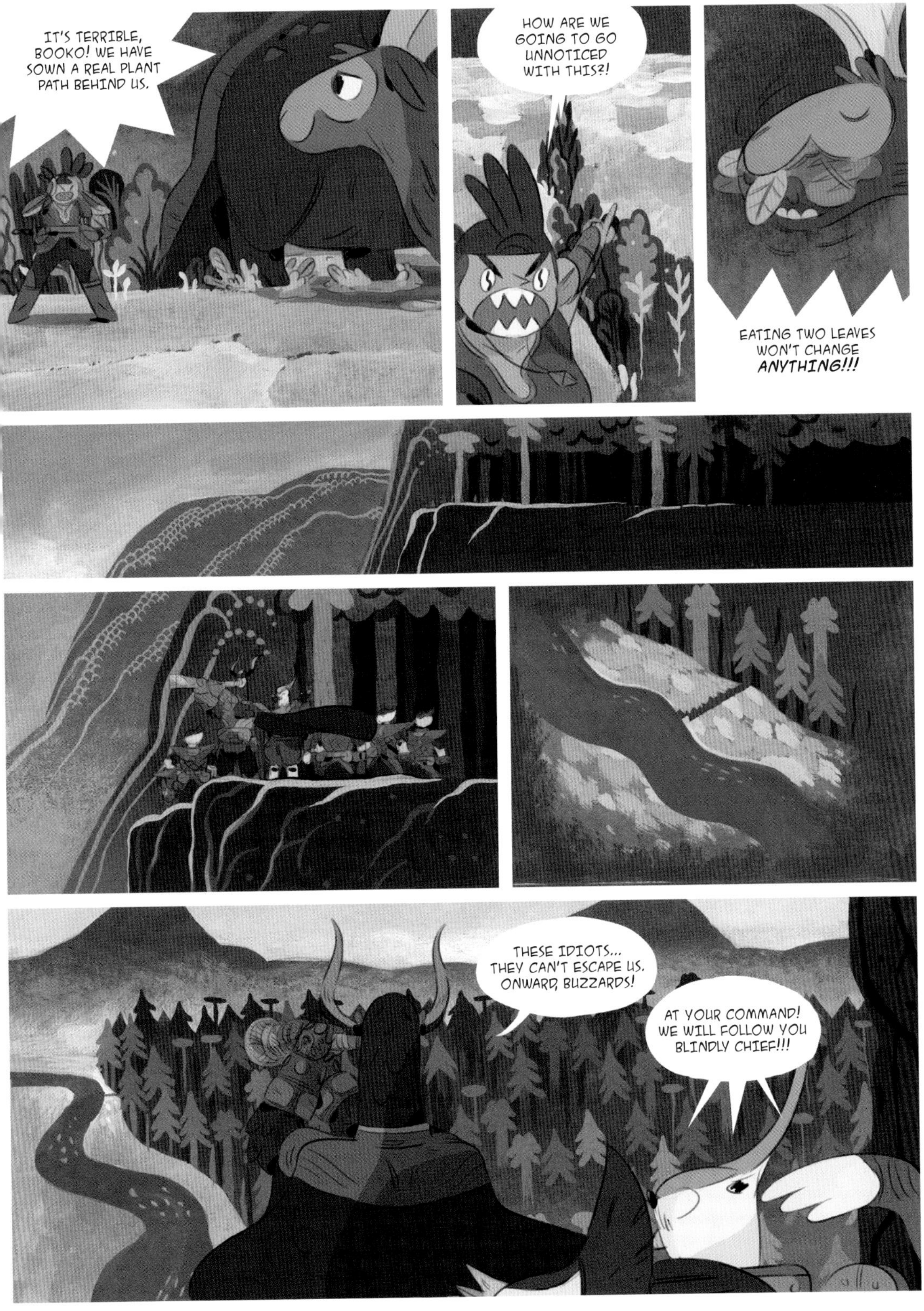

IT'S TERRIBLE, BOOKO! WE HAVE SOWN A REAL PLANT PATH BEHIND US.
HOW ARE WE GOING TO GO UNNOTICED WITH THIS?!
EATING TWO LEAVES WON'T CHANGE ANYTHING!!!
THESE IDIOTS... THEY CAN'T ESCAPE US. ONWARD, BUZZARDS!
AT YOUR COMMAND! WE WILL FOLLOW YOU BLINDLY CHIEF!!!

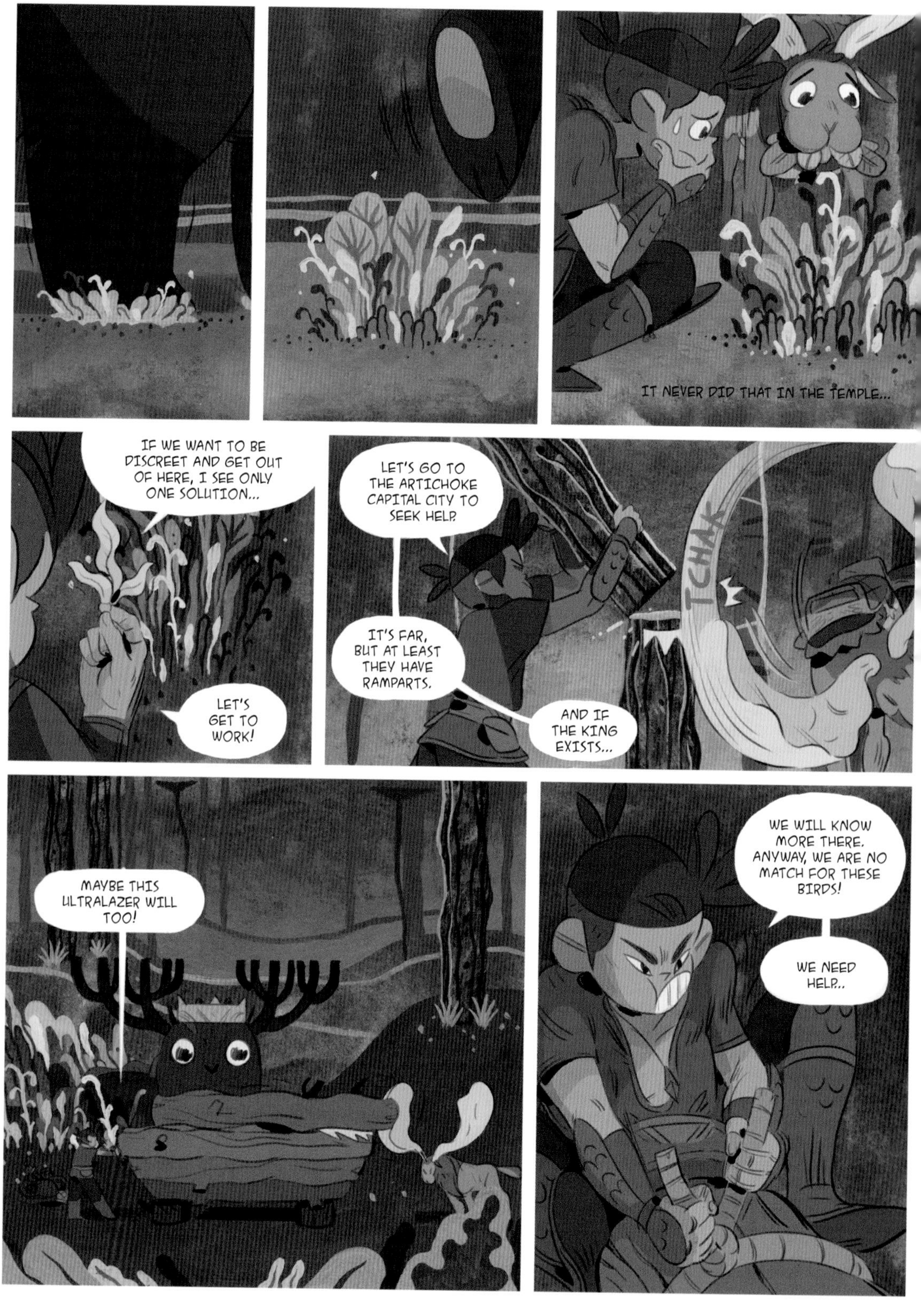
IT NEVER DID THAT IN THE TEMPLE...
IF WE WANT TO BE DISCREET AND GET OUT OF HERE, I SEE ONLY ONE SOLUTION...
LET'S GET TO WORK!
LET'S GO TO THE ARTICHOKE CAPITAL CITY TO SEEK HELP.
IT'S FAR, BUT AT LEAST THEY HAVE RAMPARTS.
TCHAK
AND IF THE KING EXISTS...
MAYBE THIS ULTRALAZER WILL TOO!
WE WILL KNOW MORE THERE. ANYWAY, WE ARE NO MATCH FOR THESE BIRDS!
WE NEED HELP...

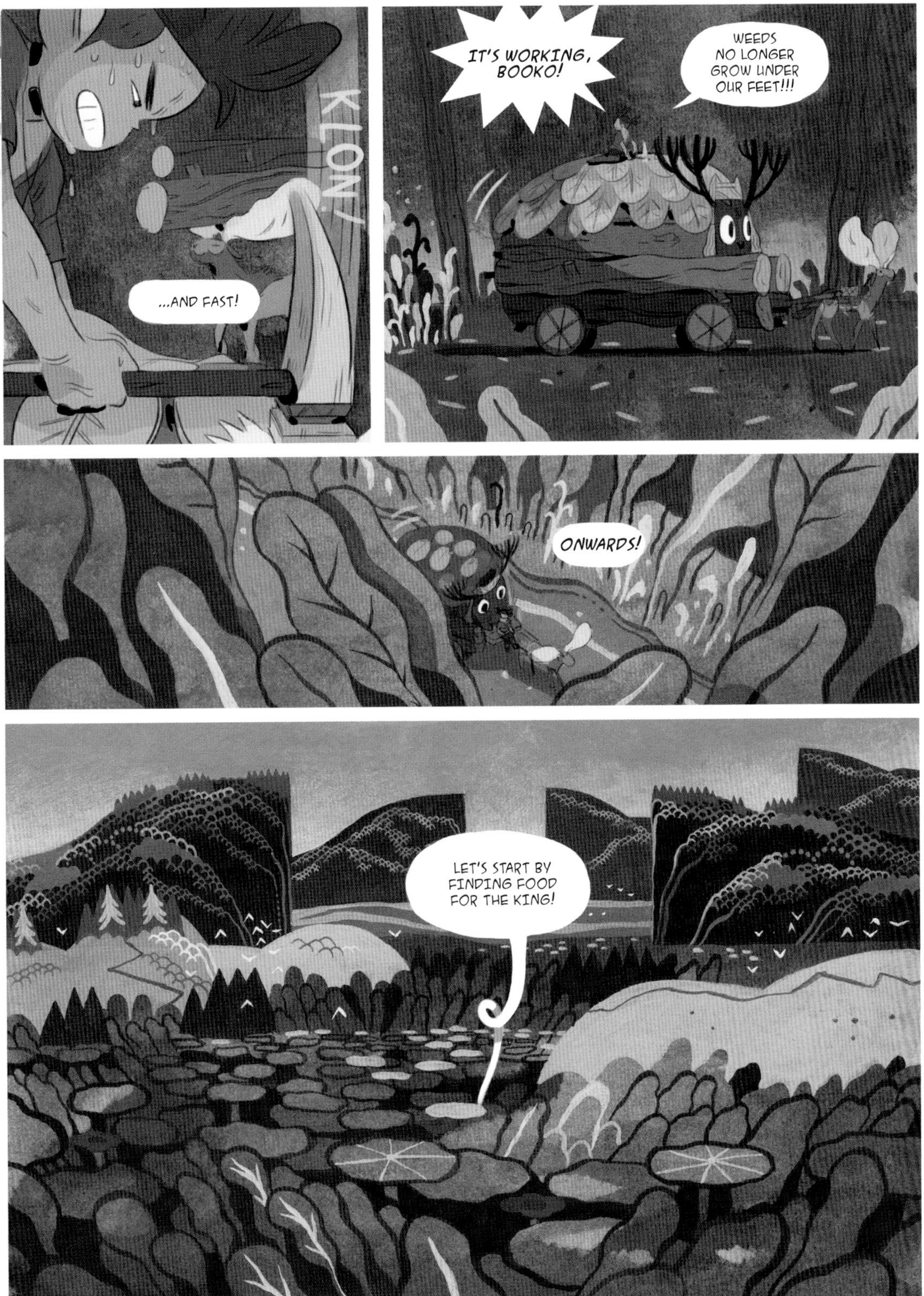
KLON!
...AND FAST!
IT'S WORKING, BOOKO!
WEEDS NO LONGER GROW UNDER OUR FEET!!!
ONWARDS!
LET'S START BY FINDING FOOD FOR THE KING!

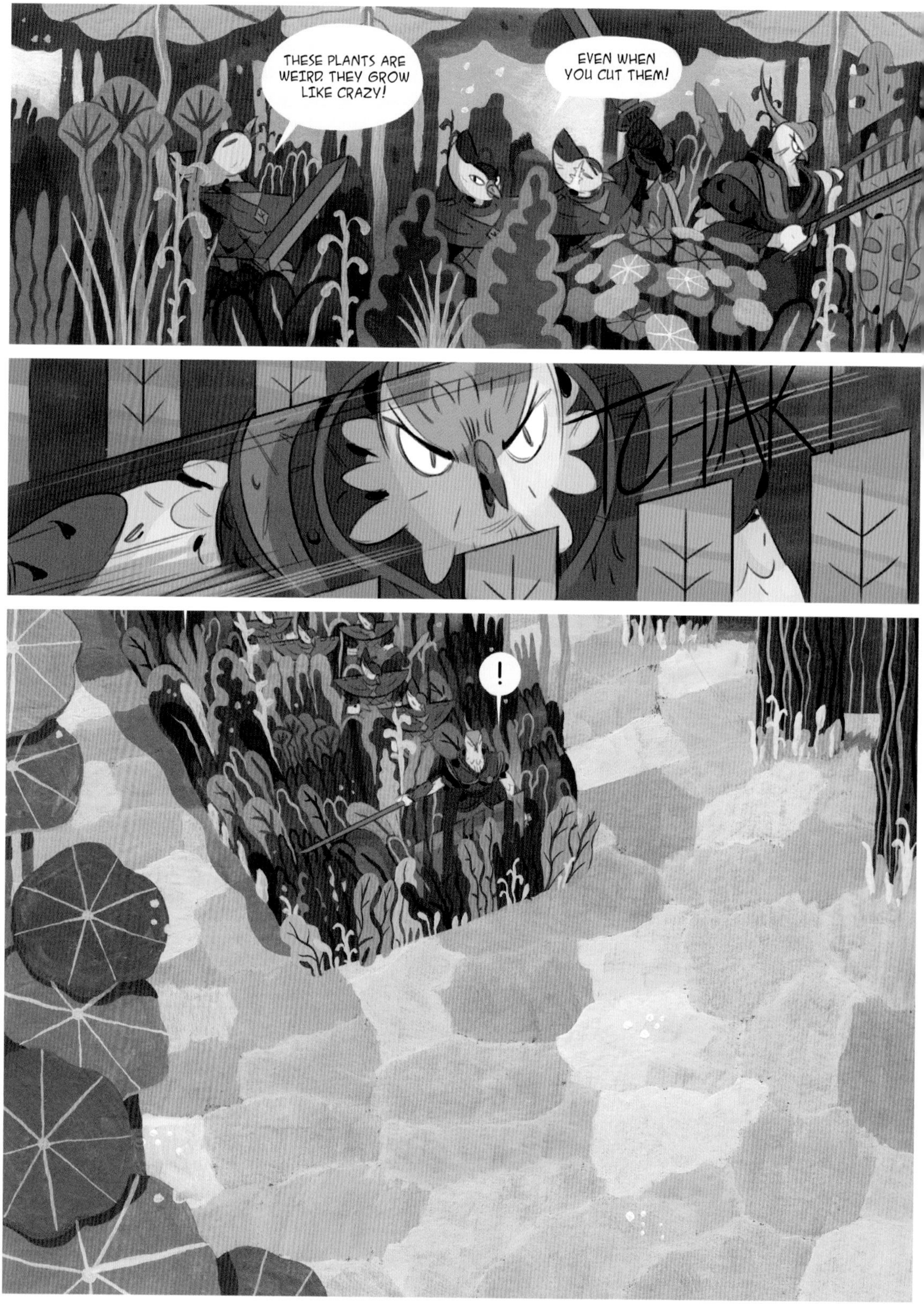
THESE PLANTS ARE WEIRD. THEY GROW LIKE CRAZY!
EVEN WHEN YOU CUT THEM!
TCHAK!
!

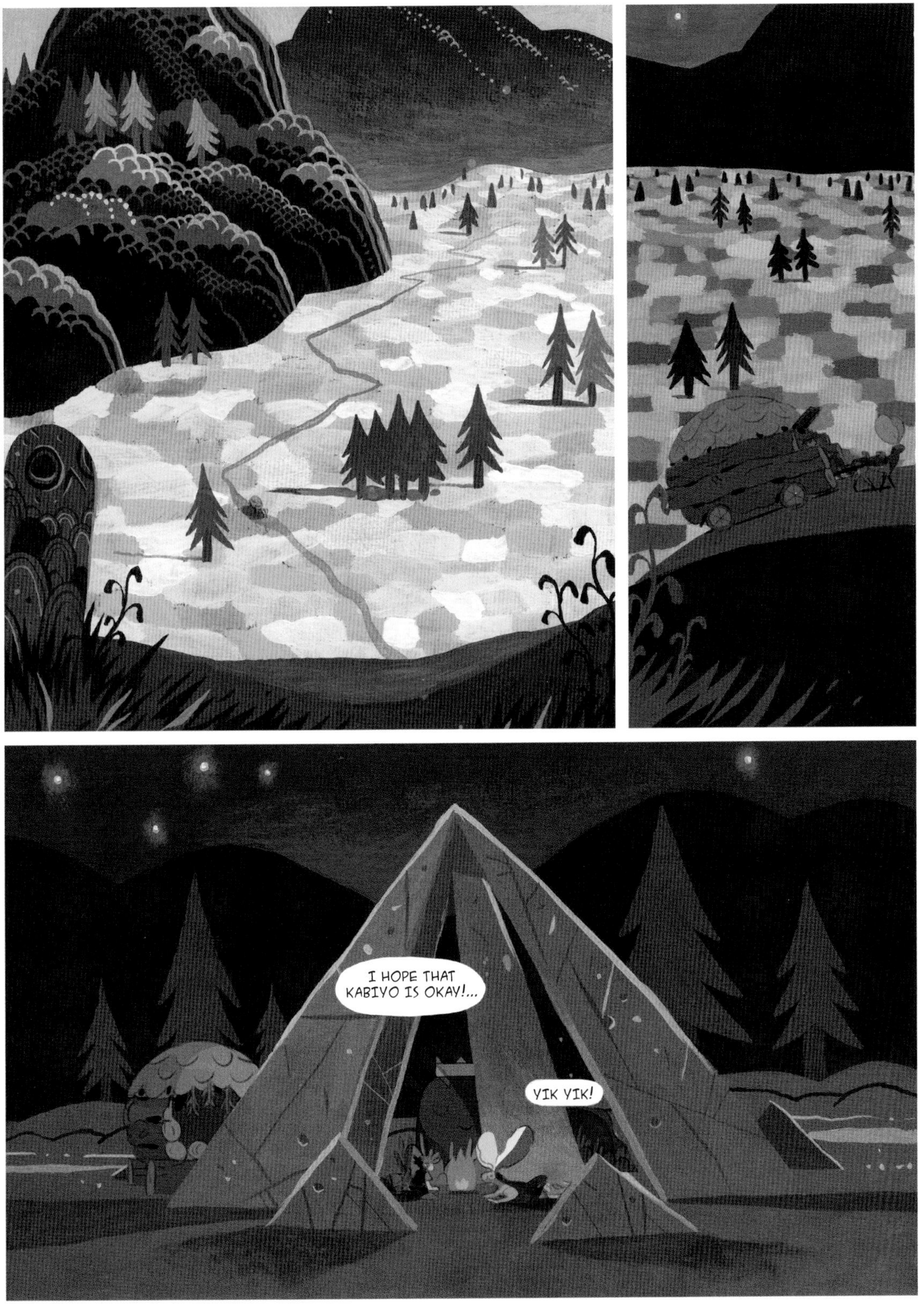
I HOPE THAT KABIYO IS OKAY!...
YIK YIK!

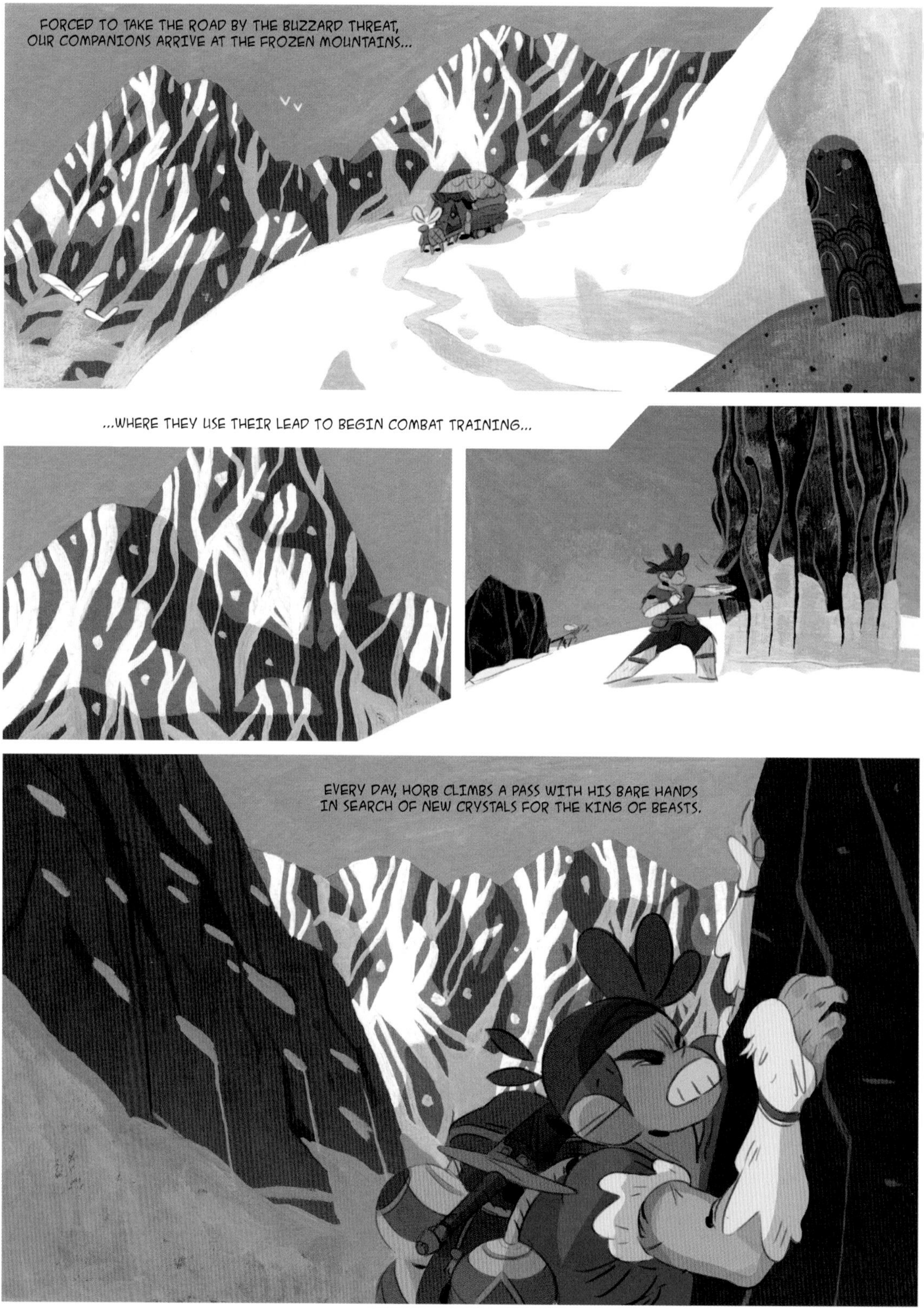
FORCED TO TAKE THE ROAD BY THE BUZZARD THREAT, OUR COMPANIONS ARRIVE AT THE FROZEN MOUNTAINS...
...WHERE THEY USE THEIR LEAD TO BEGIN COMBAT TRAINING...
EVERY DAY, HORB CLIMBS A PASS WITH HIS BARE HANDS IN SEARCH OF NEW CRYSTALS FOR THE KING OF BEASTS.

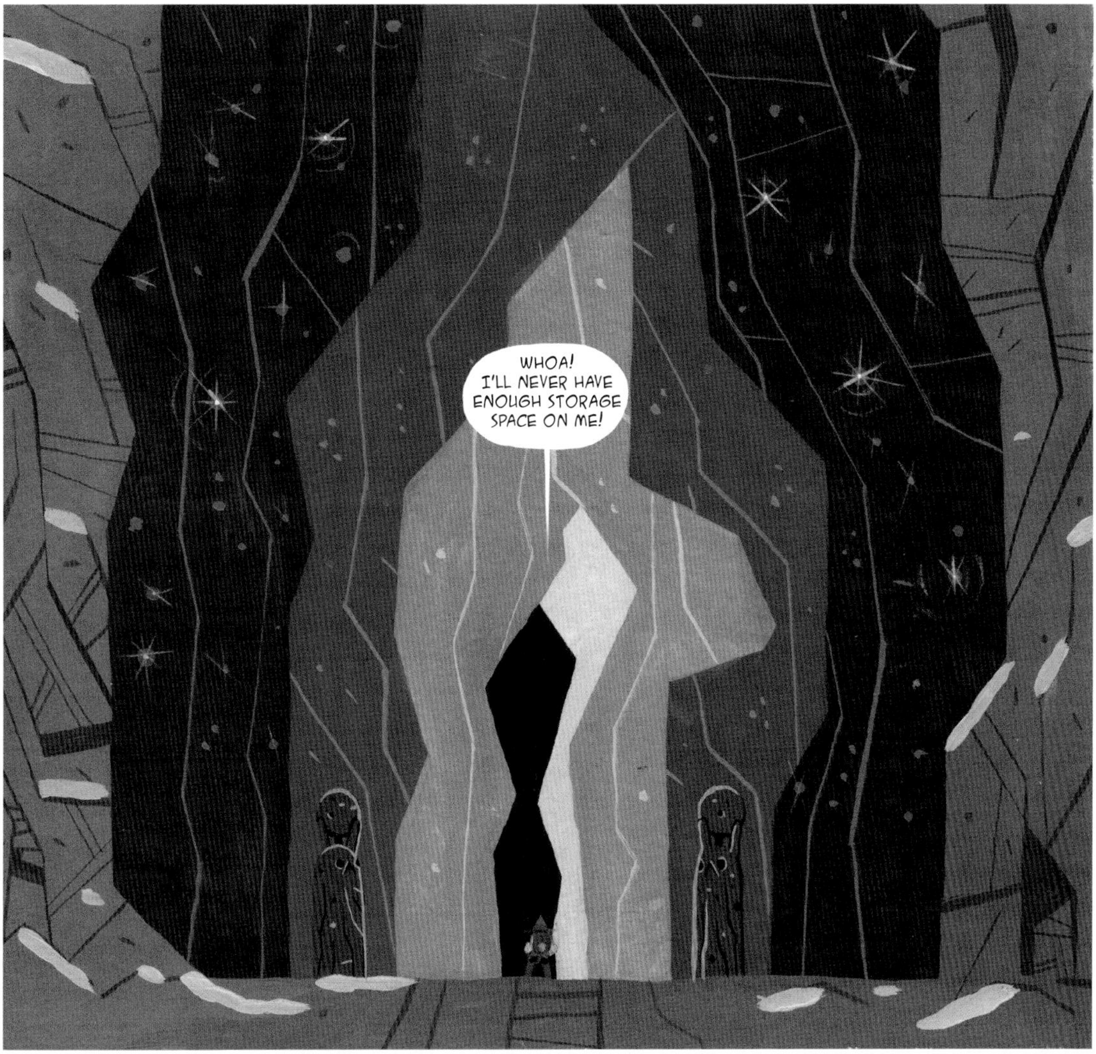
WHOA! I'LL NEVER HAVE ENOUGH STORAGE SPACE ON ME!

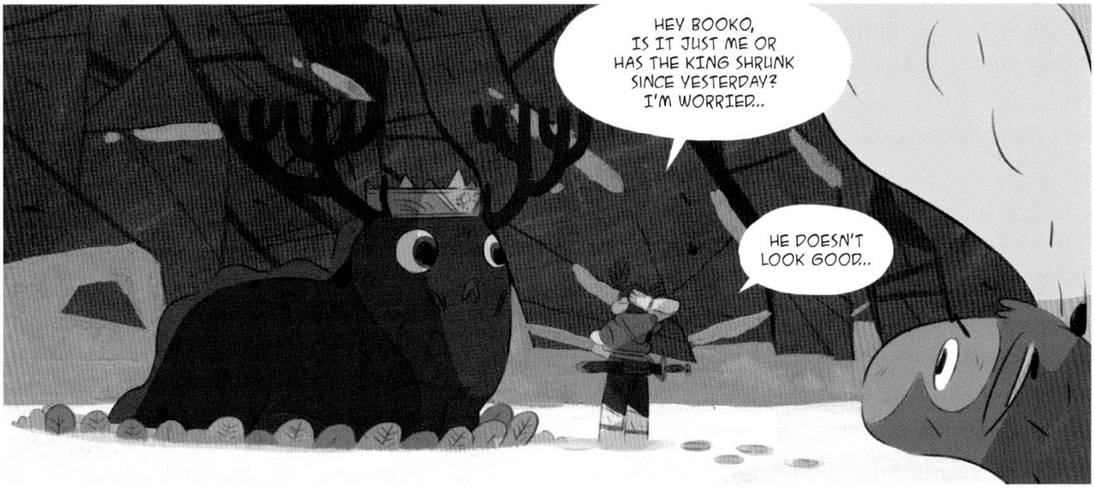
HEY BOOKO, IS IT JUST ME OR HAS THE KING SHRUNK SINCE YESTERDAY? I'M WORRIED...
HE DOESN'T LOOK GOOD...

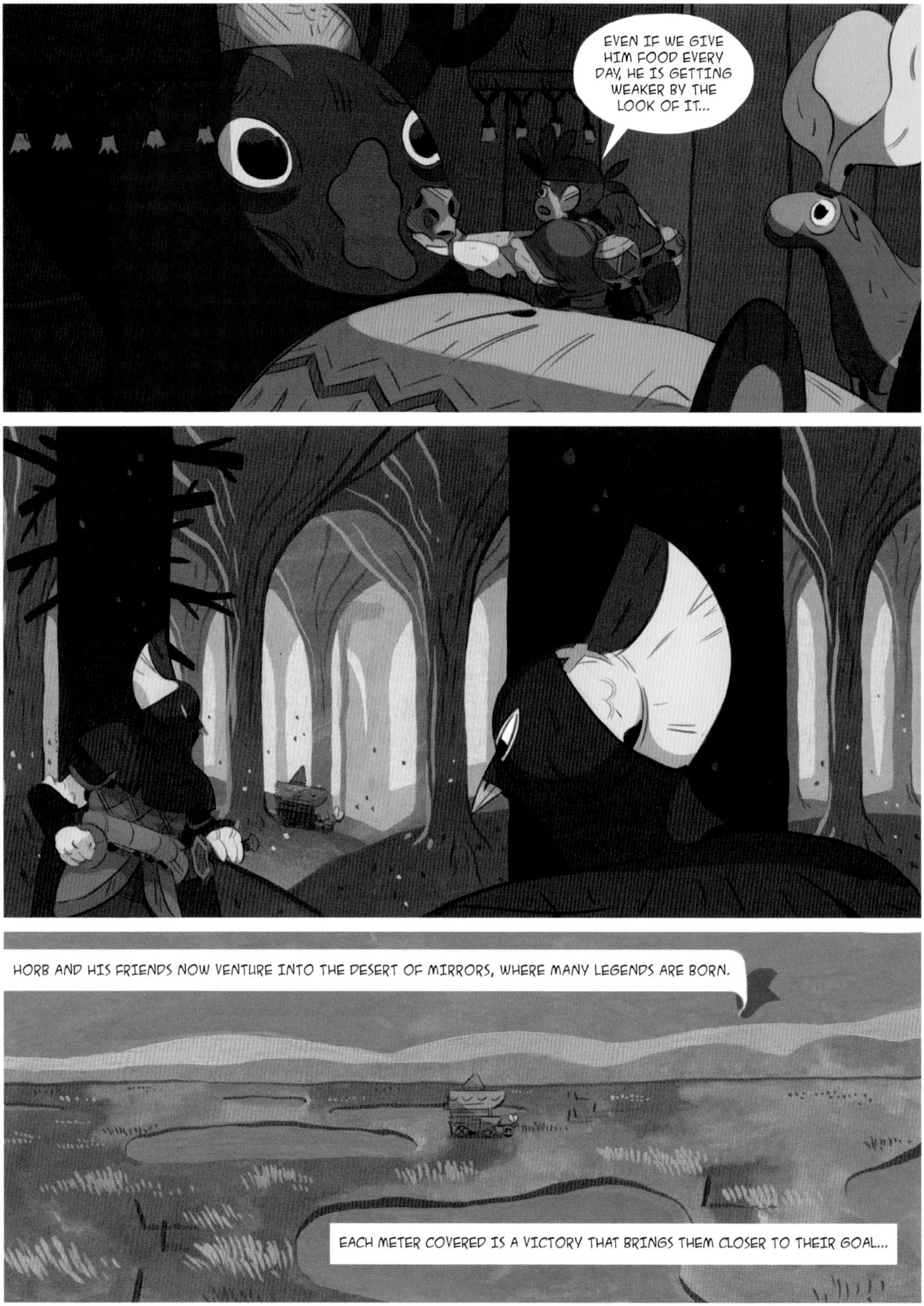
EVEN IF WE GIVE HIM FOOD EVERY DAY, HE IS GETTING WEAKER BY THE LOOK OF IT...
HORB AND HIS FRIENDS NOW VENTURE INTO THE DESERT OF MIRRORS, WHERE MANY LEGENDS ARE BORN.
EACH METER COVERED IS A VICTORY THAT BRINGS THEM CLOSER TO THEIR GOAL...

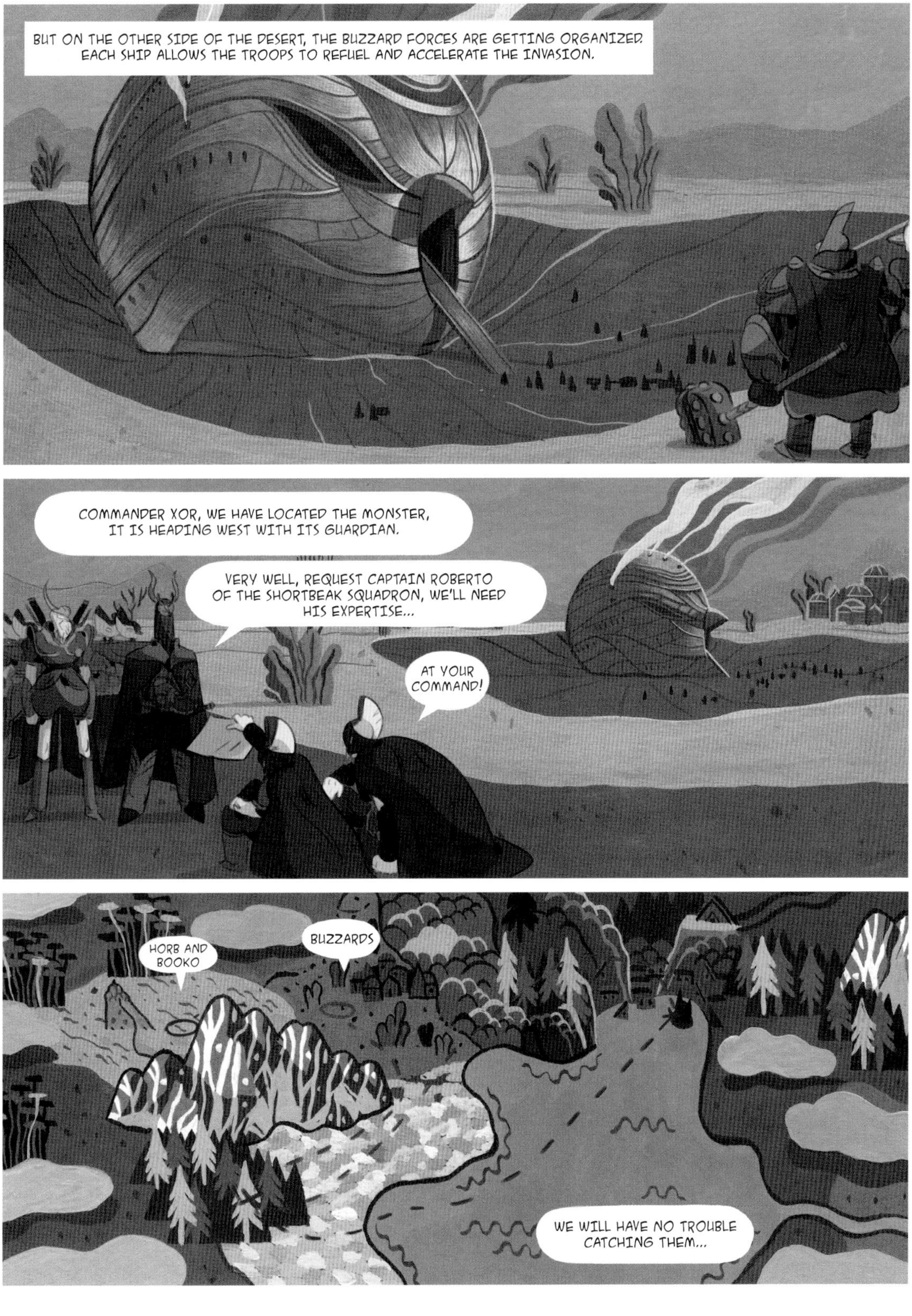
BUT ON THE OTHER SIDE OF THE DESERT, THE BUZZARD FORCES ARE GETTING ORGANIZED. EACH SHIP ALLOWS THE TROOPS TO REFUEL AND ACCELERATE THE INVASION.
COMMANDER XOR, WE HAVE LOCATED THE MONSTER, IT IS HEADING WEST WITH ITS GUARDIAN.
VERY WELL, REQUEST CAPTAIN ROBERTO OF THE SHORTBEAK SQUADRON, WE'LL NEED HIS EXPERTISE...
AT YOUR COMMAND!
HORB AND BOOKO
BUZZARDS
WE WILL HAVE NO TROUBLE CATCHING THEM...

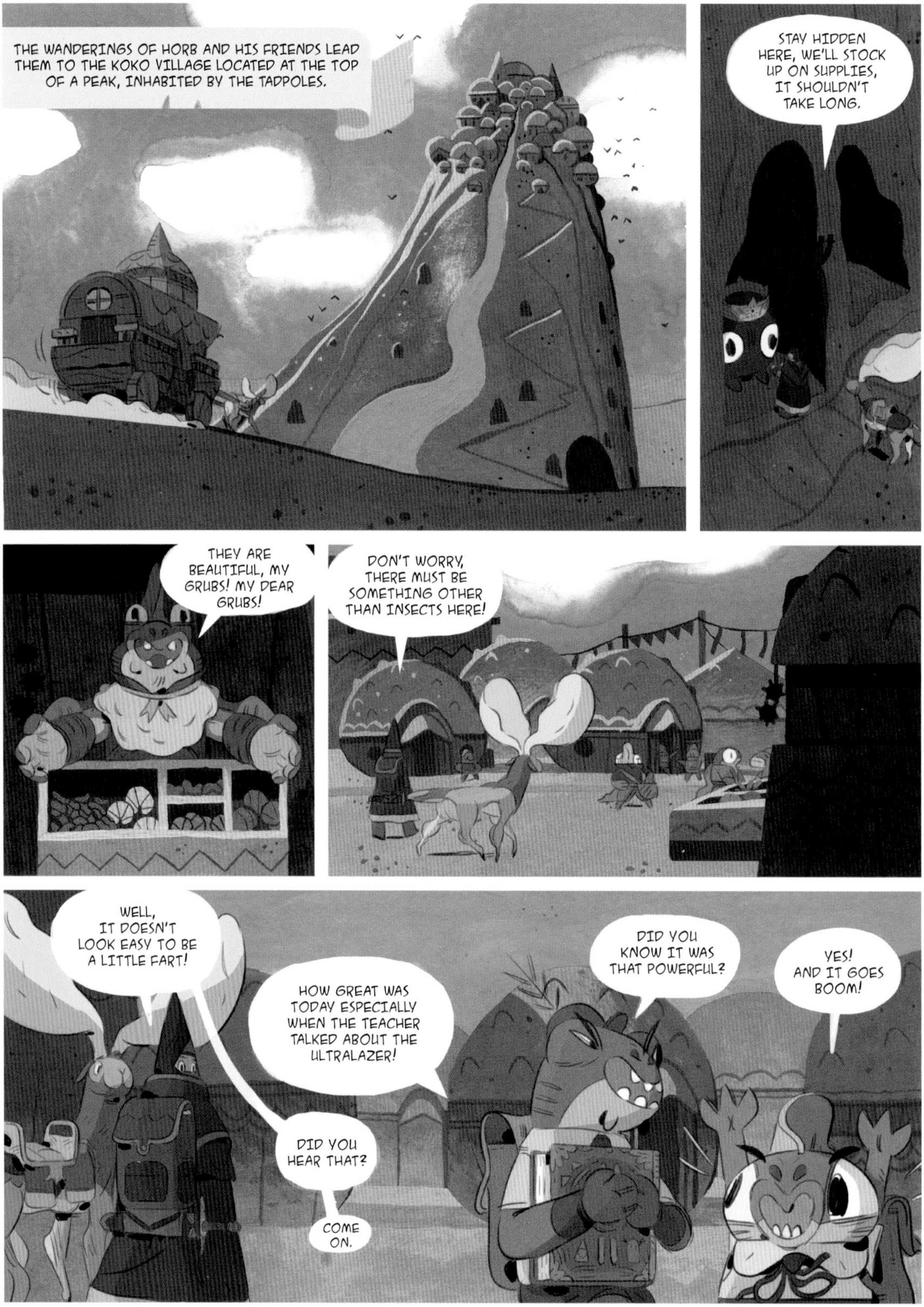
THE WANDERINGS OF HORB AND HIS FRIENDS LEAD THEM TO THE KOKO VILLAGE LOCATED AT THE TOP OF A PEAK, INHABITED BY THE TADPOLES.
STAY HIDDEN HERE, WE'LL STOCK UP ON SUPPLIES, IT SHOULDN'T TAKE LONG.
THEY ARE BEAUTIFUL, MY GRUBS! MY DEAR GRUBS!
DON'T WORRY, THERE MUST BE SOMETHING OTHER THAN INSECTS HERE!
WELL, IT DOESN'T LOOK EASY TO BE A LITTLE FART!
HOW GREAT WAS TODAY ESPECIALLY WHEN THE TEACHER TALKED ABOUT THE ULTRALAZER!
DID YOU HEAR THAT?
COME ON.
DID YOU KNOW IT WAS THAT POWERFUL?
YES! AND IT GOES BOOM!

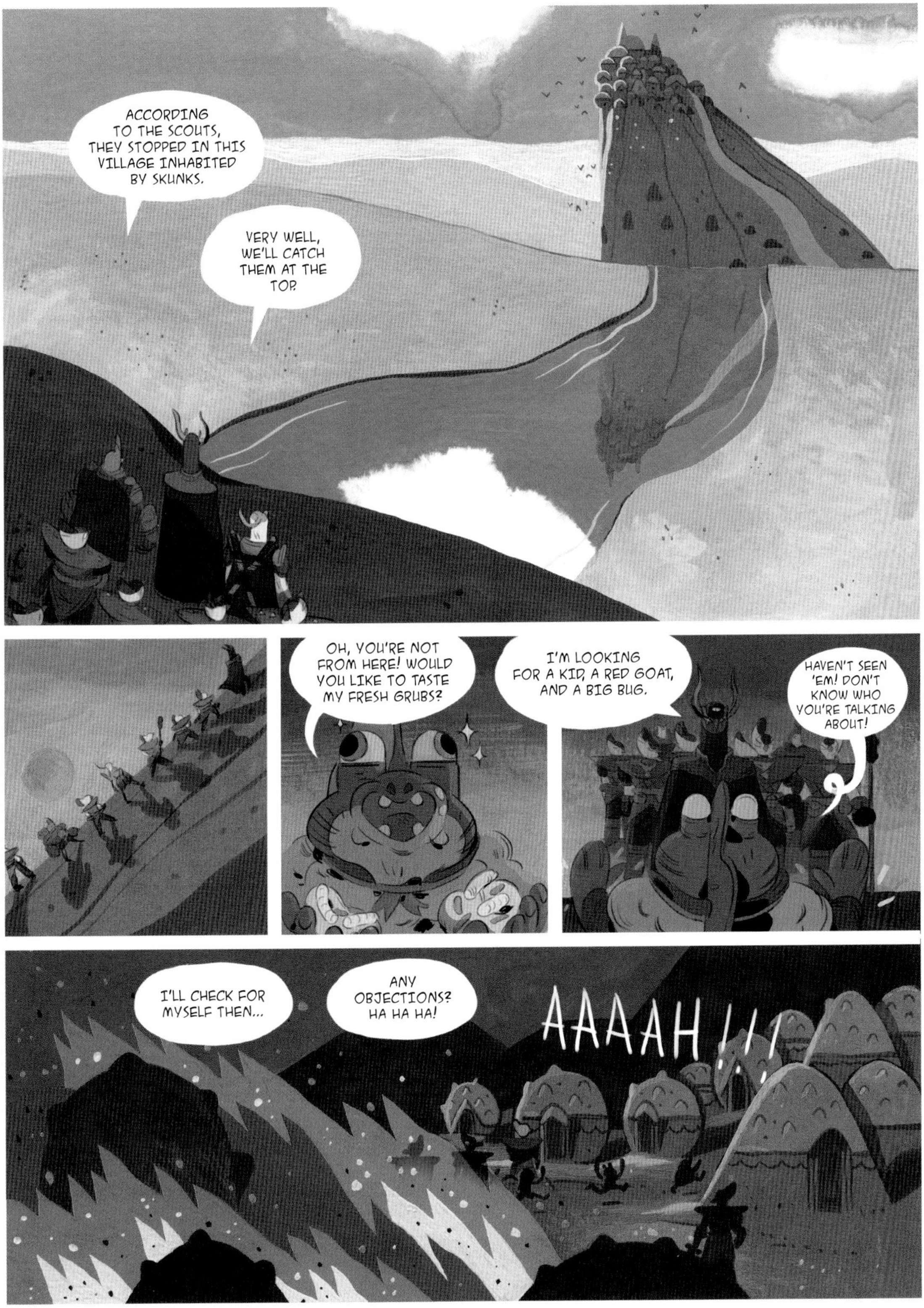

ACCORDING TO THE SCOUTS, THEY STOPPED IN THIS VILLAGE INHABITED BY SKUNKS.
VERY WELL, WE'LL CATCH THEM AT THE TOP.
OH, YOU'RE NOT FROM HERE! WOULD YOU LIKE TO TASTE MY FRESH GRUBS?
I'M LOOKING FOR A KID, A RED GOAT, AND A BIG BUG.
HAVEN'T SEEN 'EM! DON'T KNOW WHO YOU'RE TALKING ABOUT!
I'LL CHECK FOR MYSELF THEN...
ANY OBJECTIONS? HA HA HA!
AAAAH!!!

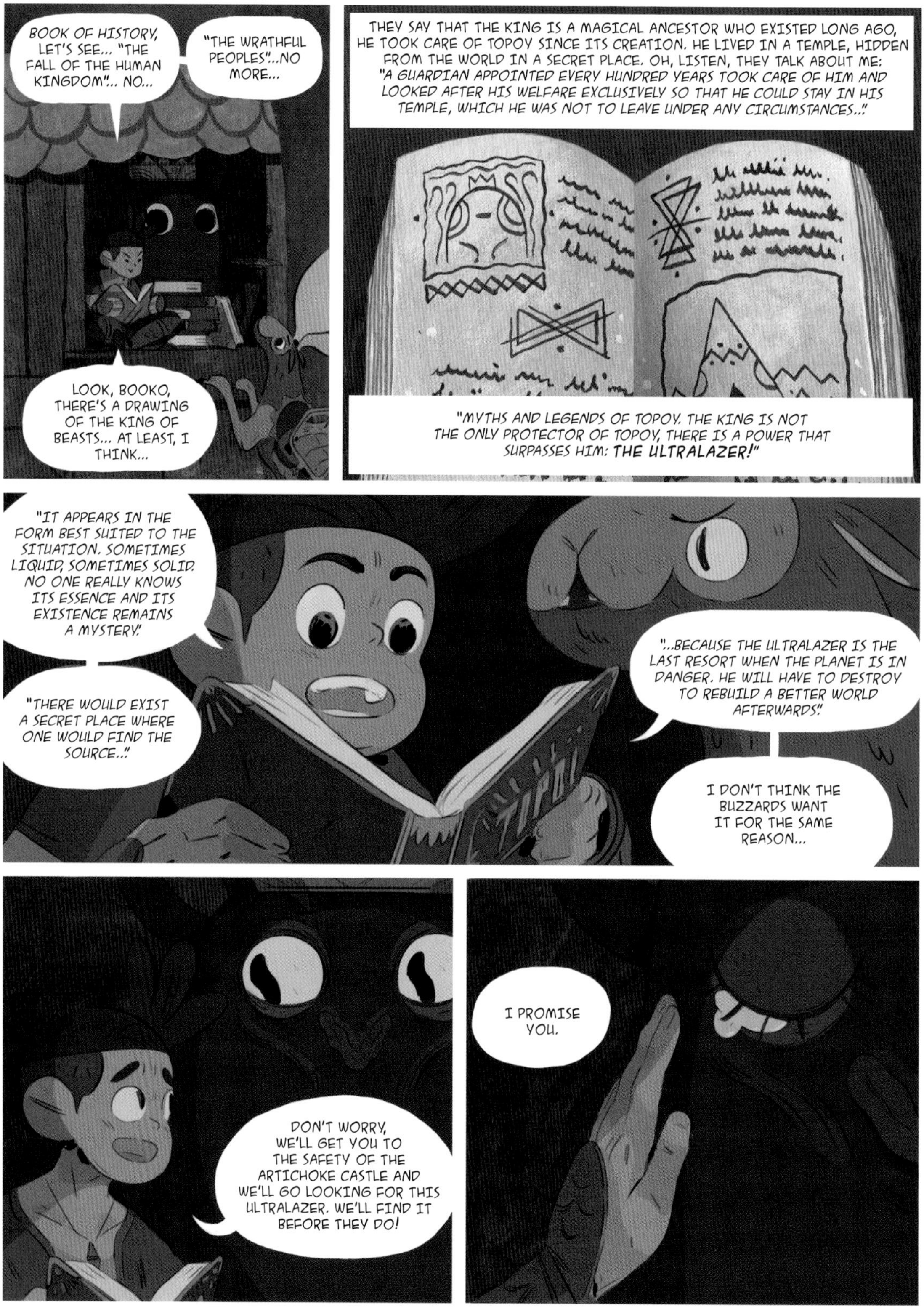

BOOK OF HISTORY, LET'S SEE... "THE FALL OF THE HUMAN KINGDOM"... NO...
"THE WRATHFUL PEOPLES"...NO MORE...
LOOK, BOOKO, THERE'S A DRAWING OF THE KING OF BEASTS... AT LEAST, I THINK...
THEY SAY THAT THE KING IS A MAGICAL ANCESTOR WHO EXISTED LONG AGO, HE TOOK CARE OF TOPOY SINCE ITS CREATION. HE LIVED IN A TEMPLE, HIDDEN FROM THE WORLD IN A SECRET PLACE. OH, LISTEN, THEY TALK ABOUT ME: "A GUARDIAN APPOINTED EVERY HUNDRED YEARS TOOK CARE OF HIM AND LOOKED AFTER HIS WELFARE EXCLUSIVELY SO THAT HE COULD STAY IN HIS TEMPLE, WHICH HE WAS NOT TO LEAVE UNDER ANY CIRCUMSTANCES..."
"MYTHS AND LEGENDS OF TOPOY. THE KING IS NOT THE ONLY PROTECTOR OF TOPOY, THERE IS A POWER THAT SURPASSES HIM: THE ULTRALAZER!"
"IT APPEARS IN THE FORM BEST SUITED TO THE SITUATION. SOMETIMES LIQUID, SOMETIMES SOLID. NO ONE REALLY KNOWS ITS ESSENCE AND ITS EXISTENCE REMAINS A MYSTERY."
"THERE WOULD EXIST A SECRET PLACE WHERE ONE WOULD FIND THE SOURCE..."
"...BECAUSE THE ULTRALAZER IS THE LAST RESORT WHEN THE PLANET IS IN DANGER. HE WILL HAVE TO DESTROY TO REBUILD A BETTER WORLD AFTERWARDS."
I DON'T THINK THE BUZZARDS WANT IT FOR THE SAME REASON...
DON'T WORRY, WE'LL GET YOU TO THE SAFETY OF THE ARTICHOKE CASTLE AND WE'LL GO LOOKING FOR THIS ULTRALAZER. WE'LL FIND IT BEFORE THEY DO!
I PROMISE YOU.

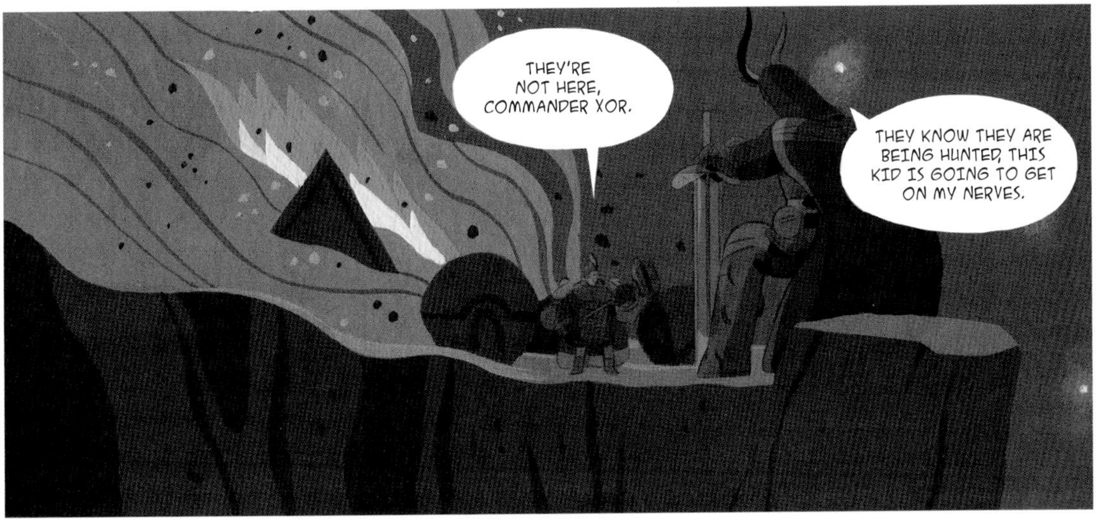
THEY'RE NOT HERE, COMMANDER XOR.
THEY KNOW THEY ARE BEING HUNTED, THIS KID IS GOING TO GET ON MY NERVES.

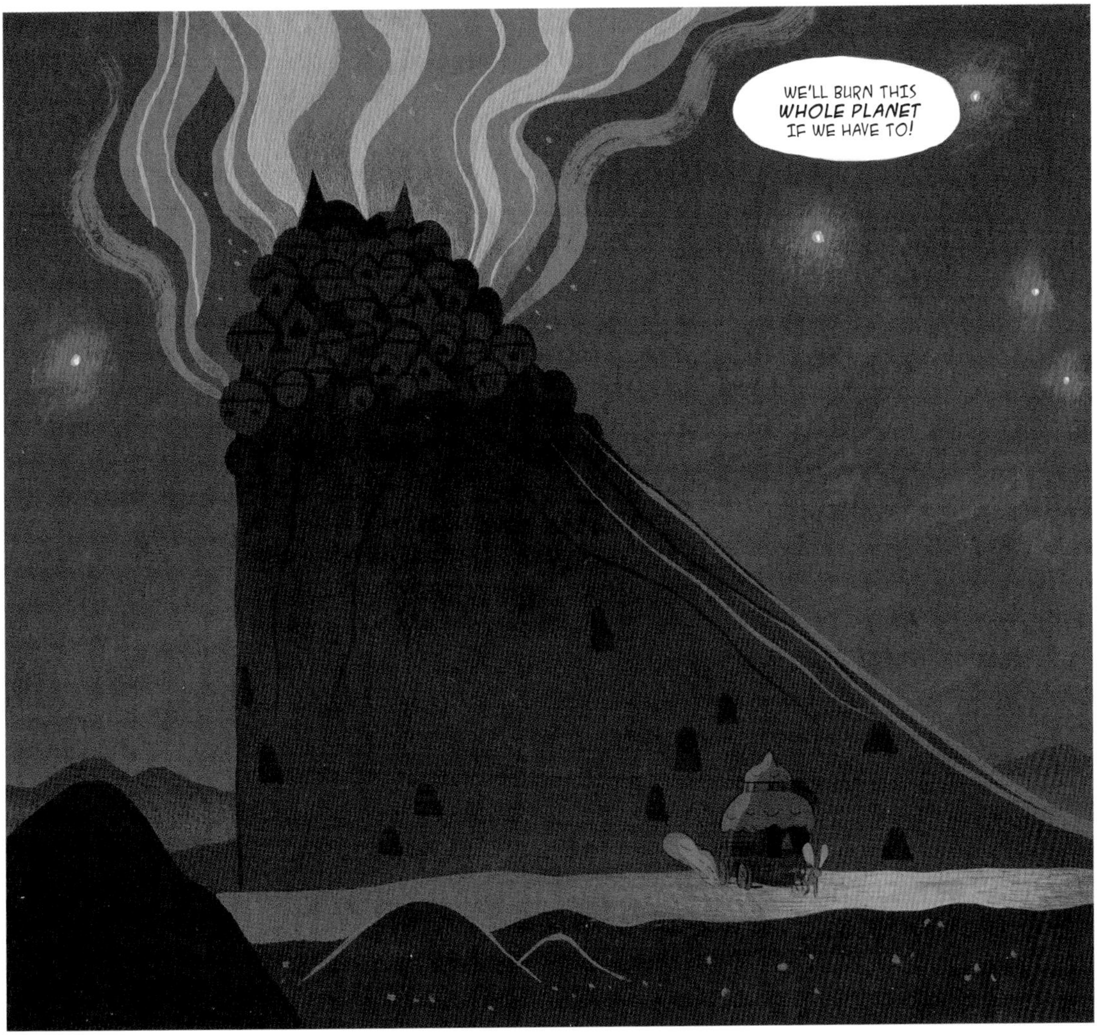
WE'LL BURN THIS **WHOLE PLANET** IF WE HAVE TO!

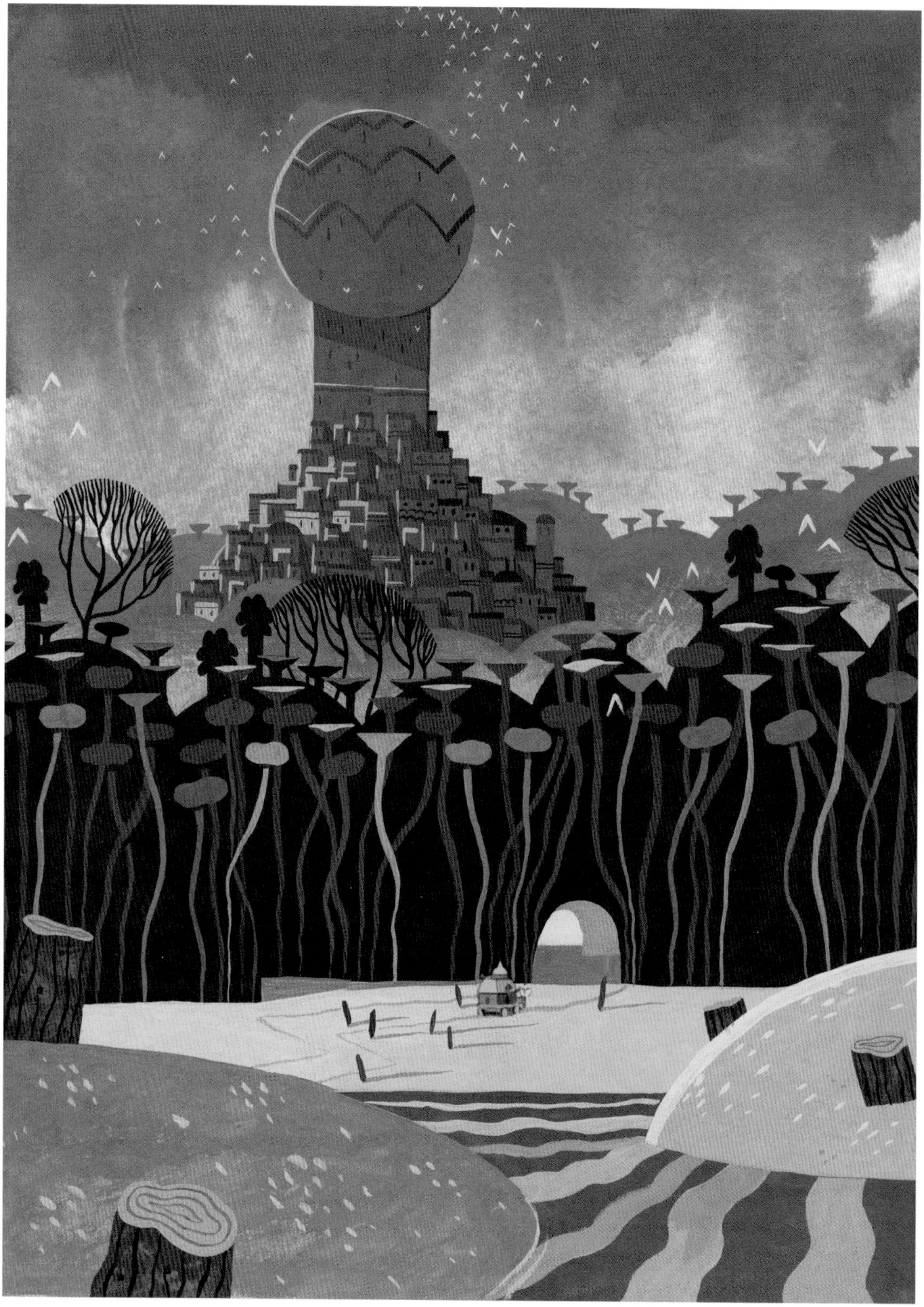

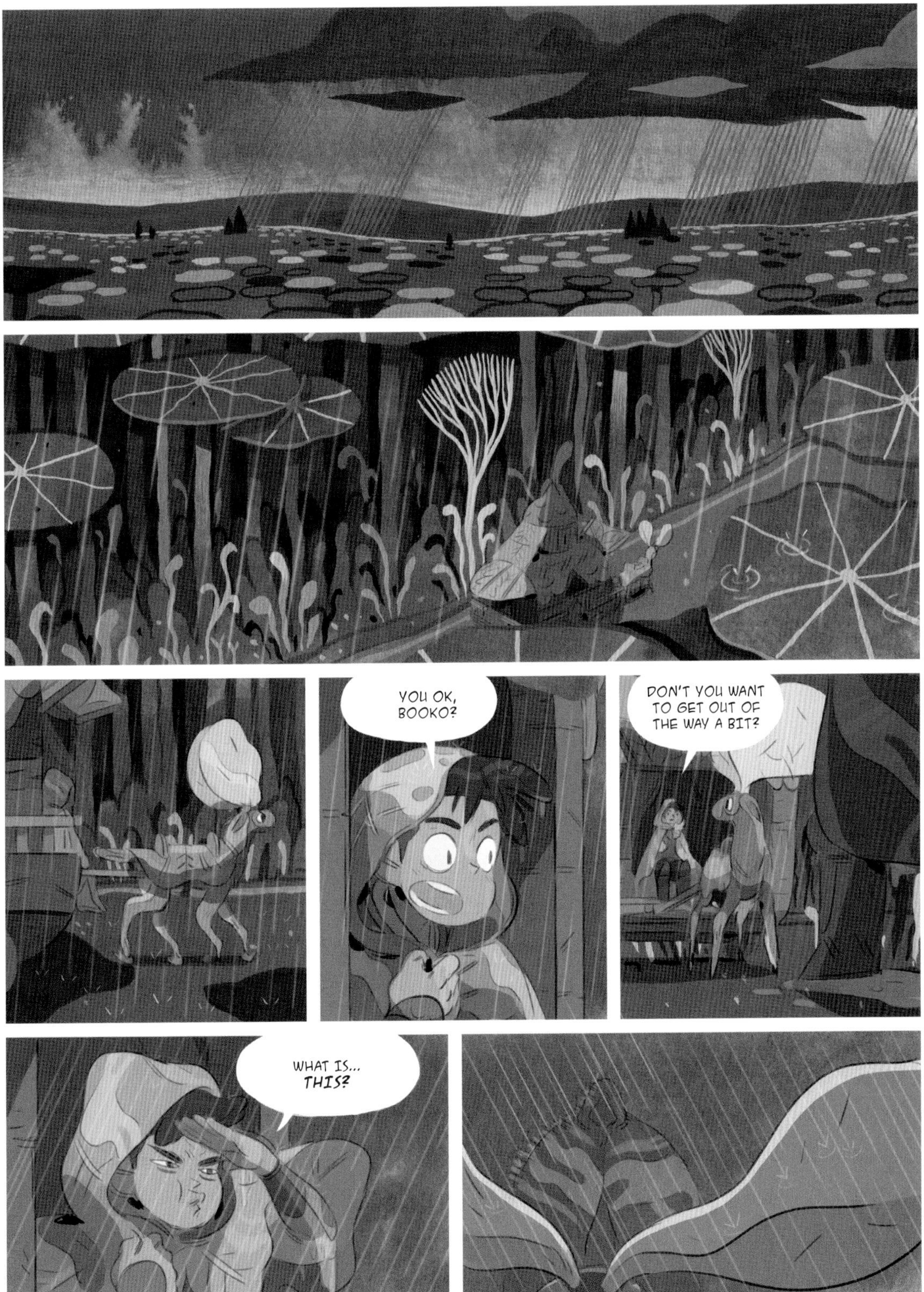
YOU OK, BOOKO?
DON'T YOU WANT TO GET OUT OF THE WAY A BIT?
WHAT IS... *THIS?*

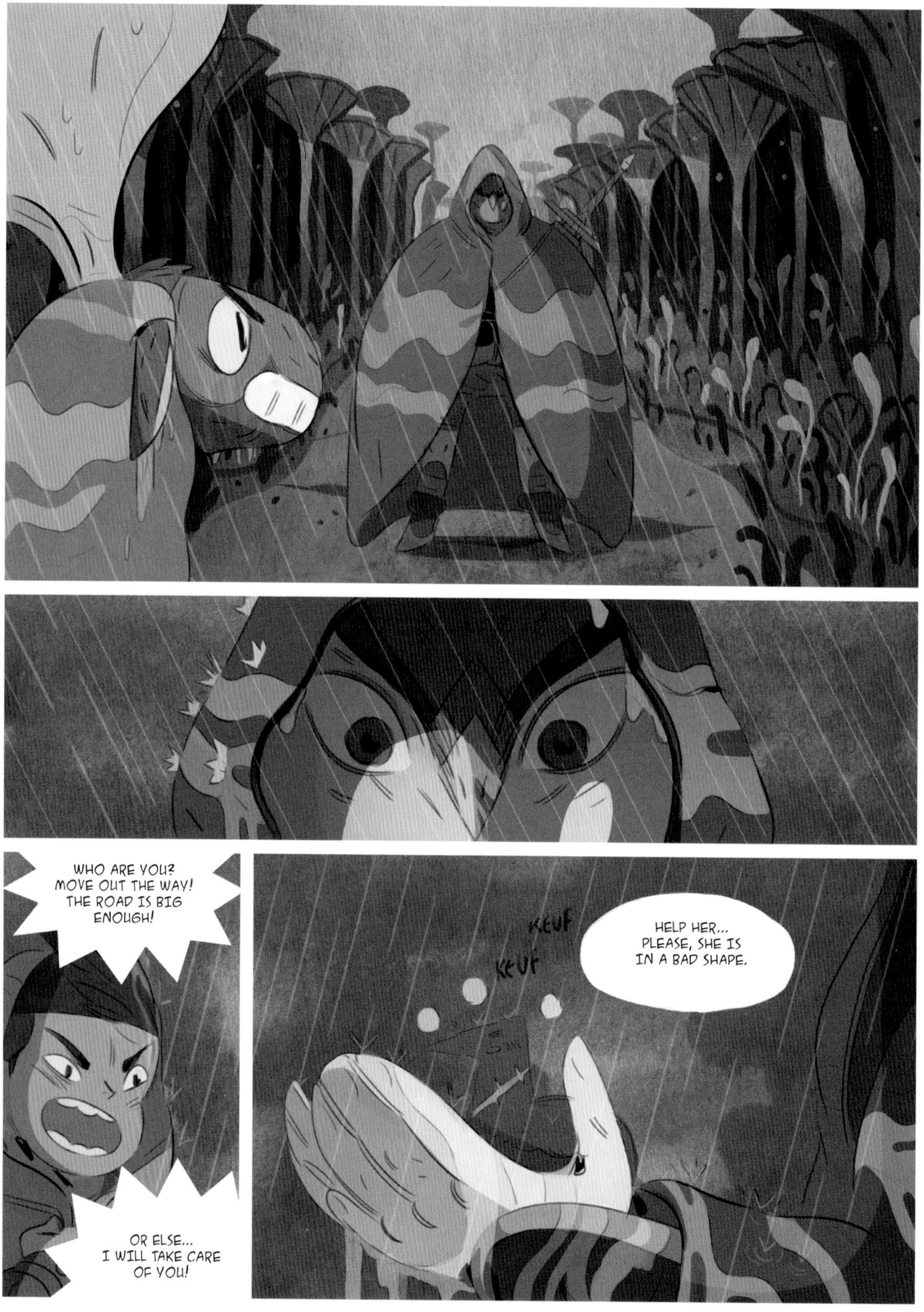
WHO ARE YOU? MOVE OUT THE WAY! THE ROAD IS BIG ENOUGH!
OR ELSE... I WILL TAKE CARE OF YOU!
KEUF
KEUF
HELP HER... PLEASE, SHE IS IN A BAD SHAPE.

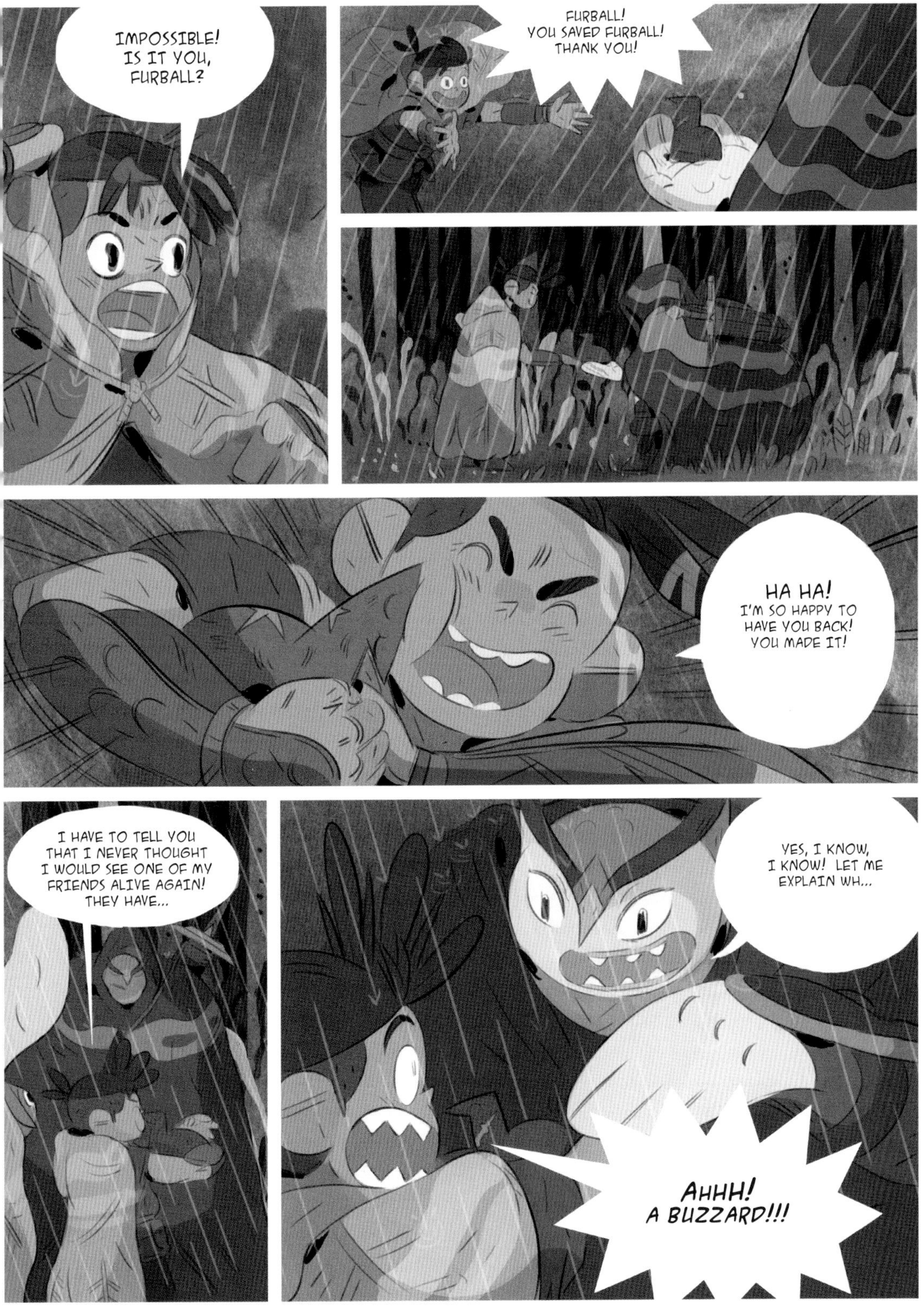
IMPOSSIBLE! IS IT YOU, FURBALL?
FURBALL! YOU SAVED FURBALL! THANK YOU!
HA HA! I'M SO HAPPY TO HAVE YOU BACK! YOU MADE IT!
I HAVE TO TELL YOU THAT I NEVER THOUGHT I WOULD SEE ONE OF MY FRIENDS ALIVE AGAIN! THEY HAVE...
YES, I KNOW, I KNOW! LET ME EXPLAIN WH...
AHHH! A BUZZARD!!!

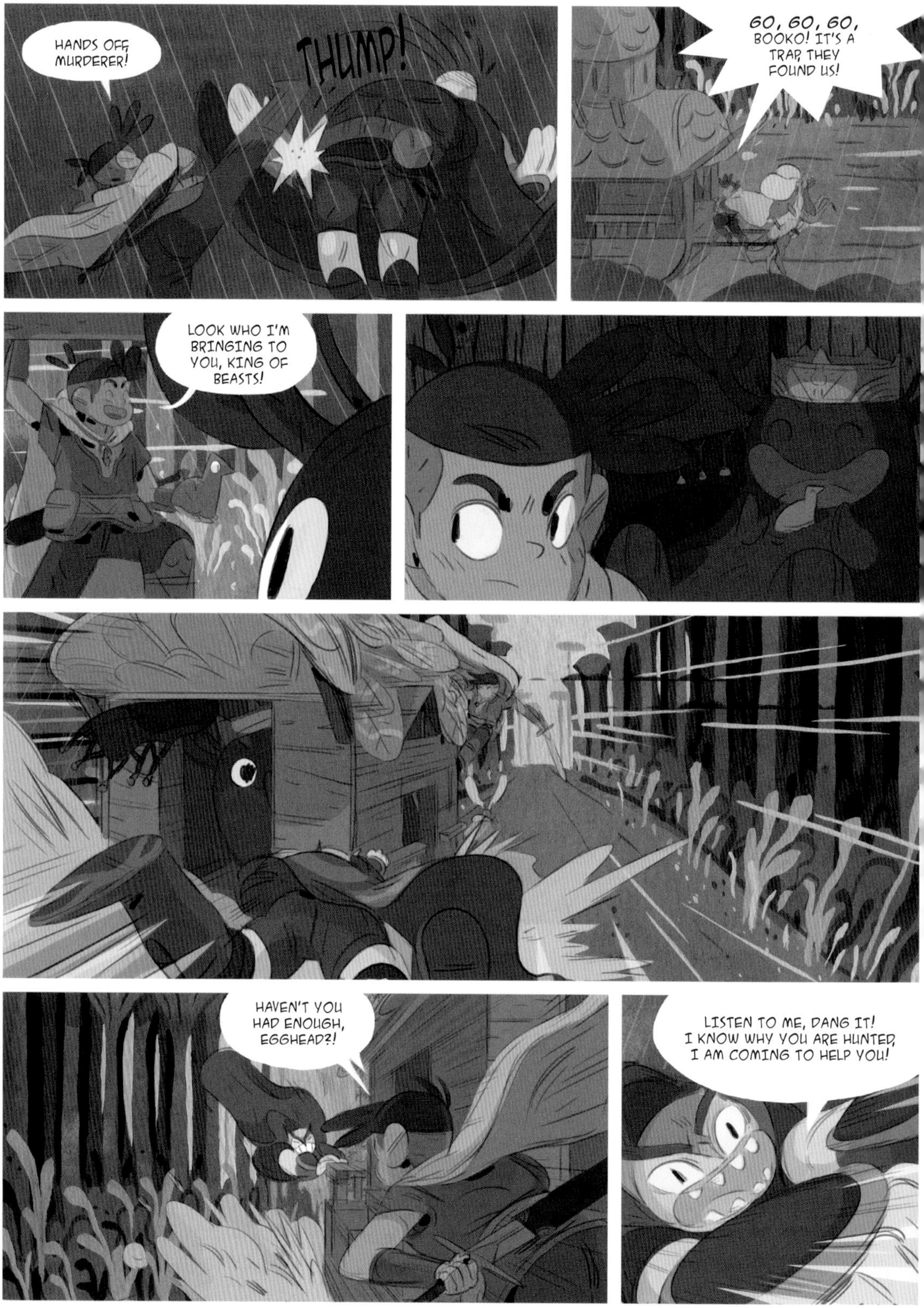

HANDS OFF, MURDERER!
THUMP!
GO, GO, GO, BOOKO! IT'S A TRAP, THEY FOUND US!
LOOK WHO I'M BRINGING TO YOU, KING OF BEASTS!
HAVEN'T YOU HAD ENOUGH, EGGHEAD?!
LISTEN TO ME, DANG IT! I KNOW WHY YOU ARE HUNTED, I AM COMING TO HELP YOU!

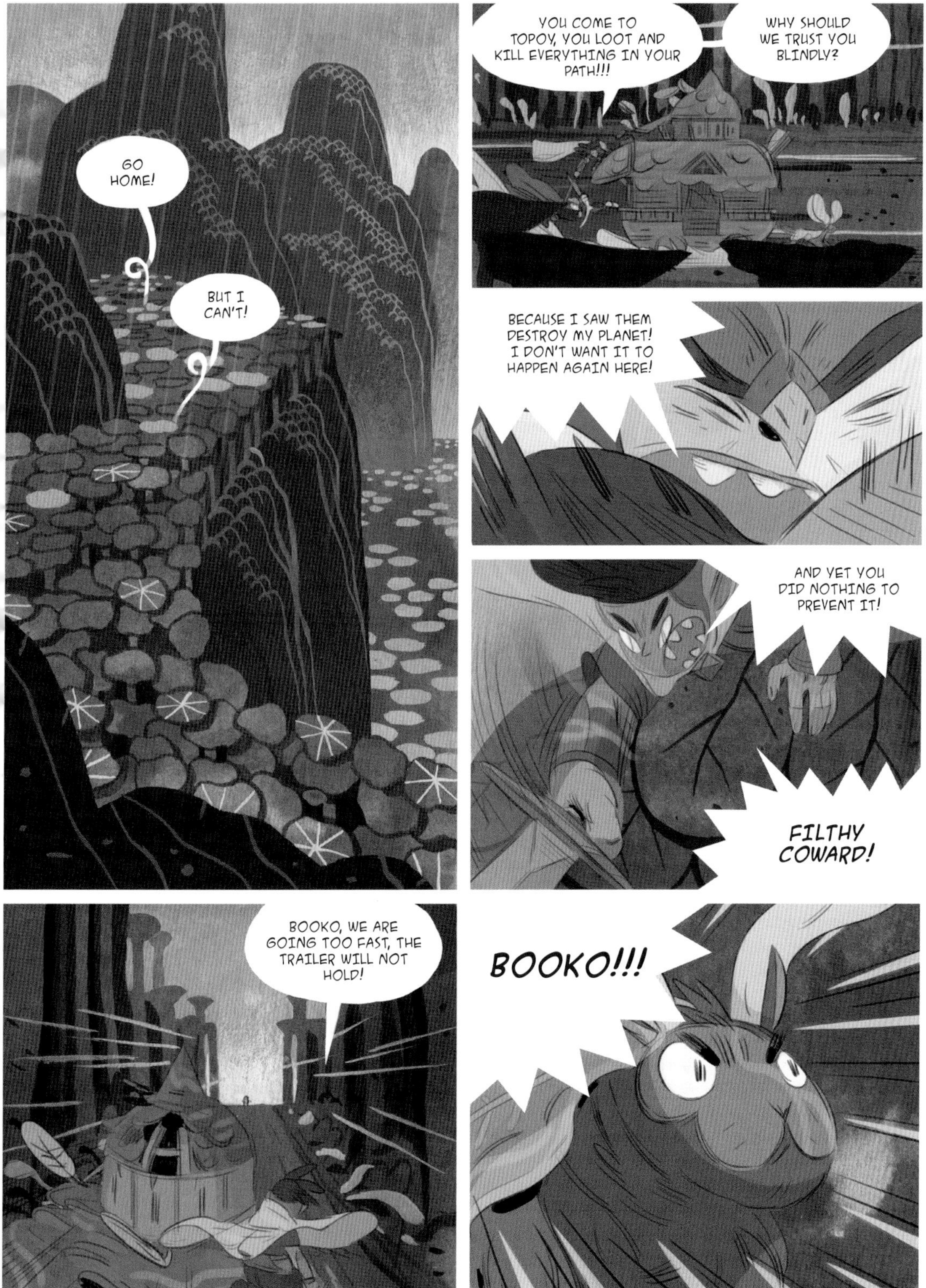
GO HOME!
BUT I CAN'T!
YOU COME TO TOPOY, YOU LOOT AND KILL EVERYTHING IN YOUR PATH!!!
WHY SHOULD WE TRUST YOU BLINDLY?
BECAUSE I SAW THEM DESTROY MY PLANET! I DON'T WANT IT TO HAPPEN AGAIN HERE!
AND YET YOU DID NOTHING TO PREVENT IT!
FILTHY COWARD!
BOOKO, WE ARE GOING TOO FAST, THE TRAILER WILL NOT HOLD!
BOOKO!!!

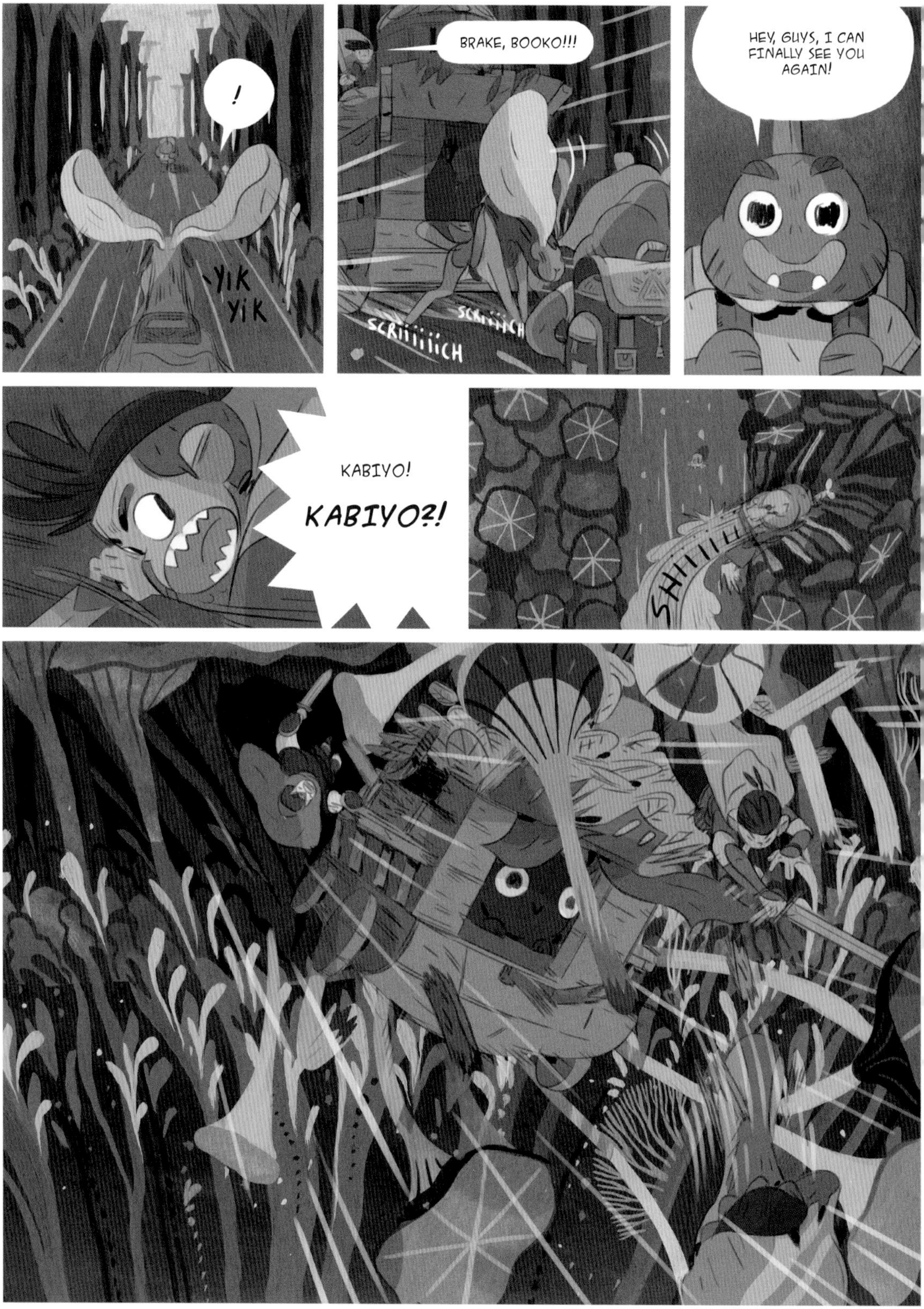
!
YIK YIK
BRAKE, BOOKO!!!
SCRIIIIIICH
SCRIIIICH
HEY, GUYS, I CAN FINALLY SEE YOU AGAIN!
KABIYO!
KABIYO?!
SHIIIII

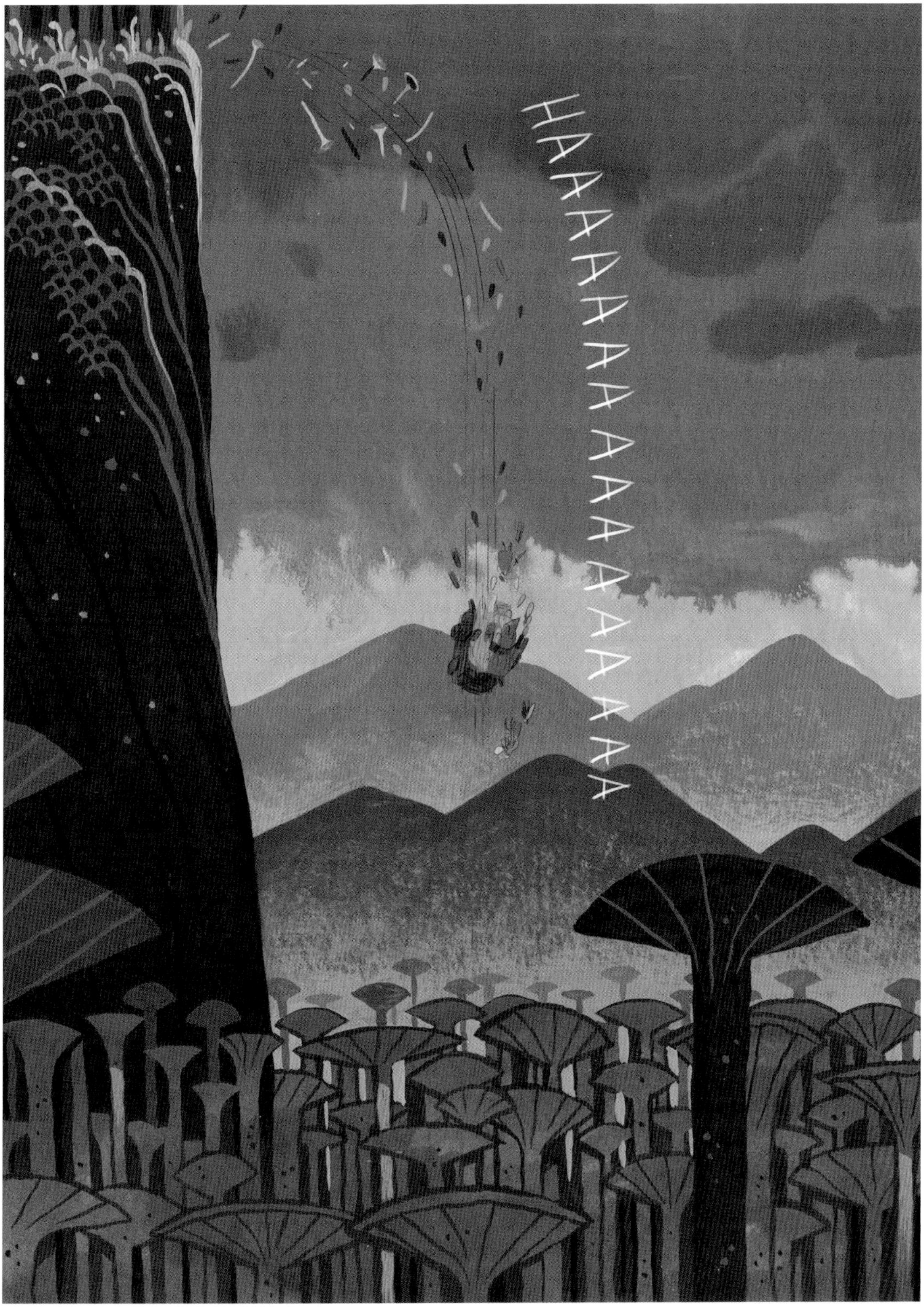
HAAAAAAAAAAAAAAA

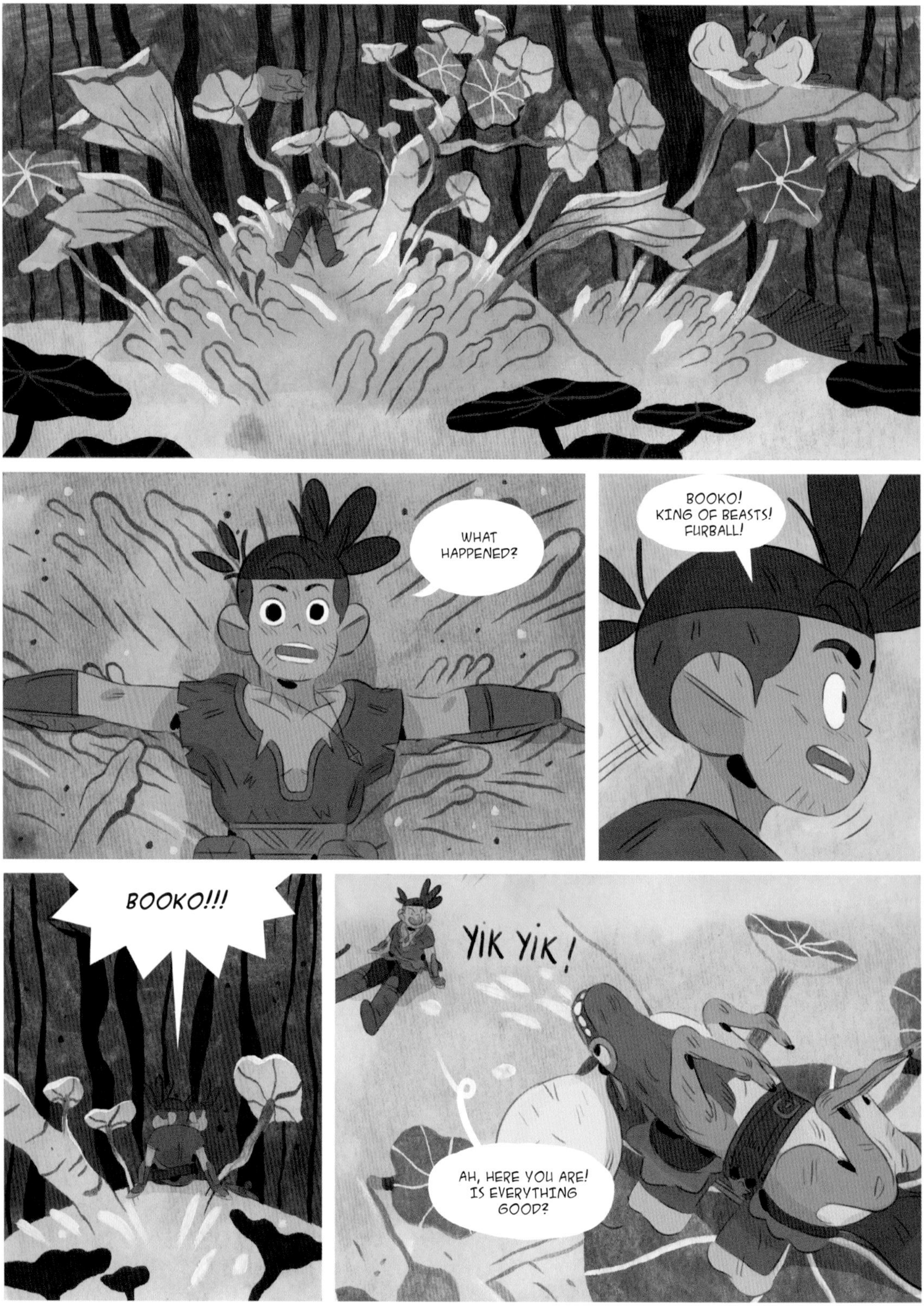
WHAT HAPPENED?
BOOKO! KING OF BEASTS! FURBALL!
BOOKO!!!
YIK YIK!
AH, HERE YOU ARE! IS EVERYTHING GOOD?

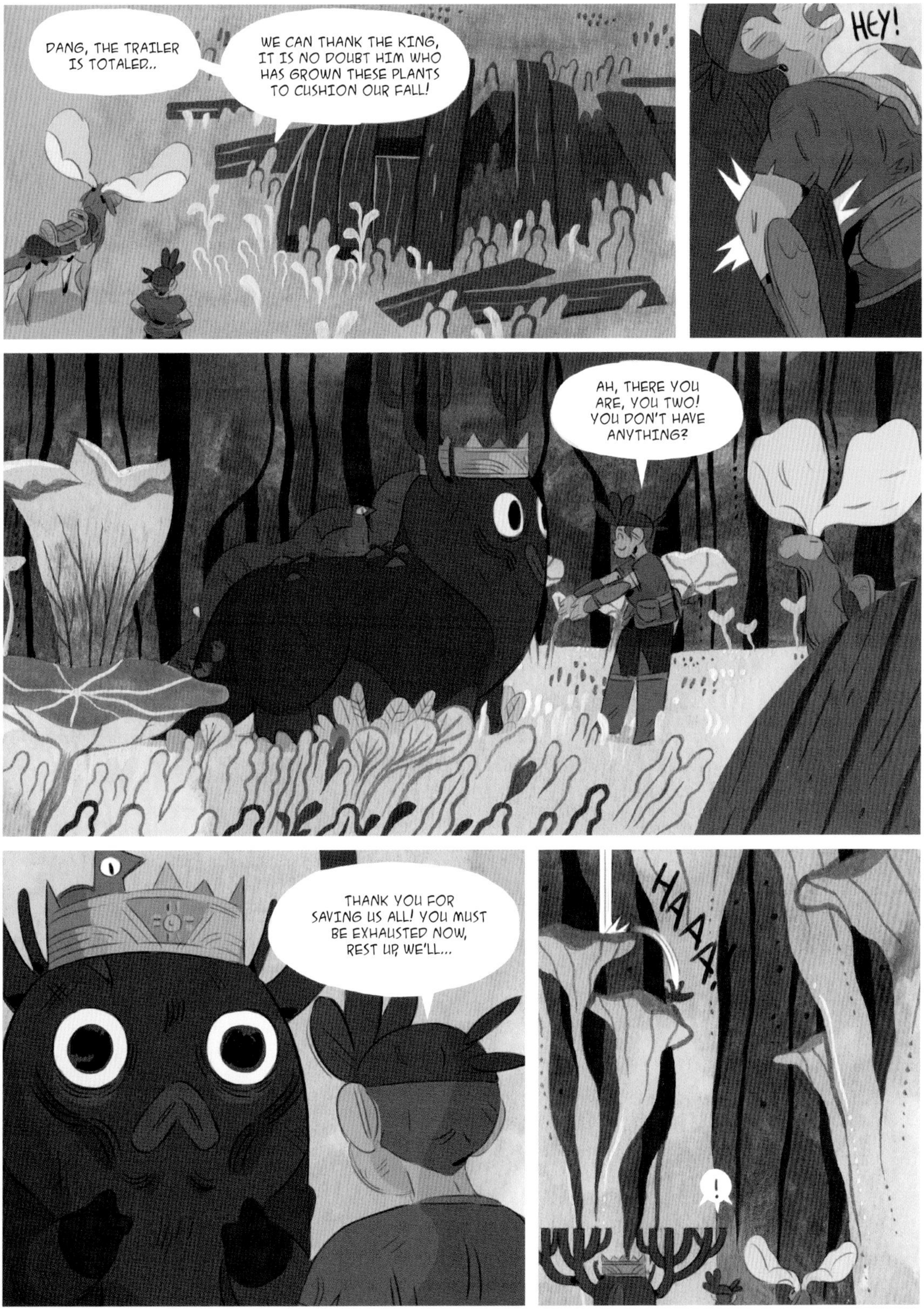
DANG, THE TRAILER IS TOTALED...
WE CAN THANK THE KING, IT IS NO DOUBT HIM WHO HAS GROWN THESE PLANTS TO CUSHION OUR FALL!
HEY!
AH, THERE YOU ARE, YOU TWO! YOU DON'T HAVE ANYTHING?
THANK YOU FOR SAVING US ALL! YOU MUST BE EXHAUSTED NOW, REST UP, WE'LL...
HAAA!
!

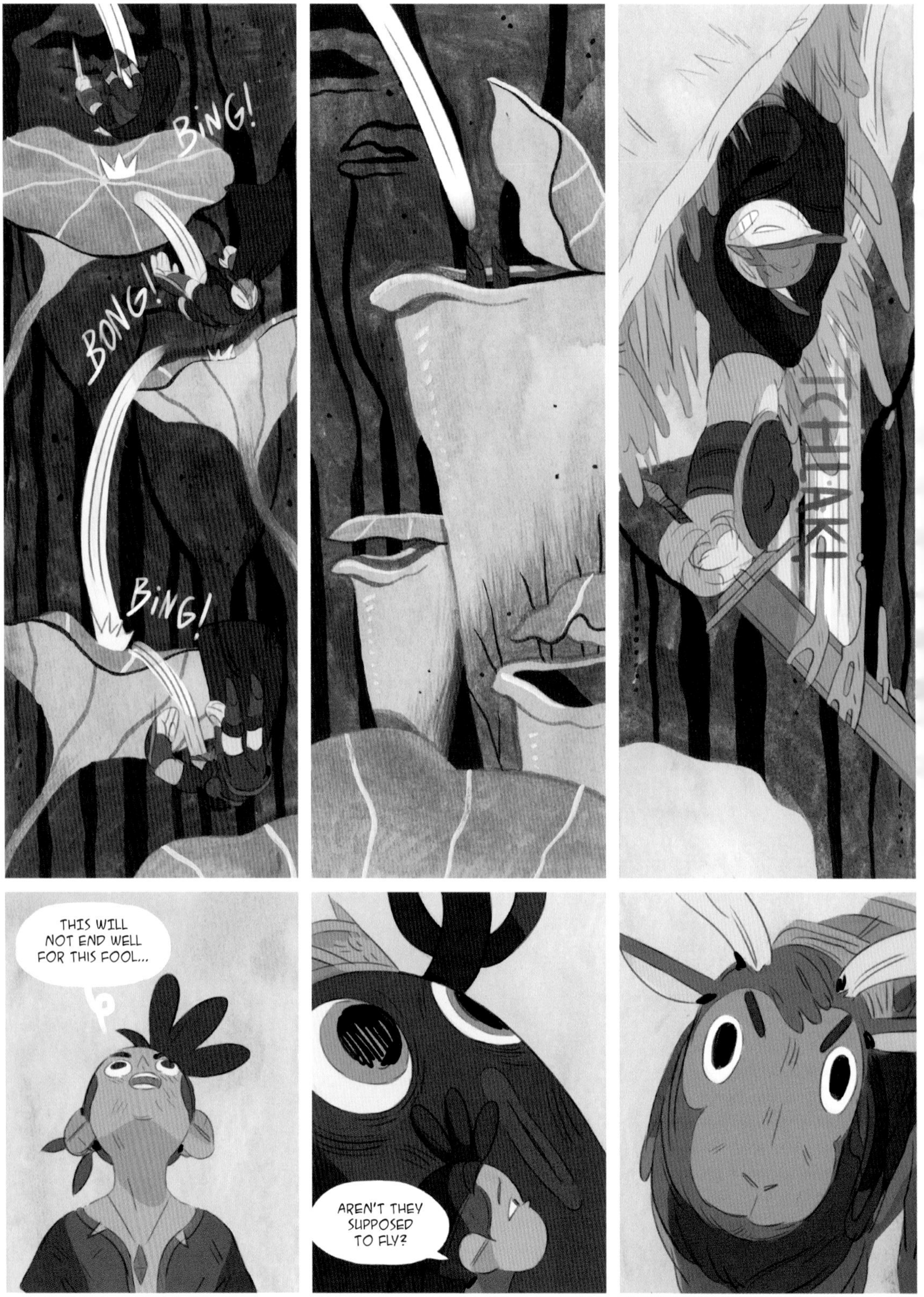
BING!
BONG!
BING!
TCHIAK!
THIS WILL NOT END WELL FOR THIS FOOL...
AREN'T THEY SUPPOSED TO FLY?

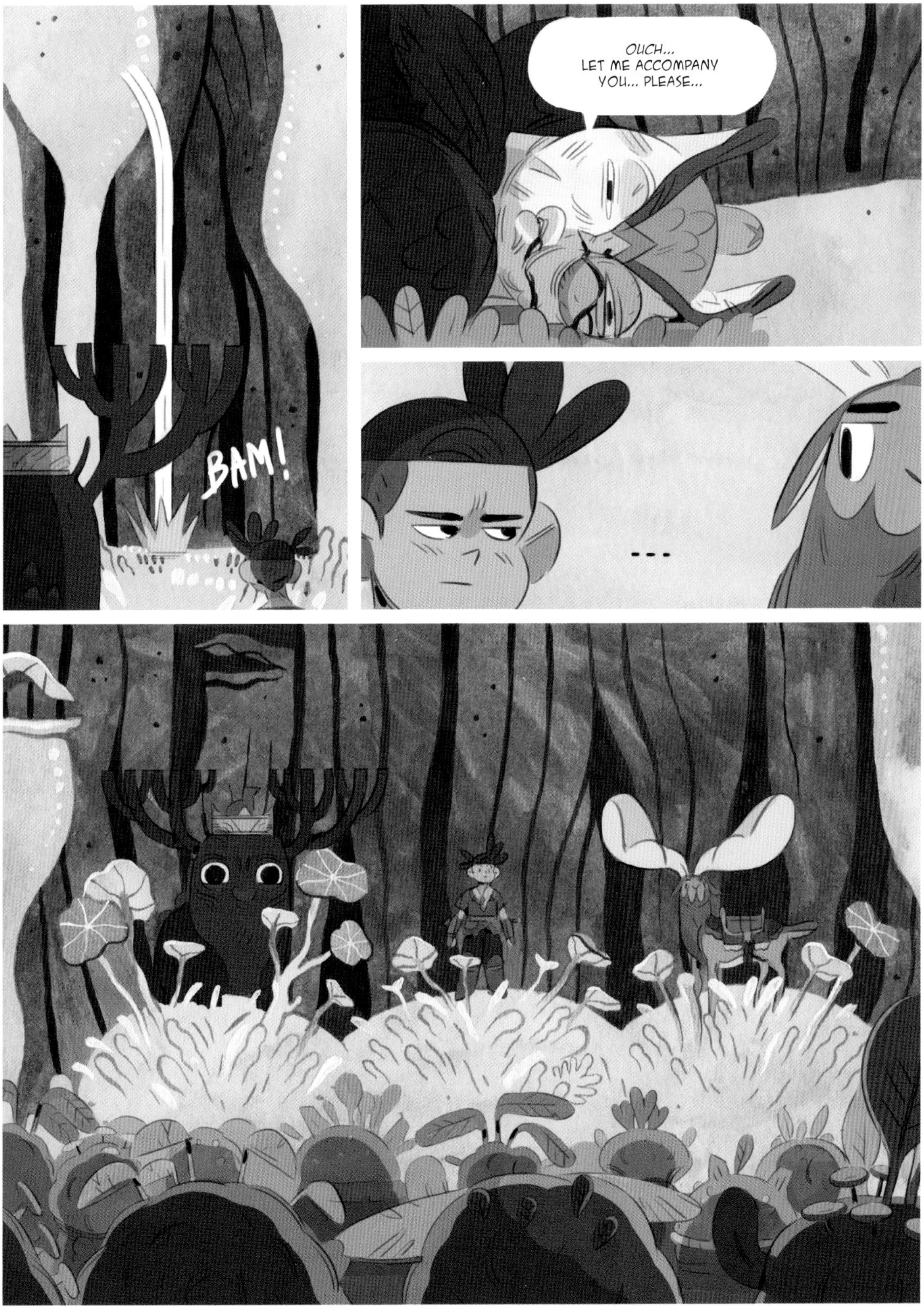
BAM!
OUCH...
LET ME ACCOMPANY
YOU... PLEASE...
...

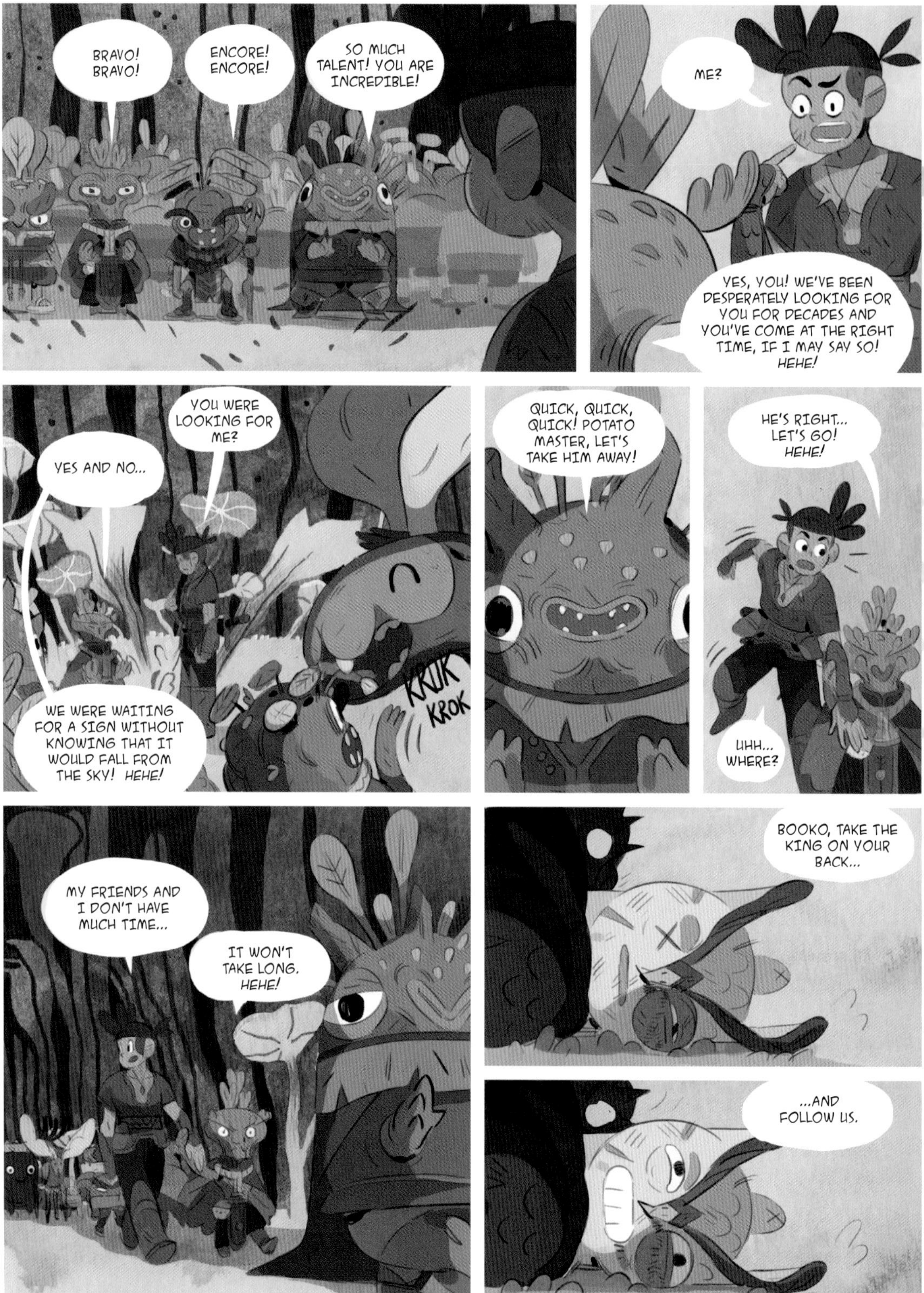
BRAVO! BRAVO!
ENCORE! ENCORE!
SO MUCH TALENT! YOU ARE INCREDIBLE!
ME?
YES, YOU! WE'VE BEEN DESPERATELY LOOKING FOR YOU FOR DECADES AND YOU'VE COME AT THE RIGHT TIME, IF I MAY SAY SO! HEHE!
YOU WERE LOOKING FOR ME?
YES AND NO...
WE WERE WAITING FOR A SIGN WITHOUT KNOWING THAT IT WOULD FALL FROM THE SKY! HEHE!
KRUK KROK
QUICK, QUICK, QUICK! POTATO MASTER, LET'S TAKE HIM AWAY!
HE'S RIGHT... LET'S GO! HEHE!
UHH... WHERE?
MY FRIENDS AND I DON'T HAVE MUCH TIME...
IT WON'T TAKE LONG. HEHE!
BOOKO, TAKE THE KING ON YOUR BACK...
...AND FOLLOW US.

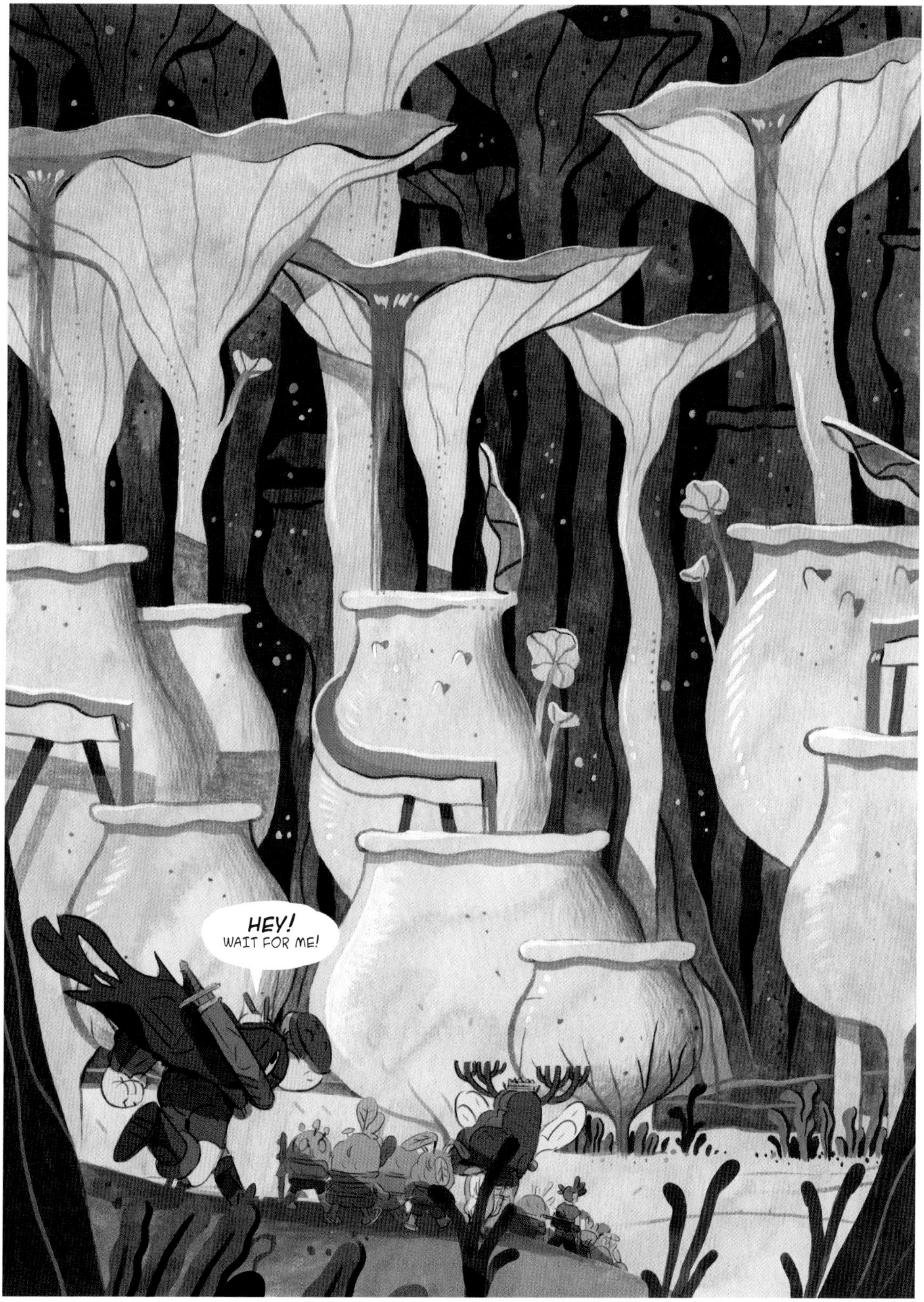
HEY!
WAIT FOR ME!

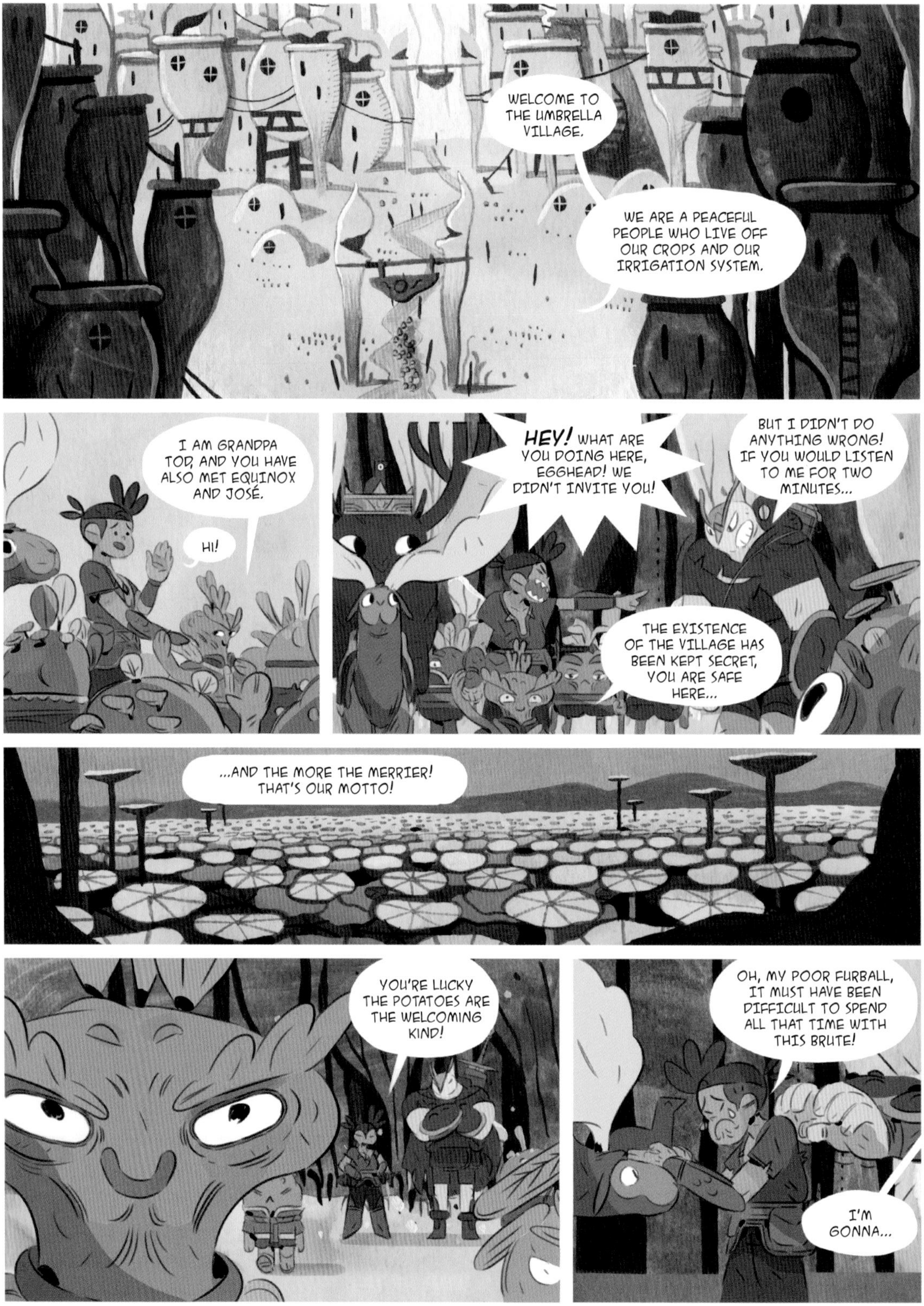
WELCOME TO THE UMBRELLA VILLAGE.
WE ARE A PEACEFUL PEOPLE WHO LIVE OFF OUR CROPS AND OUR IRRIGATION SYSTEM.
I AM GRANDPA TOD, AND YOU HAVE ALSO MET EQUINOX AND JOSÉ.
HI!
HEY! WHAT ARE YOU DOING HERE, EGGHEAD! WE DIDN'T INVITE YOU!
BUT I DIDN'T DO ANYTHING WRONG! IF YOU WOULD LISTEN TO ME FOR TWO MINUTES...
THE EXISTENCE OF THE VILLAGE HAS BEEN KEPT SECRET, YOU ARE SAFE HERE...
...AND THE MORE THE MERRIER! THAT'S OUR MOTTO!
YOU'RE LUCKY THE POTATOES ARE THE WELCOMING KIND!
OH, MY POOR FURBALL, IT MUST HAVE BEEN DIFFICULT TO SPEND ALL THAT TIME WITH THIS BRUTE!
I'M GONNA...

WE'RE HERE!

HERE IS A DORMANT SEED PLANTED A LONG TIME AGO. IT WILL GERMINATE IN FIFTY YEARS.

YOUR VILLAGE IS AMAZING, BUT THIS PLANT IS EVEN MORE AMAZING!

YES, IT'S ONE OF OUR TREASURES...

IT'S A MAGIC LOCK THAT LETS YOU INSERT VEGETATION STONES. BUT THEY'RE BECOMING RARE LATELY.

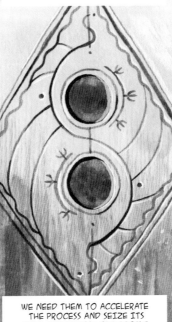

...BUT WE CAN'T WAIT FIFTY YEARS... WE MUST MAKE IT GERMINATE!

SEE THESE MARKS ON THE TRUNK?

WE NEED THEM TO ACCELERATE THE PROCESS AND SEIZE ITS CORE. OTHERWISE OUR PEOPLE WILL DISAPPEAR.

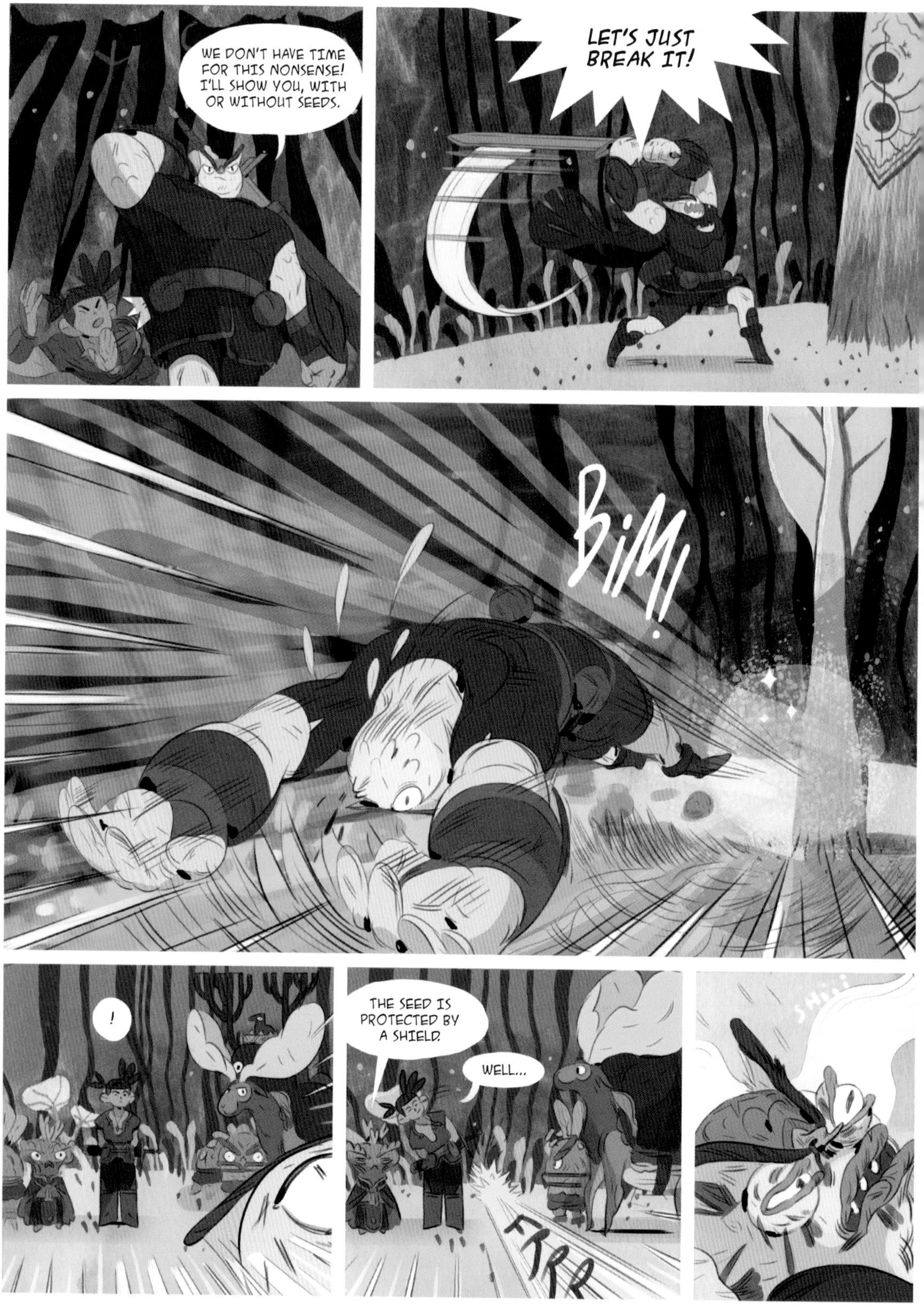
WE DON'T HAVE TIME FOR THIS NONSENSE! I'LL SHOW YOU, WITH OR WITHOUT SEEDS.
LET'S JUST BREAK IT!
BIM!
!
THE SEED IS PROTECTED BY A SHIELD.
WELL...
FRRR

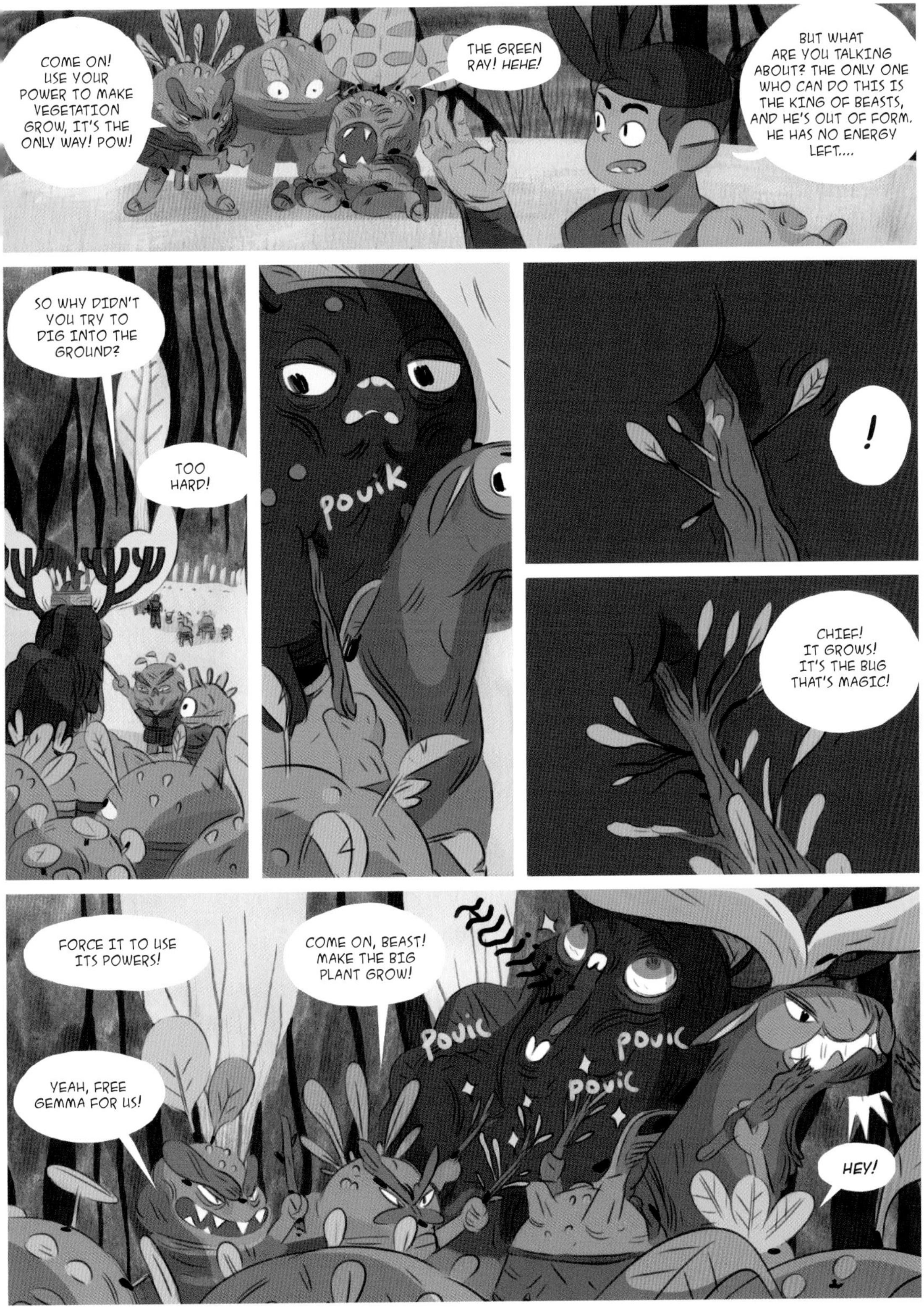

COME ON! USE YOUR POWER TO MAKE VEGETATION GROW, IT'S THE ONLY WAY! POW!
THE GREEN RAY! HEHE!
BUT WHAT ARE YOU TALKING ABOUT? THE ONLY ONE WHO CAN DO THIS IS THE KING OF BEASTS, AND HE'S OUT OF FORM. HE HAS NO ENERGY LEFT....
SO WHY DIDN'T YOU TRY TO DIG INTO THE GROUND?
TOO HARD!
POUIK
!
CHIEF! IT GROWS! IT'S THE BUG THAT'S MAGIC!
FORCE IT TO USE ITS POWERS!
COME ON, BEAST! MAKE THE BIG PLANT GROW!
YEAH, FREE GEMMA FOR US!
POUIC
POUIC
POUIC
HEY!

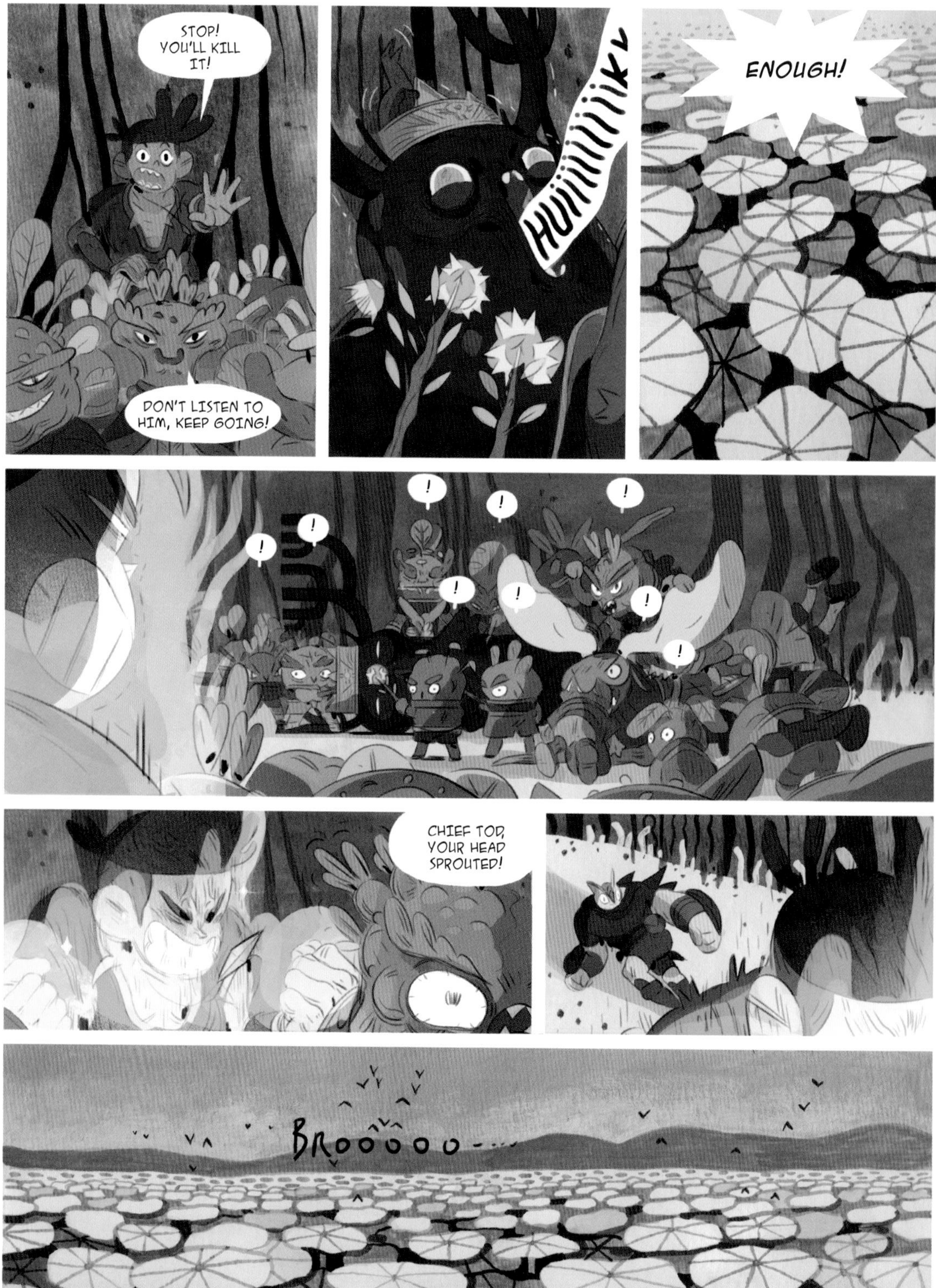

STOP! YOU'LL KILL IT!
DON'T LISTEN TO HIM, KEEP GOING!
HUIIIIIIIKL
ENOUGH!
!
!
!
!
!
!
!
!
CHIEF TOD, YOUR HEAD SPROUTED!
BROOOOO

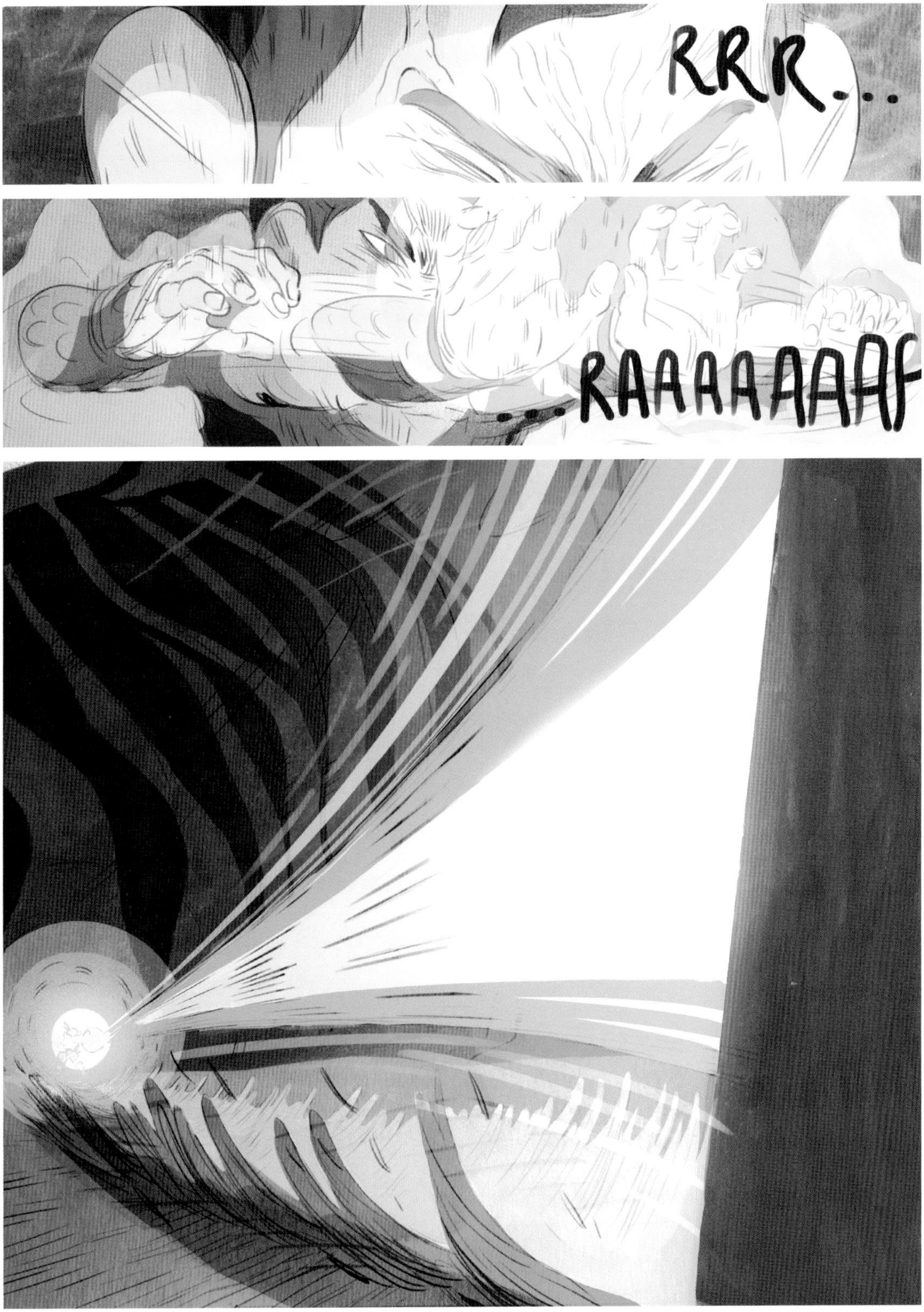
RRR...
...RAAAAAAAF

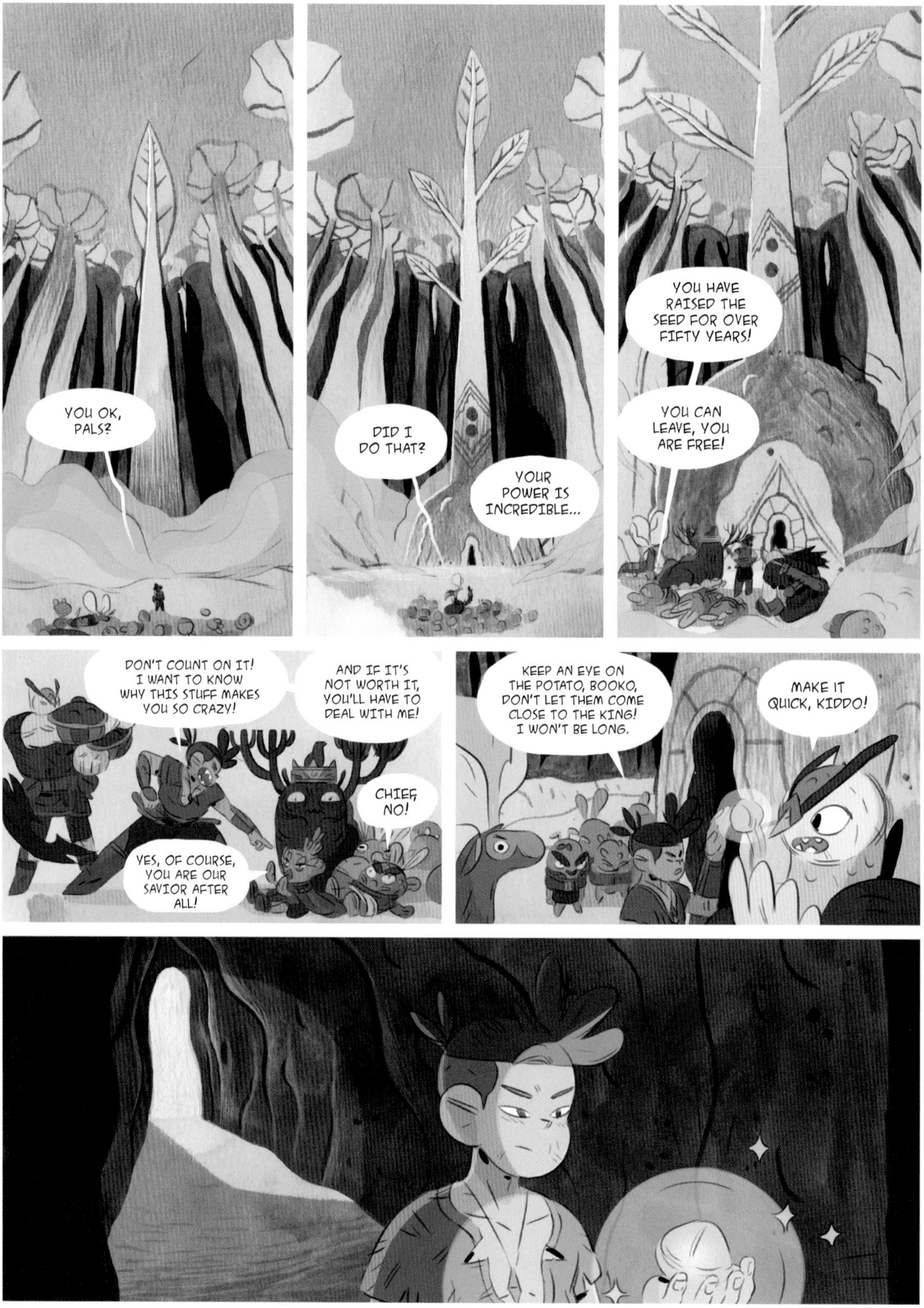
YOU OK, PALS?
DID I DO THAT?
YOUR POWER IS INCREDIBLE...
YOU HAVE RAISED THE SEED FOR OVER FIFTY YEARS!
YOU CAN LEAVE, YOU ARE FREE!
DON'T COUNT ON IT! I WANT TO KNOW WHY THIS STUFF MAKES YOU SO CRAZY!
AND IF IT'S NOT WORTH IT, YOU'LL HAVE TO DEAL WITH ME!
CHIEF, NO!
YES, OF COURSE, YOU ARE OUR SAVIOR AFTER ALL!
KEEP AN EYE ON THE POTATO, BOOKO, DON'T LET THEM COME CLOSE TO THE KING! I WON'T BE LONG.
MAKE IT QUICK, KIDDO!

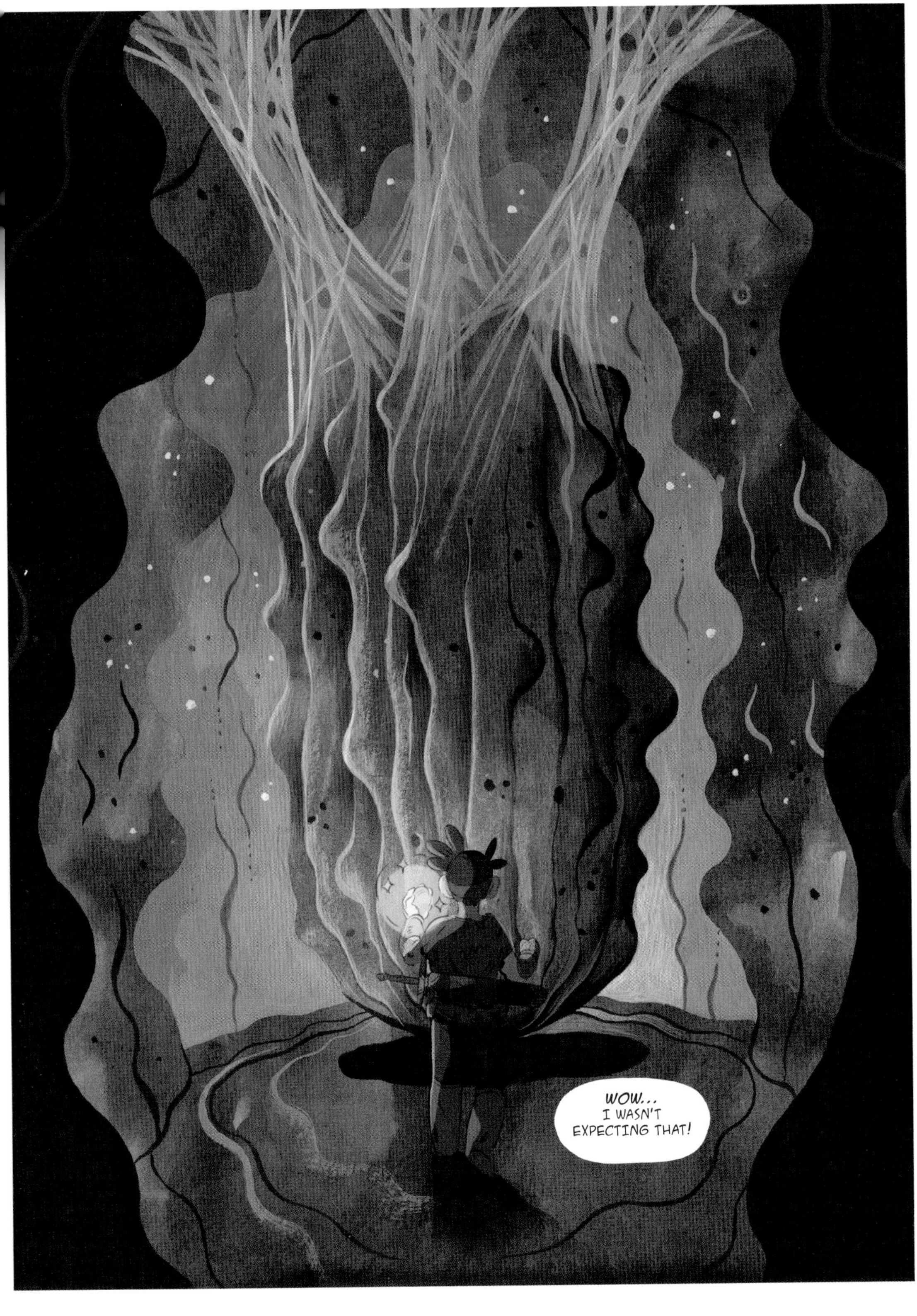
WOW... I WASN'T EXPECTING THAT!

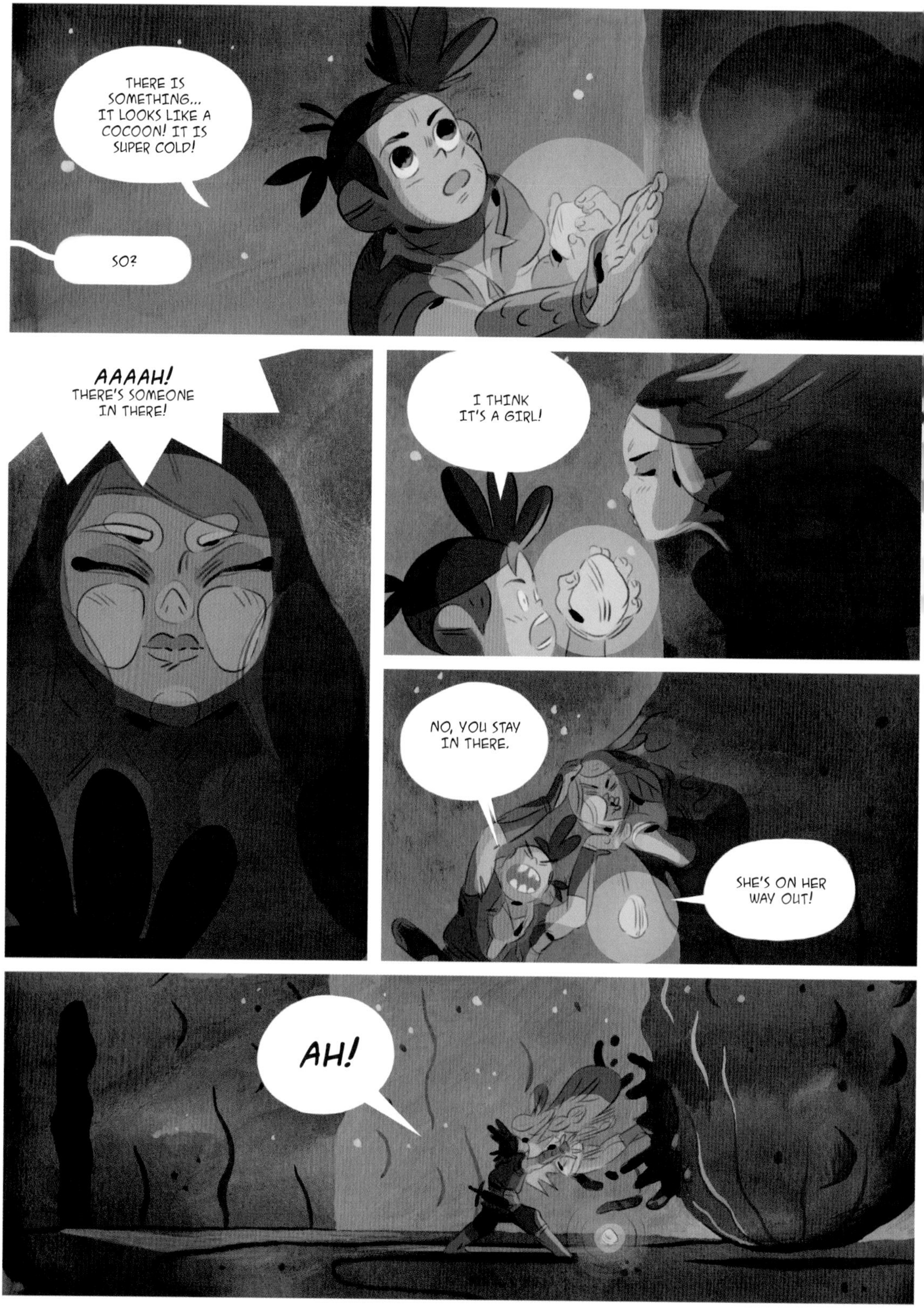
THERE IS SOMETHING... IT LOOKS LIKE A COCOON! IT IS SUPER COLD!
SO?
AAAAH! THERE'S SOMEONE IN THERE!
I THINK IT'S A GIRL!
NO, YOU STAY IN THERE.
SHE'S ON HER WAY OUT!
AH!

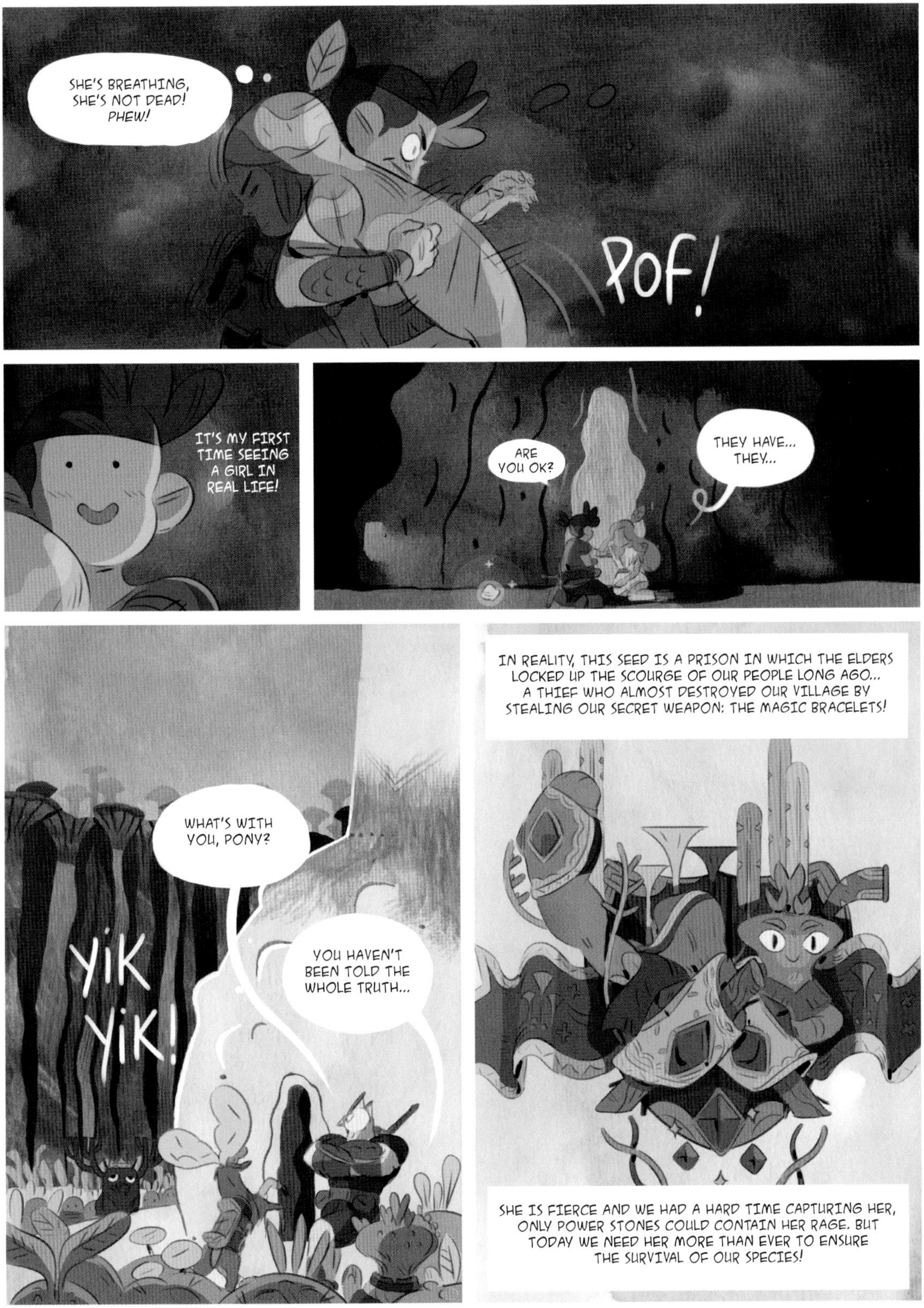
SHE'S BREATHING, SHE'S NOT DEAD! PHEW!
POF!
IT'S MY FIRST TIME SEEING A GIRL IN REAL LIFE!
ARE YOU OK?
THEY HAVE... THEY...
WHAT'S WITH YOU, PONY?
YIK YIK!
YOU HAVEN'T BEEN TOLD THE WHOLE TRUTH...
IN REALITY, THIS SEED IS A PRISON IN WHICH THE ELDERS LOCKED UP THE SCOURGE OF OUR PEOPLE LONG AGO... A THIEF WHO ALMOST DESTROYED OUR VILLAGE BY STEALING OUR SECRET WEAPON: THE MAGIC BRACELETS!
SHE IS FIERCE AND WE HAD A HARD TIME CAPTURING HER, ONLY POWER STONES COULD CONTAIN HER RAGE. BUT TODAY WE NEED HER MORE THAN EVER TO ENSURE THE SURVIVAL OF OUR SPECIES!

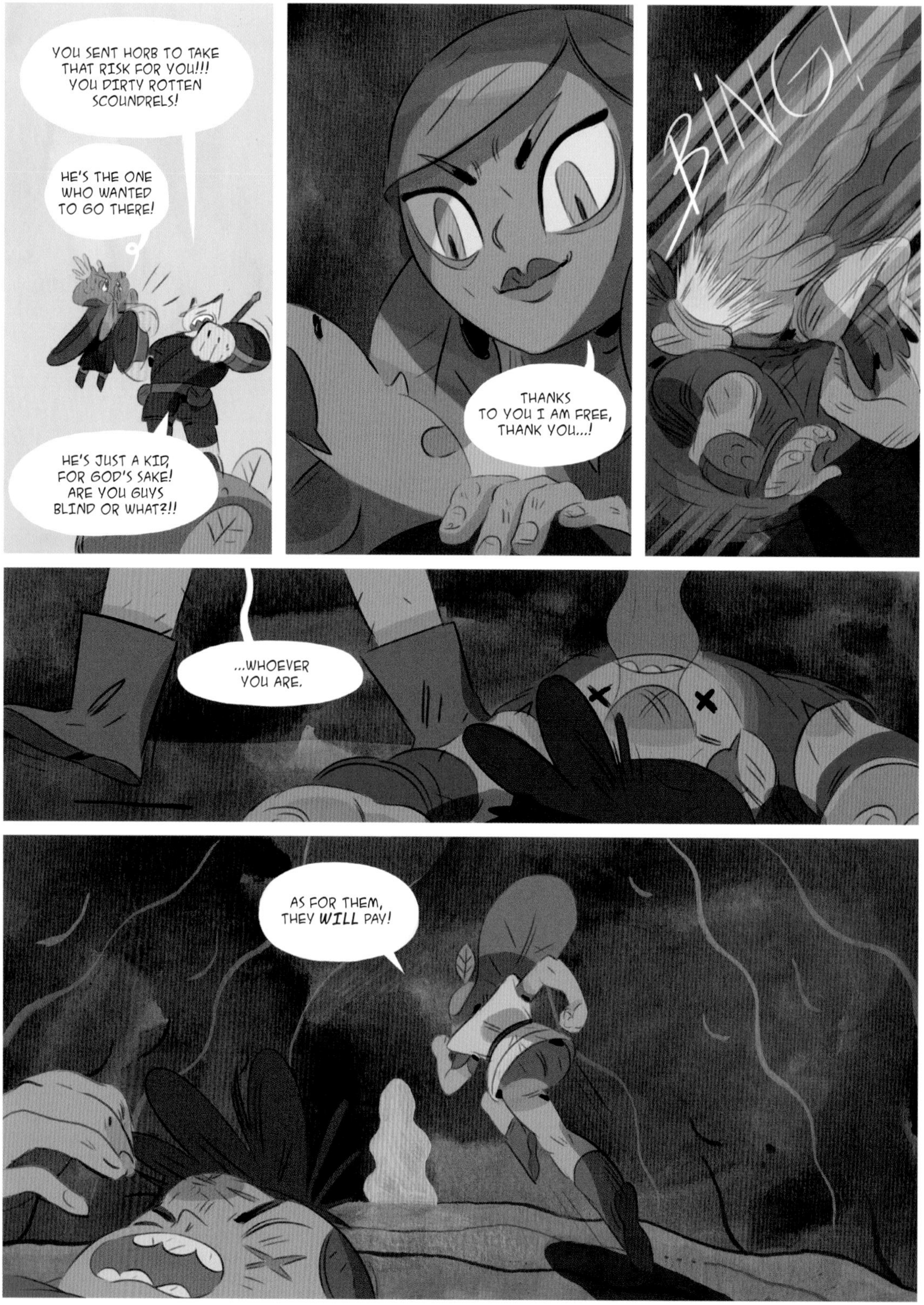
YOU SENT HORB TO TAKE THAT RISK FOR YOU!!! YOU DIRTY ROTTEN SCOUNDRELS!
HE'S THE ONE WHO WANTED TO GO THERE!
HE'S JUST A KID, FOR GOD'S SAKE! ARE YOU GUYS BLIND OR WHAT?!!
THANKS TO YOU I AM FREE, THANK YOU...!
BING!
...WHOEVER YOU ARE.
AS FOR THEM, THEY WILL PAY!

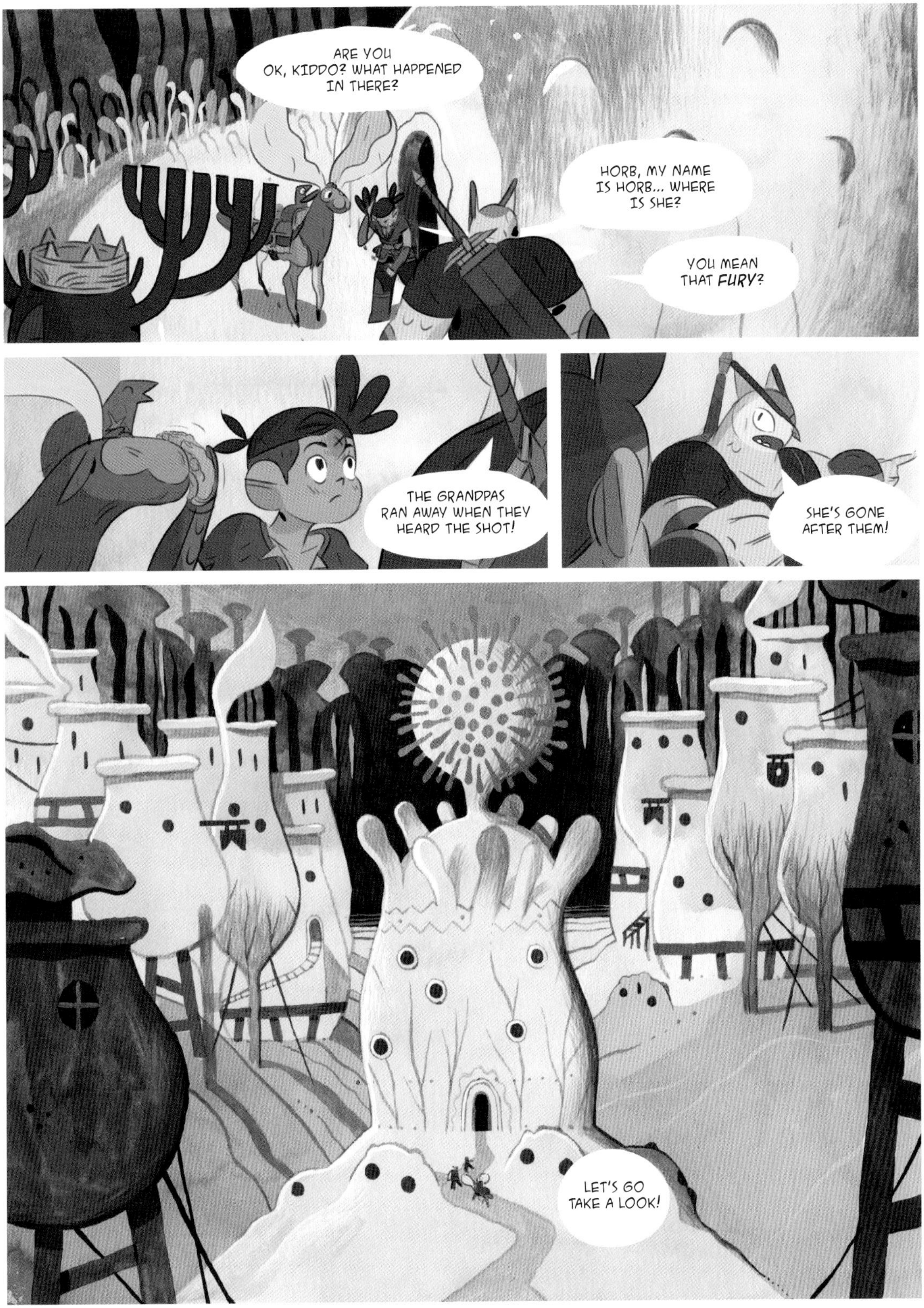
ARE YOU OK, KIDDO? WHAT HAPPENED IN THERE?
HORB, MY NAME IS HORB... WHERE IS SHE?
YOU MEAN THAT FURY?
THE GRANDPAS RAN AWAY WHEN THEY HEARD THE SHOT!
SHE'S GONE AFTER THEM!
LET'S GO TAKE A LOOK!

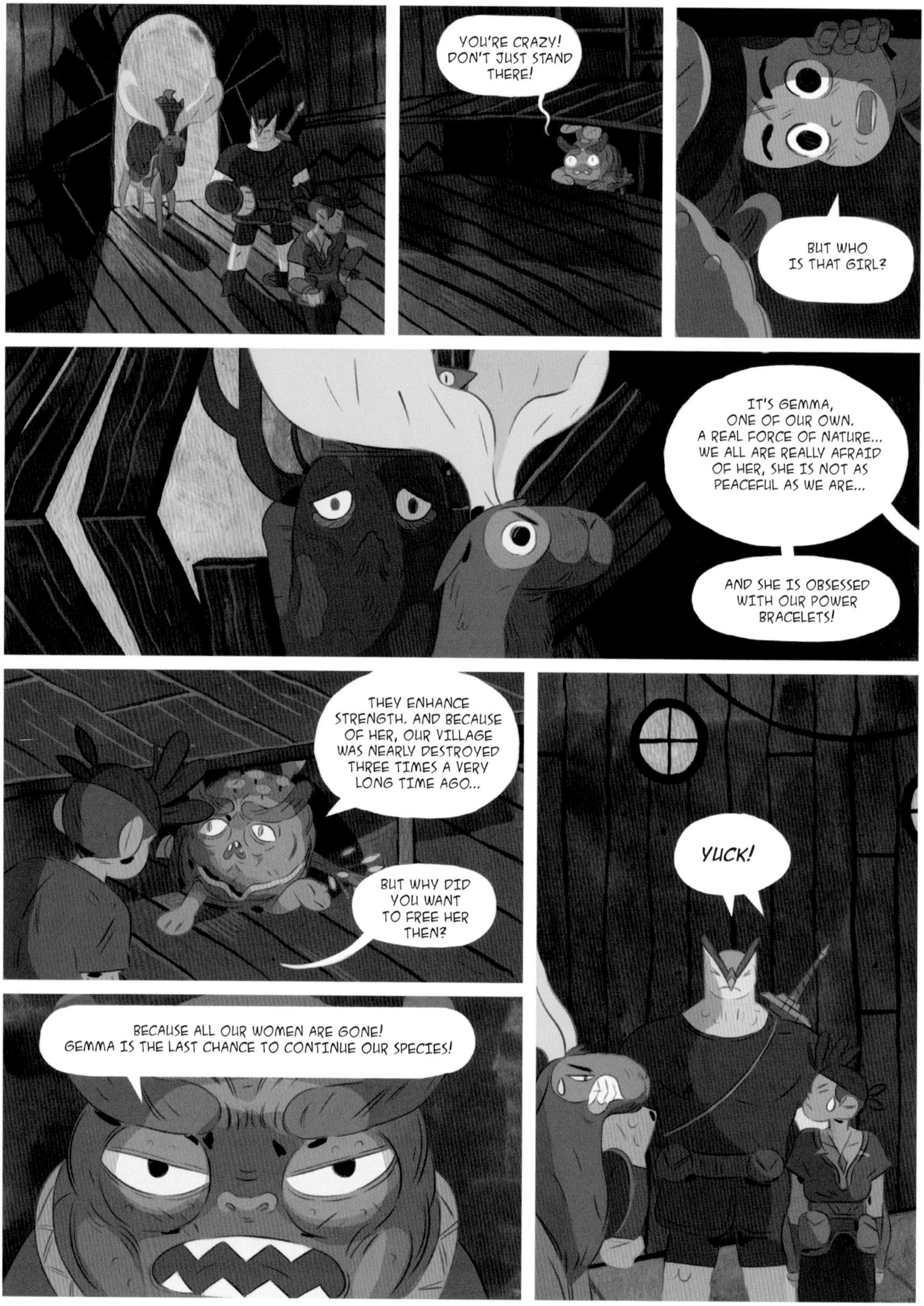
YOU'RE CRAZY! DON'T JUST STAND THERE!
BUT WHO IS THAT GIRL?
IT'S GEMMA, ONE OF OUR OWN. A REAL FORCE OF NATURE... WE ALL ARE REALLY AFRAID OF HER, SHE IS NOT AS PEACEFUL AS WE ARE...
AND SHE IS OBSESSED WITH OUR POWER BRACELETS!
THEY ENHANCE STRENGTH. AND BECAUSE OF HER, OUR VILLAGE WAS NEARLY DESTROYED THREE TIMES A VERY LONG TIME AGO...
BUT WHY DID YOU WANT TO FREE HER THEN?
YUCK!
BECAUSE ALL OUR WOMEN ARE GONE! GEMMA IS THE LAST CHANCE TO CONTINUE OUR SPECIES!

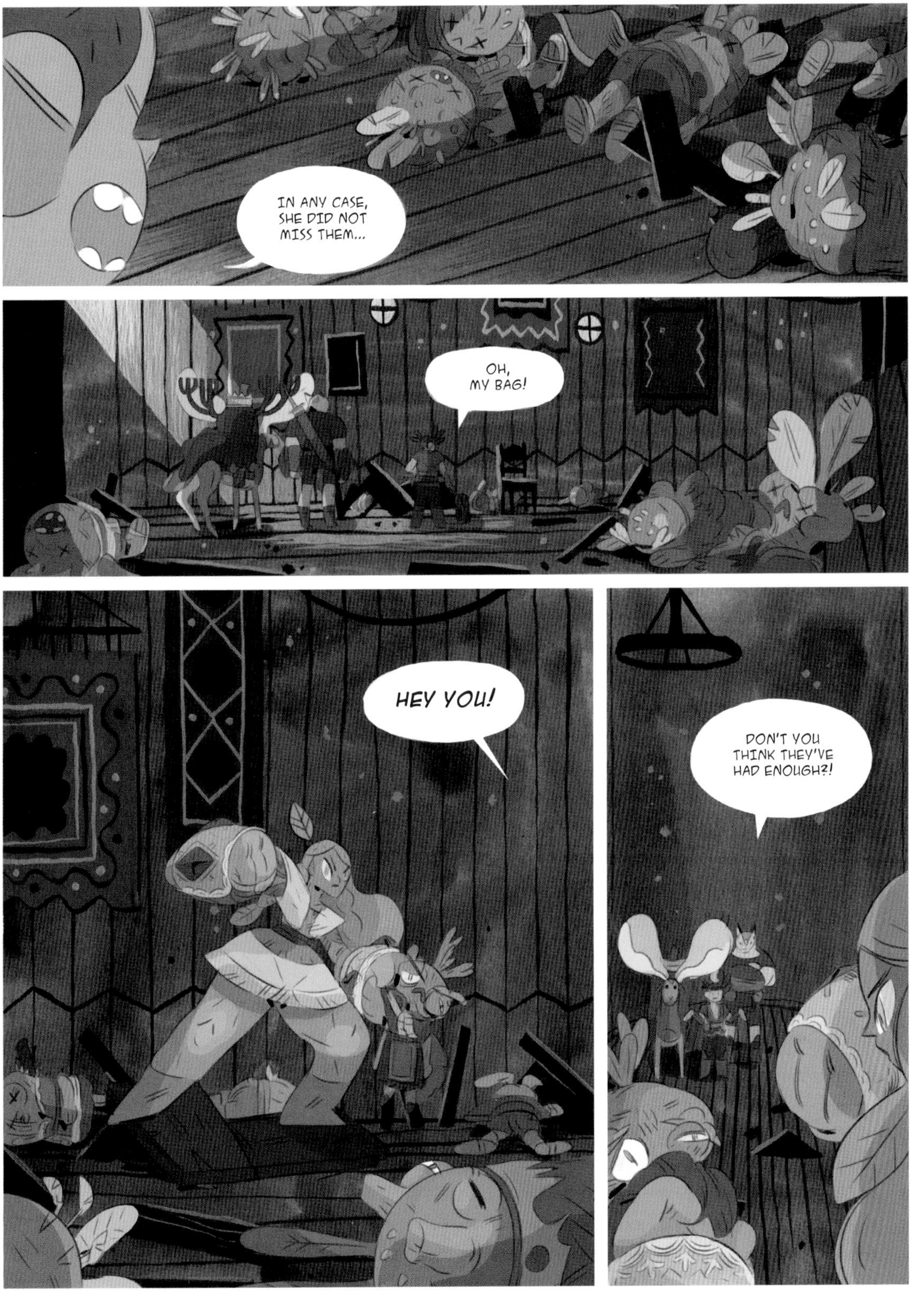
IN ANY CASE, SHE DID NOT MISS THEM...
OH, MY BAG!
HEY YOU!
DON'T YOU THINK THEY'VE HAD ENOUGH?!

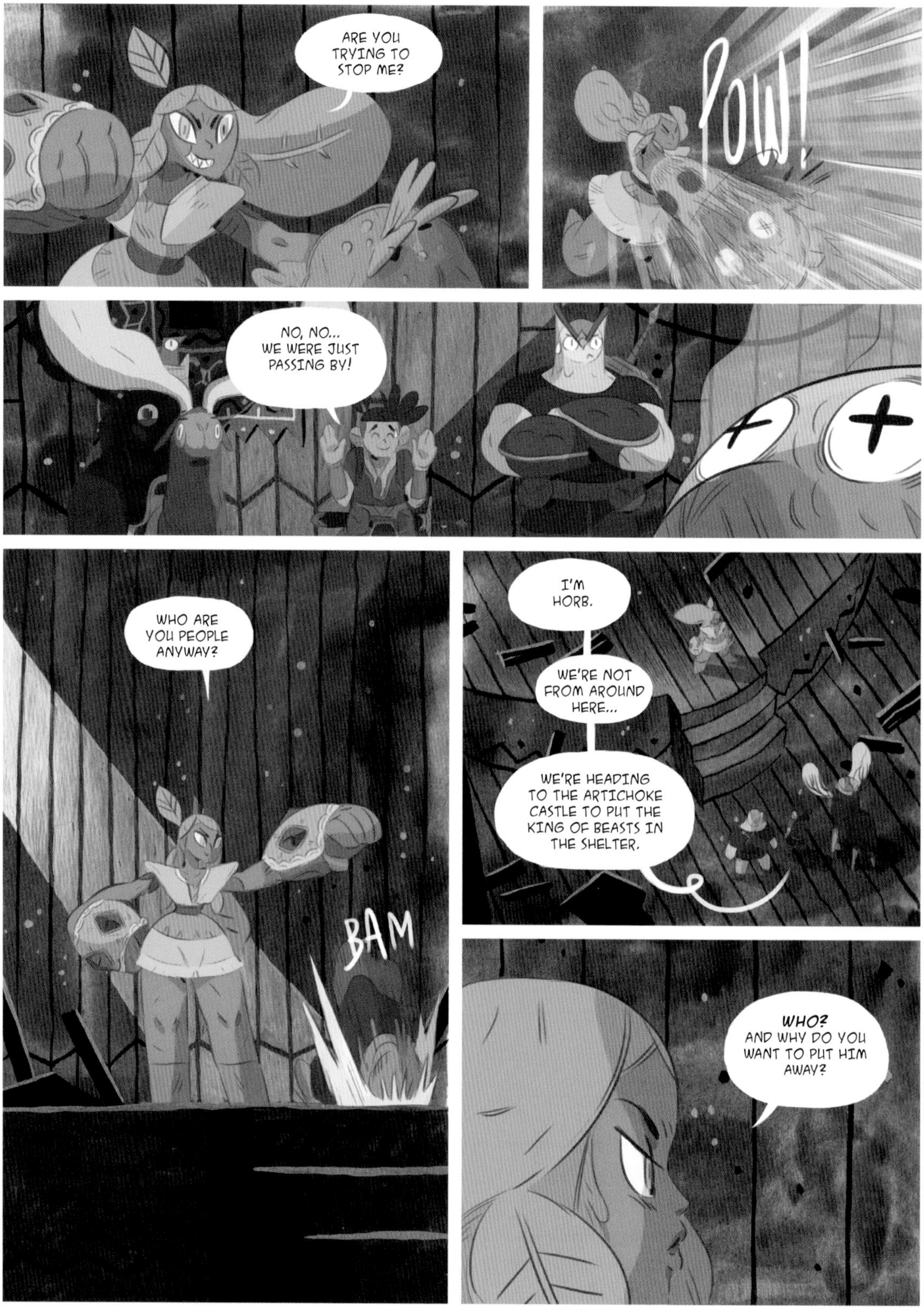
ARE YOU TRYING TO STOP ME?
POW!
NO, NO... WE WERE JUST PASSING BY!
WHO ARE YOU PEOPLE ANYWAY?
BAM
I'M HORB.
WE'RE NOT FROM AROUND HERE...
WE'RE HEADING TO THE ARTICHOKE CASTLE TO PUT THE KING OF BEASTS IN THE SHELTER.
WHO? AND WHY DO YOU WANT TO PUT HIM AWAY?

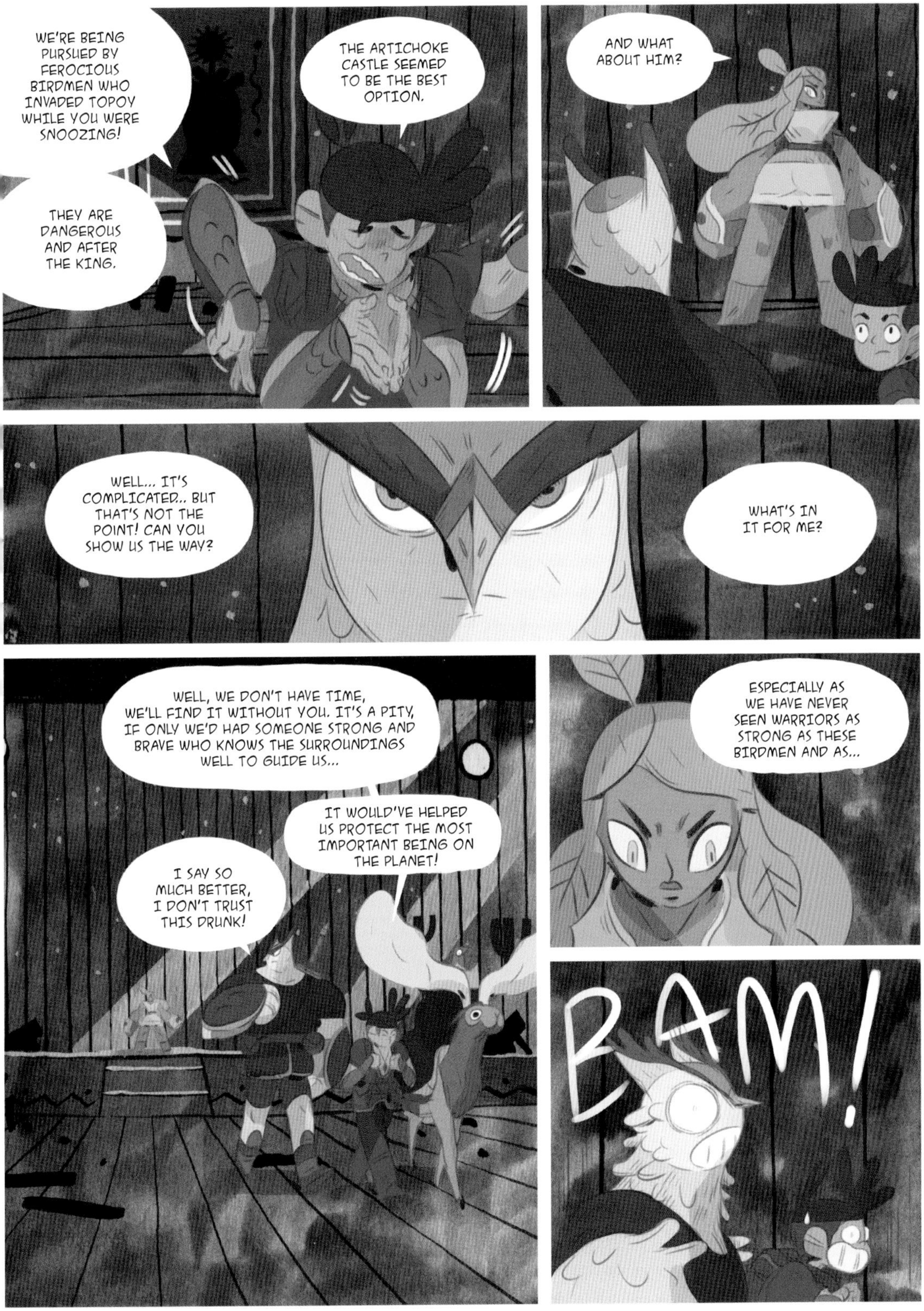
WE'RE BEING PURSUED BY FEROCIOUS BIRDMEN WHO INVADED TOPOY WHILE YOU WERE SNOOZING!
THEY ARE DANGEROUS AND AFTER THE KING.
THE ARTICHOKE CASTLE SEEMED TO BE THE BEST OPTION.
AND WHAT ABOUT HIM?
WELL... IT'S COMPLICATED... BUT THAT'S NOT THE POINT! CAN YOU SHOW US THE WAY?
WHAT'S IN IT FOR ME?
WELL, WE DON'T HAVE TIME, WE'LL FIND IT WITHOUT YOU. IT'S A PITY, IF ONLY WE'D HAD SOMEONE STRONG AND BRAVE WHO KNOWS THE SURROUNDINGS WELL TO GUIDE US...
IT WOULD'VE HELPED US PROTECT THE MOST IMPORTANT BEING ON THE PLANET!
I SAY SO MUCH BETTER, I DON'T TRUST THIS DRUNK!
ESPECIALLY AS WE HAVE NEVER SEEN WARRIORS AS STRONG AS THESE BIRDMEN AND AS...
BAM!

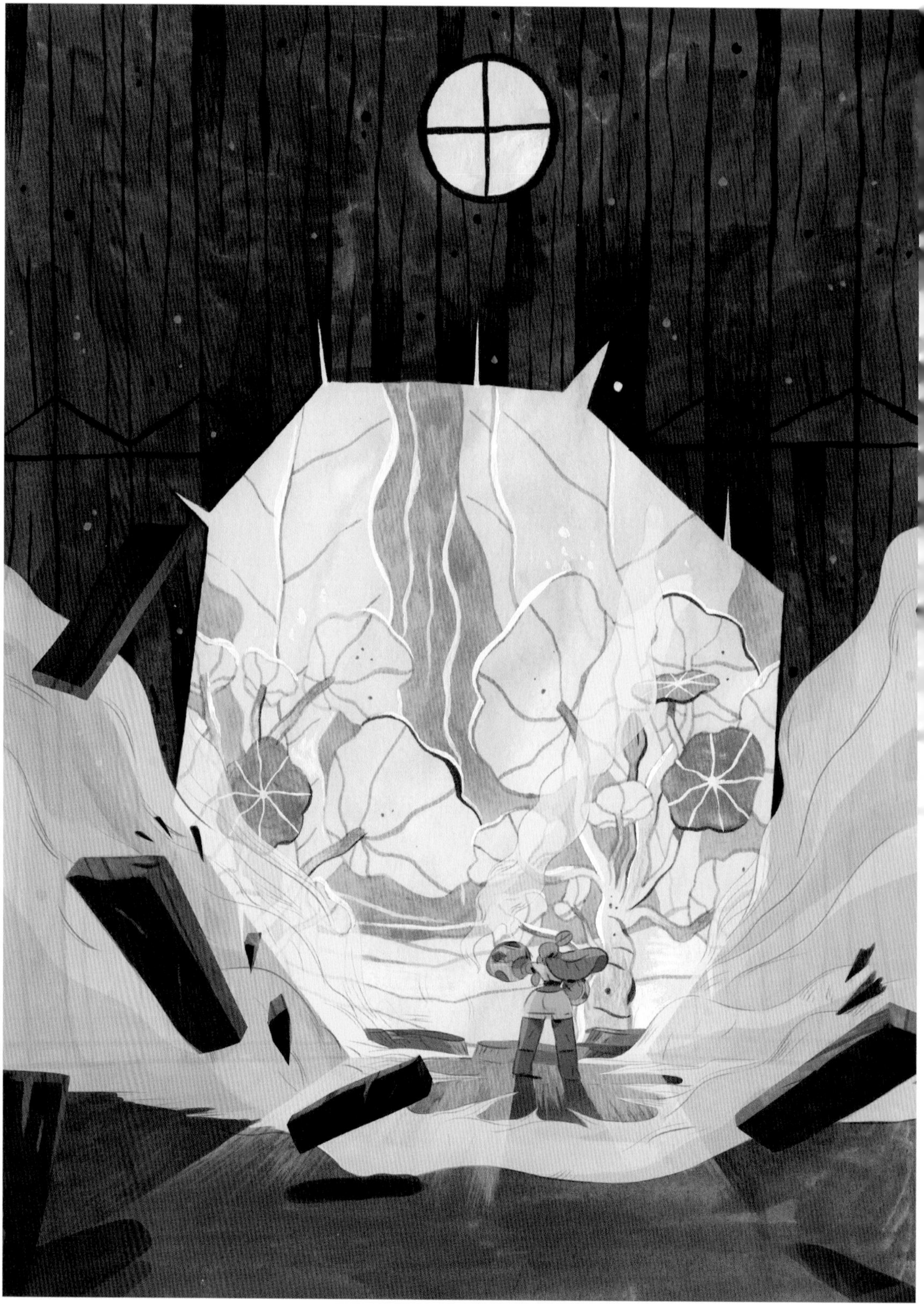

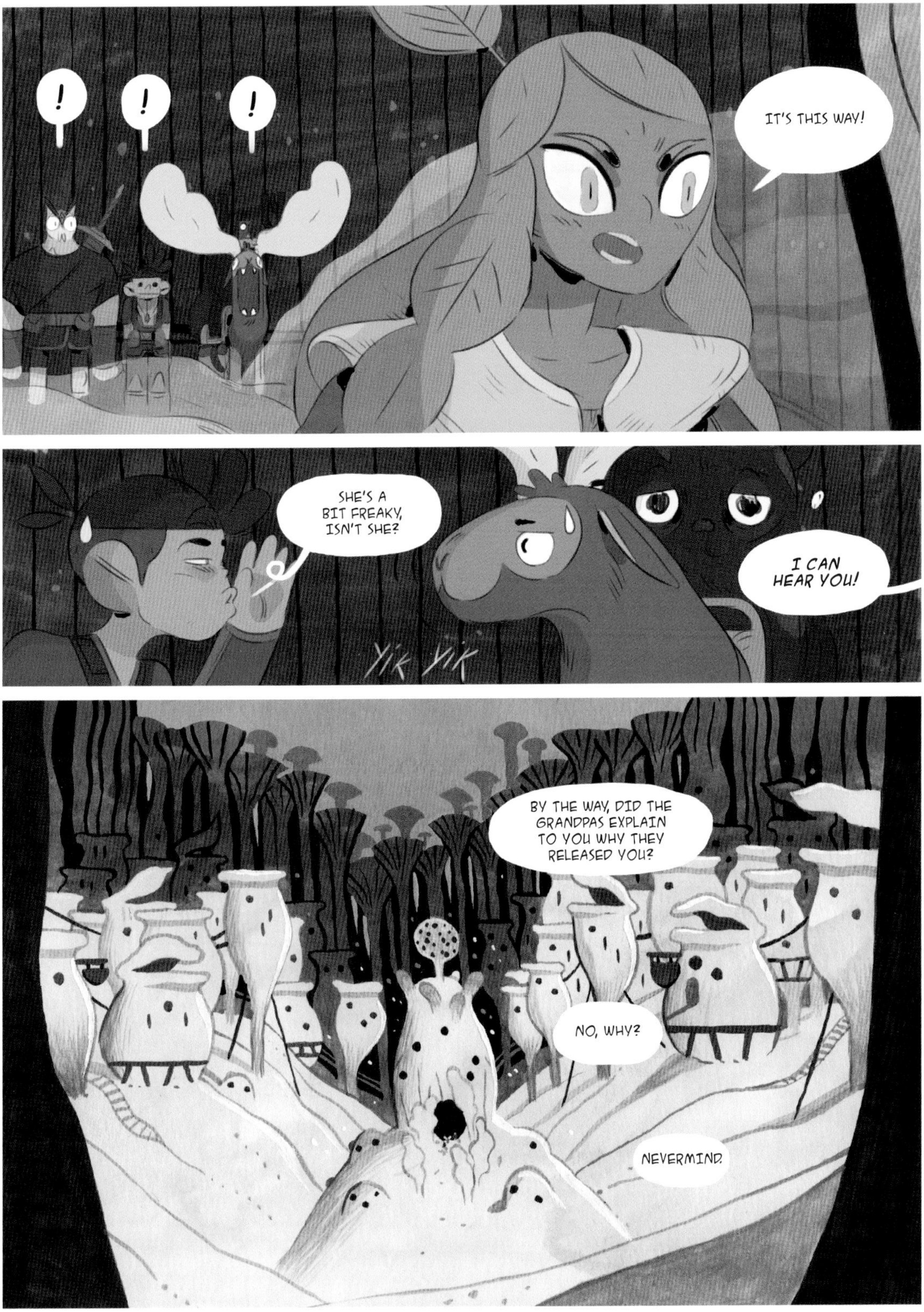
!
!
!
IT'S THIS WAY!
SHE'S A BIT FREAKY, ISN'T SHE?
I CAN HEAR YOU!
YIK YIK
BY THE WAY, DID THE GRANDPAS EXPLAIN TO YOU WHY THEY RELEASED YOU?
NO, WHY?
NEVERMIND.

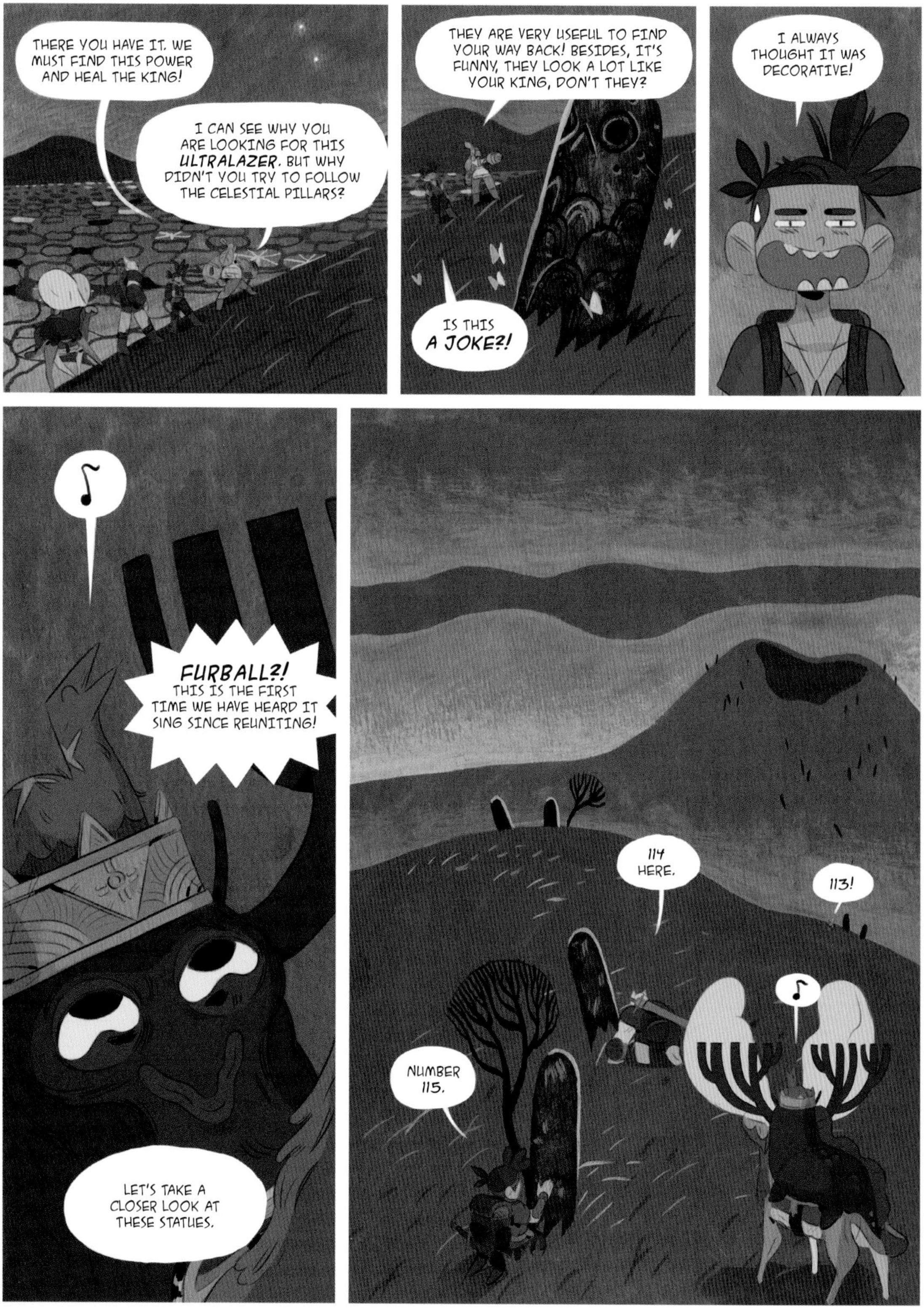
THERE YOU HAVE IT. WE MUST FIND THIS POWER AND HEAL THE KING!
I CAN SEE WHY YOU ARE LOOKING FOR THIS ULTRALAZER. BUT WHY DIDN'T YOU TRY TO FOLLOW THE CELESTIAL PILLARS?
THEY ARE VERY USEFUL TO FIND YOUR WAY BACK! BESIDES, IT'S FUNNY, THEY LOOK A LOT LIKE YOUR KING, DON'T THEY?
IS THIS A JOKE?!
I ALWAYS THOUGHT IT WAS DECORATIVE!
FURBALL?! THIS IS THE FIRST TIME WE HAVE HEARD IT SING SINCE REUNITING!
LET'S TAKE A CLOSER LOOK AT THESE STATUES.
114 HERE.
113!
NUMBER 115.

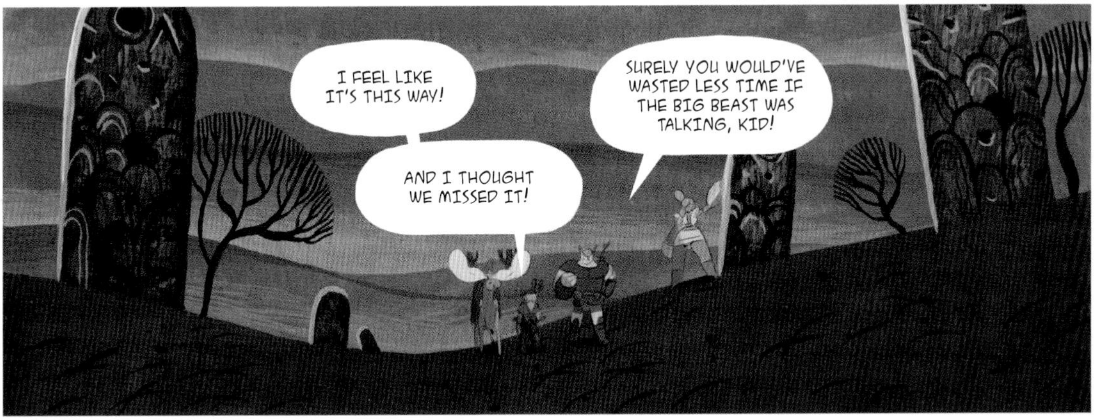
I FEEL LIKE IT'S THIS WAY!
AND I THOUGHT WE MISSED IT!
SURELY YOU WOULD'VE WASTED LESS TIME IF THE BIG BEAST WAS TALKING, KID!

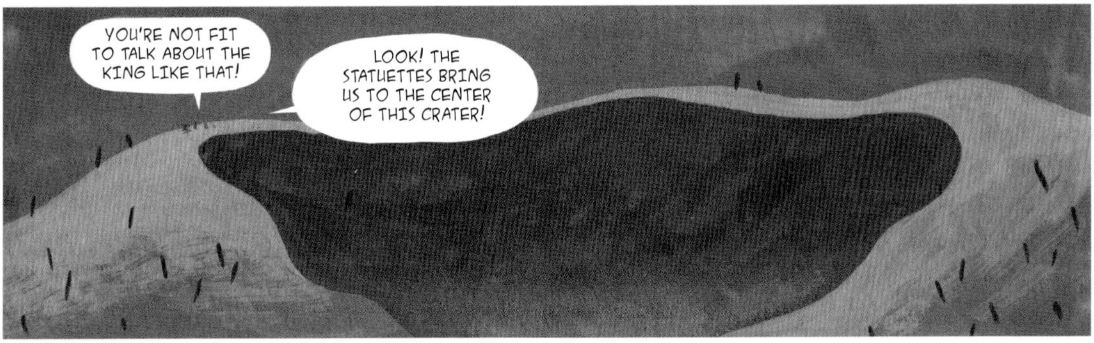
YOU'RE NOT FIT TO TALK ABOUT THE KING LIKE THAT!
LOOK! THE STATUETTES BRING US TO THE CENTER OF THIS CRATER!

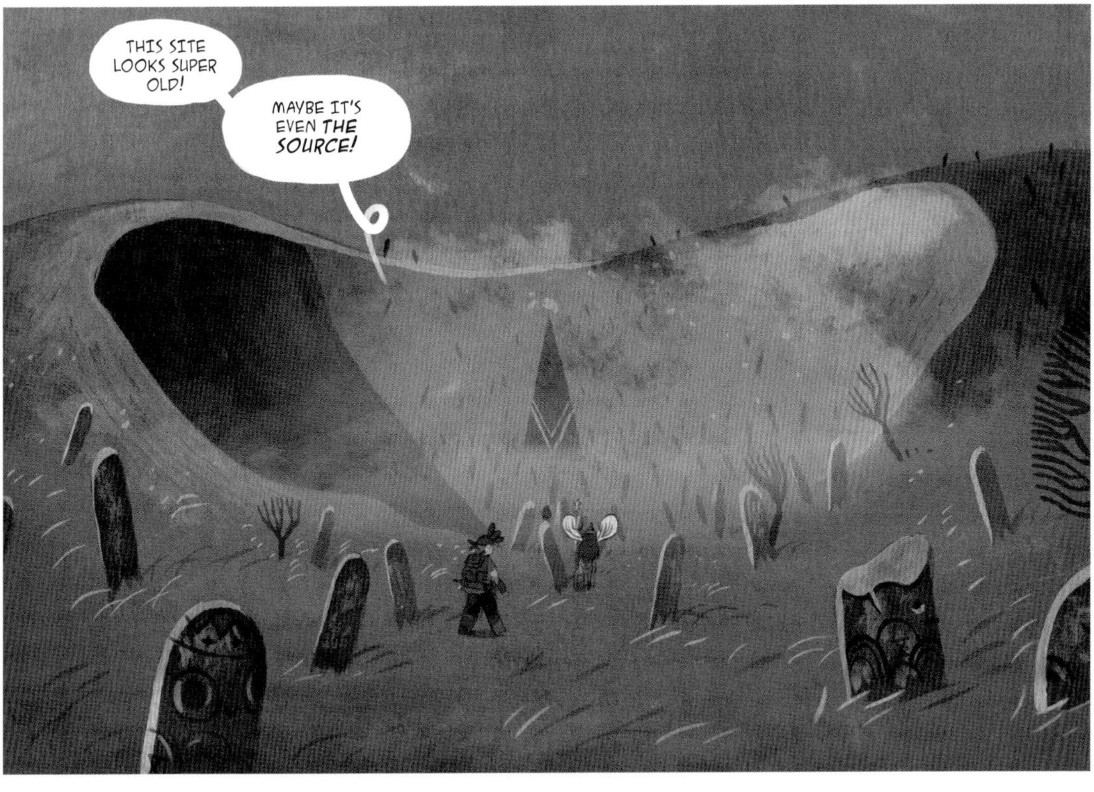
THIS SITE LOOKS SUPER OLD!
MAYBE IT'S EVEN **THE SOURCE!**

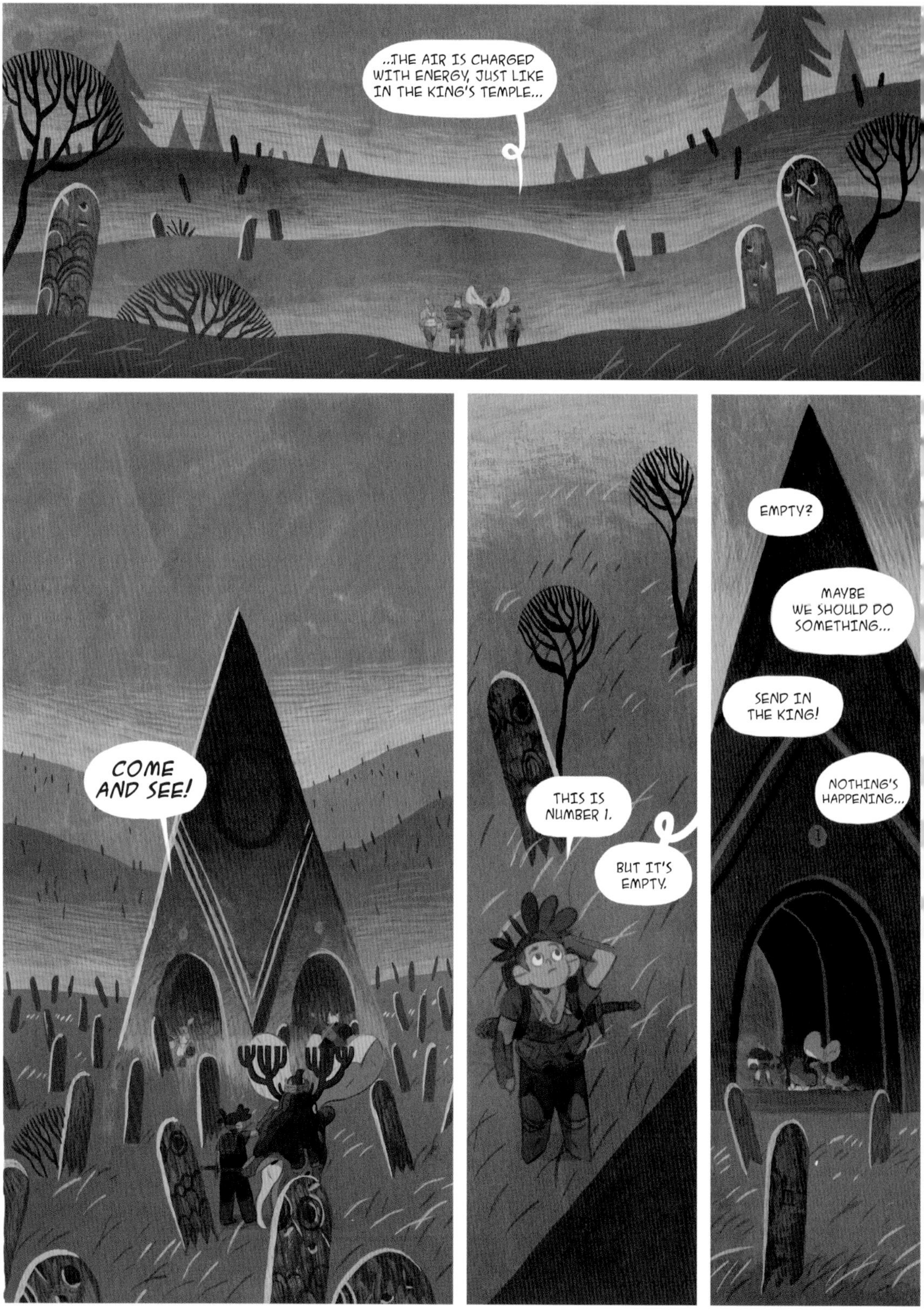

..THE AIR IS CHARGED WITH ENERGY, JUST LIKE IN THE KING'S TEMPLE...
COME AND SEE!
THIS IS NUMBER 1.
BUT IT'S EMPTY.
EMPTY?
MAYBE WE SHOULD DO SOMETHING...
SEND IN THE KING!
NOTHING'S HAPPENING...

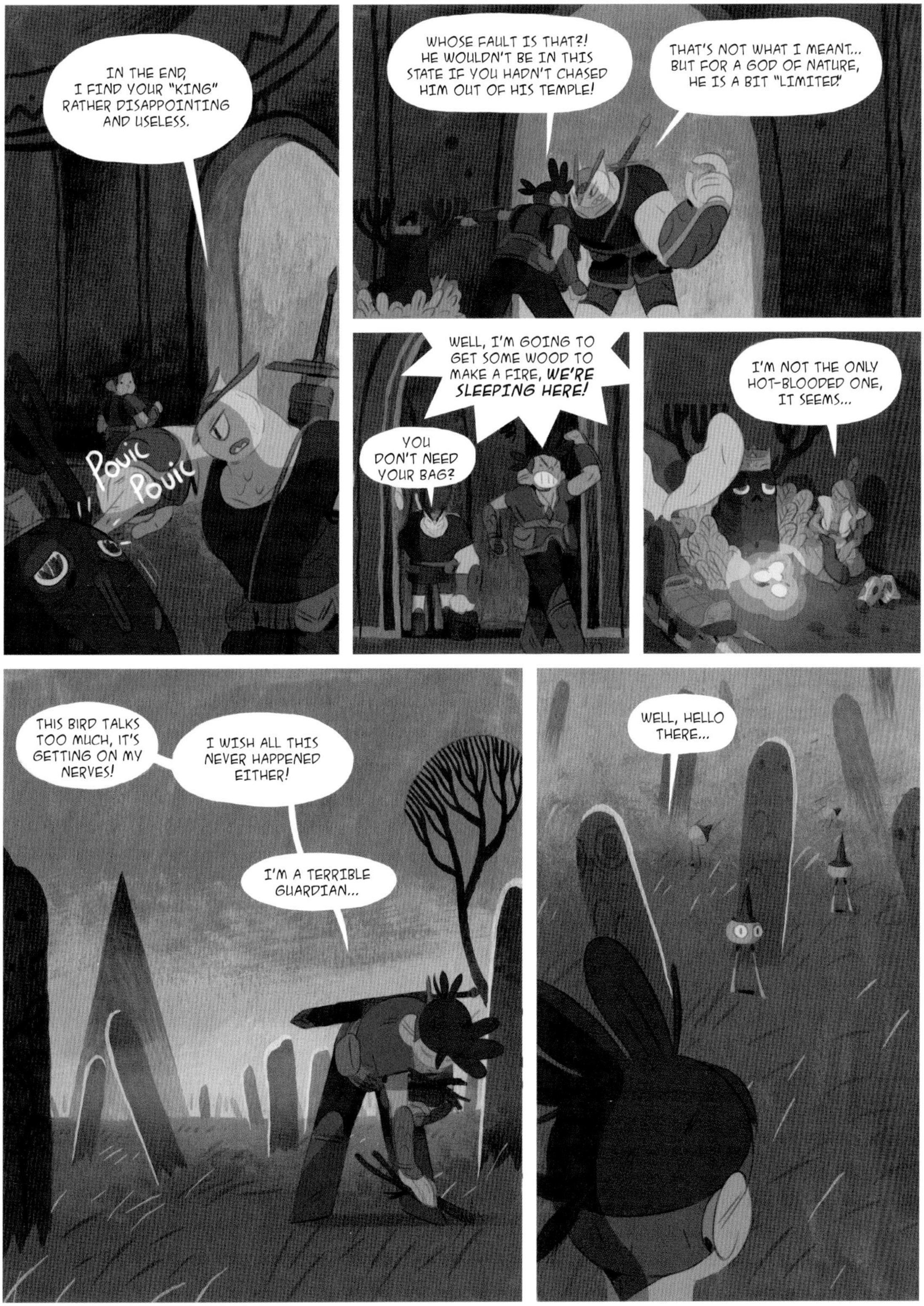
IN THE END, I FIND YOUR "KING" RATHER DISAPPOINTING AND USELESS.
POUIC POUIC
WHOSE FAULT IS THAT?! HE WOULDN'T BE IN THIS STATE IF YOU HADN'T CHASED HIM OUT OF HIS TEMPLE!
THAT'S NOT WHAT I MEANT... BUT FOR A GOD OF NATURE, HE IS A BIT "LIMITED."
WELL, I'M GOING TO GET SOME WOOD TO MAKE A FIRE, ***WE'RE SLEEPING HERE!***
YOU DON'T NEED YOUR BAG?
I'M NOT THE ONLY HOT-BLOODED ONE, IT SEEMS...
THIS BIRD TALKS TOO MUCH, IT'S GETTING ON MY NERVES!
I WISH ALL THIS NEVER HAPPENED EITHER!
I'M A TERRIBLE GUARDIAN...
WELL, HELLO THERE...

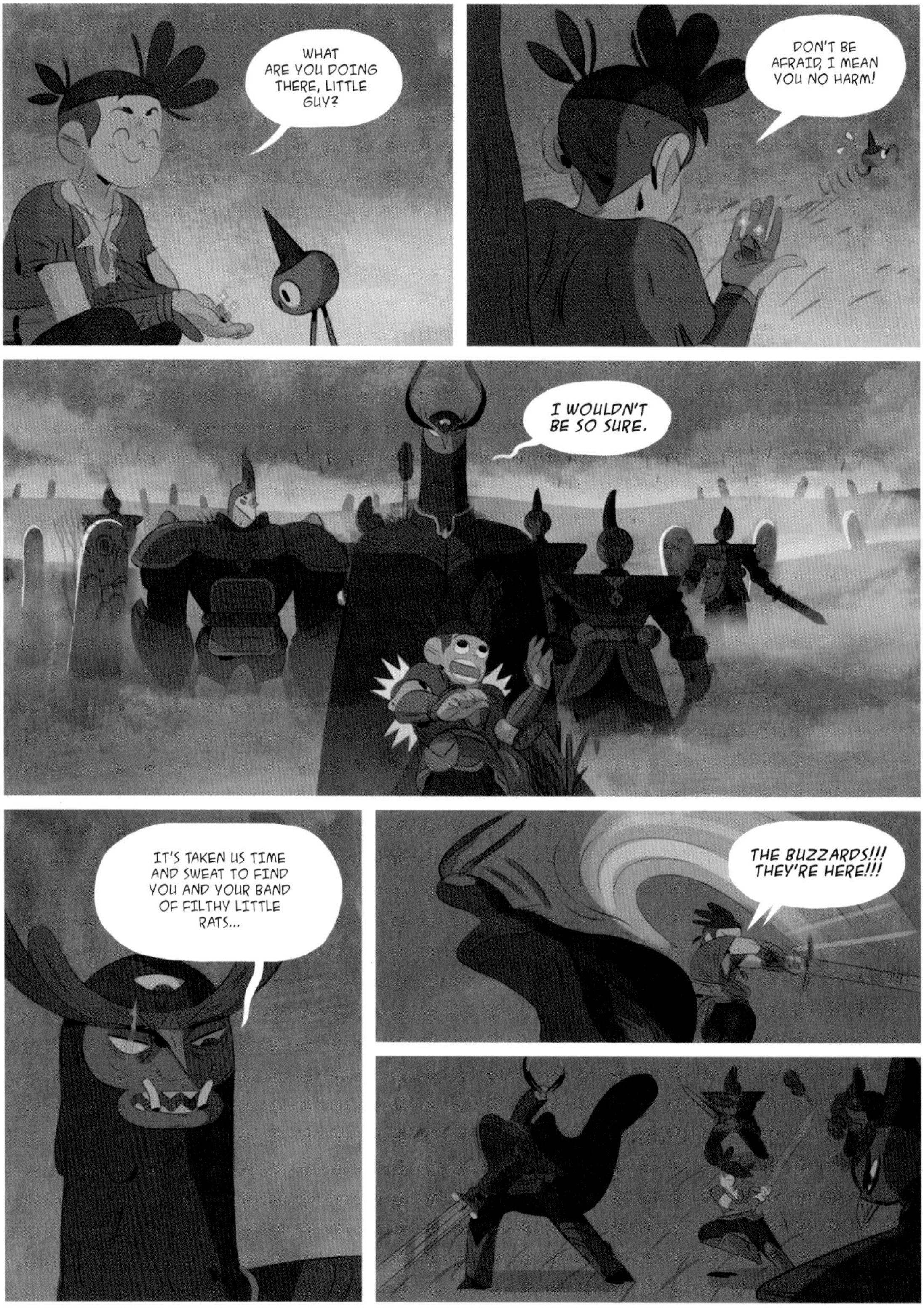
WHAT ARE YOU DOING THERE, LITTLE GUY?
DON'T BE AFRAID, I MEAN YOU NO HARM!
I WOULDN'T BE SO SURE.
IT'S TAKEN US TIME AND SWEAT TO FIND YOU AND YOUR BAND OF FILTHY LITTLE RATS...
THE BUZZARDS!!! THEY'RE HERE!!!

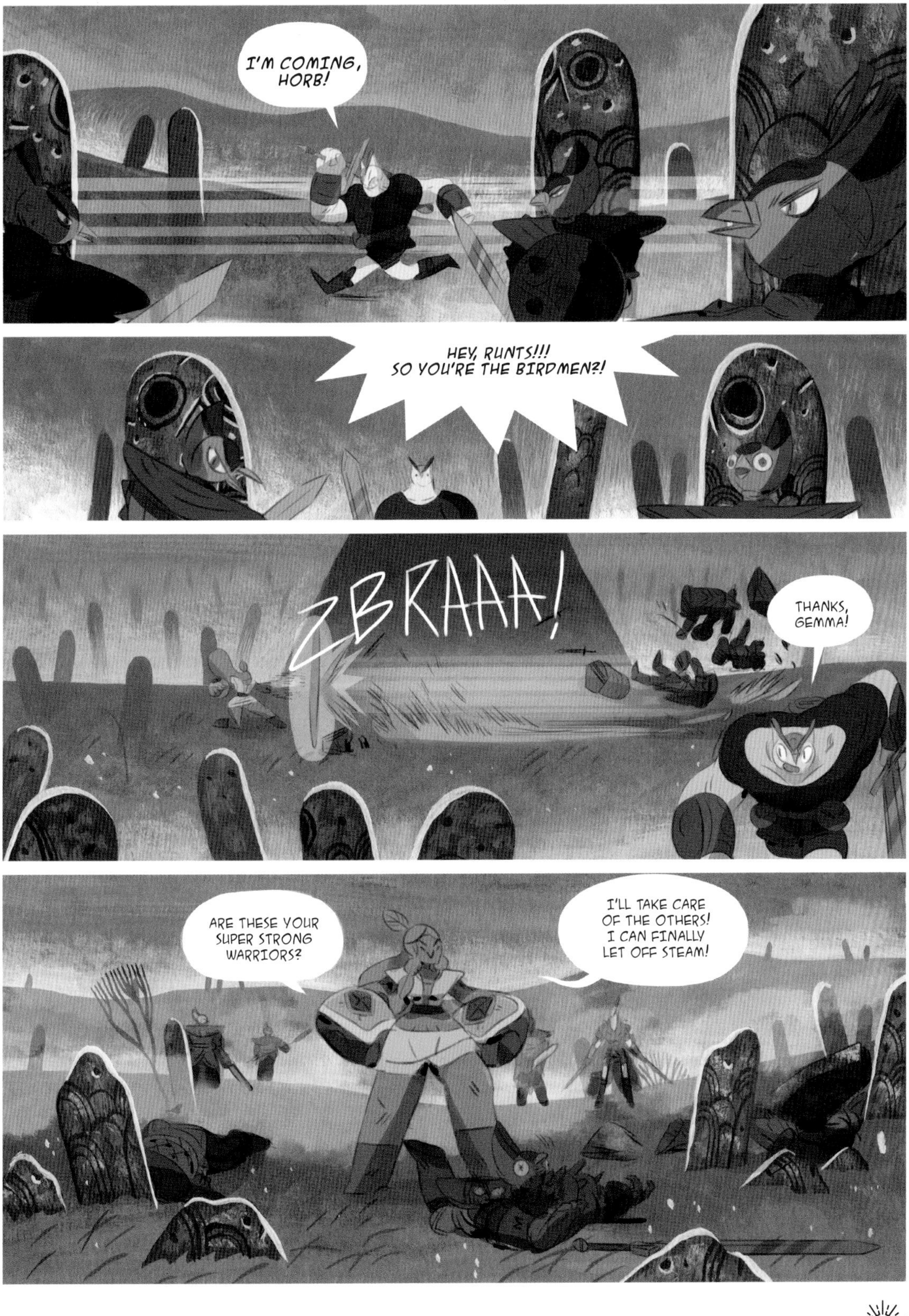
I'M COMING, HORB!
HEY, RUNTS!!! SO YOU'RE THE BIRDMEN?!
ZBRAAA!
THANKS, GEMMA!
ARE THESE YOUR SUPER STRONG WARRIORS?
I'LL TAKE CARE OF THE OTHERS! I CAN FINALLY LET OFF STEAM!

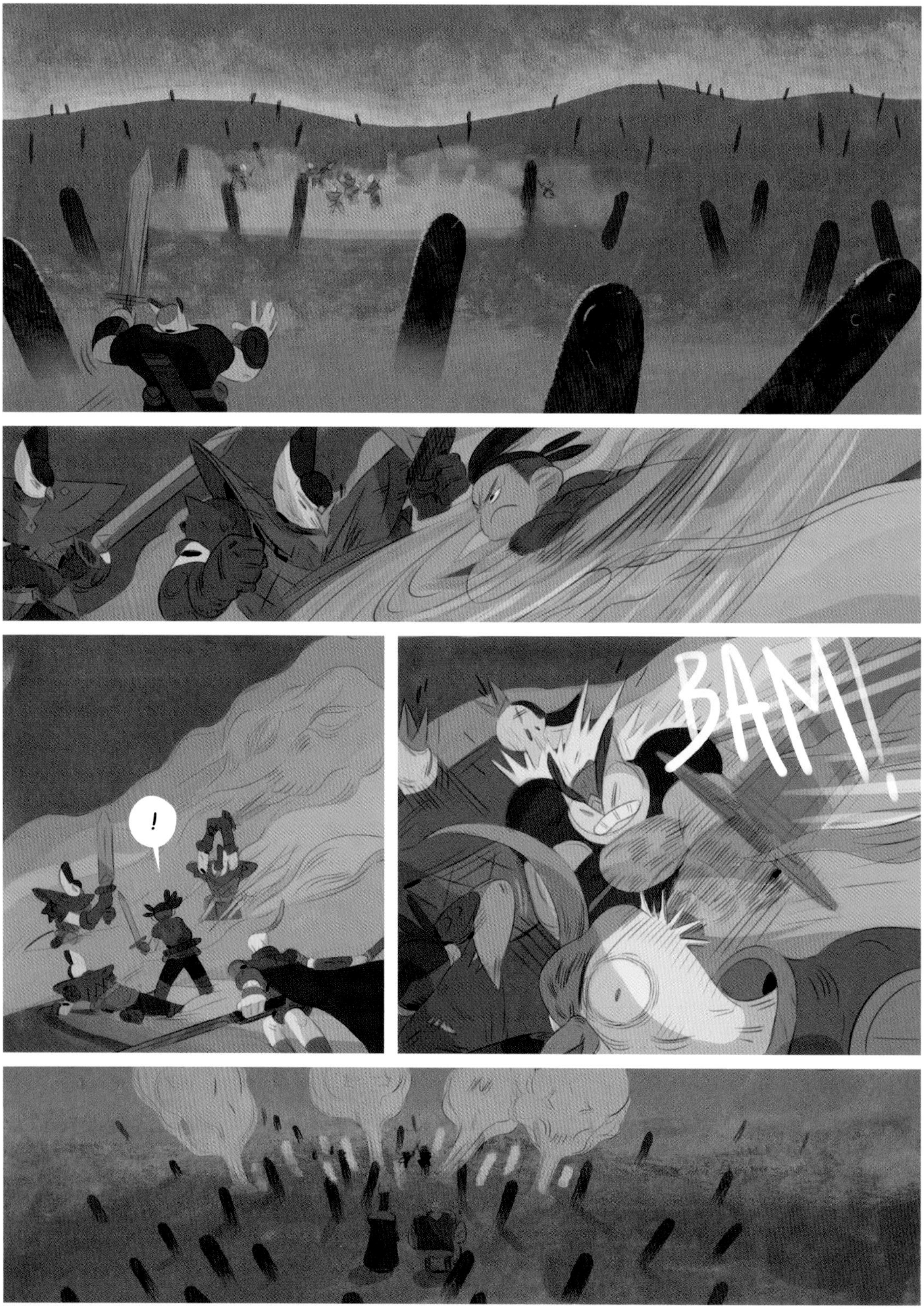

!
BAM!

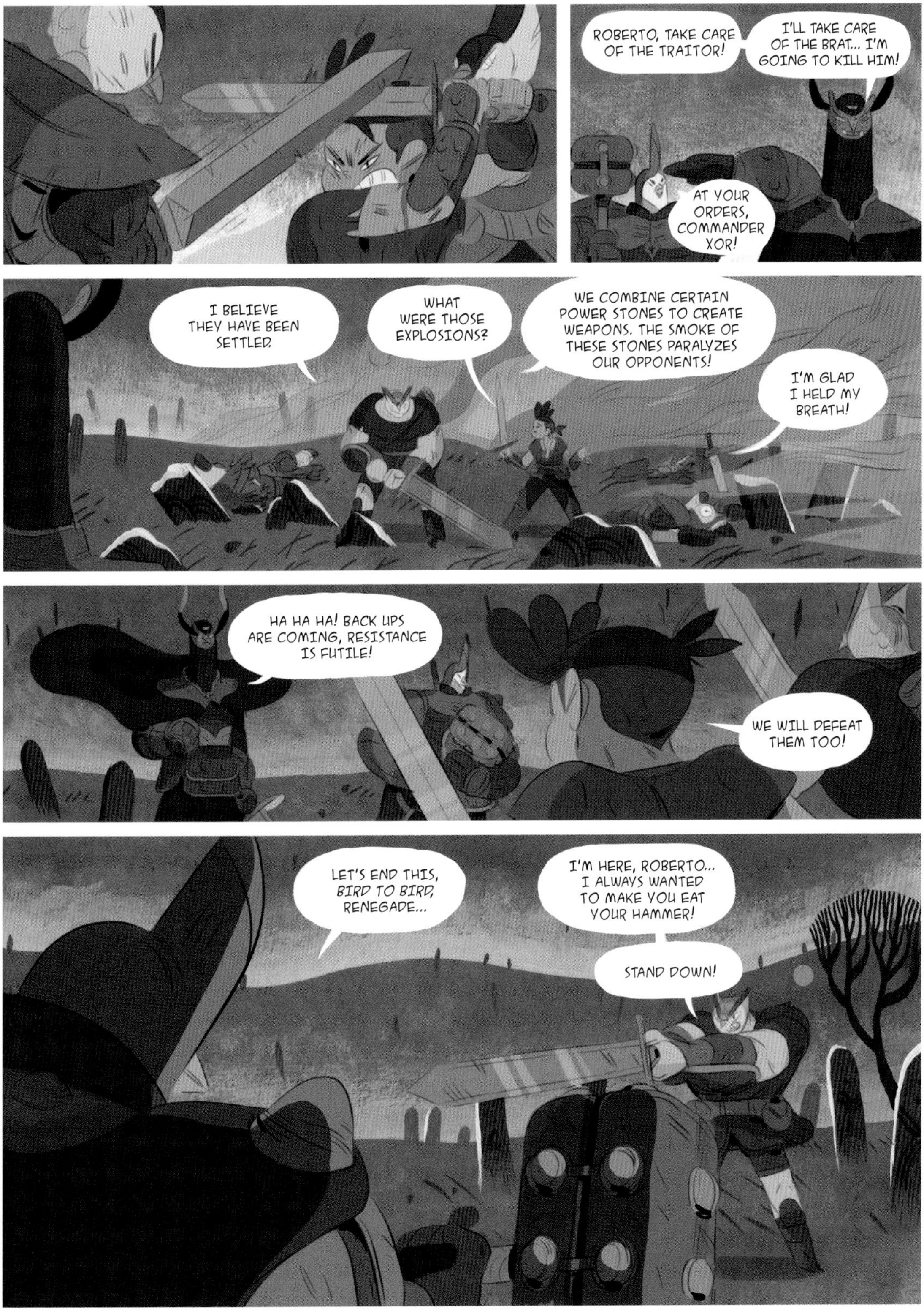
ROBERTO, TAKE CARE OF THE TRAITOR!
I'LL TAKE CARE OF THE BRAT... I'M GOING TO KILL HIM!
AT YOUR ORDERS, COMMANDER XOR!
I BELIEVE THEY HAVE BEEN SETTLED.
WHAT WERE THOSE EXPLOSIONS?
WE COMBINE CERTAIN POWER STONES TO CREATE WEAPONS. THE SMOKE OF THESE STONES PARALYZES OUR OPPONENTS!
I'M GLAD I HELD MY BREATH!
HA HA HA! BACK UPS ARE COMING, RESISTANCE IS FUTILE!
WE WILL DEFEAT THEM TOO!
LET'S END THIS, BIRD TO BIRD, RENEGADE...
I'M HERE, ROBERTO... I ALWAYS WANTED TO MAKE YOU EAT YOUR HAMMER!
STAND DOWN!

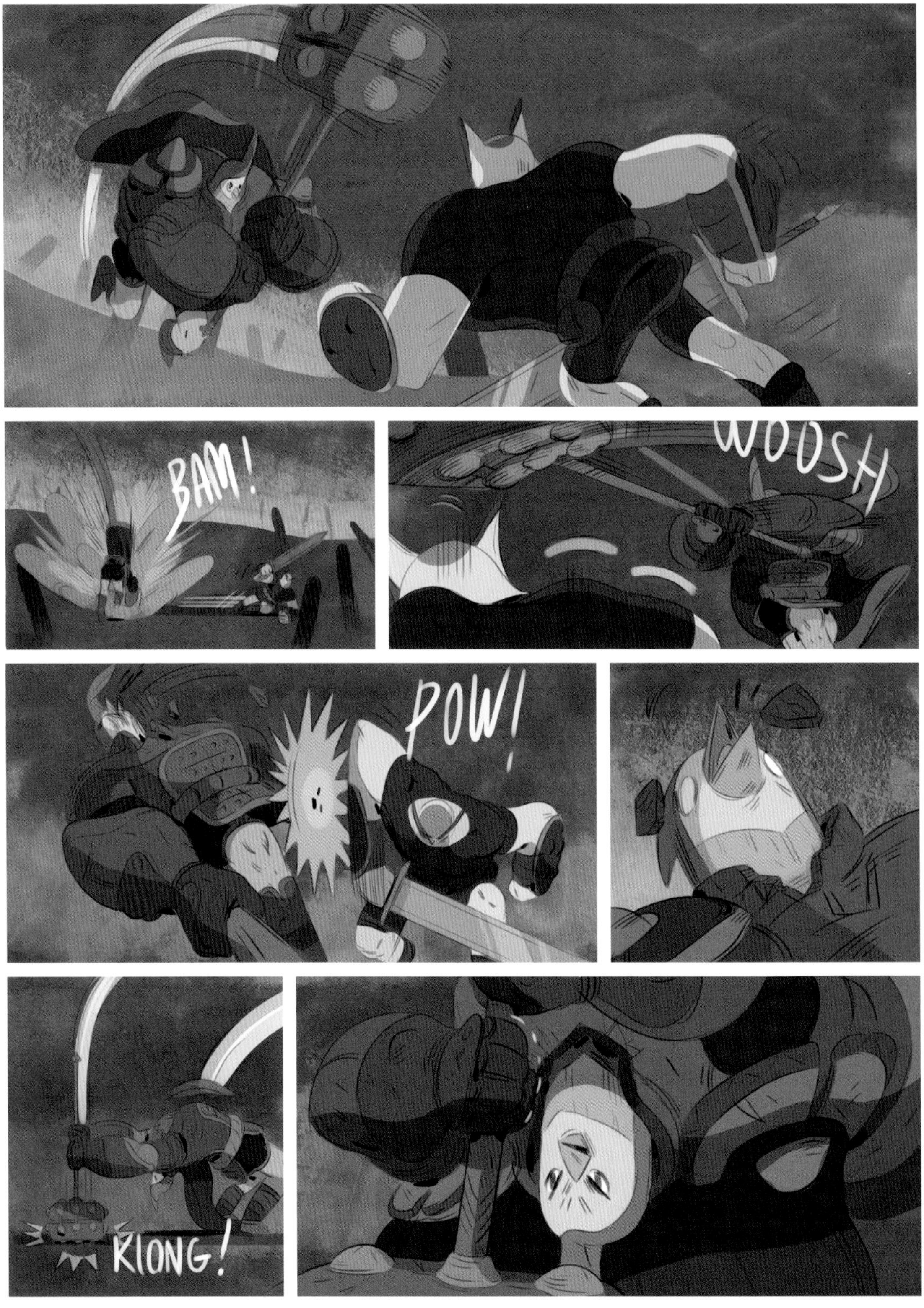
BAM!
WOOSH
POW!
KLONG!

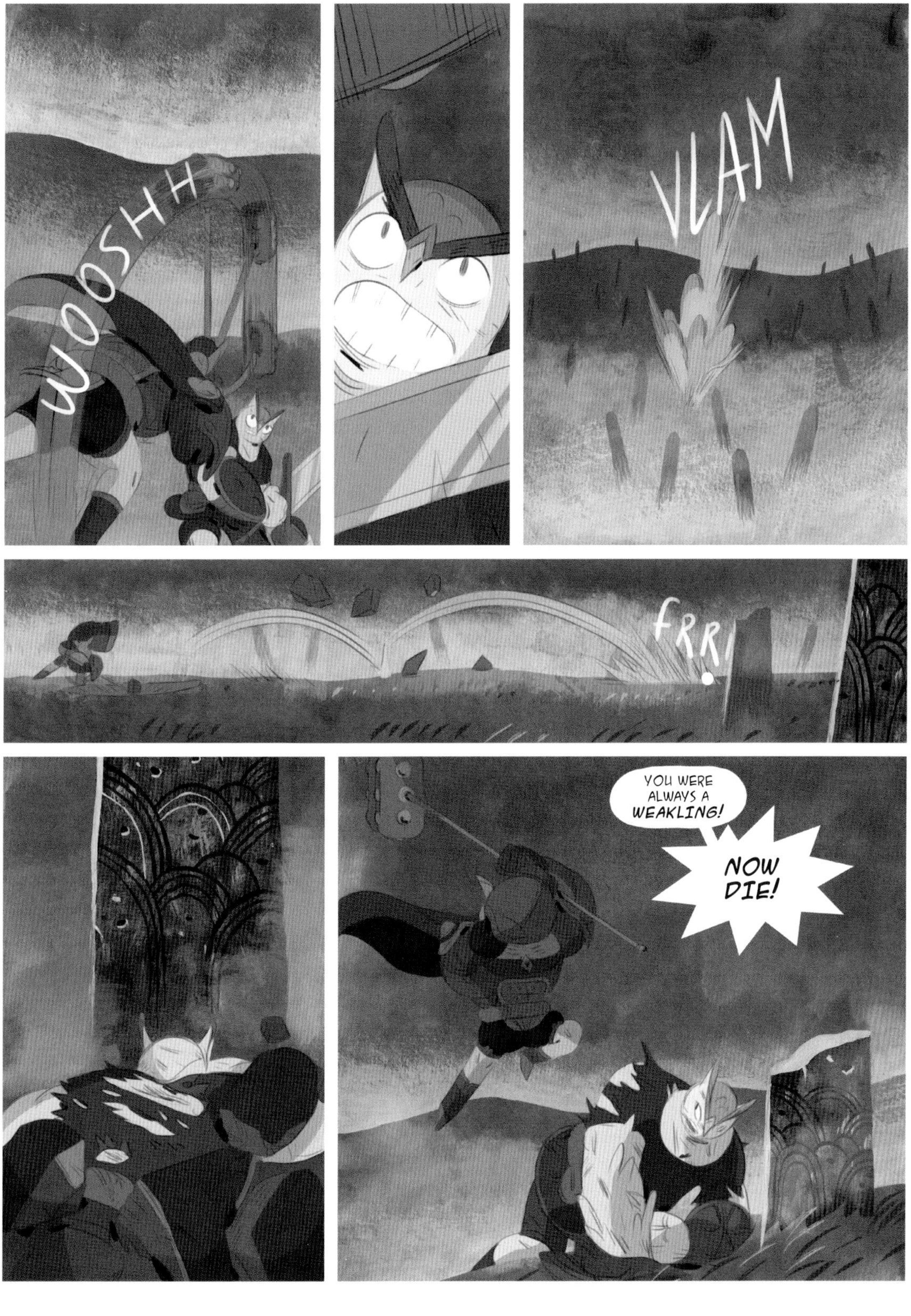
WOOSHH
VLAM
FRRI
YOU WERE ALWAYS A WEAKLING!
NOW DIE!

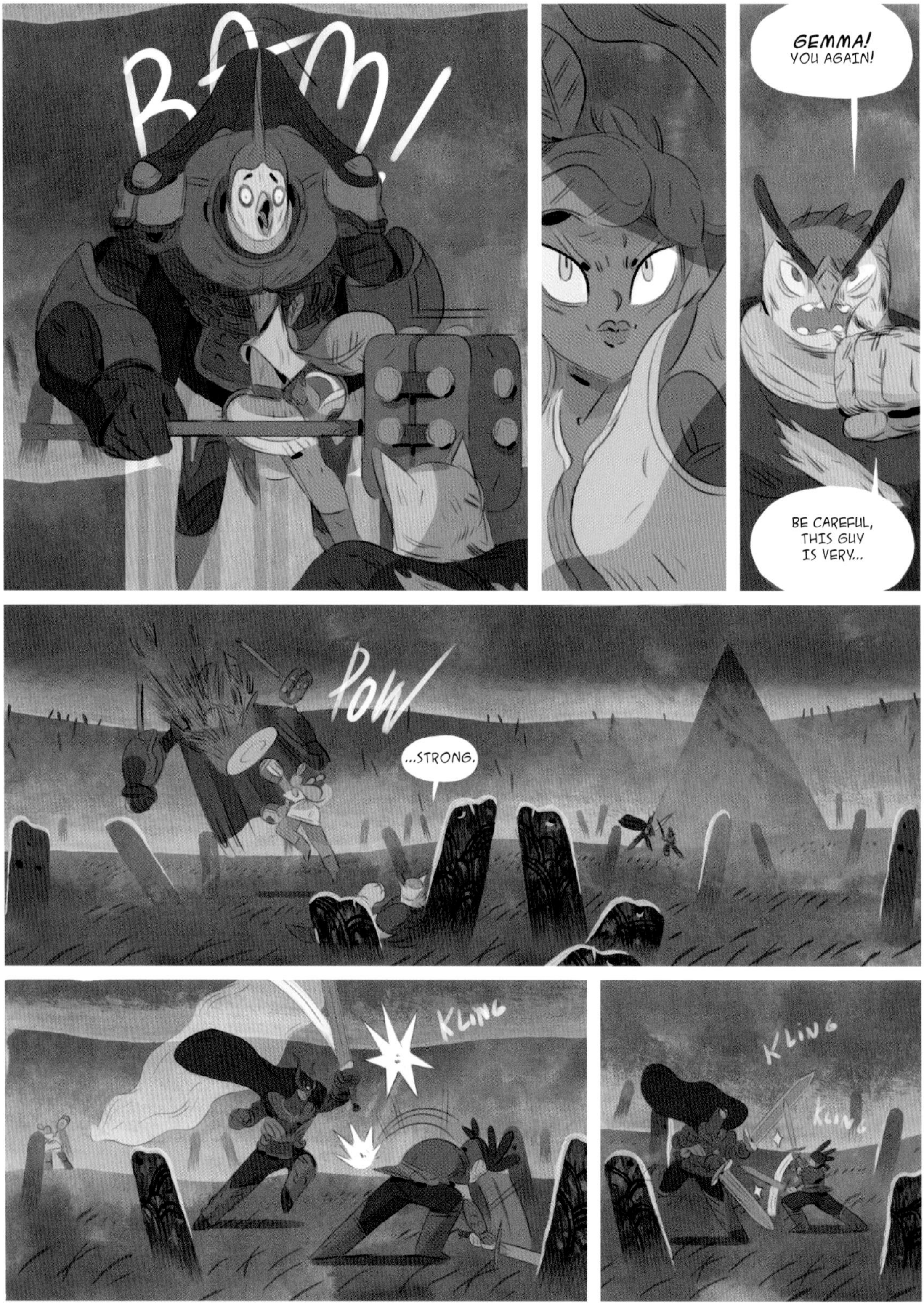
BAM!
GEMMA! YOU AGAIN!
BE CAREFUL, THIS GUY IS VERY...
POW
...STRONG.
KLING
KLING
KLING

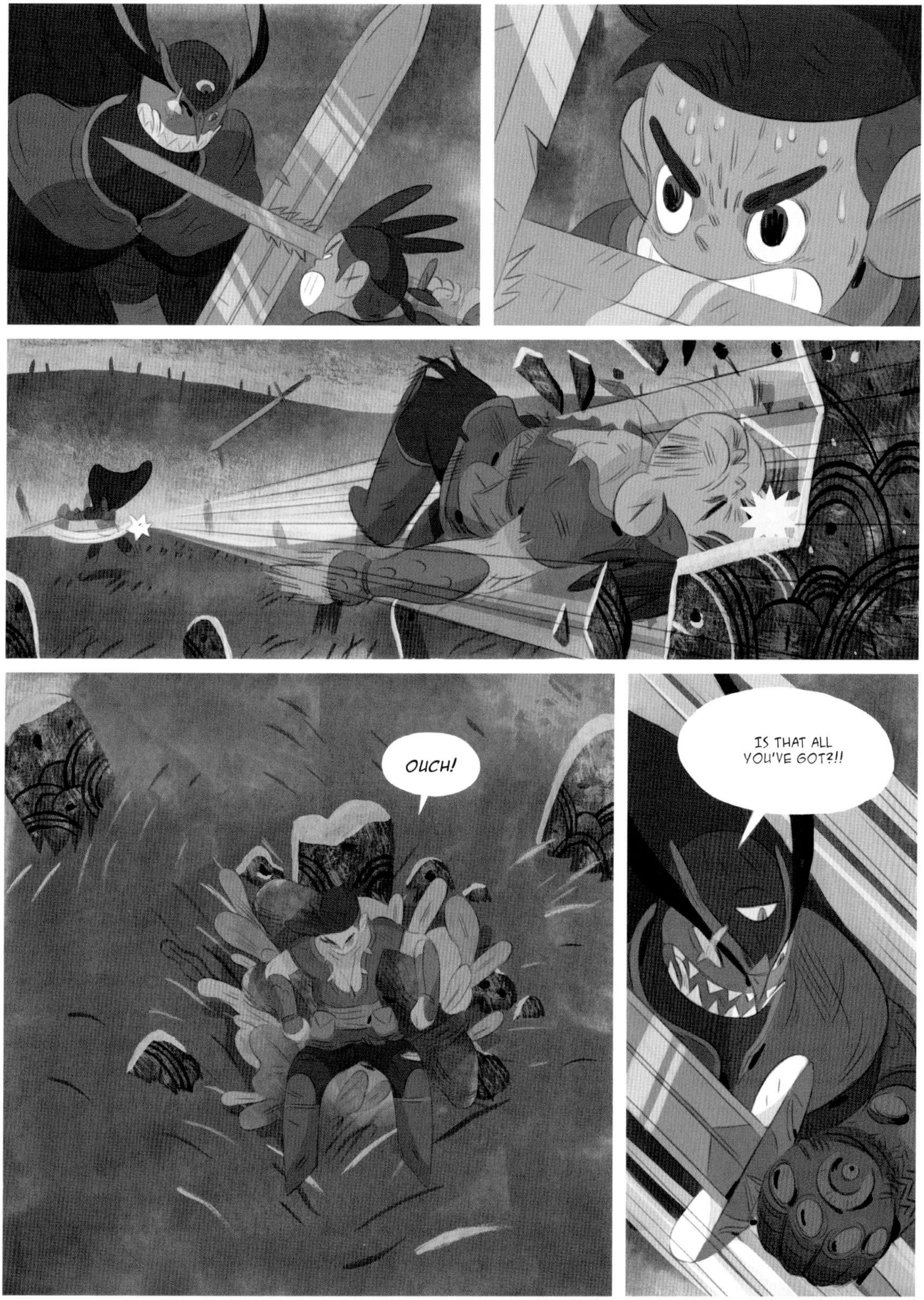
OUCH!
IS THAT ALL YOU'VE GOT?!!

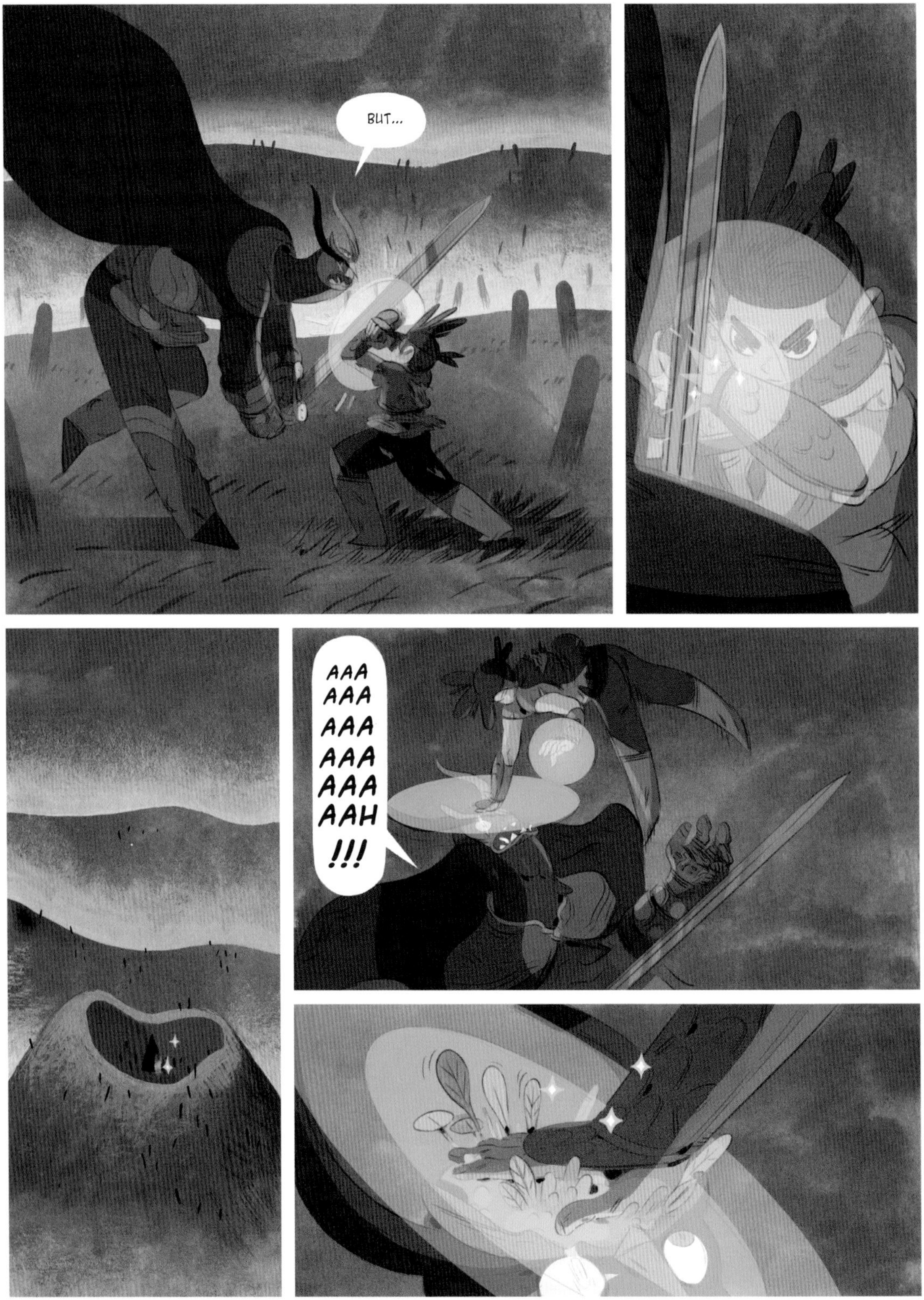
BUT...
AAA AAA AAA AAA AAA AAH !!!

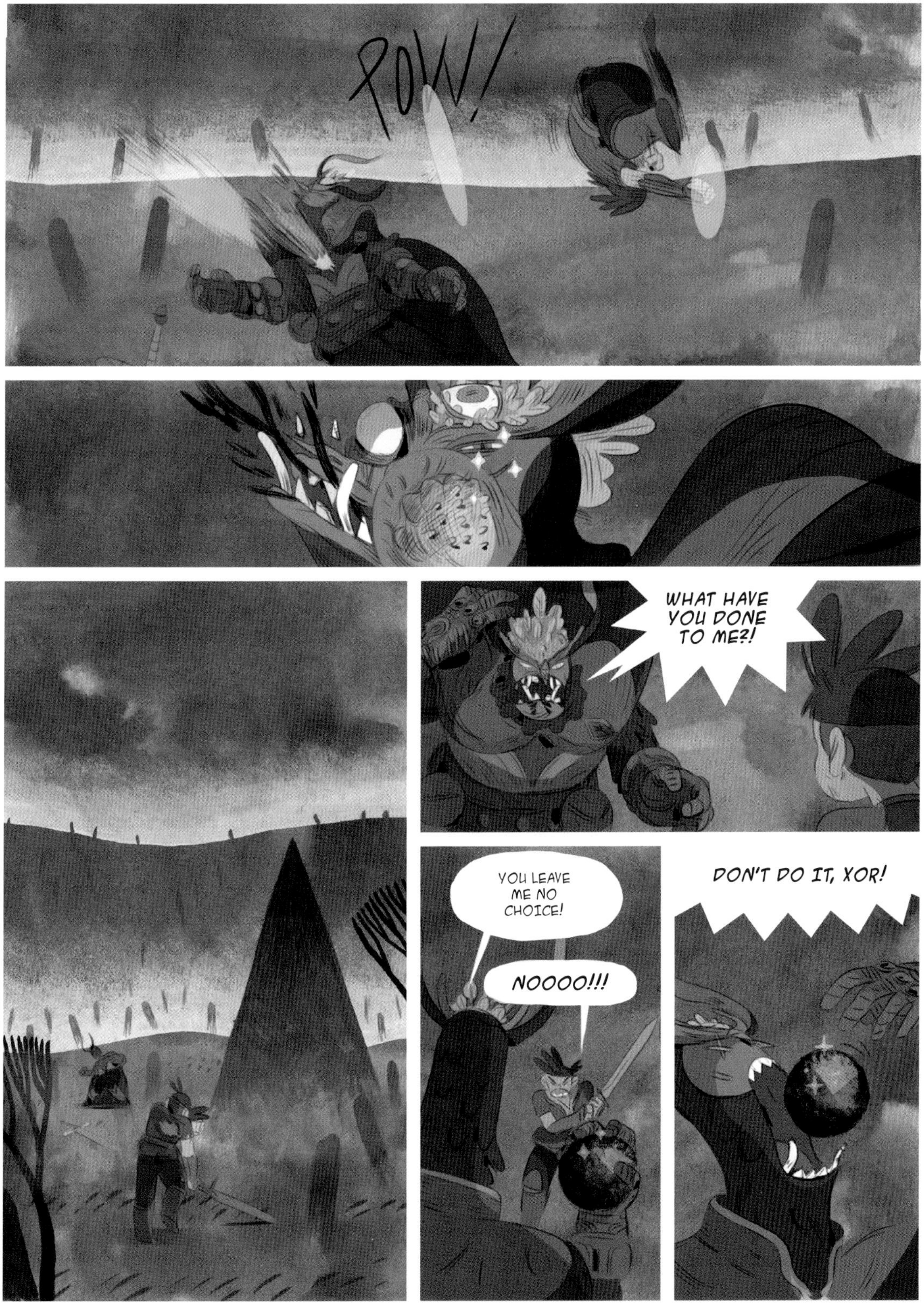
POW!
WHAT HAVE YOU DONE TO ME?!
YOU LEAVE ME NO CHOICE!
NOOOO!!!
DON'T DO IT, XOR!

HE'S... HE'S SWALLOWED A STONE?!

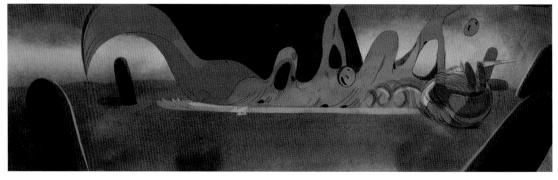

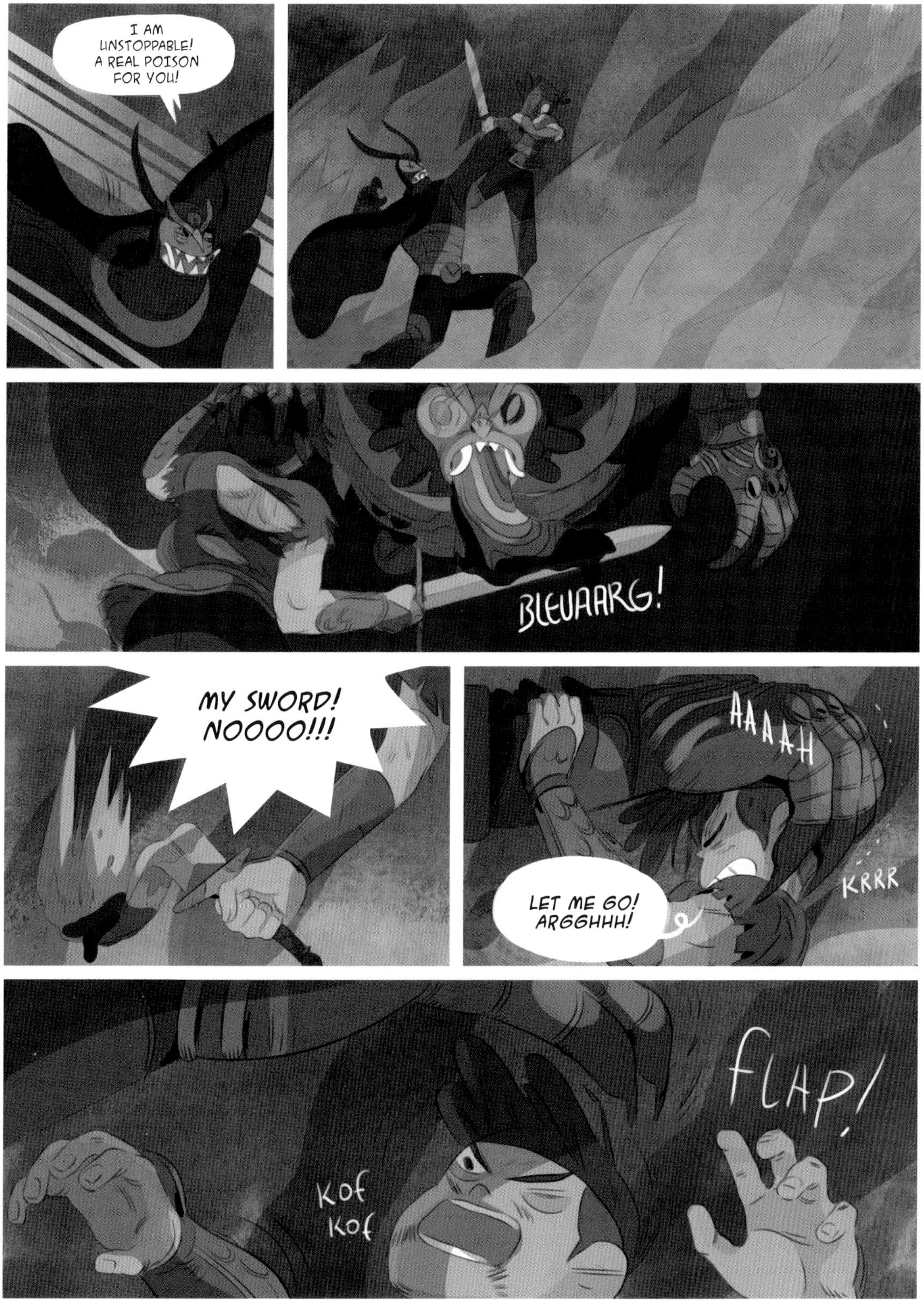
I AM UNSTOPPABLE! A REAL POISON FOR YOU!
BLEUAARG!
MY SWORD! NOOOO!!!
AAAAH
KRRR
LET ME GO! ARGGHHH!
FLAP!
KOF KOF

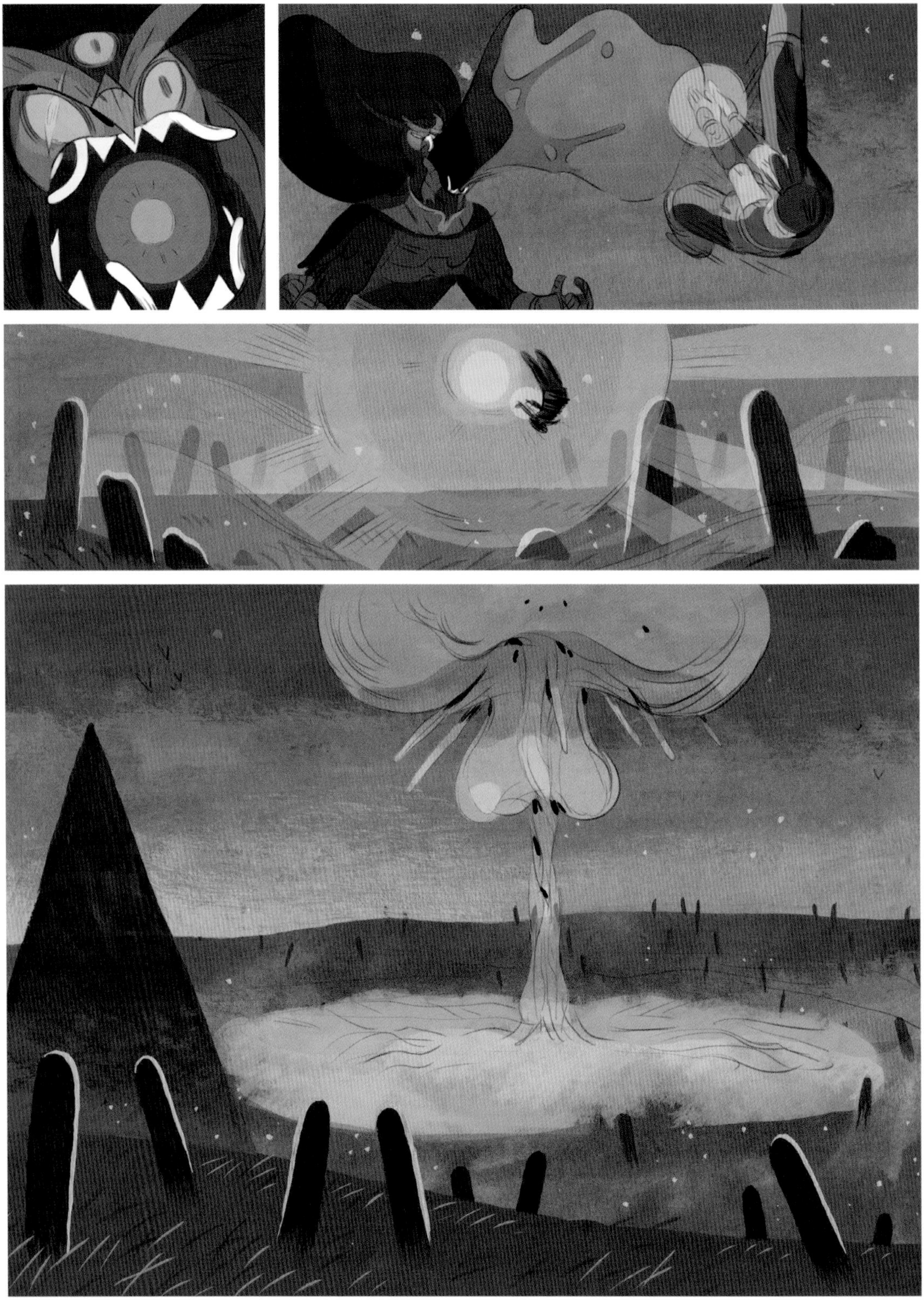

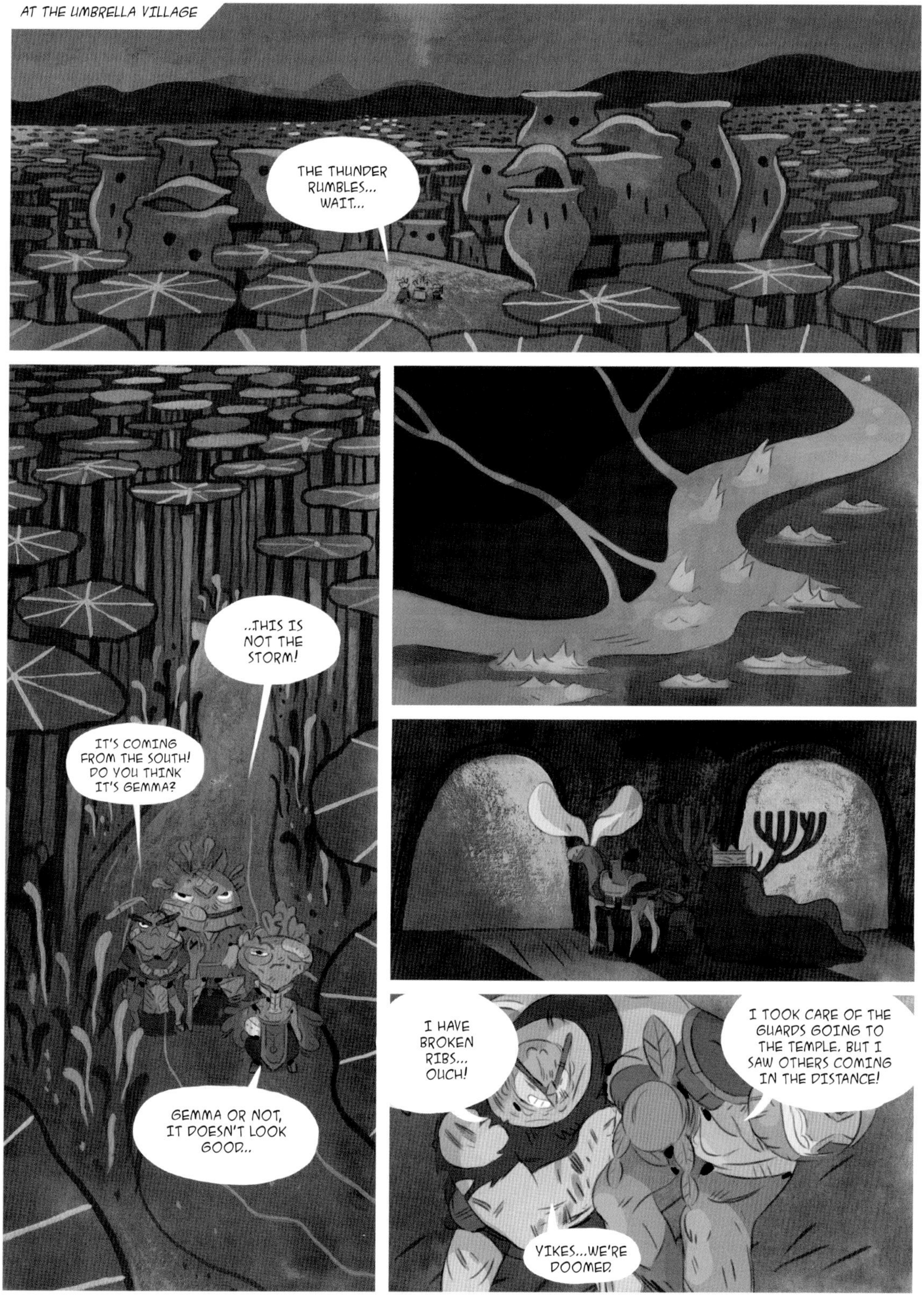
AT THE UMBRELLA VILLAGE
THE THUNDER RUMBLES... WAIT...
..THIS IS NOT THE STORM!
IT'S COMING FROM THE SOUTH! DO YOU THINK IT'S GEMMA?
GEMMA OR NOT, IT DOESN'T LOOK GOOD...
I HAVE BROKEN RIBS... OUCH!
I TOOK CARE OF THE GUARDS GOING TO THE TEMPLE. BUT I SAW OTHERS COMING IN THE DISTANCE!
YIKES...WE'RE DOOMED.

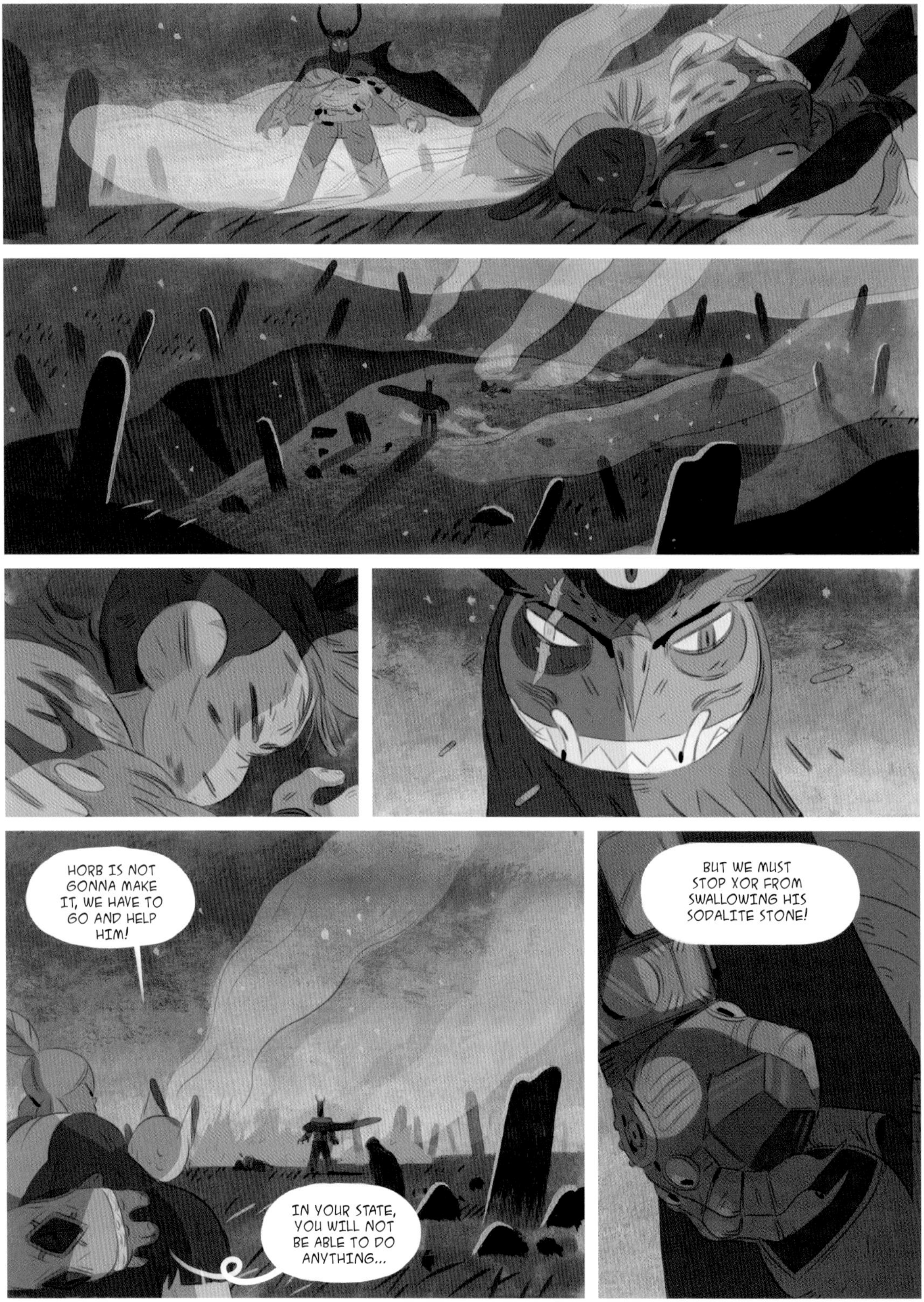
HORB IS NOT GONNA MAKE IT, WE HAVE TO GO AND HELP HIM!
IN YOUR STATE, YOU WILL NOT BE ABLE TO DO ANYTHING...
BUT WE MUST STOP XOR FROM SWALLOWING HIS SODALITE STONE!

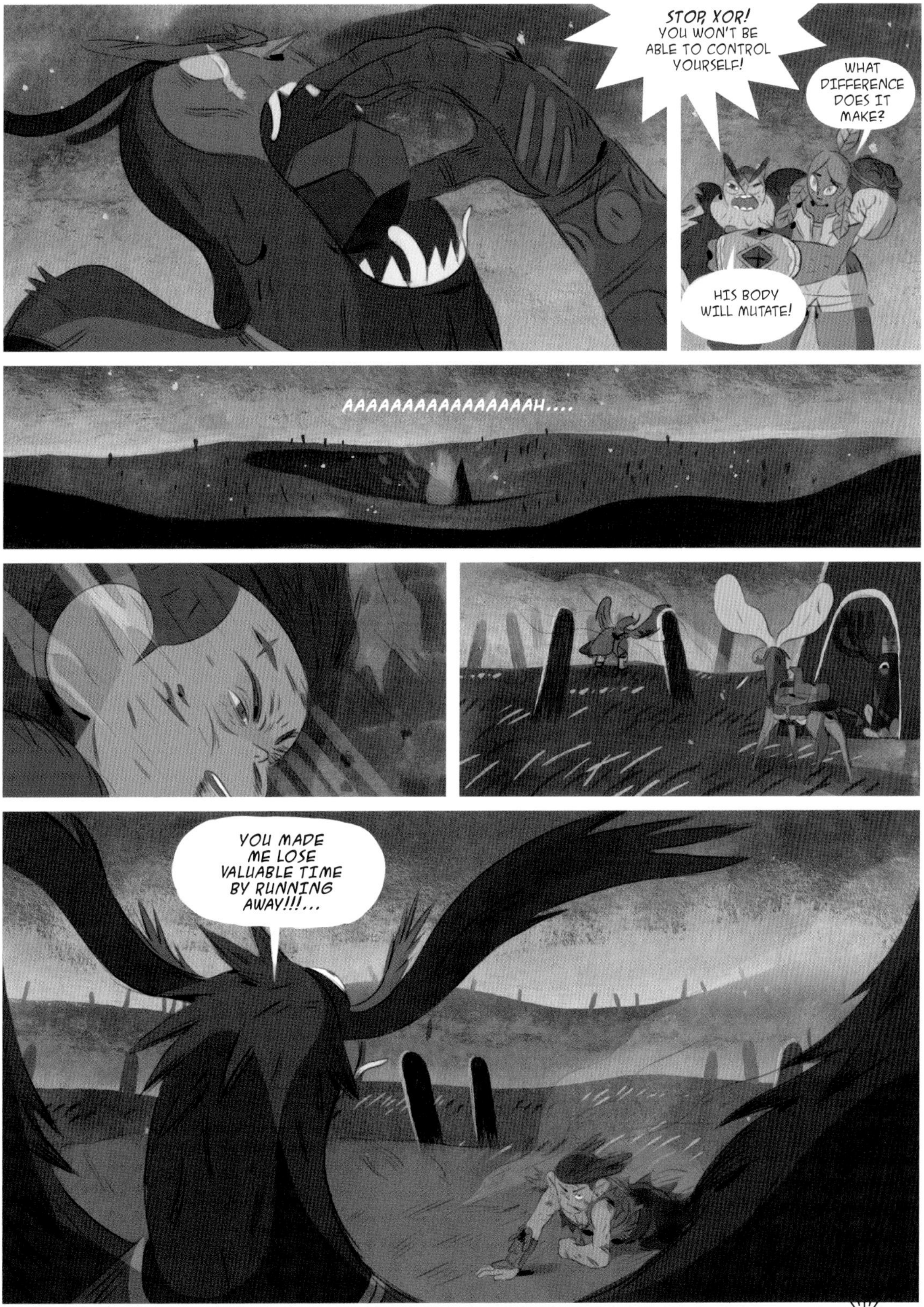
STOP, XOR!
YOU WON'T BE ABLE TO CONTROL YOURSELF!
WHAT DIFFERENCE DOES IT MAKE?
HIS BODY WILL MUTATE!
AAAAAAAAAAAAAAAAH....
YOU MADE ME LOSE VALUABLE TIME BY RUNNING AWAY!!!...

ROOO OOO...

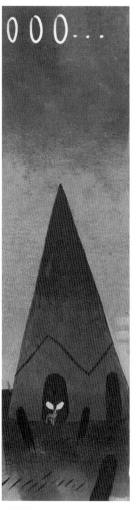

I DON'T HAVE THE STRENGTH TO FIGHT ANYMORE, I GIVE UP..

BOOKO!!!

BOOKO! WHY DID YOU COME? HE IS TOO STRONG, WE FAILED...

GRRRRR

HA HA HA! LOOKS LIKE ANOTHER ONE OF YOUR FRIENDS WILL DIE PROTECTING YOU!

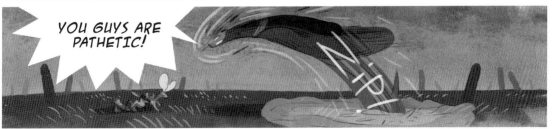

YOU GUYS ARE PATHETIC!

ZIP!

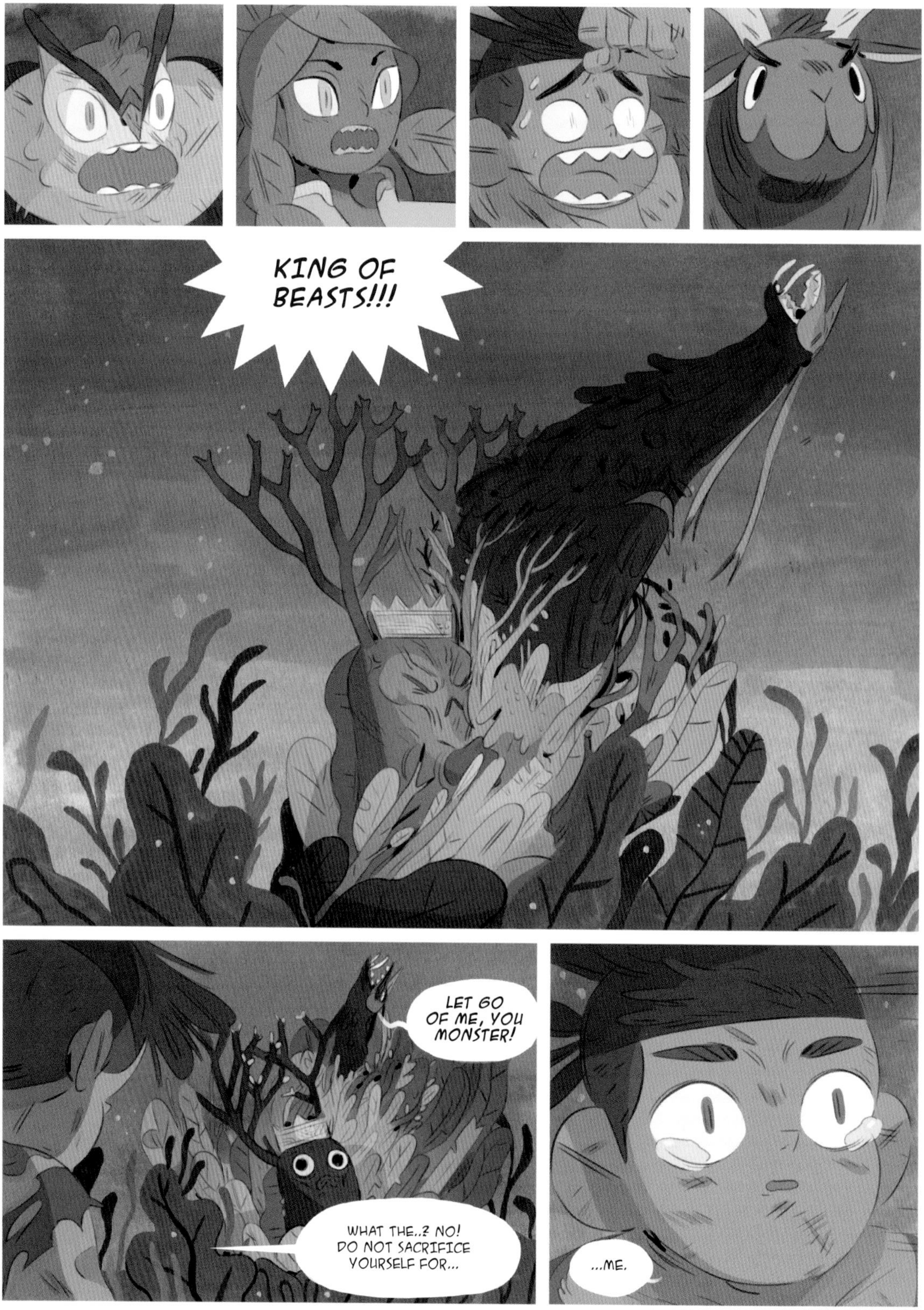
KING OF BEASTS!!!
LET GO OF ME, YOU MONSTER!
WHAT THE..? NO! DO NOT SACRIFICE YOURSELF FOR...
...ME.

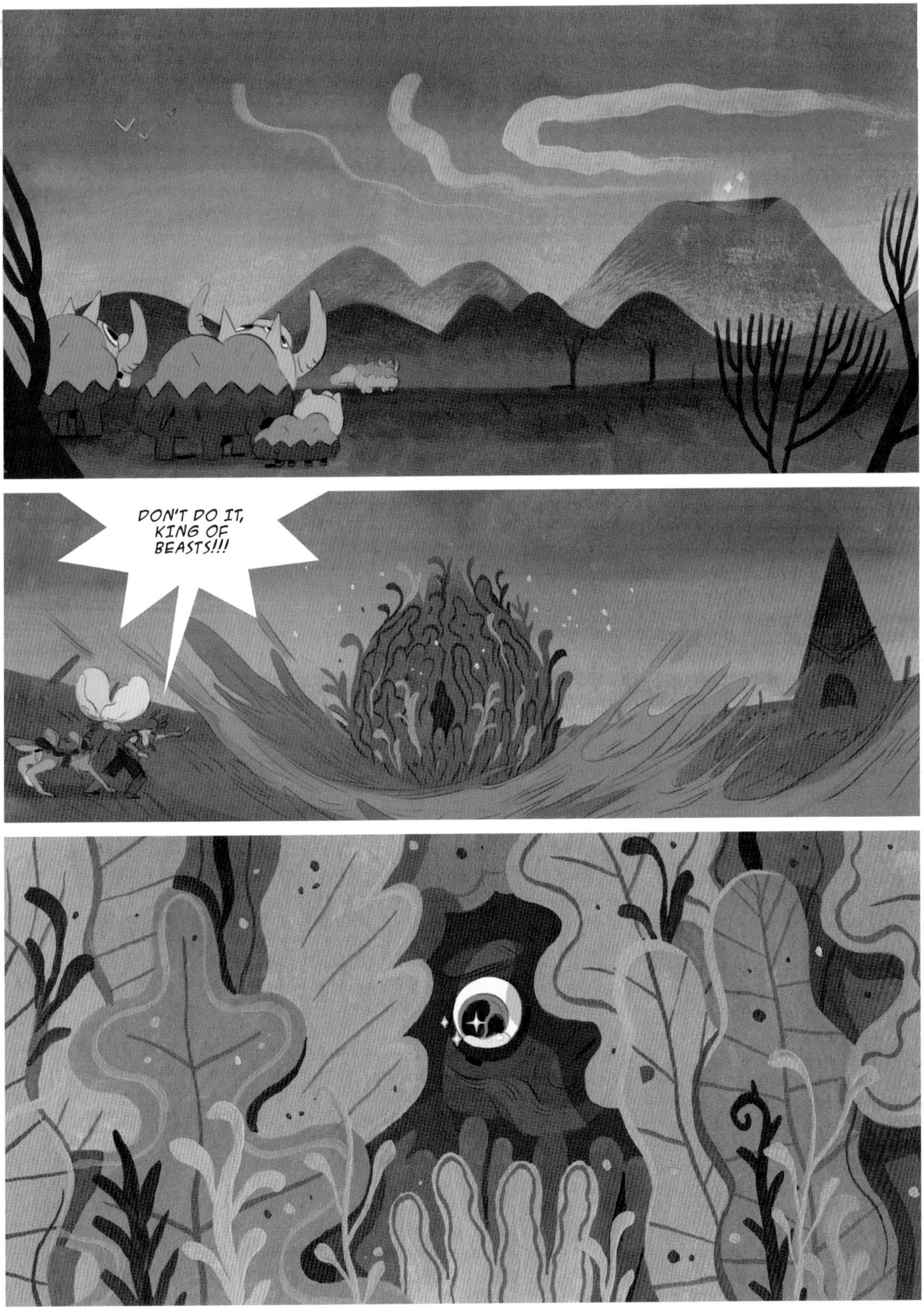
DON'T DO IT, KING OF BEASTS!!!

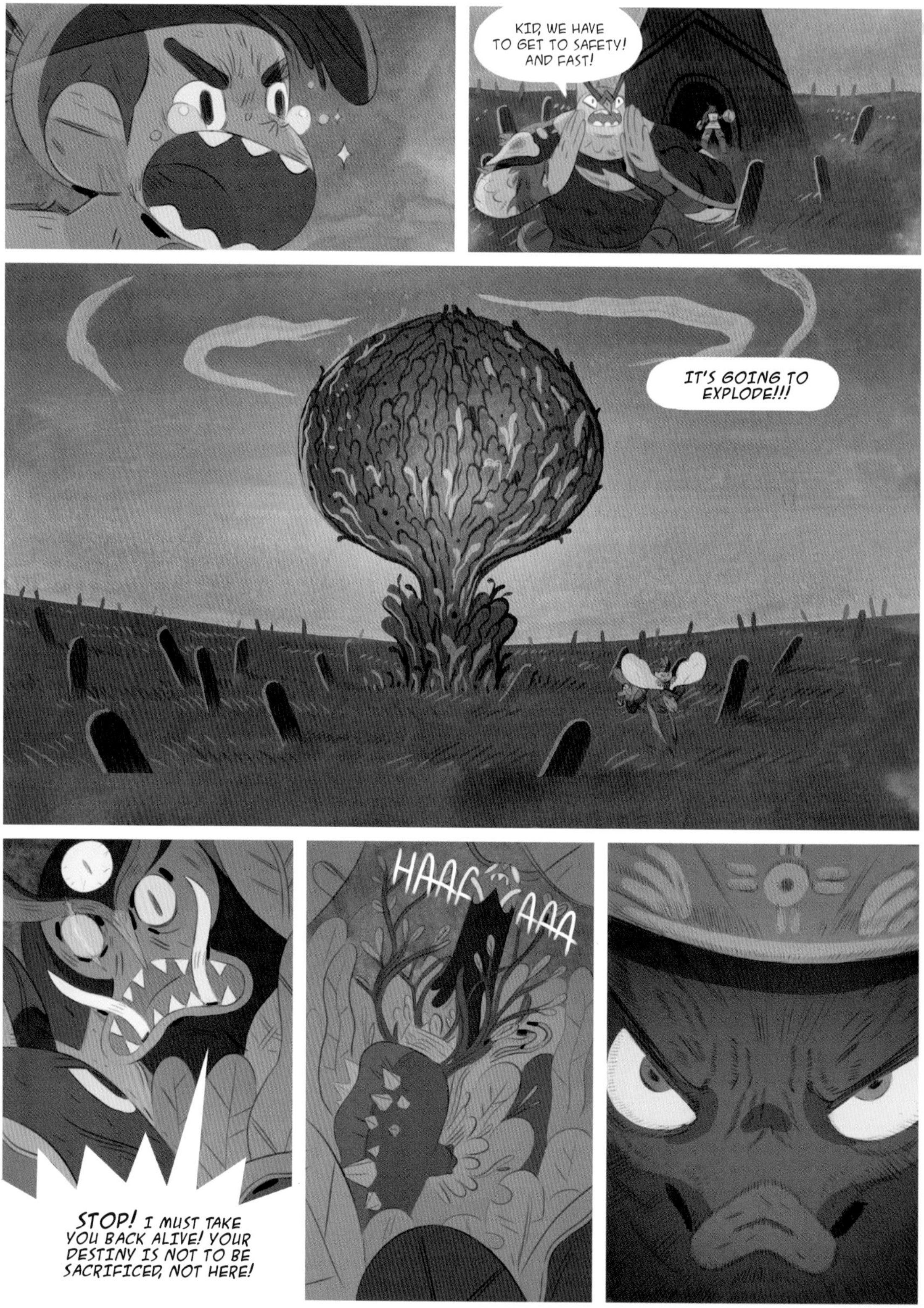
KID, WE HAVE TO GET TO SAFETY! AND FAST!
IT'S GOING TO EXPLODE!!!
STOP! I MUST TAKE YOU BACK ALIVE! YOUR DESTINY IS NOT TO BE SACRIFICED, NOT HERE!
HAAA AAA

THOSE WALL INSCRIPTIONS ARE GLOWING! WE HAVE AWAKENED SOMETHING HERE!

WHAT?! THE DOOR IS CLOSING ON US!

KIDDO, DO YOU KNOW WHAT'S GOING ON?!

HE'S PRETTY BANGED UP.

THE... TEMPLE...

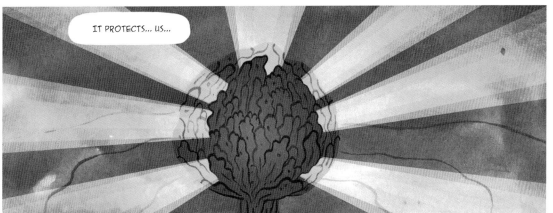

IT PROTECTS... US...

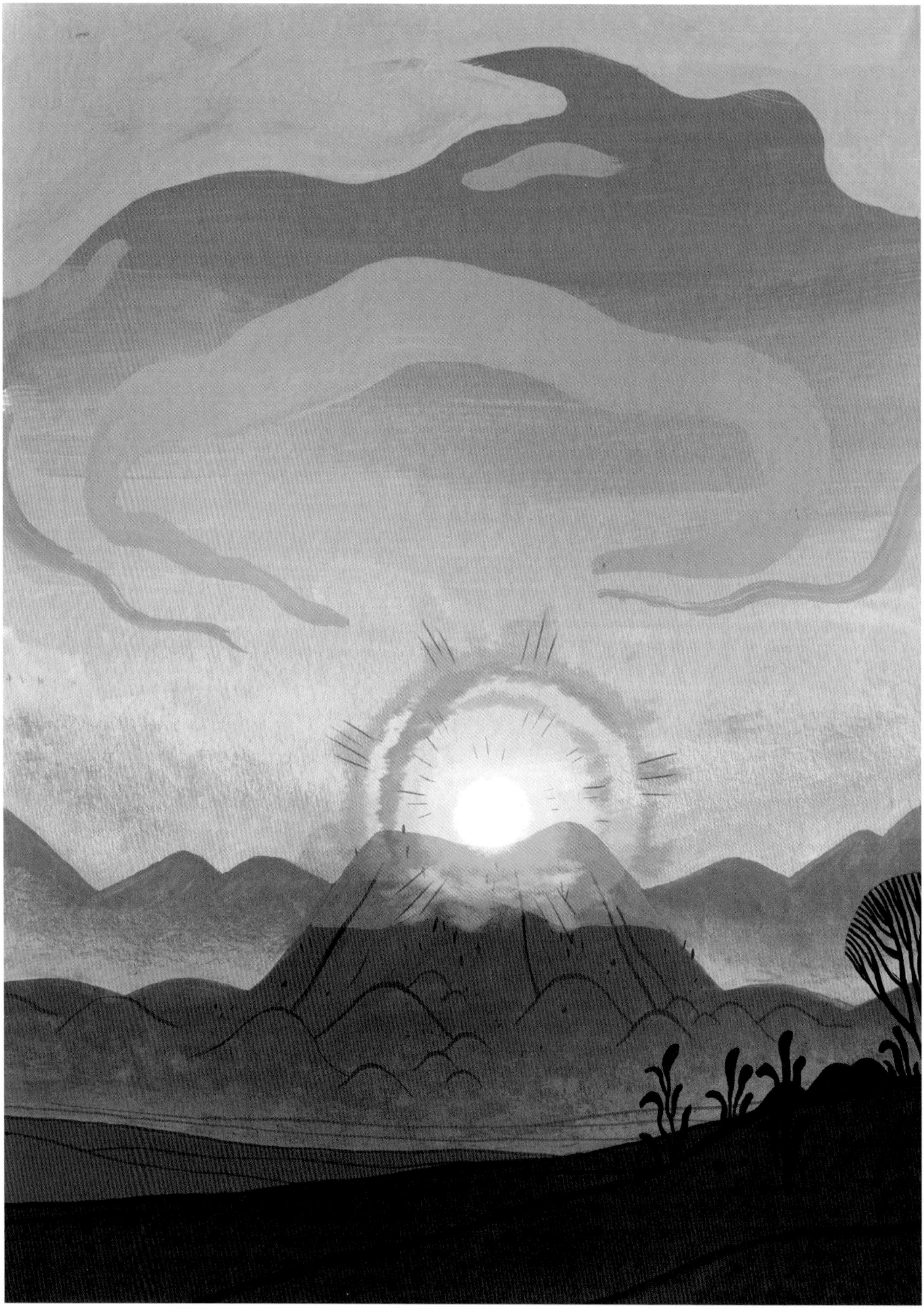

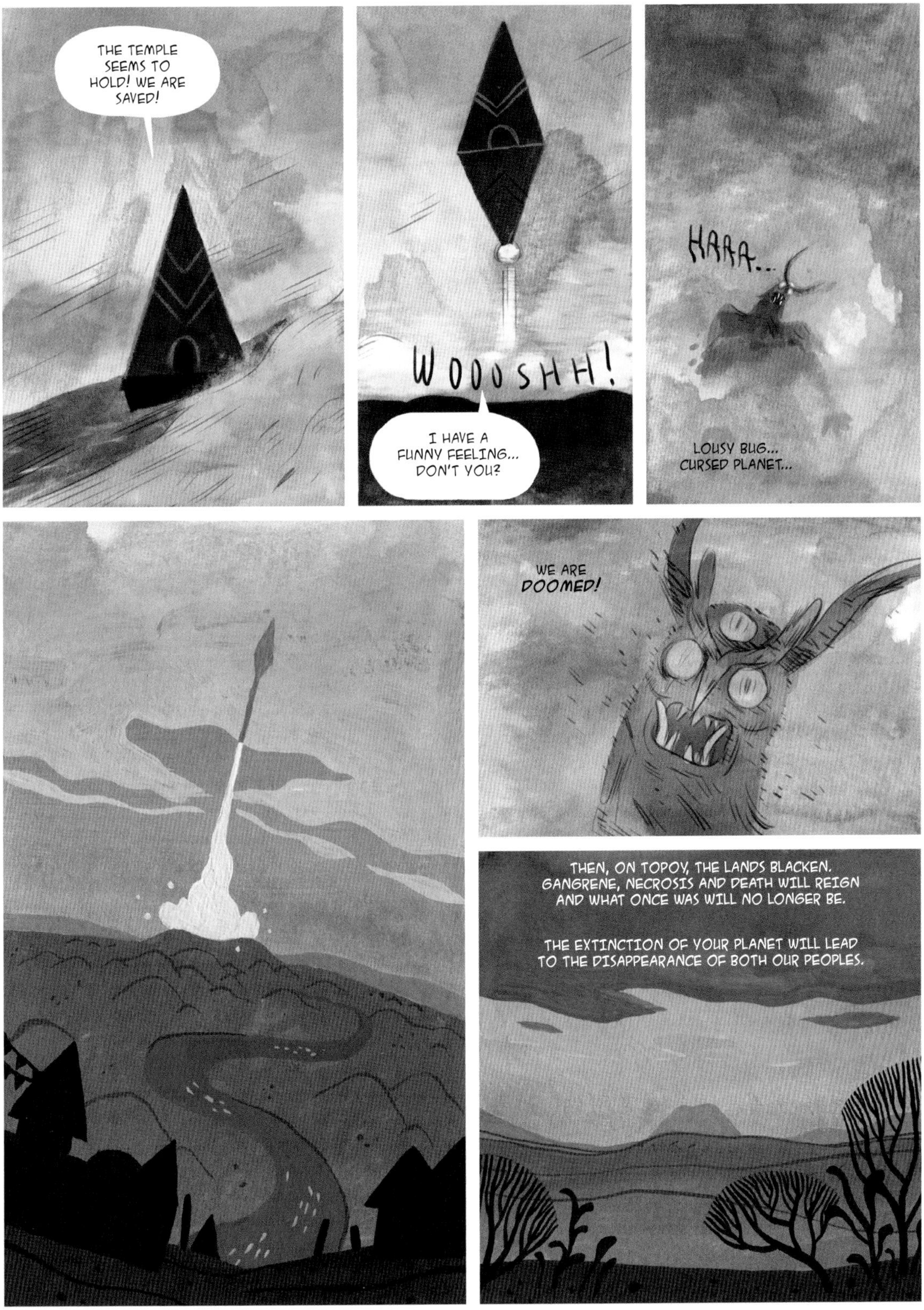
THE TEMPLE SEEMS TO HOLD! WE ARE SAVED!
WOOOSHH!
I HAVE A FUNNY FEELING... DON'T YOU?
HARR...
LOUSY BUG... CURSED PLANET...
WE ARE DOOMED!
THEN, ON TOPOY, THE LANDS BLACKEN. GANGRENE, NECROSIS AND DEATH WILL REIGN AND WHAT ONCE WAS WILL NO LONGER BE.
THE EXTINCTION OF YOUR PLANET WILL LEAD TO THE DISAPPEARANCE OF BOTH OUR PEOPLES.

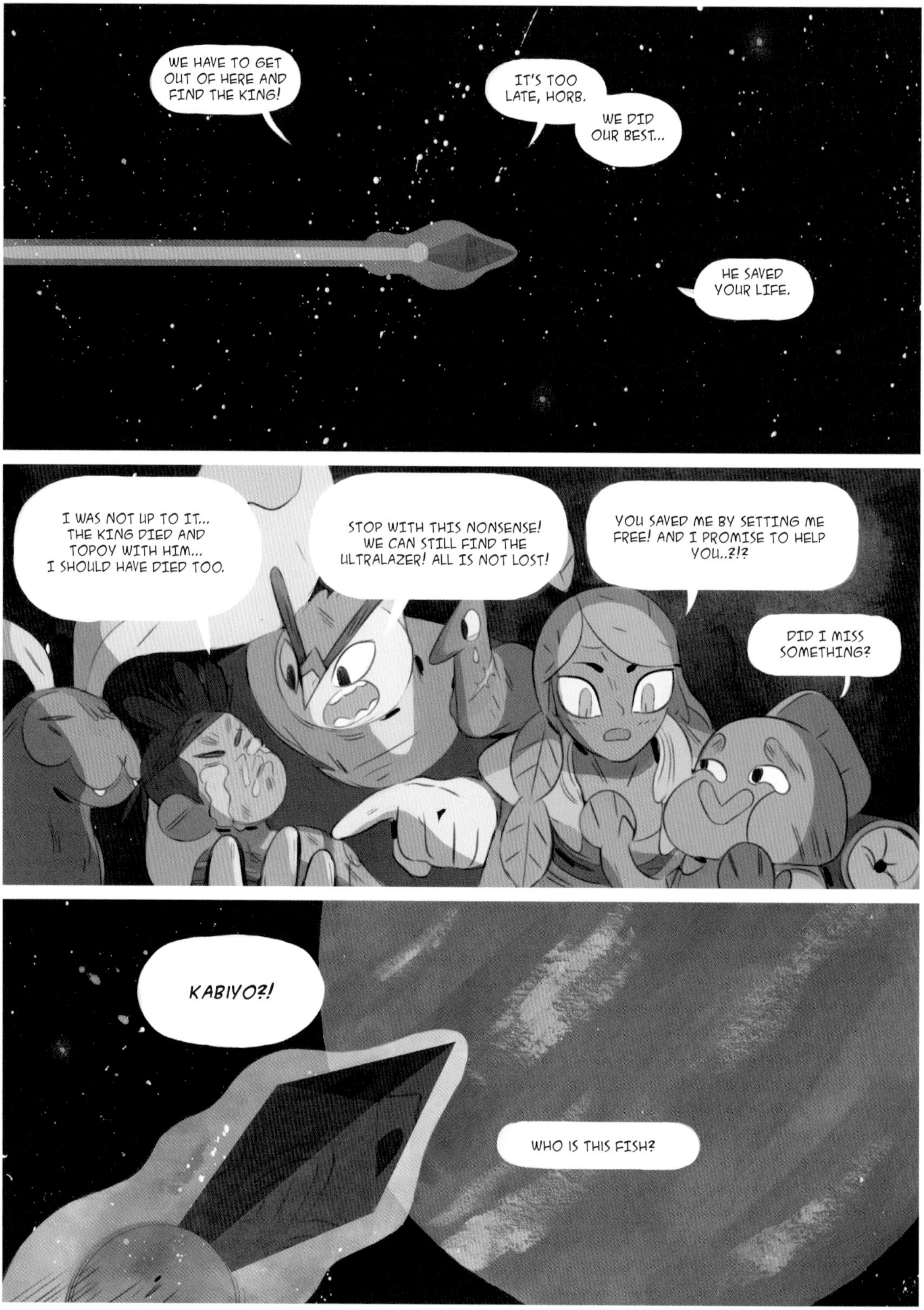
WE HAVE TO GET OUT OF HERE AND FIND THE KING!
IT'S TOO LATE, HORB.
WE DID OUR BEST...
HE SAVED YOUR LIFE.
I WAS NOT UP TO IT... THE KING DIED AND TOPOY WITH HIM... I SHOULD HAVE DIED TOO.
STOP WITH THIS NONSENSE! WE CAN STILL FIND THE ULTRALAZER! ALL IS NOT LOST!
YOU SAVED ME BY SETTING ME FREE! AND I PROMISE TO HELP YOU..?!?
DID I MISS SOMETHING?
KABIYO?!
WHO IS THIS FISH?

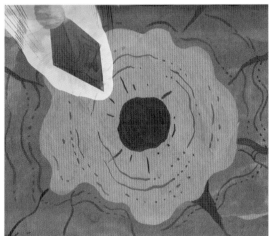

BUT WHERE DID THE VOLCANO GO?

THE EXPLOSION MUST HAVE BEEN MASSIVE... IT DOESN'T LOOK LIKE TOPOY ANYMORE.

WE TOOK A RIDE IN A SPACESHIP?!

DON'T BE SILLY, MOLLUSK BOY.

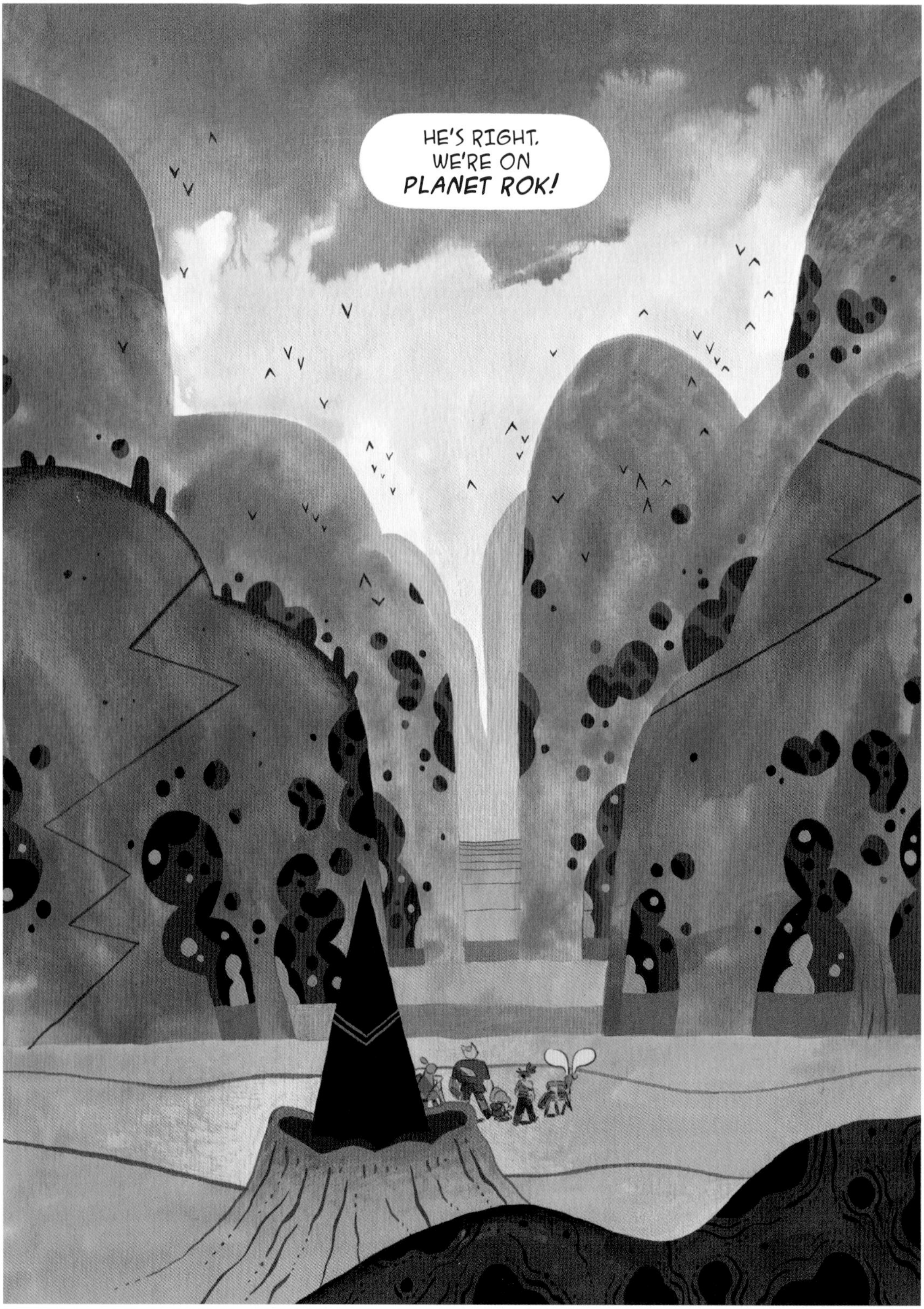
HE'S RIGHT. WE'RE ON PLANET ROK!

TO BE CONTINUED...

Hardness
Density
Color

Kayoux Inventus I

#01 Moss Stone
Hardness: 4½-5

Density: 0.3 oz/in³
Color: 💧💧💧

Hemimorphite

Explosion : creates a solid blue mass

Ingestion : allows to breathe under water

◆◆◆◆

#02 Mushy Stone 
Hardness: 2
Density: 0.84-1.02 oz/in³
Color: 💧💧💧

Glauconite

Explosion : makes all sorts of mushrooms grow.

Ingestion : vegetal absorbtion power

◆◆◆◆

#03
Hardness: 6½-7

Density: 1.16-1.51 oz/in³

Olivine

Explosion : spreads a bouncing green shield

Ingestion : makes the body untouchable.

◆◆◆

#04 Vine Stone
Hardness: 3½-5½

Density: 0.88 oz/in³
Color: 💧💧💧

Serpentine

Explosion : creates powerful roots

Ingestion : makes body as strong as steel

◆◆◆◆

#05 Melt Stone
Hardness: 1½-2
Density: 0.95 oz/in³
Color: 💧💧💧

Vivianite

Explosion : can melt any type of vegetal

Ingestion : projects toxic mist through skin pores

◆◆◆

#06 Geyser Stone
Hardness: 5-6

Density: 0.67-0.81 oz/in³
Color: 💧💧💧💧

Opale noble

Explosion : hydro-explosive stone, explodes when touches water

Ingestion : makes the body untouchable.

◆◆◆◆

#07 Spark Stone
Hardness: 5-6

Density: 0.88 oz/in³
Color: 💧

Haüyne

Friction : gives off a powerful light

Ingestion : allows all power stones to be revealed

◆◆◆◆

#08 Magma Stone
Hardness: 7-7½

Density: 1.26 oz/in³
Color: 💧💧

Pyrope

Explosion : creates lava rivers

Ingestion : allows user to spit torrents of magma.

◆◆

#09 Force Stone
Hardness: 6

Density: 0.81 oz/in³
Color: 💧💧💧

Sodalite

Explosion : turns water into salt

Ingestion : increases levels, but distorts the body

◆◆◆

◆◆◆◆ Common   ◆◆◆ Rare   ◆◆ Ultra rare   ◆ Unique   ◆ Legendary

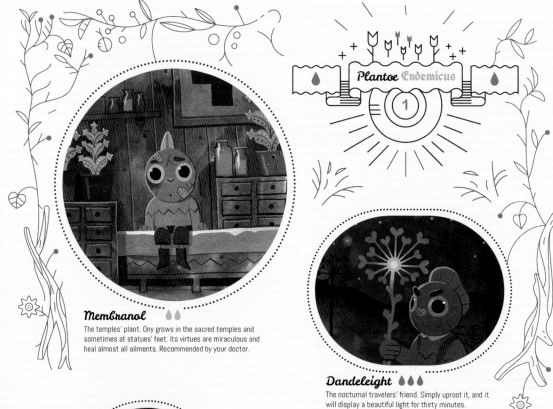

Plantoe Endemicus

1

Membranol 🌢🌢

The temples' plant. Ony grows in the sacred temples and sometimes at statues' feet. Its virtues are miraculous and heal almost all ailments. Recommended by your doctor.

Dandeleight 🌢🌢🌢

The nocturnal travelers' friend. Simply uproot it, and it will display a beautiful light for thirty minutes.

Neverlost 🌢

A type of aquatic bulb whose tips form compositions resembling celestial bodies. This plant helps in finding one's way by indicating the cardinal points. However, one must already know them in order to benefit from it.

Spysee 🌢

Certain regions of Topoy have entire fields of these highly unsettling plants with eyes. Some speculate that they might be connected to each other through a collective consciousness.

 Rare